PRAISE FOR OLIVIA CUNNING'S
RED-HOT SINNERS ON TOUR SERIES

HOT TICKET

"The heat and hunger between the two leads creates a palpable tension that will keep readers turning pages with reckless abandon and begging for more from this sizzling series."

—*RT Book Reviews*

"Cunning develops her characters into real people who engage in a compelling and satisfying erotic romance. Their relationship builds amid a dramatic series of unexpected events."

—*Publishers Weekly*

"I said it for the first book and I'll say it again, these yummy guys are so hot that you'll want to rip your clothes off and join them. I hope this tour never ends."

—*Night Owl Reviews*, Top Pick

"As Jace's story is told in *Hot Ticket*, the reader is provided with the heart-wrenching and powerful backstory that formed the Jace we saw in the first two books of this series."

—*The Romance Reviews*, Top Pick

DOUBLE TIME

"Snappy dialogue, dizzying romance, scorching hot sex, and realistic observations about life on tour make this a winner."

—*Publishers Weekly*

"Whether you like rockers or not, this story will get you thinking about becoming a groupie!"

—*Night Owl Reviews*

"Hot rock stars, hotter sex, and some of the best characters I've read this year."

—*Guilty Pleasures Book Review*

"*Double Time* gives us Trey's much anticipated happy ending, and all the sexual adventures along the way."

—*Fresh Fiction*

ROCK HARD

"The sex is incredible and the love is even better. Each rocker has a piece of my heart… an excellent read."

—*Night Owl Reviews,* Reviewer Top Pick

"Readers will love the characters and enjoy their scorching love scenes and passionate fights."

—*RT Book Reviews,* 4 stars

"Sizzling sex, drugs, and rock 'n' roll… absolutely perfect."

—*Fresh Fiction*

"I just can't seem to get these rockers out of my system. I can't wait to read each band member's book."

—*A Buckeye Girl Reads*

"Olivia Cunning has written a perfect erotic romance... amazingly hot."

—*About Happy Books*

BACKSTAGE PASS

"So sensual, sexy, and yummy."

—*Night Owl Romance,* Reviewer Top Pick

"Extremely well written... I honestly fell in love with each of the band members. Oh, the glorious plot! So good, so yummy, so hot!"

—*Sexy Women Read*

"What caught me by surprise was the laugh-out-loud humor and intense relationships... the romance was sweet, sexy, and had my heart racing."

—*Fiction Vixen*

"An erotic foray into the behind-the-scenes world of a heavy metal band... Olivia Cunning has created intriguing characters and a Rock 'n' Roll world that feels genuine."

—*Fresh Fiction*

"A plot that rocks with sexy romps that keep on rolling."

—*My Overstuffed Bookshelf*

ALSO BY OLIVIA CUNNING

BACKSTAGE PASS

ROCK HARD

DOUBLE TIME

HOT TICKET

SINNERS ON TOUR

Wicked BEAT

OLIVIA CUNNING

sourcebooks
casablanca

Published by Sourcebooks Casablanca, an imprint of Sourcebooks, Inc.
P.O. Box 4410, Naperville, Illinois 60567-4410
(630) 961-3900
FAX: (630) 961-2168
www.sourcebooks.com

Library of Congress Cataloging-in-Publication Data

Cunning, Olivia.
  Wicked beat : sinners on tour / Olivia Cunning.
     pages cm
  (trade paper : alk. paper) 1. Rock musicians—Fiction. 2. Man-woman
relationships—Fiction. I. Title.
  PS3603.U6635W54 2013
  813'.6—dc23
                              2013008568

Printed and bound in the United States of America
VP 10 9 8 7 6 5 4 3 2 1

Dedicated to the memory of
Jimmy "The Rev" Sullivan,
who will continue to rock the rhythm of my heart
foREVer.

Chapter 1

REBEKAH ADJUSTED THE PILLOW beneath her older brother's head. She smoothed the blanket over his lap. Plucked a stray hair from his hospital gown and flicked it onto the powder-blue carpet. Shifted his arm into a more natural position at his side. Licked her thumb and rubbed at a spot of mustard near the corner of his mouth.

Wincing, Dave turned his head, trying to escape her spit bath. "Will you knock it off, Reb?"

"Sorry," she said. "I'm just nervous. Are they really coming?"

"Of course they're coming. They're back on tour next week and haven't fired me yet." Dave scowled and clutched his blanket with one hand. He could almost grip it tightly now. Rebekah wavered between pride and despair when confronted by how far Dave had come since his accident and how far he had left to go in his recovery. "And they are never going to go for this plan, Reb. Never."

"I'll just be filling in for you temporarily, Dave. Until you can go back on tour with them. You're unquestionably the best front of house engineer on the planet, and you've come up with the perfect solution for their dilemma. They're not going to fire you."

"They don't really have a choice, Reb. I can't continue as their FOH if I can't reach my soundboard. And even if I could reach it, there's no way I can adjust the sliders fast enough to keep up with the band during a live show."

"But you will, Dave. You just need more time to recover. I can work your soundboard until you're ready to go back to work. I'm happy to help you out." In reality, he was helping her as much as she was helping him. No metal band wanted to hire a female live sound engineer. Dave had warned her before she started school. Told her she'd be stuck mixing pop music at mall concerts. She'd been determined to show him otherwise, but so far, determination had gotten her a long way toward nowhere. If someone would just give her a chance, she would show them that a woman could be just as metal as a man.

"I know how much you want to help, sis, but I don't think they're going to agree to this. You've got to start at the bottom and work your way up, not expect to land a job with one of the biggest bands in the industry straight out of school."

Heart sinking, she sighed. Tried not to pout *too* much. She knew he was right, but patience had never been Rebekah's greatest virtue. Actually, patience didn't even know where she lived.

"But I will do my best to make them see that this is a viable solution," he said. "That you're good enough to take my place."

She smiled a make-big-brother-feel-like-a-superhero smile. "Really?"

"Just don't be too disappointed if they say no."

It would crush her. She worshipped Sinners and every note of every song that had ever been produced by their talented hands, fingers, mouths, feet, and any other body part they used to create music. In college, Rebekah had done her capstone project on Sinners. It had been proclaimed brilliant and propelled her to the head of her graduating class. Dave smiled, his gaze moving from hers to her recently dyed hair. He cringed.

"Has Mom seen your hair?" he asked.

Rebekah grinned and smoothed her platinum blond, shoulder-length hair with one hand. She'd recently dyed the under-layer cobalt blue. Since she'd regrown hair, she liked doing things that brought attention to it. Strange how being entirely bald at twenty-four would do that to a girl. Besides, Rebekah had always loved putting her mother into apoplectic fits, even if it meant being subjected to regular exorcisms. "Do you think she'll like it?"

"Um, no."

"Good." She giggled. "So are *all* the band members coming to visit you?" Her heart thudded with excitement.

Dave grinned at her. "Will Trey be with them, you mean?"

Busted. She sorta had a panting-lust-thing for Sinners' rhythm guitarist, Trey Mills, and Dave knew it. Probably because every time she talked to Dave, texted, or emailed him, she always asked how Trey was doing. Dave would always tell her *who* Trey was doing instead. It had not managed to decrease her interest even a little. On the contrary, Trey's long list of conquests had made him more intriguing. Rebekah was sure he could teach her a thing or two in the bedroom, and she was sorely in need of some attention in that department.

"I'm not sure if Brian's back in town yet," Dave said. "He's probably still in Kansas City with his wife, but I'm pretty sure the rest of them will stop in. Including Trey-Can't-Keep-It-In-His-Pants Mills. You'd do best to stay away from him, Reb."

Uh, no, that would not be best by any stretch of the imagination. The man was made to be devoured whole. Who cared about the following indigestion? Not her.

A set of knuckles rapped against the door.

Was that them? Rebekah's heart skipped a beat.

"Come in," Dave called.

The door swung open and the man of Rebekah's wet dreams poked his head into the room. Jet-black hair obscuring one sultry green eye, sexiness oozing from every pore, Trey Mills scanned Rebekah from head to toe. Her entire body flushed with heat. Trey offered Dave a crooked grin. Her temperature rose another few degrees.

"Sorry to interrupt the festivities, dude." Trey lifted both dark brows, one pierced with a tiny silver hoop. "We'll come back later."

He closed the door.

Oh my God, he's getting away!

Rebekah raced across the room and jerked the door open. "Wait, don't go. There are no festivities. I'm Dave's younger sister, Rebekah."

—◦◦◦—

Eric dropped his hand from Jace's forehead and gaped.

At her.

For like five minutes.

He forgot why he'd had Jace in a stranglehold. Something about an engagement ring and Jace's dominatrix girlfriend, Aggie. Forgot that he couldn't wait to pick up a new custom-made cymbal for his drum kit after they visited what's-his-name—*Dave!*—who'd just been brought home from the hospital. Forgot that walking required a sequence of left foot, right—not left foot, left, left, stumble, right foot. Forgot that in order to inhale, his chest had to expand.

Eric choked on his own tongue.

It was her. Standing right there. About shoulder high. Petite. Feminine. Blond-and-blue-haired. Both beautiful and adorable in her mismatched tube socks, a purple tank top, and a green miniskirt. It really was her. The woman of Eric's wet dreams.

And she was gushing all over Trey.

Son of a bitch.

Wait, Eric thought. Maybe he was jumping to conclusions. Perhaps the signs were all wrong. He'd never actually seen her before, so he had to be sure. Eric lifted the long lock of hair that he dyed a different vibrant color every forty-nine days without fail and stared at it. His memory had served him correctly. It was currently cobalt blue—the exact same shade as the under-layer of *her* hair. What were the chances? It had to be kismet. Destiny. Fate. Providence. All of the above…

She'd said her name was Rebekah. That was Eric's favorite name. At least, now it was.

Rebekah tore her eyes off Trey long enough to notice Eric examining his own hair like an idiot. "Nice color," she said with a devilish grin.

Eric gaped.

At her.

For like five minutes.

Conversation continued all around him, but he couldn't stop staring. His eyes grew dry and itchy because he refused to blink.

Something slapped him alongside the head. Eric started and turned his head to find Sed, Sinners' lead vocalist, looking at him as if waiting for something. "Well?"

"Well, what?"

"Do you think we should give her a chance?" Sed asked.

Apparently, Eric had missed something while he'd been gaping, stumbling, asphyxiating, gaping some more, and not blinking—in that order.

Jace pounded Eric on the back. "You okay in there, Sticks?" he asked. "Did you have some bad cheese?"

Cheese? What the fuck is cheese?

Eric's brain usually worked pretty well, but apparently not with that sexalicious creature in the room.

"I promise to do my best," Rebekah said, her soft voice mixing all sorts of strange emotions in Eric's chest. She released Trey's arm and moved to stand directly in front of Eric. The strawberry scent of her shampoo made his knees weak. Or maybe it was that pair of baby blue eyes gazing up at him from beneath thick, black lashes. "Will you let me work for you?" She touched the center of his chest and his heart leapt against her fingertips. "You won't regret it."

Eric swallowed hard. He had no idea what she was talking about, but her working for him in any capacity sounded fine and dandy to him. "Yes."

She emitted a happy little squeal, wrapped her arms around him, and squeezed. She almost set him off balance as she hopped up and down excitedly. Before he could sweep her into his arms and carry her off to the nearest justice of the peace to recite eternal vows, she released him and hugged Jace, then Sed. Eric cringed when she plastered herself to Trey. It was one hundred percent obvious who she wanted. Now that he and Trey Mills were the only two single guys left in this band, Eric thought he would have pretty good odds of picking up a nice girl for himself.

No such luck.

Trey whispered something in her ear. She giggled and whispered, "Not here."

Eric turned, found the nearest wall, and repeatedly banged his head against it.

Chapter 2

REBEKAH CARRIED HER SUITCASE up the stairs of the tour bus and came to a screeching halt. This was not the bus that had been ripped in half and caught on fire in Canada, was it? It couldn't possibly be, but who could tell beneath the piles of debris that littered the aisles and every available surface?

A black-haired, tattooed man, wearing a pair of black, baggy jean shorts over red plaid boxers, emerged from one of the piles. He had various chains connecting his nipple piercings to God-only-knew-what in his pants. Rebekah hadn't even noticed him sitting there on what might have been a sofa or a cardboard box or a stuffed grizzly bear trophy.

"You must be the new FOH engineer."

A thrill of pride made her chest swell. Sure, it was mostly due to her brother's misfortune that she, Rebekah Esther Blake, was Sinners' temporary front of house soundboard operator, but she was here and ready to prove herself worthy. "That's me," she said, beaming. She quickly forced the ear-to-ear grin from her face. She should probably try to act a little more butch or these tough roadie guys would eat her for breakfast.

"I'm Travis. That's Jake. Marcus should be here soon."

Rebekah scanned the piles of debris until she saw the movement of a blond mohawk near what appeared to be a dining table under a mountain of laundry and beer cans.

Jake stood, wiped his hand on his black T-shirt, and then extended it in her direction. "Dave's sister, right?"

"Um, yeah." She took his hand and shook it. "I'm Rebekah, but most people call me Reb."

"Are you sure that's not short for rebel?" Jake asked as he took in her funky clothes and blue hair.

Travis laughed. "That would make more sense, if you and straightlaced Dave come from the same family."

"My mother has disowned me no less than a hundred times." Rebekah grinned over memories of all those small victories. "She's only disowned Dave about a dozen."

Travis laughed, dark eyes twinkling with merriment, and shook her hand.

"So, where do I sleep?" she asked, wondering if there were even beds in this mess. And then she realized the mess *was* beds. Bunk after bunk filled with spare pillows, blankets, potentially clean clothes, and obviously dirty clothes. Obvious, because she could smell them from where she stood.

Someone stomped up the steps behind her. "I've come to rescue you," a deep voice said behind her.

She turned and found Sinners' drummer, Eric, standing behind her. She smiled at him, and he smiled back, looking like he'd just discovered the puppy he'd always wanted under the Christmas tree. "Rescue me? From what?"

"Do you really think we'd make you stay on the pigsty bus?"

"I don't mind," she said.

"The place is highly toxic to sensible females."

She laughed and slapped him on the arm. "Then I'll be perfectly fine."

Eric paused and raked a hand through his crazy hair.

For some inexplicable reason she wanted to run her fingers through it too. Like a work of art, Eric Stick's hair demanded attention. It was long on one side—something to hold on to. The other half was sheared off short. She imagined it would feel soft and silky beneath her fingertips. A row of inch-long spikes ran from forehead to nape, separating long locks from short fuzz. It was shiny and ebony except for the long lock that curled around his throat and hung down to his left collarbone. By some strange coincidence it was dyed the same blue she'd chosen to dye hers—for the sole purpose of ticking off her mother—not a week ago.

She wondered if his was real hair or fake extensions. She reached up and ran a finger over the long, blue strands. They felt real. Silky. Smooth. Warm from his body heat. She stroked the lock again between her fingers and his throat. His Adam's apple dipped as he swallowed hard. She cocked her head at him, really seeing him for the first time. When she really looked at him, he was actually very attractive. Why hadn't she ever noticed him before? Obscenely tall (from her low vantage point) and lean. Rugged features. Strong jaw. Straight nose. Thin lips with a ready smile and a sexy cleft in the middle of his chin that begged to be stroked with her fingertip. He was no Trey Mills, but…

Rebekah's gaze lifted to Eric's eyes, which were the color of a clear winter sky. "Will Trey be on the other bus?" she asked.

Eric's slim black brows drew together into a scowl. "Yeah," he said. "Of course."

"Then I'm there."

She turned, brushed past Eric, and trotted down the bus steps.

"Later, Reb," she heard Travis call from inside the pigsty bus.

Eric loped down the steps and came to a halt beside her. She glanced around the parking lot looking for another bus. She'd only seen one bus when the taxi had dropped her off. It wasn't like a big ol' tour bus was something she could have easily overlooked. Behind the pigsty bus, she spotted the large, black moving van with Sinners' red logo painted on the back, but nope, there was no other bus in sight. "Where's the other bus?"

"Sed's bringing it. He called and said he was on his way. And before you ask, yes, Trey is with him." He rolled his eyes skyward and shook his head.

She set her suitcase at her feet to wait. Rebekah took another glance around the parking lot and noticed a vintage Stingray Corvette parked under a palm tree. That hadn't been here when she'd arrived. She'd have noticed it for sure. The car was a real beauty that had been manufactured in 1965. Maybe '66. Shiny emerald green paint. Its convertible top had been left down. Good thing it didn't rain often in Southern California.

"*Sweet!*" she said, practically salivating over the car's beauty and the raw power she knew would be under its hood.

"What?" Eric asked.

She pointed enthusiastically across the parking lot. "That gorgeous hunk of metal over there."

Eric's gaze followed the tip of her finger. He scratched behind his ear when his eyes located the object of her obsession. "You mean my car?"

She glanced at him, eyes wide. "That's yours?"

He grinned and nodded. "Yeah. I'm so proud of her. She died at only two stoplights today." He held up two fingers.

"She died?"

Eric scratched behind his ear again and stared up at the clear sky. "I can't seem to get her timing right. Or maybe I didn't gap those new spark plugs correctly. I'm not sure."

"Mind if I take a look?" Rebekah left her suitcase by the bus and was heading across the parking lot before he could answer. He caught up with her in two long-legged strides.

Before Rebekah's failed stint as an oil-rigger and a crab fisherman, um, fisher*wo*man, she'd had a failed stint as an auto mechanic. Not because she had been bad at it, but because no one took her seriously. She *had* been bad at rigging oil and fishing crab—five-foot-two and a hundred and six pounds soaking wet did not make her suitable for many of the jobs she insisted she wanted.

When she reached the car, her heart sank. The camel-colored, leather interior was totally trashed. "What did you do to her?" she bellowed and turned on Eric, who took a step backward, his smile fading.

"She was like that when I got her."

"And you just left her like this? How long have you had her?"

Eric tipped backward at the hips, lifted his toes off the ground, and stared at his black Converse high-tops. "Uh, around ten…"

"Ten days?"

"Uh…" He shook his head.

"Ten *weeks*?"

Eric cleared his throat. "Um… ten… years." He whispered the last word.

She slapped him on the chest with the flat of her hand. "How *could* you? She's a priceless work of art and you treat her like junk."

"Junk? No, not junk. She's my baby." He patted the door affectionately.

"Your baby? That pisses me off even more." Rebekah moved around to the front of the car to pop the hood. "If the engine looks as bad as the interior, I'm gonna scratch your eyes out."

Eric covered his eyes with both hands.

And he had reason to. "Oh, dear," Rebekah gasped as she tried to make heads or tails over what someone had done to the once glorious V-8 engine. "Is that? Is that… a *coat* hanger holding open the carburetor choke?"

"I tried to fix her," Eric said, his eyes still protected by his long-fingered hands.

He looked ridiculous. And somehow endearing. She smiled to herself and propped up the hood with a metal rod—another coat hanger.

"Are you sure *you* should be the one trying to fix her?"

"I have a repair manual for this model," he said. "A really good one."

"We're going to need it to figure out how to straighten out this disaster."

He lowered his hands from his eyes. "*We're* going to need it?"

"I'm sorta a mechanic. Or I used to be. If you want, I'll help you get her running properly. I don't do interiors though."

He hesitated.

"Do you have a better suggestion?" she asked, running a finger along the side of the engine block and finding seeping oil. Blown head gasket. *Wonderful.* She sighed heavily. This poor car. How could he claim that it was his baby?

Eric moved to stand beside her, looking at the completely fucked up engine with something that bordered on pride. "When I had her towed to my house from the junkyard, I promised myself that I'd do all the work on her myself. She *does* start now." He glanced at Rebekah. "Sometimes."

"I'm surprised she runs at all."

He flushed and looked across the parking lot. Rebekah stared at him, perplexed. He hadn't been this cute ten minutes ago, had he? Maybe because he was so close, she was able to get a better look at him. And he smelled good. A hint of leather and aftershave and something utterly male. She suddenly wanted him to notice her. As a woman.

Rebekah shifted sideways and brushed her arm against his, pretending it was an accident. He didn't move away, but he didn't increase the contact between them either.

"You can keep that promise. If I do help you," she said, "you'll be the one doing all the work. I'll just supervise."

His bright, genuine smile did something strange to her heart. It soared upward, fluttering in her throat or thereabouts.

"That sounds like a plan, Reb."

His hand slid across her lower back. A thrill of excitement raced up her spine.

"I don't expect you to volunteer your help," he said. What would you like in repayment for your assistance?"

His thumb rubbed a small circle at the base of her spine. Her breath caught. Why were her nipples suddenly erect? She thrust her breasts forward, wanting him to observe them, and not sure why the thought of him seeing her arousal excited her. She chanced a glance at him and found his eyes closed. Her heart sank a little. He wasn't paying attention to her. She turned away from him slightly. Not exactly out of his one-armed embrace, but to be less... *engulfed* by the man. He stood over a foot taller than her, which made her feel very feminine and small. She wasn't sure she liked that feeling.

"Uh, what did you have in mind?" she asked breathlessly.

"I give a pretty good massage," he said, his low voice drawing goose bumps along the side of her neck. His eyes opened and immediately fixated on the small bumps at the front of her thin tank top. His breath caught. She tugged the hem of her shirt down, giving him a nice view of her cleavage as well. She pretended that was accidental too. He was definitely paying attention now.

Which would make *now* a good time to grab hold of the long side of his hair and pull those easy-to-smile lips against her throat.

Wait. What was *she* thinking? Trey—all cool, suave, and sexy—was the band member she wanted to tease mercilessly, not this silly guy with the... with the... mesmeric hands. Oh. Just his thumb rubbing in circles along her lower back had her muscles melting. Her belly quivering. Her nipples straining.

Eric moved behind her, and his long fingers dug into her shoulders with just enough pressure to have her swaying back toward those wonderful hands in bliss. His thumbs massaged either side of her spine as he worked his way lower. Lower. Lower. Mmmmm, lower.

"Sold!" she cried as a deep shudder shook her entire body. Dear God, this man's hands...

Eric chuckled and those strong, long-fingered hands moved around her waist to splay over her belly. He drew her against his lean-muscled body. She tilted her head back and found his gaze locked on her neckline. He bent his head closer to her ear. "I'm good at other things too," he murmured.

I'll bet you are. "Just not fixing cars," she teased.

His hands rubbed her belly, and she longed for him to move them a bit higher to massage her aching breasts. If his hands felt that good on her back and belly, what would they feel like there? Oh, and down there.

"That wasn't nice, little Reb."

"Who said I was nice?"

"You look very nice to me," he murmured.

She tugged the neckline of her shirt a little lower. Her nipples were scarcely covered now.

Eric drew a shaky breath through his teeth. Did he want her? She wanted him to want her. More like needed him to.

A loud, low rumble drew Rebekah's attention. Thunder? On a sunny Californian day? A red Harley entered the parking lot and headed across the expanse of concrete in their direction. It pulled to a stop beside them, and its rider, dressed all in leather, shifted the bike on its kickstand.

"Tripod!" Eric greeted.

"Tripod?" Rebekah echoed.

The rider removed his helmet, revealing the cutest member of Sinners, bassist Jace Seymour. Jace was a perfect ten on the hottie scale. That dark beard stubble and bleached blond, spiked hair totally worked for him. Rebekah found each member of Sinners attractive in his own way. Lead guitarist Brian, with his cover model good looks, was a perfect ten. Vocalist Sed, all hunky and handsome, was another perfect ten. Rhythm guitarist Trey, sultry, sexy, with a heap of bad boy thrown in for good measure, was at least an eleven. And then there was Eric. Their drummer. She'd never really paid much attention to him. Too busy drooling over Trey. Trey—hummina, hummina, hummina—Mills. She wondered when he'd arrive.

Jace unhooked an elastic cord from the back of his bike and the cargo net snapped free. He tugged a duffel bag off the back of the seat and tossed it to Eric.

"If you're trying to impress her with your car, man," Jace said, "I think you should reconsider your strategy." He snorted as he attempted to withhold a laugh.

"She loves it," Eric said.

"She's just saying that so you don't cry."

Rebekah shook her head. "No, he's right. I do love it. I can't wait to help him restore the engine."

Jace lifted one brown eyebrow at her. "*You're* going to help him restore it?"

Before she could take Jace down a peg about women's lib and all that, Eric said, "Apparently, she has mad mechanic skills. Right, Reb?"

"Uh, yeah. I guess." She blushed. "Well, I get auto mechanics, but sometimes I'm not strong enough to… But I do have little hands, so I can reach into small places easily." She held up her hands, fingers splayed wide, and tapped her fingertips together. "I prefer to work with big hunks of metal—"

"Big hunks of metal? You've signed up with the right band," Eric said.

Jace snorted and slapped Eric's shoulder.

She rolled her eyes at Eric and tried not to laugh. "As I was saying, I'm not a fan of electronic components. That's why I love these older cars so much." When she beamed a smile at Eric, he got that melty look that Dave sported when he gazed at his adorable little sister with sappy affection. Ugh! She hated when guys looked at her like that. Rebekah was *not* Eric's adorable little sister. She was a strong-willed, sharp-minded, tough, independent, sensual creature, and he'd damned well better remember it.

Rebekah grabbed Eric by the front of his white T-shirt and pulled him down to eye level, prepared to give him a good tongue-lashing. "J-just because I'm s-small doesn't mean I'm not capable of t-taking care of myself or that I'm not s-sexy." She hated how she stammered when she was perturbed. It sorta took the significance from her words.

Eric just grinned at her, the heart-meltiness in his look intensifying. "Are you sure about that, precious?"

Maybe she'd get her point across better if she did something other than lash him with her tongue. She wasn't precious. She wasn't. She was bold. Daring. And more impulsive than strong-willed, sharp-minded, tough, independent, *or* sensual. Her free hand found the long hairs at the nape of his neck. She grabbed them with enough force to draw his lips against hers. He put up no resistance to her unexpected kiss, but didn't exactly respond the way she'd hoped, or at *all* for that matter.

Rebekah kissed him hungrily, with an open mouth and a seeking tongue, as if they were red-hot lovers rather than barely acquainted.

Eric made a strange sound in the back of his throat, dropped Jace's duffel bag between his feet, and drew her against him with both arms. Plastered against the solid length of his body, her feet rose off the ground as he stood straight. One strong hand pressed against the middle of her back, and the other slid down over her ass as he drew her closer and kissed her senseless.

Whoa! She hadn't meant for this to happen. She'd meant it to be more of an exercise in "don't underestimate my power" than "make my toes curl and my heart race." Rebekah's hands loosened their hold on Eric's shirt and hair to slide over his solid shoulders. Yeah, solid. Everything about this guy felt solid. Well, at least bodily.

"Um," a deep, quiet voice said from somewhere near Rebekah's shins, "if you'll just… let me… get my bag." There was a loud *umph* as Jace pulled his duffel bag from beneath her feet. "I'll get out of your way."

Regaining a few of her marbles, Rebekah tugged her mouth away from Eric's and opened her eyes. "Let that be your lesson," she whispered breathlessly.

His lashes fluttered as he opened his eyes to gaze at her. "My lesson?"

"I'm *not* the most precious, adorable, little thing you've ever seen in your life."

"Oh, yes… you are," he murmured and closed the narrow gap between their lips to kiss her again.

Um… whoa! What the fuck? Her entire body was thrumming with unexpected sexual energy. She eased away, kissing Eric intermittently to wean her mouth slowly from the delight his gently sucking lips instigated. She even put a hand on his face and pushed in an attempt to restrict her mouth's access to his. It was not very effectual, really. Even when he leaned back at her prompting, she leaned forward to follow. Damn, the man had strong lips. And hands. Dear Lord, they felt good against her ass and lower back.

Rebekah forced her lips to break contact with Eric's. Her hand slid to cup his cheek while she stared into his irresistible blue eyes. "I'm not adorable," she assured him, her eyes drifting closed again as she leaned in to steal another kiss. She just needed one more and she'd be set. Just one more. "I'm… I'm sexy and… Mmmm…" Or two. She kissed him again. And again. Shuddering when his tongue brushed her upper lip, she pulled away and then bit her bottom lip to make it behave and stop herself from craving his mouth so thoroughly. Rebekah opened her eyes, immediately got lost in his gaze again, and forgot what her point had been in the first place. "I'm sexy and… sensual and…" *Still a woman.*

"No arguments from me, little Reb. I just didn't know if you were sure."

A loud horn blared as a solid black tour bus with Sinners' cherry red logo painted on the side turned into the parking lot and pulled to a halt next to the pigsty bus.

Eric lowered Rebekah to her feet and released her. He held onto her arm until she regained her balance and then turned to drop the hood on the Corvette before going around to the back of the car to open the trunk.

She was a bit confused by his sudden brusqueness. He'd probably lost all respect for her after she'd thrown herself at him like that. It wasn't like she attacked good-looking guys on a regular basis. Or ever, actually. She just hadn't expected to enjoy Eric's kiss quite that much. She really had intended to use it to drive home her point. Which had been that... um... What had her point been? She touched her heated cheeks with cool fingertips.

Eric pulled a large duffel bag from the trunk and closed the hatch.

When he noticed her standing there uncertainly, he said, "Well, come on. Don't you want to see the inside of the new bus?"

She smiled and nodded enthusiastically.

He bit his lip and shook his head at her. "I still say you're the most precious, adorable, little thing I've ever seen."

She gasped indignantly. Oh yes. *That* had been her point. "Eric Sticks, you don't want me to teach you another lesson, now do you?"

He grinned and Rebekah's heart raced.

"Yeah, actually, I do," he said.

Chapter 3

MUCH TO ERIC'S DELIGHT, the new tour bus had six curtained bunks instead of four, and the mattresses were at least a foot wider. Bliss for someone obscenely tall and forced to sleep in a compartment de-signed for an average-sized toddler. Being perfect gentlemen—*yeah, right*—the guys let Rebekah choose her bunk first. She selected the bottom bunk closest to the bathroom where Sed used to sleep on the old bus. Trey immediately claimed the bunk over hers, which had been Eric's.

"This way I get to be on top of Rebekah night after night after night," Trey said. He bit his lip and leaned toward her, but didn't touch her. Her eyelids fluttered, lips parted, and she swayed toward him. Under Trey's spell already. Son of a bitch. The guy had the uncanny ability of knowing how to seduce anyone. Except Brian. He'd been trying to get in their lead guitarist's pants for years. As far as Eric knew, he'd never quite managed it.

Rebekah flushed and giggled like most women did when Trey gave them the slightest notice. If Eric had said that exact same thing to her, she probably would have punched him in the teeth for being a pig.

Eric picked the bunk across the aisle from Rebekah's. Because he was sick of sleeping in a top bunk, not because he kept replaying her little *lesson* over and over in his mind. And not because those thoughts were making his dick all tingly with excitement. And defi-nitely not because he might catch a glimpse of her while she slept. Um, yeah.

Jace tossed his duffel bag into the bunk above Eric's. "I finally get my own bunk," he said. In the past, he'd had to take whichever bunk happened to be unoccupied, which changed depending on which band member had claimed the queen-sized bed in the only bedroom for a particular night.

Sed took the bottom bunk across from the bathroom, leaving the bunk above him for Brian, whenever he happened to show up.

"Does this bus have a bedroom?" Trey asked. He slipped the strap of Rebekah's tank top over her shoulder with one finger. Again, with the flushing and giggling on her part. But her nipples weren't hard. Not like when Eric had massaged her back. And she wasn't teaching Trey any lessons. At least, not yet.

"Of course it has a bedroom," Sed said. He opened the door at the end of the hall. "But now that we each have our own bunk, we don't have to fight over it."

Eric turned his attention to Jace, who had this totally annoying, empathetic expression on his beard stubble-covered face. Jace glanced from Trey to Rebekah and then rolled his eyes at Eric. So Jace had figured out that Eric was jonesing over Rebekah. Twerp. Eric supposed it wasn't too hard to figure out, but it was easy enough to remedy. If she wanted Trey, what did he care? Trey could have her. Um, yeah.

The group inspected the bedroom, which was slightly smaller than the one on their last bus. This one still had a queen-sized bed, but there was no room for a dresser. Eric shoved Jace in the shoulder and grinned. He pointed at the ceiling. "No hook for your bondage games, Tripod. How will you ever get your jollies off?"

"I'll save it up for when I get home. Aggie's dungeon should be finished by the time we finish this leg of the tour." Jace flushed, as he was wont to do whenever the subject drifted to anything sexual or romantic. Considering the hard-core kink the guy enjoyed, his embarrassment was kind of strange.

Eric was pleased to find that though the bedroom was smaller, the bathroom was larger. You could actually turn around without dislocating your elbow on the wall. The rest was similar to their old bus, except the colors were different throughout. The dining benches, the sofa, and captain chairs had black leather upholstery instead of cream. The carpet was red instead of beige. Black granite countertops. Shiny, black paneling. Black apartment-sized appliances. The curtains that hid the bunks were red. The bedding? Red. Framing around the bunks? Black.

Everywhere Eric looked: red and black.

"Um, Sed?" Eric scratched behind his ear. "Did you have this thing custom-made in Sinners' colors?"

"Yeah. It was Jerry's idea. Cool, huh?"

This nightmare-inducing color palate had been their manager's idea? Knowing Jerry, he was probably using it in some advertising campaign. "I guess…" Eric shook his head.

"I like it," Rebekah said. "It looks classy, yet metal."

"Exactly!" Sed smiled so broadly that both dimples showed. His goofy grin faded into a scowl when his eyes met Eric's. "Metal," he said in a low growl.

Eric's amusement died when Trey leaned into Rebekah's personal space again. Her cheeks went pink, and she fidgeted with the bangles on her wrist. Maybe if Eric told her that he found her fidgeting absolutely adorable, she'd teach him another lesson. He could use another one. Or a million or two.

"What in the hell?" Brian said from near the bus entrance. He rubbed a hand over his face as he took in the new bus's décor.

"Brian!" Trey was down the aisle hugging and pounding Brian on the back before Eric could blink.

Eric caught Rebekah's bewildered expression before she'd managed to hide it with a friendly smile. She followed Trey to be introduced to Brian. Trey was asking his friend a million questions a minute, leaving Rebekah to stand awkwardly waiting for her opening.

Now that Brian was here, maybe Eric had a chance to catch her attention again. Trey didn't have time for some chick when his best bud, Brian, was within reach.

"Did you have fun in Aruba?" Trey asked. Brian had finally had time to take a real honeymoon with his wife of five months.

"Of course. I was with Myrna," he said, as if that explained everything. "Why is our logo painted all *huge* on the outside of the fucking bus?"

"Because our logo is awesome," Trey said, initiating a fist bump with Brian.

Brian knocked knuckles with Trey, but still looked less than thrilled about their new bus's paint job. "We'll have a convoy of groupies following us everywhere we go."

"So the roadies can sell them T-shirts when we stop at rest areas." Sed shrugged.

"And we can auction off the utilization of Trey's lips for beer money," Eric added.

Trey's eyes widened. "Uh, no. What if some whacko wins?"

"Then I'll hold you down until she gets her money's worth," Eric said.

"At a rest area, I'd be more concerned about some lonely truck driver winning," Rebekah said.

Eric laughed. "Or a sexually frustrated politician."

Rebekah burst out laughing. "Or a demented circus clown."

"Or an escaped convict."

"Are you two finished?" Trey said, crossing his arms over his chest.

"Who's this?" Brian asked, nodding in Rebekah's direction.

"Our temporary FOH," Sed explained.

Brian's jaw dropped. "Our new front of house is a chick?"

"Thanks for noticing." Rebekah smiled and extended a hand in his direction.

Brian shook it slowly, pinning her with those intense brown eyes of his. When she flushed and lowered her gaze, he shook his head as if to clear it of cobwebs. He dropped her hand and then turned his attention to Sed. "How did we end up with her as our FOH? I thought Marcus was going to stand in for Dave." He glanced from one bandmate to the next, looking entirely perplexed.

"I have a degree in audio engineering," Rebekah assured him. "I graduated in June."

"As in June of this year?" Brian's voice cracked at the end.

Trey grabbed Brian's arm to gain his attention. "Dave's little sister," he whispered out of the corner of his mouth. "He trusts her with his trade secrets. No one else. Just her."

Rebekah lowered her eyes. "Yeah, he gave me thorough instructions on how to set up and run the entire show." Eric wasn't sure why she looked so depressed about that. Dave was a wizard at mixing a live show. The audio engineers of other bands would have paid big money to learn his methods, especially for his seamless mixing of a rhythm and lead guitar in a dueling solo.

"But our set list is changing to accommodate the new single," Brian reminded them. "Totally uncharted territory for us. Piano intro. Bass solo. A vocal duet." Which frankly made Eric a bit queasy. He'd be singing vocals *live* and, at the same time, maintaining the insanely fast drum track of their newest single, "Sever."

Rebekah brightened at the mention of a new song, her blue eyes flashing with excitement. "I'll make it sound awesome!" She thrust a fist in the air. "Just you watch."

Eric grinned at her enthusiasm. Absolutely adorable. But not metal. Like, at all.

"Dave needs to work out the new mix, not some freshly graduated coed. Ummmm," Brian said. "What's your name, miss?"

"Reb," she supplied.

"Reb, I need to have a little meeting with my band." He swept a hand at them. "Would you excuse us for a minute?" He glanced pointedly over his shoulder toward the exit.

Rebekah's bottom lip trembled. For a second, Eric thought she was going to burst into tears, and then she straightened her spine. She nodded curtly. "Of course."

She started toward the exit. Eric's first instinct was to follow her and make sure she was okay. Brian had been too hard on her. Eric figured it was mostly the shock of knowing his complicated sound would be at the mercy of some amateur. Master Sinclair expected perfection in his live sound and so did Sinners' fans. But he shouldn't have said those things in front of Rebekah. She glanced over her shoulder with longing and then grabbed the handrail to start her decent of the steps. Eric couldn't stand to see someone so full of life look so downtrodden.

"Hey, Reb," Eric called.

She glanced over her shoulder, her pale eyebrows raised in question.

"Would you do me a huge favor?"

She grinned deviously and his heart skipped a beat. "Depends."

"Um, could you move my car into storage? Travis can show you where to park it."

She smiled and nodded eagerly. Eric tossed her his keys and she caught them. She cradled them against her chest and hopped down the stairs with a spring in her step. Eric grinned. He just prayed his stubborn car would start for her.

"Uh oh," Sed said in his typical, low baritone growl.

"Houston, we have liftoff," Trey said. He cupped his hands around his mouth and made CB radio scratch noises. "Head in the clouds confirmed. Roger."

Eric turned his attention to his bandmates who were staring at him with wide grins.

"What?" Eric asked.

"Someone has a little crush," Sed said.

"Nah."

"Dude, you let her drive your car," Trey said. "You don't let *any*one drive your car."

"Drive is a relative term in the case of that piece of shit." Sed chuckled.

"Fuck you, Sed," Eric grumbled.

Sed just laughed harder.

Eric shook his head. "That isn't why I let her drive it. I don't *like* her, like her."

Jace choked on a laugh. Eric sent him a look of warning. No one needed to know he had already locked lips with Rebekah. And oh yeah, he'd *liked* it, liked it.

"She just looked…" Eric sought the right word to explain why he'd broken his no-one-drives-my-car rule. "…sad."

"If you do like her, and I'm not saying you do, but if you think you might, do *not* let her walk all over you like the others," Trey advised.

"I don't like her," he insisted. "Besides, she has a thing for you, Trey."

"Does she?" Trey grinned. "I guess I'll have to use that to its greatest advantage."

"What do you mean?"

Trey's grin widened. "You'll see."

"I didn't call a band meeting to discuss Eric's nonexistent love life," Brian interrupted. "How could you guys just hire her without consulting me?"

"You were unreachable," Sed said.

"That's bullshit, Sed. You could have called me. This isn't some trivial decision you make on the fly. Have you even seen her work?"

Sed crossed his arms over his broad chest. "Well, not exactly, but Dave vouched for her. That makes her okay by me."

"Of course Dave vouched for her. She's his sister."

"So what do you suggest we do?" Sed asked.

"Find someone who knows what the fuck they're doing. How about that?"

"I think we should give her a chance before we fire her," Jace said.

Everyone hesitated, still not used to Jace speaking his opinion. It wasn't that they didn't respect it. They just didn't expect him to voice it so readily. Jace's woman had somehow managed to break through the impenetrable wall he'd hidden behind since he'd become a member of the band. Aggie should consider a job in top secret military weapons development or something. If she could break through Jace's defenses, she could break through anything.

"I agree," Eric said. "I think Reb will do fine. Dave wouldn't throw her off a cliff without a safety harness."

"Does Marcus know about this?" Brian asked.

Shit. Wow, look at that new carpet. Very nice. Eric noticed the black flecks in the red for the first time as he stared at it to avoid Brian's accusatory glare.

"I'll take that as a no." Brian sighed. "You know Marcus wants the FOH position. As monitor engineer, he has seniority."

"I'd agree, except Dave's coming back," Sed said. "We're not giving Dave's job to Marcus. We owe Dave that. This is just temporary, until he gets back."

Brian rubbed a hand over his face. "You know I hope you're right, man, but let's face facts. Dave's paralyzed. How likely is it for him to ever return?"

"He can move now," Jace said. "We saw him a few days ago. He was moving. Wasn't he, guys?"

Trey nodded slightly. "Yeah. A little." Trey stared down at his hands and flexed them into tight fists before lifting his head to look at Brian. "We've got to give him more time to recover before we do anything hasty."

"So we're going to give Rebekah a chance then?" Eric prompted.

"I have a bad feeling about this," Brian said.

"I have a bad feeling about your face, but we still let you hang around," Eric said.

Brian crossed his arms over his chest, and after a long tense moment, nodded. "Fine. We'll give her chance. I just hope I won't be saying, 'I told you so' in three days."

Eric grinned. "Great, I'll go tell her."

"Nope, I'm going to tell her," Trey said and sprinted down the steps.

Eric dashed after him.

Chapter 4

REBEKAH SHUT OFF ERIC'S Corvette and glanced up to find Trey Mills grinning at her from beside the car. His sultry, green eyes held a spark of orneriness. Her heart skipped a beat. He always looked like he'd just crawled out of bed after a night of fantastic fucking. Rebekah wouldn't mind volunteering to keep him in that look. The man was too fine for his own good. Or her own good, she wasn't sure which.

"Hey." Trey's deep, teasing tone sent a shiver of delight down her spine.

She flushed, wondering why this man just had to look at her to get her all hot and bothered. A bit belatedly, she noticed that Trey had Eric in a headlock with his hand over Eric's mouth. Eric poked Trey in the ribs, which made Trey squirm, but he didn't release him.

"What are you doing to Eric?" Rebekah asked.

"You can't take this obnoxious guy anywhere," Trey said. "Brian's decided you'll do a fine job as our soundboard operator."

She grinned and shook her head. "Liar."

When she opened the car door, Trey stepped back, forcing Eric to move with him. Eric made a sound of protest against Trey's hand.

Trey got a strange look on his face and then laughed. "You think licking my hand will make me release you, Sticks?"

"So what did Brian *really* say?" Rebekah asked.

She took one of Eric's hands in both of hers. Looking up at Trey, she drew her tongue over Eric's palm. Eric shuddered.

"He said you deserved a chance," Trey said. "Brian is a really great guy, you know. Fair. Considerate."

Eric said something against Trey's hand that earned him an elbow to the ribs.

Rebekah still didn't believe Trey. Brian didn't want her there and she knew it. She'd just have to show him that she could excel at this job and change his mind about her ability as an audio engineer. Show him that great things came in small packages. That you shouldn't judge a book and/or FOH by her cover. And any other relevant clichés that came to mind.

Rebekah traced Eric's lifeline with the tip of her tongue, and his fingers curled. Trey's hand muffled the little sound of torture Eric made in the back of his throat.

"What are you doing?" Trey asked, his green eyes following the motion of her tongue as she slowly licked Eric's fingers one at a time. Strong fingers that gave wonderful massages. Eric's entire body was trembling by the time she reached his little finger.

"I thought you might release him if I licked *his* hand." She sucked Eric's middle finger into her mouth.

Trey watched her draw Eric's finger deeper into her mouth. He bit his lip and held a hand in her direction. "My turn."

His mouth now free, Eric wriggled out of Trey's stranglehold and stood upright. Her plan had worked. And she'd gained Trey's attention as a bonus.

"If you're trying to make my fly too tight, little Reb," Eric said, "you are succeeding." He adjusted his jeans with a pained wince.

She grinned around his finger. That hadn't been her original intention, but she liked how he readily admitted her effect on him. She needed to feel desirable. She hadn't felt that way for a long while. Too long. Her body had healed after her surgery, but she knew she was missing something. She felt different. Empty. And when her long-term boyfriend Isaac had tried to make love to her, he had made her feel the loss of her womb to the depths of her soul. He hadn't been intentionally cruel, but it had wounded her nonetheless. No matter how much she'd once loved Isaac, she'd had no choice but to leave him after that.

Rebekah reached for Trey's outstretched hand and tugged him closer. She released Eric's finger from her mouth and drew Trey's inside. When Eric started to move away, she held his hand firmly. She didn't want him to go. She wanted Eric to want her. And she wanted Trey to want her as well. She wasn't sure she wanted either of them to do anything about their desire. She just needed to know it existed.

While Eric seemed content to let her suck on his finger alternately with Trey's, Trey wasn't so patient. When she shifted her attention to Eric for a second time, Trey moved to stand behind her. Trey's hands rubbed over her rib cage and hip bones, urging her to lean back. She felt it against her lower back—the hard ridge of Trey's cock within his jeans—and she shuddered.

She wanted to feel Eric's desire for her as well. She urged him toward her until there were scant inches between their bodies. She wrapped both arms around Eric and pulled his long, hard body against hers. Just like he'd said, he was hard. For *her*. She felt his hard cock against the heated flesh of her belly. Two handsome, sexy men who could have just about any woman they wanted, desired... *her*.

Yeah, but for how long? If they knew how useless her body was, that would send them running in opposite directions. Tears sprang to her eyes, and she tilted her chin down to press her forehead against Eric's hard chest. She couldn't let him see that she was emotional when she should be nothing but aroused.

Trey's hands slid between her and Eric to rub the under-curves of her breasts. He used his chin to brush her hair aside so he could suck on her neck just under her ear. Her thoughts scattered as she lost herself in the moment.

"Oh," she gasped. She hadn't expected Trey to move so fast, but his mouth, his hands, the solid strength of his body behind her felt so good, she only considered stopping him for a millisecond.

Trey bent his knees so that his erection slid down the crack of her ass.

"Oh!" She tilted her head back and looked at Eric. His vibrant blue eyes were partially concealed by heavy lids as he gazed down at her. The sultry look that came so naturally to Trey looked even better on Eric. His hands slid between Trey's hip bones and her butt to draw her closer. Eric lifted her feet off the ground, dragging her up his cock until it pressed against her mound. Trey followed her upward motion, keeping his cock pressed firmly against her ass. Rebekah couldn't think of anything more exciting than being pressed between these two strong and sexy men. Couldn't think of anything more exciting *until* Eric lowered his head to kiss her. She clung to his back and opened her mouth to his questing tongue.

While Eric had her distracted, Trey's hands slid from her breasts to the waistband of her leggings. He slowly eased them down. His fingers against the bare skin along both hips brought her back to her senses.

She jerked her mouth from Eric's and moaned, "No."

"Yes," Trey whispered into her ear. "You mean yes. Say yes, Rebekah."

"Yes," she gasped.

"That's a good girl." Trey looked over Rebekah's shoulder at Eric. "Please tell me you have a couple condoms on you. I got nuthin' with me."

Condoms? Why did he need a couple condoms? She was especially confused by his need for more than one. When realization struck her, Rebekah's entire body stiffened. Trey thought she'd do *that?* Here? With him *and* with Eric? Simultaneously? Was that even possible? How would they... Take turns? Or would they both... Rebekah's heart thudded so hard she expected it to burst right through her sternum.

"Let me go," she whispered.

"Shh, shh, sweetheart, we've got you," Trey murmured. His warm breath against her ear sent shivers of delight down her spine. "Just relax. We'll make you feel so good."

Panic setting in, Rebekah struggled for her freedom. Eric took a step back and lowered her feet to the ground. "You don't have to if you don't want to," he murmured. He removed his hands from her butt and moved one to cup her face.

The strange thing was that somewhere inside she *did* want to. She wanted Trey to slide his cock up her ass and Eric's to plunge upward into her hot, achy pussy. Thrusting into her. Together. It wasn't *that* idea that made her stop them, but the thought that they'd find out. That they'd know. Know she wasn't whole anymore.

Isaac had stood beside her all through her cancer treatments and surgery. Been endlessly patient and understanding while she'd healed. When they'd finally gotten intimate again, he'd lost his erection, saying she felt weird inside. So weird that he hadn't wanted her anymore. She supposed she couldn't blame him. He'd wanted kids. She couldn't give them to him no matter how much she wanted to. And now, she couldn't help but think that no man would ever want her. Sure, they might when they didn't know the truth about her, but as soon as they found out her womb had been taken...

Rebekah couldn't stop shaking. She felt like she was going to collapse.

"I d-don't want to," she whispered. A lie. But better than them finding out and making her feel the way Isaac had made her feel. Empty. Useless.

"Cock tease," Trey muttered under his breath. He pushed away from her and stormed out of the garage.

Rebekah watched him stalk off, not sure why it upset her so much. "He'll hate me now," she whispered.

"He'll get over it." Eric wrapped an arm around her back and rubbed her upper arm encouragingly. "You okay? You're shaking all over."

She swallowed her threatening tears and nodded. She closed her eyes and took several deep breaths to calm herself. Eric's steady strength comforted her more than he could possibly realize. That he didn't demand to know why she was so upset and stupid won the guy so many brownie points, he could have led every Girl Scout troop in the contiguous forty-eight states. Not that she could ever mistake him for a girl. Not after feeling that stone-hard cock against her mound. And he was still threatening to bust the zipper of his pants. Not that she was staring at it or anything.

"So you got her started?" he asked.

Rebekah jerked and tore her eyes off the bulge in Eric's pants, erm, her *shoes* to glance at him in question. "Huh?"

"My car."

She smiled, grateful for the subject change. It helped her bury all the hurt and distract her from the white elephant in his pants, erm, in the *room*. "Yeah, she started right up."

"She must really like you."

Rebekah's smile broadened. "You think so?"

"Oh yeah. She has excellent taste in women."

Rebekah felt her cheeks grow pink. "Has she started for a lot of women then?" Surely a handsome, successful musician like Eric Sticks had a harem of women at his disposal. She glanced at him and found him staring at her through half-closed lids. Her nipples pebbled under his attention. She swallowed and averted her gaze. Even when Trey had been stroking her breasts, her nipples hadn't gotten that hard. Why Eric? There was no denying he was handsome, but Trey... Whoa. She'd always thought Trey Mills was finer than Royal Copenhagen china. Maybe that was the problem. Maybe some Corelle dinnerware was more practical. Maybe Eric could be her everyday dish, and she could take Trey out for special occasions. If ever. He'd sure look nice in her china cabinet stored safely behind the glass.

Eric grinned, obviously unaware that she was mentally comparing him to tableware. "My baby doesn't kiss and tell."

She laughed. "Fair enough."

"You ready to get on the road?"

"Heck yeah, I am," she said.

"You have your CDL, I assume."

"CDL?"

"Commercial Driver's License. You'll need it to drive the bus."

Rebekah's heart slammed into her ribs. "I can't drive the bus!"

"Then who's going to drive? Dave used to be our regular driver."

"Not me." Dave had crashed said bus and nearly died. He would have died if Jace hadn't pulled him from the fiery wreckage or if Eric hadn't resuscitated him by giving him CPR. As she and Eric walked out of the garage and back toward the tour bus, she paused and took his arm to draw him to a halt. "Eric?"

He looked down at her and her heart started thudding again. Why did it keep doing that? He was just standing there. Yes, he looked at her like she was his favorite dish and he was starving to death, but that didn't explain her reaction to him.

"Yeah?" he asked.

Her grip on his arm tightened. She wanted him to feel her gratitude. See it in her eyes. "Thank you for saving my brother's life. Thank you from the bottom of my heart. If there's anything I can do to repay you…" And she did mean anything. Well… with the exception of threesome quickies in a storage area.

He shrugged, but couldn't hide the pleased little smile on his lips. "No big. That CPR stuff comes in real handy around this band.

Are you certified? You never know when someone's going to have a grand mal seizure, crash a bus, or pass out in their own vomit."

Ew. Rebekah's stomach rolled. "Um. Vomit?"

"No worries. I'll take care of all the vomity ones."

She chuckled and then broke into delighted laughter.

He grinned. "You get that I'm joking?"

"Well, of course you're joking. Vomity ones." She laughed again. "Too funny."

"Most people don't get my jokes. Say they're inappropriate." He finger-quoted *inappropriate.*

"Are they idiots?"

"Arguably."

She laughed again.

"A woman who gets my jokes…" His pleased little grin turned into a broad smile. "Can I buy you a coffee sometime? Or a jet?"

"A jet?" She laughed until her stomach ached and she had to bend over with her hands on both knees to catch her breath. "You're killing me."

"Gives me an excuse to practice my CPR. So nice of you to volunteer your soft and tasty lips."

When he leaned closer, she halted his seeking lips with a hand in his face. "Easy there. Do I look like CPR Annie to you?"

"Not at all. But if it will make you feel better, I can close my eyes and pretend."

Actually, she was already feeling better. She didn't need to pretend. Eric Sticks was like a refreshing breeze, blowing away all the clouds that insisted on blotting out her sunshine. Too bad she still had her heart set on Trey.

Chapter 5

STOMACH PROTESTING ITS EMPTINESS, Eric opened the small refrigerator and hunted for something edible. There was one good thing about losing their previous bus. All the suspicious-looking, past-their-expiration-date condiments had been replaced with new bottles. Unfortunately, Eric's secret stash of hot dogs had not. Neither had most of the beer. The stuff currently stocking the fridge looked suspiciously like vegetables and raw meat.

Eric leaned back and waved a hand at the refrigerator. "What's up with the food? Where are my hot dogs?"

Jace rose from the booth around the dining table and stood beside him, his brow crumpled with confusion. "Are those vegetables?"

"Looks like it."

Trey and Brian came to stand in their little huddle before the open refrigerator door. The four of them stood there staring into the fridge as if assessing a piece of modern art for deeper meaning.

"Wait. Is that… cauliflower?" Brian asked, reaching in and poking the package of cauliflower as if he expected it to bite him.

"Sed!" Trey called to Sed, who was driving the bus in Dave's absence. They'd already decided they needed to hire a new driver as soon as possible, but this arrangement would work for now.

"What?" Sed called from the driver's seat.

"Do you know anything about the vegetables in the refrigerator?"

"Jessica says I need to eat better."

"So putting this stuff in the fridge makes her think you're actually going to eat it?" Trey asked.

"I guess."

"Did she forget that none of us can cook?"

"I can stir up some scrambled eggs," Eric said. It was the one thing he knew how to cook. And they could be flavored with just about anything. He enjoyed trying new spices. Perhaps nutmeg and sage this time.

Eric reached for the carton of eggs.

Jace karate chopped his wrist, and Eric's fingers went numb. "Step away from the eggs, Sticks."

Eric might have complained, but Rebekah giggled at his expense and his concentration shattered. He glanced at her sitting in one of the captain's chairs with her feet curled beneath her. Her mismatched socks barely showed from beneath the ginormous sweatshirt she was swimming in. The faded red garment must have once belonged to a four-hundred-pound linebacker. She'd insisted that she was cold when he'd teased her about wearing it earlier. She was already so goddamned adorable, and that huge garment made her seem even more petite. He suppressed the urge to sweep her into his arms and bury his face in her neck. And lose his hands inside that baggy sweatshirt to see if her pert nipples were hard again.

"Maybe there's a frozen pizza in there," Brian said, opening the freezer. He leaned in for a closer inspection. "Chicken? Why is there chicken in the freezer?"

"Jessica's idea," Sed called from the driver's seat.

"I thought she was supposed to be a smart chick," Trey said. "Does she really think we're going to eat this complicated stuff?"

"She *is* a smart chick. She's marrying me," Sed called.

Eric and the rest of the guys busted out laughing. "That proves she's dumb as a post."

Sed stomped the brakes, and his four bandmates ricocheted off each other like bowling pins. Eric sobered immediately; memories of wrenching metal, fear of death, and agonizing pain in his ankle took all the humor out of the situation. He'd limped for days after the bus accident, but all things considered, with the exception of Dave's injury, they'd been lucky.

Rebekah untangled her legs from beneath her sweatshirt and slipped between the guys to peer into the fridge. "I can probably throw something together."

Brian's head swiveled in her direction. "You know how to cook?"

"I've been in the kitchen a time or two." She smiled at them.

When her eyes fell on Trey, he turned and moved to the front of the bus. He leaned against the dashboard, crossed his arms over his chest, and struck up a conversation with Sed. Eric saw the pain in Rebekah's troubled eyes before she covered it with a bright smile. "Go sit down, guys. I'll make dinner."

Rebekah's eyes opened wide when Brian grabbed her in a crushing embrace. "Thank you." He planted a kiss on her temple and squeezed her enthusiastically, swaying side to side with glee.

Eric wedged an arm between Brian and Rebekah. "What about Myrna? Sheesh!"

Brian released Rebekah, looking puzzled. "What do you mean? It's all Myrna's fault in the first place. She's spoiled me so much with her cooking that I don't think I can make myself eat the usual crap we consume on the road."

So Brian was just thinking about keeping his stomach happy? Eric wasn't sure why Brian's hug and platonic kiss pressed all his jealousy buttons. Maybe because Rebekah looked so pleased about it. Did she have a thing for Brian too? Lots of chicks wanted the Brian/Trey combination. Maybe that's why she'd freaked out in the storage unit earlier. Maybe she'd wanted to be the filling in a Brian/Trey sandwich, and Eric had been the wrong kind of bread.

Eric's heart skipped a beat when she gripped his right hand in both of hers.

She looked up at him, a twinkle in her blue eyes. "You're going to help me, right, Eric?"

"Help you?"

"Yeah. You can cut vegetables and stuff, right?"

Not *exactly*. He grinned regardless. He doubted he was capable of telling this woman no. "Sure."

Rebekah rummaged around in the refrigerator to take inventory.

Eric couldn't take his eyes off her ass as she bent at the waist and sorted through ingredients. He stood directly behind her, imagining his cock buried in her warm, slick depths. Her smooth, naked skin beneath his fingertips as she allowed his exploration. His possession. Her warmth against his thighs as he thrust deep. Deep. So deep that his balls pressed against her. He clenched his hands into fists at his sides to prevent himself from grabbing her and showing her the effect that little wiggle of her hips was having on his thoughts and his fly. It was probably a good thing she had that baggy sweatshirt on. If he could actually see her slim thighs and the division between them, his fist-clenching would have done little to keep his hands off her. She backed up unexpectedly, and her luscious little ass bumped into his thighs. He didn't have the mental faculties to take a step back. Instead, his arms slid around her hips and pulled her closer. She stood upright.

"Sorry about that," she said.

Even though she had to feel how hard he was against her lower back, she didn't move away. She tilted her head back to look at him. "I should probably take off this baggy sweatshirt. It's kind of a fire hazard."

As far as Eric was concerned, her body was a much greater fire hazard. He was definitely about to burst into flames. The sweatshirt brushed over his face as she lifted her arms and pulled it over her head. Her scent bombarded his senses. He bit his lip to keep from moaning aloud. Dear lord, he wanted her. Even more so when his gaze settled on the twin bumps of her nipples straining against her tank top. It took every shred of his willpower not to stroke them with his thumbs.

"It is chilly in here," she murmured, taking a deep breath that made her cleavage swell above the neckline of her top.

"Fuckin' A," he groaned and lifted his hands with the intention of cupping those two succulent globes of flesh. Of rubbing those erect nipples between his thumbs and forefingers until she begged him to suck them into his mouth and flick his tongue against them. Rebekah stepped away before he could claim his prize package.

"How does roast sound?" she asked Brian.

"Oh God, yes," Brian murmured.

Eric had forgotten the guys were even present. He glanced over his shoulder self-consciously. Had they noticed him pressing against their little cock tease of a soundboard operator? And enjoying it immensely? Her coyness might piss off Trey, but it had Eric entirely spellbound. His cheeks pink, Jace offered Eric a knowing grin. That would be one in the "totally noticed it" column. Brian seemed more interested in the lean roast Rebekah set on the counter.

The consistent hum of the bus engine lowered several pitches as Sed directed the bus off the road and into a rest area. Eric braced himself as they drew to a halt and reached for Rebekah to steady her. She smiled her gratitude at him and he grinned like a giddy fool.

"Eric," she said, "you wash and cut these red potatoes into large chunks."

He wasn't sure if he could hold a knife in his trembling hand, but he couldn't help but be happy that Rebekah had chosen him to help her cook. Not Trey. Eric stifled the urge to stick his tongue out at Sir Fucks-a-lot, who was still chatting with Sed at the front of the bus. Sed stood from the driver's seat, stretched his arms over his head, and nodded at Trey.

Rebekah tumbled half a bag of potatoes into the sink and left Eric to figure out how to wash and cut them on his own. She heated some oil in a pan and unwrapped the roast. Spellbound, Eric watched her massage spices into the meat, imagining her tiny hands digging into his ass as he gyrated his hips to fuck her deep. And hard. Would she like it hard? Eric was accustomed to having intensely sensual thoughts frequently. His mind had always been the center of his sexuality, but he didn't usually get this turned on by *every*thing a woman did. When she tossed the meat into the hot grease and it sizzled loudly, Eric finally snapped back to his senses. He didn't want *that* to happen to his ass, thank you very much.

She glanced at him. "You have no idea what you're doing, do you?"

He hated to admit it, but he didn't. He didn't want her to get exasperated and shoo him out of the kitchen. He wanted to help her. To be close to her. Special to her. "Show me."

She washed a potato, moved it to the cutting board built into the countertop, and cut it into several large pieces. "Do you think you can handle that?" She looked at him from beneath her thick lashes.

Handle what? "Yeah."

"That smells fantastic already," Brian crooned from the dining area.

"It won't be ready for a couple hours."

Brian covered his belly with both hands when it rumbled with hunger. "I think my stomach will digest itself by then."

"We used to go days without a decent meal. Myrna has spoiled you," Jace said and chuckled.

Brian smiled at him. "And not just with her cooking."

Rebekah turned the meat to sear its other side and searched the fridge for vegetables. Eric almost cut his thumb off as he watched her wriggling backside, which was no longer hidden by her sweatshirt.

"Mercy, woman," he growled.

She glanced at him, her eyebrows raised in question.

"You have one seriously fine ass." Eric bit his lip. Sometimes things popped out of his mouth before he had a chance to edit them. Well, they always did, actually.

Instead of chastising him, she grinned and gyrated her hips. "You think so?"

The pain of the knife slicing through the pad of his thumb barely registered.

"Way to go, lover boy. Now you're bleeding all over our fucking dinner," Trey said. He nudged Rebekah aside and found a bag of apples in the refrigerator. He tossed one to Brian and claimed one for himself.

"Oh dear." Rebekah yanked the knife out of Eric's hand and tossed it in the sink. She grabbed his wrist and kept his hand elevated as she tugged him into the bathroom. She searched frantically through the medicine cabinet. "Don't you guys have anything but pain relievers in here?"

"We tend to nurse a lot of hangovers." Eric's chest constricted over her concern. No one gave a shit about him. Ever. "There should be a first-aid kit under the sink."

Blood was now dripping down the side of his hand, but the wound didn't hurt much. She located the kit and wrenched it open. She grabbed a can of antiseptic spray, popped the lid off, and sprayed his wound as if she was an '80s hairdresser with a can of Aqua Net. Stinging pain shot up his arm.

"Ow! Fuck!" Eric tucked his hand against his chest to protect it from her overzealous disinfection.

"Hold still." She turned on the water and forced his hand beneath the flow. "Let me see it."

"Um, Rebekah!" Sed called from outside the bathroom. "I think the roast is burning."

"Just turn off the burner!" she bellowed. "Eric is more important."

Eric is more important? Did she really feel that way?

Rebekah inspected his thumb and sucked a breath through her teeth. "It's not all that deep, but you practically filleted it."

"If someone hadn't distracted me with her seriously fine ass…"

She stiffened and lifted her guilty gaze. "I'm sorry. I'll go put my sweatshirt back on."

He shifted her back against the sink counter so they were facing each other and pinned her there with his body. "I'd rather you didn't."

He brushed her platinum and cobalt hair behind one ear, his uninjured thumb brushing over her high cheekbone. The tension drained from her body and she watched him, her lips slightly parted. She was close enough that he could feel her heart thudding in her chest and recognized that his was thudding just as hard. He lowered his head, closing the distance between their lips.

"I finished cutting the potatoes," Jace said and pushed the door open. "Are you okay, Eric?"

Rebekah squirmed from between the counter and Eric's body. "I think it just needs a bandage," she said. "What do you think?"

Jace and Rebekah inspected the cut on Eric's thumb while Eric tried to get his raging hard-on under control. Damn, this woman had him turned every which way but right side up.

"I don't think it needs stitches either," Jace was saying.

Another painful spray of disinfectant and a rather large bandage later, Eric followed Jace and Rebekah out of the bathroom. Eric watched her add water to the roast and set it to simmering. She refused to let Eric help her this time, but Jace, the little bastard, somehow weaseled himself into her assistant's role. Jace didn't need help figuring out how to peel and cut carrots. It was almost as if he'd cooked before.

"You've been holding out on us," Brian accused as he watched Jace cut onions like a master chef.

Jace glanced over his shoulder, flushed, and changed his technique to awkwardly cutting the onions into uneven chunks.

"You can cook, and you let us starve?" Trey hit Jace in the middle of the back with his apple core.

"I'm not any good," Jace insisted quietly.

"Better than Eric," Brian said. "You haven't cut off your thumb yet."

Eric laughed. "Fuck you, Sinclair."

"Sorry, Sticks. I save it all for Myrna."

With an indulgent grin on his face, Sed shoved Brian's shoulder. "Is she pregnant yet?"

Brian shrugged. "Don't know. If not, it's not from a lack of trying."

Eric averted his gaze. He never thought he'd see the day when one of Sinners would talk about having kids. He caught sight of Rebekah staring at Brian as if someone had ripped her heart out. She noticed that Eric was staring at her again and turned back to the stove. She added the vegetables to the roast, covered the Dutch oven with a lid, and closed herself in the bathroom. Eric wondered what was bothering her.

"Slow down, buddy," Trey said. It took Eric a moment to realize he was talking to him.

"Huh?"

"If you really want her, slow down."

"What? You mean Rebekah?"

"Is there any other *her* on the bus? Just play it cool."

"But she wants you."

Trey winked at him. "And I'm still planning to use that fact to its fullest."

Chapter 6

REBEKAH CHECKED HER REFLECTION in the bathroom mirror to make sure none of the guys would be able to tell she'd been crying. So stupid that she'd been crying anyway. She couldn't let herself turn into a blubbering mess every time someone mentioned having babies. Saving her life was more important than being able to have children. She knew that. Sometimes it didn't feel that way. She'd always wanted to be a mom. Just another dream that had been crushed. Her latest dream, to be the best front of house soundboard operator in the business, was what she needed to focus on. She'd been given a chance. She had to use it and do her best. She prayed her best was good enough.

Rebekah let herself out of the bathroom and went to check on the roast. When she lifted the lid, five hungry rock stars groaned in unison. She grinned to herself. She could totally get used to this. She put the lid back on the pot and turned to face the guys crammed in the two booths around the dining table.

"Do you want a beer, Rebekah?" Sed asked and took a sip from his brown bottle.

"No, thanks. I need to go over Dave's notes some more."

She retrieved Dave's precious notebook from the chair she'd left it in and settled in the seat with the pages of diagrams and text. How on earth was she supposed to remember all this? She'd thought the guitars would be her biggest challenge, but they didn't compare to how many mics had to be set up and adjusted for Eric's massive drum kit. She looked up and caught Eric staring at her. He didn't look away. His pale blue gaze seemed to caress her skin as he watched her with undisguised interest. She didn't understand why, but she liked the way he looked at her. It was as if she was forbidden fruit, and he was one second away from getting himself ejected from the Garden of Eden.

Rebekah glanced at Trey, hoping he might also show a bit of interest, but he was wedged against Brian in the dining booth going over something about the new song they were adding to the show. She wished she hadn't balked back in the storage garage. Trey was the one she'd always had a crush on. Every slight movement he made was like he was playing an orchestra of sensuality. Unfortunately, he didn't want to play with Rebekah at all.

She forced her attention back to her notebook, using a pencil to carefully scribe notes in the margins. She wished the band trusted her enough to come up with her own setup rather than emulating her brother's, but there was no sense in redoing something that already worked. She couldn't wait to get to the venue and work on setting up the piano and Eric's vocal mic. Those would be her own. Maybe with time they'd let her explore more of her ideas. For now, she just had to live up to their expectations. Her big brother's shoes were a lot to fill.

When dinner was ready, the guys crowded around the stove.

"Sed, don't take half the roast!" Brian said.

"My woman bought it, so it's mine. You're lucky I let you have any."

"Save me some carrots." Trey poked one of the carrots on Sed's plate and added it to his own. "They're sweet."

"Hey!" Sed complained.

While Sed's attention was on trying to retrieve the stolen carrot, Brian helped himself to some of Sed's roast. Jace saw his opening at the stove and began to divvy up the remaining food between his plate and Eric's. Rebekah decided she'd be lucky to get the leavings at the bottom of the pan.

When the scuffle ended and all were satisfied that they had gotten everything they had coming to them, they headed for the table. The pan on the stove was completely empty. Rebekah stood there watching with wide eyes. The five of them noticed her at the same time. Each paused with their forks halfway to their mouths.

"Rebekah didn't get any," Eric said. He slid from the end of the bench and waved her toward his vacated seat. "Have mine."

She heard his stomach rumble from where she stood. "No, you eat. I'll be fine."

"Get her a plate," Sed said. "We'll all share."

"That isn't nec—" The eager looks on their faces stifled her protests.

Eric retrieved a plate and set it in the center of the table. Each gave her some of their food until her plate was fuller than any of theirs. She didn't know why it touched her so much. "Thank you."

"Sit," Eric insisted. He picked up his plate and moved to the living area. He sat on the sofa and balanced his plate against his chest so he could shovel food into his mouth with his free hand.

There was a narrow spot beside Trey on the bench. He glanced at her and then at Eric in the living room. Instead of scooting over to give her more room, he moved further from Brian so that there was no place to sit. Rebekah decided he didn't want her to sit beside him. She bit her lip, not sure why Trey's rebuffs hurt so much. She took her plate from the table and went to sit next to Eric on the sofa.

"That was rude," Sed commented.

"Shut up," Trey murmured.

Rebekah ignored him. It wasn't hard when Eric gifted her with a brilliant smile. She'd rather sit with him anyway. Otherwise, he'd be eating alone.

"God, this is good," Brian said with a full mouth. "I think Reb deserves a raise."

Rebekah flushed with pleasure and set her plate on her lap. "I'm glad you like it."

"Love it," Sed said in his deep baritone.

"Thanks for cooking for us," Jace added with an adorable smile.

Trey silently shoveled food into his mouth, but Eric nudged her gently with his elbow. "If you feed them good food, they'll love you forever."

She supposed she could handle that. "Well, since I can't drive the bus, I guess I'll take the cooking duties."

Several hollers of appreciation came from the dining area.

"But you guys get to wash the dishes," she added.

The appreciative cheers turned to grumbles.

Someone's phone rang. There was a scuffle as Trey snatched Brian's phone out of his hand and answered. "Hi, Myrna. Watcha doin'?" Trey said in a teasing tone. "Oh, he's much too busy to talk right now."

"Give me the phone," Brian insisted.

"Are you knocked up yet?" Trey asked. His face fell, and he hurriedly handed the phone to Brian. "She's crying."

"Great," Brian grumbled and shoved Trey out of the booth with both hands. Brian headed toward the bedroom with his phone. "Don't cry, sweetheart," he said to his wife. "We have plenty of time. We'll keep trying."

Brian closed the bedroom door behind him.

Rebekah pushed her food around her plate, her appetite suddenly lacking. She doubted she could swallow around the knot in her throat anyway.

"Dipshit," Sed grumbled at Trey.

"I didn't mean to make her cry. How was I supposed to know she started her period?"

"She told you that?" Sed cocked an eyebrow at him.

"How else is she going to know she's not pregnant?"

"Was she really crying?" Jace asked.

"Yeah…"

"Maybe we should ask her to come on tour with us again," Sed said. "How is she supposed to get pregnant if she's in Kansas City and Brian is touring all over the country?"

"He could always jack off into an empty beer bottle and FedEx it to her," Eric said.

While everyone else rolled their eyes at him, Rebekah burst out laughing.

"He can put it on dry ice, and then she can warm it up in the microwave when it arrives."

Rebekah laughed harder, almost dropping her plate in the process.

"Oh my God, Rebekah," Sed grumbled, "would you please not encourage him? He's bad enough already."

She glanced from Sed to Eric, and her smile faltered. "That was not funny, Eric," she said seriously. She turned her head so no one but Eric could see her expression. "Yeah, it was," she whispered.

Eric grinned. "Are you going to eat any of that?" He pointed at her plate with his fork.

Her appetite had already returned. "Yeah. Making me laugh won't earn extra food from me."

The guys around the table had already finished their food and were picking at Brian's. Rebekah couldn't blame them. The roast was tender and juicy. The flavor rich and savory. It was one of the best meals she'd ever cooked.

"Hey, what's that?" Eric pointed to the back of the bus.

While her attention was elsewhere, Eric attempted to steal from her plate. Her hard stare stopped him with his fork hovering millimeters from one of her potatoes. "Busted."

"You're just picking at it, and it's so good," he said. "I wouldn't want it to go to waste. Can't I have just a little bite?"

She considered him for a moment. She really didn't mind sharing, but he was so fun to tease. "How about a trade?"

"I don't have anything you want."

He had plenty she wanted, but she didn't want to be too greedy. "Foot massage."

"For one potato?" He shook his head. "That's worth a bite of roast, two potatoes, and a carrot. At least."

"You're a master negotiator. You'd better do a good job." She fed him off her plate, knowing there was no way she could possibly eat it all anyway, but hey, she got a foot massage from the man with the magic hands out of the deal. She was definitely getting the better end of this bargain.

He chewed each bite slowly, as if trying to avoid his task.

When he'd finished, she continued to eat and he rose to put his empty plate in the sink. Returning a moment later, he knelt on the floor at her feet. He took her socked foot in both hands and looked up at her. Their eyes met and her heart began to race. When his uninjured thumb rubbed her instep with just the right amount of pressure, she moaned.

Eric got a strange look on his face, lowered his nose to her foot, and took a hesitant sniff. "Jeez, woman, are you trying to kill me?"

"My feet do not stink," she said indignantly.

"Must be the sock." He stripped it from her foot and tossed it aside.

His thumb against her bare skin was almost too wonderful to bear. She stretched her toes and closed her eyes to relish the sensation. After a minute he stopped and moved to sit beside her on the sofa. She opened her eyes to look at him. "What about the other one?"

"You said foot massage, not *feet* massage."

She scowled. "But my other foot wants some attention."

He looked at her plate pointedly.

"You can't possibly still be hungry," she said

"I am," Sed said in his low baritone. "That was fucking fantastic. I'll massage your other foot for second helpings."

Eric's eyes opened wide, and he flopped down on the floor again. "Jessica will kick your ass if you touch another woman."

"Worth it. Have you tried Jessica's cooking?" Sed made a face of horror.

Rebekah giggled. Eric Sticks and Sed Lionheart competing to massage her feet? She didn't remember dying and going to heaven, but it could be the only logical explanation. If only Trey would show some interest. He was sucking on a red lollipop and staring at the bedroom door where Brian had disappeared moments before.

"I'll make more next time. I'm not used to cooking for five men." Or anyone but herself since she'd broken up with Isaac.

"When we catch up with the other bus and the equipment truck, you'll be cooking for seventeen men," Eric said.

"Seventeen?"

"And one very adorable woman."

"I'm not adorable," she insisted.

"And also for yourself."

"There's another woman on tour?" She said it before she realized he was teasing her again. "You better get busy massaging, or I'll be sharing this delicious piece of roast with Sed." She pushed a large piece of roast to the edge of her plate.

"I'm so there," Sed said.

"Hey, Sed," Trey said around his sucker. "Come here. I need to tell you something."

Sed hesitated and then returned to the table and leaned close to Trey who said something in his ear. Rebekah lost concentration when Eric stripped off her other sock and massaged her neglected foot. She speared her meaty offering with her fork and fed him. He grinned while he chewed and passed Sed a smug look. Sed had settled at the table next to Jace. Apparently, he'd changed his mind about competing for the rest of Rebekah's supper. When she finally finished, Eric took her plate and set it in the sink.

He then settled next to her on the sofa. "I don't think I'll ever get the smell of Reb foot off my hands." He sniffed his fingers and made a face of displeasure.

"Hey!"

"Do you play video games?" Sed was suddenly standing over her and handing her a controller.

"A little," she admitted. She took the controller from Sed.

"Awesome." Sed handed a second controller to Eric and then plopped on the sofa next to him. "You playing, Jace?" he called to their bassist.

"Yeah, why not?"

Jace squeezed in on Sed's opposite side. "Scoot over, Sticks. I can't breathe," Sed complained.

Eric moved closer to Rebekah. His arm and thigh rested against hers. She scooted toward the arm of the sofa to give Eric a bit more room. Sed's massive frame shifted into Eric again. "What part of get the fuck out of my personal space don't you understand?" Sed said to Eric.

By the time Sed was satisfied with his personal space, Rebekah was halfway on Eric's lap. Eric hesitated and then wrapped an arm around her back. Her heart thudded as she shifted completely onto Eric's lap. His arms circled her as he gripped his controller in front of her body.

"That's better," Sed said. He and Jace exchanged devious grins.

Rebekah wasn't sure what was going on, but she decided trying to shoot aliens was twice as hard when she was engulfed by Eric's body heat and his masculine scent. She couldn't concentrate with him this close. Not that she minded.

Brian came out of the bedroom and sat next to Trey in the booth. Rebekah's attention was cut in half again as she tried to follow their conversation. Even Eric's attempts to protect her from the enemy aliens in the game didn't save her avatar from certain death.

"Everything okay?" Trey asked.

"Myrna's pretty upset," Brian said. "I told her I'd fly to Kansas City and see her in ten days or so. You know, when she's fertile. Maybe no sex for ten days will up my sperm count or something."

"Too much information, bro." Trey chuckled.

"One of these days you'll be in my shoes, and I'm going to give you a hard time."

"Trying to have kids? No way in hell. I don't want any kids. Not my idea of a good time."

Rebekah's avatar met an untimely end as she took her eyes off the TV to look at Trey. He didn't want kids? She was just the woman not to give them to him.

"I love kids," Eric said. "They're so much fun."

Rebekah scowled. Her avatar regenerated on screen, and she blasted an unlucky alien to bits.

Chapter 7

IN THE DARKNESS, REBEKAH rolled onto her back and stared at the bunk overhead. Trey slept up there. She could hear his soft snores. He hadn't spoken a word to her all evening. She'd had fun with the other guys, but Trey was obviously avoiding her. She rolled onto her side, restless and horny. She regretted making Trey and Eric stop their combined seduction more and more with each passing minute. Maybe they wouldn't notice that her body was weird. It had been almost two years since her surgery. Maybe things were better now. How could she know if she didn't try?

Feeling claustrophobic in her little curtained bunk, she tugged the curtain back. Across the way, the light in Eric's bunk was on. He looked up from the book he was reading. When she tried to see the title on the spine, he shifted it so she couldn't read it. The tease. Like her. Did Trey really think she was a cock tease? She hadn't meant to be. It had just sort of happened that way.

Thinking about what had almost transpired in the garage made her skin hot. And being on a bus with five virile men all evening didn't do much to cool her off. She kicked off her covers and rolled onto her back again. She caught movement out of the corner of her eye and turned her head enough to catch Eric watching her. She followed his piercing gaze to her cleavage. The way he looked at her made her want to feed his desire. Maybe she should try sex with Eric. He'd probably be less critical of her body than Trey would be. She wasn't sure what compelled her to tug her loose tank top down until one bare nipple appeared above the neckline. Eric's excited gasp made that nipple bud into a hardened point.

Jeez, why did her nipples get hard every time that guy looked at them? Annoyed, she rubbed a hand over her breast, trying to get her reaction under control. It only managed to make her nipple harder. Probably because it felt so good. Damn, she was horny. Her sex drive had been nonexistent for almost two years. This was a welcome, though unexpected, change.

Eric's book tumbled to the floor, and she looked down at it. Shakespeare? Really? She glanced at him and found him watching her with a look of unquenchable desire on his ruggedly handsome face. Did he like watching her rub her own breast that much?

She plucked at her nipple with her fingertips to see how Eric would react. He shifted in his bunk and took a deep, shuddering breath. If she kept going, would he get excited enough to touch himself? She licked her lips. Their eyes met. She wanted him to become so aroused that he couldn't help but touch himself.

She used her toes to yank her curtain open farther. She then pulled her top down in front until both breasts were fully exposed. Pretending she wasn't putting on a little show for Eric, she pressed her breasts together, rubbed them with her palms, and plucked at her nipples until they were both standing at rigid attention. She licked her fingers and slid the wetness over her pebbled flesh. She wondered what Eric's strong fingers would feel like against her nipples. The memory of his thumb against her lower back and the instep of her foot had her attempting to copy his technique. She cupped one breast in each hand and rubbed her thumbs over both nipples in firm, repetitive circles. While no substitute for the real thing, it did feel good. Knowing he was watching her made it feel a thousand times better. Her eyes drifted closed, head tilted back, mouth dropped open. "Oh, yes," she whispered.

Across the aisle, Eric gasped brokenly.

Did he think she was sexy? Or just pathetic?

"Eric." She hadn't meant to say his name. She bit her lip and peeked at him through one half-closed eye.

His blue eyes were glazed with desire. For *her*? She slid a finger into her mouth and sucked. He pressed his tongue against his upper lip then eased his curtain open, revealing a hard-muscled, long, and lean torso. He had perfectly sculpted arms, shoulders, and chest. A drummer's body. She could see the hint of his washboard abs. A small ring pierced one nipple. Unfortunately, the curtain obscured his lower body. Was he entirely naked? She wished he would open his curtain and let her see the rest of his body. His cock. She wanted to see it. Was he hard?

She slid her finger into her mouth to wet it. She then rubbed it over her aching nipple and down the center of her belly. Eric's chest rose and fell with excited breaths. He shifted and fumbled with something behind the curtain below his waist. He sucked a breath between his teeth, and his eyes drifted closed in bliss. Oh God, was he touching himself now? She couldn't see what he was doing below the waist, but his arm was moving rhythmically.

His eyes opened and he rubbed his face against his pillow, his mouth open. Wow, he looked sexy. Did she look that sexy to him? She lowered her hand and cupped her mound through her pajama bottoms. She was hot. And getting wet. It took a lot to get her wet, but that look on his face had her fluids flowing freely. She wanted to touch herself while Eric touched himself. And she wanted him to see her do it.

She glanced at the bunk above Eric's where Jace slept to make sure his curtain was closed completely. Heart thudding with excitement, Rebekah pushed her curtain open farther. She glanced across the aisle, waiting for Eric to reciprocate. He watched her, his head tilted back slightly, his arm still moving with the same rhythm, but he didn't open his curtain, didn't show her what she wanted to see. She could tease too.

Rebekah removed her tank top and matching pajama bottoms, leaving her in nothing but her panties. She rolled onto her side, presenting her back to Eric. She played with her breasts, not sure which excited her more: knowing he was watching, or the actual attention she paid to her flesh. Okay, who was she kidding? Knowing he was watching was all the appeal.

She heard his curtain slide. She looked over her shoulder wondering if he'd shut her out. No, he'd opened it farther. She could see Eric's navel now and his forearm moving against his belly as he stroked his cock, but she still couldn't see what she really wanted to see.

Her back still to Eric, she ran one hand over her ass. Eric sucked a breath through his teeth. He liked that, did he? Would he like to see more?

She rolled to face him and thrust her breasts forward, rubbing her hands over her belly, sides, and hips with a featherlight touch. When she covered her mound with one hand and squeezed, Eric's entire body jerked with excitement. She wanted to show him more. Show him everything.

Rebekah eased her panties down her thighs, removed them, and tossed them across the aisle into Eric's bunk. His breath caught. He picked up her panties with his free hand and pressed them to his nose. He inhaled deeply and then shuddered.

"Oh dear God," he groaned.

Trembling, Rebekah spread her thighs and tested her excitement. Her pussy was delightfully wet. Her lips swollen and achy. She brushed two fingers against her clit and jerked with excitement. She hadn't been this worked up since before her surgery. The doctor had said she'd never get her sex drive back. Heh, wrong, Doctor Dumbass.

Rebekah rubbed her breast with one hand, the excited flesh between her thighs with the other. Her pleasure built until she was writhing with excitement in her bunk. Oh. Oh? Was she going to come? She couldn't do that anymore, could she? She hadn't been able to with Isaac after her hysterectomy. *Don't think about him*, she chastised herself.

Rebekah rolled onto her back and ran her hands down over her belly and between her thighs. She opened her legs and slid two fingers inside her pussy. She was so wet. Couldn't remember ever being this turned on. She wanted Eric to see. To see her plunging her fingers into her own body. She turned around in her bed so that her head was at the foot and rolled onto her stomach, trying to find a position where he would be able to see the most. She moved her bent legs up under her belly, her knees just under her ribs, and spread her legs wide.

"So beautiful," he murmured.

She moved her arm beneath her body, down its center, between her legs. She stroked at her throbbing clit, undulating her hips in excitement. Could he see what she was doing? She plunged her fingers deep inside, and Eric cursed under his breath. Oh yeah, he could see everything. She turned her head, her left cheek pressed against her mattress so she could watch his face. Her excitement built as she stroked her clit and drove her fingers deep into her slick passage. She bit her lip to keep from crying out as her body convulsed with release. She felt the clenching of her pussy around her fingers as the ripples of pleasure pulsed through her. Rebekah collapsed and stretched out on her side, still trembling with the aftereffects of her orgasm. The first she'd had in a long time. Way too fucking long.

Eric pushed his curtain back, revealing his long cock. She watched him stroke himself for several minutes, his fingers wrapped around his flesh, drawing up and down its length with gentle, fast strokes. She strained her ears to hear the sounds of flesh on flesh and the excited hitch in his breath. She had the sudden urge to want to come with him. She opened her legs again and stroked her clit with the same rhythm he used. She decided watching the look on his face was almost as sexy as watching his hand slide over his cock, almost as sexy as thinking about it between her lips. She sucked on the fingers of her free hand, wanting him in her mouth, wondering what his cum would taste like. She slid the fingers of her other hand in and out of her pussy, imagining him thrusting into her, longing to have his slim hips between her quaking thighs. The involuntary arch in Eric's back told her he was close to release. She stroked her clit more vigorously, afraid she'd miss her chance to come with him. Watching the fluids erupt from his body, watching him catch his cum in his free hand, watching him rub it over his cock from tip to base while he stared at her through half-lowered lids sent her over the edge. She cried out as a second orgasm pulsed through her body.

The curtain above her opened, and Trey's face appeared upside down over the edge of his bunk. "What are you doing down there?" His eyes drifted over her nude body, to the fingers she still had buried in her pussy. "Fuck yeah, that's what I'm talking about." He flipped himself out of his bunk and onto the floor. Still senseless with spent desire, she watched Trey reach in his bunk. She couldn't figure out why he was inserting a metal stud through his tongue and securing it in place with a metallic ball. Couldn't figure it out until he leaned over her body and buried his face between her thighs. He rubbed the bit of metal over her clit, and she cried out in surprise. She grabbed two fistfuls of his longish hair, intending to push him away, but within seconds she was too busy writhing in pleasure to consider stopping him.

Trey's tongue flicked against her with such perfectly timed precision, she became delirious. Rebekah shook her head side to side, knowing this much pleasure must be wrong. Trey's hands glided up her body, hands skimming over her heated flesh. Goose bumps rose along his gentle paths. Her panting became gasping and then moaning. She had no sense of place.

Trey's thumbs brushed over both nipples, and she cried out.

"Will you two take it to the bedroom and shut the fucking door?" Sed yelled from his bunk.

Trey lifted his head and Rebekah cried out again, this time in protest. He placed a kiss along the inner ridge of her hip bone. "Come on," he murmured, his voice husky with desire. For her. Trey Mills wanted her. She couldn't quite grasp the concept.

Trey climbed to his feet, and her eyes fell on the tent in his shorts. Trey was hard. Excited by her body. A surge of lust flooded the apex of her thighs, and she shuddered. He offered her a hand and helped her to her feet.

"You coming, Eric?" Trey asked, catching Eric's eye and nodding toward the bedroom.

Rebekah's heart lurched. "What?"

"He likes to watch. You want him to, don't you?"

She stared at Eric, who was still lounging in his bunk. She couldn't read his expression. Bewilderment? Frustration? "Yeah. I want him."

Trey tugged Rebekah toward the bedroom at the back of the bus.

Chapter 8

ERIC JERKED THE CURTAIN of his bunk closed and buried his head under his pillow. He wanted her. Rebekah. Wanted to watch her touch herself again. Damn, that had been so hot. He'd seen a lot of things in his day, well, mostly his nights, but watching Rebekah pleasure herself had turned him on like nothing in his experience. He didn't only want to watch her though. He wanted to touch her. Kiss her. Taste her. Smell her. Hold her. Laugh with her. Cry with her. He wanted *her*. And she wanted fucking Trey. Everyone wanted fucking Trey.

Eric yelled, "Fuck!" into his pillow and tossed it aside.

He knew it would be pure torture to watch Trey touch Rebekah, taste her, make love to her. Watch Trey do all the things he wanted to do. But Eric couldn't resist her invitation. He knew she meant to say that she wanted him to *watch*, not that she actually wanted him, but Eric couldn't help but get his hopes up. When Trey was finished with her, Eric could try to scrape together whatever was left of her and make it his. It had never worked in the past, but maybe this time would be different.

Eric tugged his boxer briefs up his thighs and tucked his half-hard cock into his underwear and down his thigh. He shouldn't have jacked off in front of Rebekah. She probably thought he was some desperate loser. He located her panties and hid them under his pillow before yanking his curtain open and climbing from his bunk. He found his book on the floor and shoved that under his pillow as well, before padding down the corridor toward the open bedroom door. He could already hear Rebekah's sighs of delight.

Frozen on the threshold, Eric stared at the bed. Rebekah lay sprawled on her back, her arms spread wide as she clung to the bed-clothes, her back arched to thrust the perfect globes of her breasts upward. Her eyes were closed tightly, but her mouth hung open in blissful abandon. Whatever Trey was doing to the flesh between her legs must have felt fucking amazing.

"Oh, oh, oh," she cried. "I'm coming. I'm coming!"

Eric's mouth went dry, his dick hard.

"Close the door!" Sed insisted, and a spare pillow hit Eric in the back of the head.

Eric stumbled over the threshold, closed the door, and leaned his back against its cold surface for support.

He could smell Rebekah's excitement—the musky scent of her wet pussy—like the scent of her panties, yet more pronounced. Eric shuddered and pressed his cock against his thigh so he didn't yank it out of his drawers and start jerking it again.

Trey lifted his head and glanced over his shoulder at Eric. "There you are. Come over here where you can see."

Eric hesitated, sparing a glance at Rebekah's flushed face for signs of protest. She gazed at him through lowered lids, biting her lip as she wriggled her hips in anticipation of Trey's pierced tongue. When Eric didn't make a move, she beckoned him closer with two fingers.

Eric sprinted to the end of the bed and came to a sudden halt next to Trey. Trey grabbed Rebekah by the hips, tugged her to the bottom of the bed, and spread her legs wide.

"Isn't she beautiful?" Trey murmured. He traced the slick skin of her red and swollen inner folds with one finger.

"Yes," Eric agreed. Eric's dick twitched as Trey's finger continued to explore Rebekah's excited flesh.

"She's hot," Trey said.

"Yes."

"Wet."

Eric nodded. Her pussy was so wet, her juices were trickling from her inner folds over her ass. Kneeling on the floor between Rebekah's parted thighs, Trey leaned forward and rubbed the stud in his tongue along one slippery lip. Her hips buckled. The other lip now. He slipped the tip of his tongue inside her, and she cried out. Eric couldn't stand it. He slipped a hand into his underwear and held the hot flesh of his cock, squeezing its head to try to abate his excitement.

Trey's tongue slid from her pussy and flicked over her clit. Rebekah cried out and grabbed Trey's head with both hands. "Oh God, Trey. Lick it fast. Fast and harder!" As she pressed Trey's face against her, her arms blocked Eric's view, which was probably a blessing in disguise.

Trey captured her hands and linked his fingers through hers. He eased her hands away so Eric could see Trey's tongue flicking that little metal ball of delight over her swollen clit.

"Oh, oh, oh, oh, oh!" Rebekah cried, each syllable growing louder and higher pitched. When her hips buckled, Trey plunged his tongue inside her. He twirled his tongue, his piercing tracing the rim of her opening in wide arcs. She sputtered and fought to free her hands from his.

Trey eased away.

"No," she moaned. "Don't stop. Please. Feels... Feels... so good." A broken sob erupted from between her lips.

"Eric can't see if you grab my head, sweetie. You want him to see, don't you?"

She nodded vigorously.

"Eric, why don't you come down here for a closer look?" Trey said, looking at Eric through his longish bangs with those emerald green bedroom eyes. Trey's lips were slick with Rebekah's juices. Juices Eric wanted to sample.

Eric forced his hand from his cock—*fuck*, he was hard—and sat on the end of the bed next to Rebekah. He tilted his head for a closer look. Watching him from beneath heavy eyelids, Rebekah shifted her leg so that her bare skin was touching Eric's thigh. His entire body went taut. Trey rubbed his tongue over her clit again, and she jerked. With several rapid strokes he had her hips undulating in torment. Her scent intensified. Eric breathed deeply through his nose, his thoughts thick with lust. He wanted to immerse himself in her. Touch her.

Eric's hand trembled as he slid it across Rebekah's lower belly. Her back arched, and she panted. "Eric."

"Eric?" Trey murmured with a crooked grin. "I'm doing all the work here." He winked at Eric and went back to work. What was Trey up to? He didn't get that ornery gleam in his eye unless he had some ulterior motive. Eric couldn't think well enough to puzzle Trey out at the moment. Not with this beautiful woman's naked body in sight.

Eric slid his hand over Rebekah's belly again. Goose bumps rose along her smooth flesh. She groaned in torment.

"Show me that you want me, Eric," she whispered. "Show me."

Her passion-glazed eyes moved to the bulge in Eric's boxer briefs. She wanted to see? Many girls got a little freaked out when they realized watching them get done by one of his friends excited him so thoroughly.

Eric eased his black boxer briefs down so that half his cock appeared above the elastic waistband. Her breath caught, and she rubbed her nipples with both hands. He imagined his hands taking the place of hers. His tongue against those taut buds. Gently scraping his teeth over them. Sucking on them until she clung to his hair.

"Do you want to taste her, Eric?" Trey asked.

Eric's cock twitched. He swiveled his head to look at Trey. "Yeah."

"How much?"

He took a stuttering breath. "So much."

Trey rose from the floor and stood over Eric. He bent close until their noses almost touched. Eric considered leaning back to get Trey out of his personal space, but he could smell her. Smell Rebekah. On Trey's lips. Eric's eyes drifted closed. He grabbed the hair at Trey's nape to keep her scent close. Trey didn't move away. He leaned closer.

"You smell her, don't you?" Trey murmured. His nose brushed Eric's. His long bangs tickled Eric's cheek. Eric couldn't move. Could only breathe in her essence. Even if it was mingled with Trey's. "Show her how far you'd be willing to go to taste her, Eric."

Eric did want to taste her. He did. He wasn't sure if he could do what Trey was suggesting, but what he wanted was so close. All he had to do was close the scant inch between his mouth and Trey's, and he could sample her flavor.

"Show her," Trey whispered.

Eric's tongue slid out between his lips. When it touched Trey's lip, he jerked back slightly. Her sweetness registered on Eric's taste buds, and he groaned in pleasure. Eric ran his tongue along Trey's upper lip. Sucked gently. He found more of Rebekah's sweet cum on the tip of Trey's tongue. Eric sampled more of what he wanted from Trey's mouth. More of what he needed. Her. He wanted her. Needed her. Rebekah made a sound of torment. Eric could only concentrate on one thing though. The taste of her juices in Trey's mouth. Eric sucked it off Trey's lips and then stroked Trey's tongue with his to collect more of her nectar. Eric started when he encountered the piercing in Trey's tongue, but was soon delving inside again.

"Oh," Rebekah purred. "Why is that so sexy? Kiss him, Eric. Taste me there."

A hand wrapped around Eric's cock. For a scant second he thought Trey was about to seduce him as he'd seduced so many men in the past, but it wasn't Trey's hand stroking his length tentatively. It was Rebekah's.

All too soon, Rebekah's taste was no longer discernible from Trey's. Eric jerked his head back.

"You're not a bad kisser, Sticks," Trey said with a crooked grin.

Eric couldn't even dwell on how disturbing he found that compliment. He'd never kissed a guy before. All Eric could think about was sampling more of Rebekah's taste.

Eric shoved Trey aside and pulled free of Rebekah's gentle grasp on his cock to kneel on the floor between her legs. He gripped her ass in both hands and pulled her delicious pussy against his face. He licked and suckled her like a starving man. He could not get enough. He writhed his tongue inside her as that seemed to stimulate her juices to flow the most freely. Rebekah's excited cries fueled him to lick her faster. The way she moved against his seeking tongue urged him to plunge it deeper inside. Her heels pressing into his back encouraged him to add suction to his probing. After a long moment, someone pushed against Eric's forehead until he lost contact with Rebekah's flesh.

"I think you've had enough," Trey said. Again with the devious grin and twinkling green eyes.

"More," Eric growled. He sometimes scared himself when he got out of control like this, but at the moment he wasn't scared of his lust. He merely wanted it appeased.

"Why don't you let her taste herself on your lips?"

Eric's heart thudded and then began to race. That would entail kissing her. Eric launched himself across the bed and landed beside Rebekah. She laughed softly and grinned up at him.

"Can I kiss you?" he asked.

She sank her fingers into the long hairs at his nape and lifted her head to claim his lips. He took that as a yes. Eric got lost in her kiss. These lips were as sweet as her others, and her scent still clung to his skin. Each inhalation of her musk ratcheted his desire to a higher level. He wanted her. So much. His hand slid over her rib cage and cupped her small breast. When his thumb brushed her hardened nipple, she gasped into his mouth.

Unexpectedly, she turned her head to the side and separated their mouths. "Wait," she cried and slid her hips across the bed. "Don't."

Eric looked down at Trey. He wasn't sure what Trey had been doing to Rebekah while he'd been distracted with her kisses, but Trey looked none too pleased about her sudden refusal.

"What do you mean 'don't'? You aren't going to leave us hanging again, are you?"

"I mean, don't. Not there," she said, her words broken by ragged gasps.

Eric looked at her and found her eyes brimmed with tears. His heart stumbled like a racehorse going down at top speed. He wrapped both arms around her and tucked her head against his chest.

"We'll stop," Eric promised. He'd definitely need to jack off, and soon, but his satisfaction was not worth this woman's tears. He kissed the top of her head.

"No," she said, "I don't want you to stop, Trey. Just not there."

"Not everyone likes anal, Trey," Eric said, tugging her more securely against him. He wasn't sure why holding her made his heart race so fast. He just wanted her closer. To absorb her into his body. What a strange thought.

"I wasn't touching her ass. I was—"

"Yes, anal. I want anal," Rebekah said, her voice muffled by Eric's chest. "I loooooove it. Give it to me in the ass, Trey."

"Ashtray?" Eric echoed, confused.

Rebekah's body shook against his as she laughed. "In the ass, *Trey*, not the ashtray."

"Oh." For some reason Eric would rather Trey fuck an ashtray.

"No pussy? You sure?" Trey asked. "That's what Eric really likes to watch."

True. That's what Eric *usually* liked to watch—some chick's swollen pussy getting stuffed with a friend's cock—but this wasn't some chick. This was Rebekah. He'd be totally okay with Trey getting lost and just watching Rebekah pleasure herself again. That had been beautiful. Magnificent. Sexy. And most importantly, for him alone.

"Maybe you want to let go of her now, Eric," Trey said, tugging on Rebekah's ankle.

No, not really, but he did anyway. Eric captured her lovely face between his hands and kissed her nose. "If you don't want to, you can tell Trey no."

"I do want to," she said breathlessly.

Damn.

Rebekah rolled away from Eric and onto her belly. She spread her ass cheeks with both hands and said, "Okay, do it. I'm ready."

Eric scooted down the bed for a better look. He'd never seen a pussy more swollen and wet. How could she possibly mean she'd rather have it in the ass? It was a very nice ass, but no comparison to her feminine folds.

Trey chuckled. "Not even close. I was prepping the wrong hole the entire time. Now I have to start over." He wet the tip of his middle finger by collecting the fluids drenching the flesh between her legs and then slipped it inside her tight ass to the first knuckle.

Rebekah tensed.

"Just as I thought," Trey said. "You've never done this before."

"Yes I have. Lots of times."

Eric watched Trey's finger slide deeper into her back passage, and then he slowly withdrew it before plunging it into her body again. Trey was right. She was entirely too tense for someone who loooooooved anal. Didn't matter to Eric, though. Watching Trey loosen her passage was damned sexy. Eric's cock began to throb incessantly. If he hadn't been worried that Rebekah would be put off by his actions, Eric would have stroked himself in time with Trey's gentle probing.

Trey leaned over Rebekah's body to whisper into Eric's ear, "Show her that she turns you on, Eric. That's what she really wants. Better yet, tell her." Trey leaned back and winked at him.

Huh? Tell her. Tell her what?

"Your ass is so sexy, Rebekah," Eric said, feeling pretty stupid for saying it.

"It is?" she panted and rocked backward to take Trey's finger deeper. Eric's cock twitched at the sight.

"Yeah. Just looking at it makes me want to touch myself."

Rebekah surprised him by grabbing the front of his underwear and tugging them down until his rigid cock sprang free. "Oh, Eric, you're so hard. Is it for me?"

Who else would he be this hard for? Trey? No chance. "Yes. For you."

She ran a single finger up the length of him and settled her fingertip in the tiny opening at the tip. Eric sucked an exited breath through his teeth.

"That's it, Rebekah. Relax." Trey had two fingers inside her ass now. "I'm hard for you too."

"You are?" She glanced over her shoulder. "Show me, Trey."

Trey whipped his hard dick out of his boxer shorts, and Rebekah's hand moved to circle Eric's cock as she stared at the evidence of Trey's excitement. She tugged Eric's cock a few times, and his eyes drifted shut.

"Touch yourself, Eric," she panted. "Please."

She released him and grabbed his hand, directing it to the smooth hot flesh of his cock.

"Look at me and touch yourself," she instructed.

He definitely wanted to touch himself when he looked at her.

Trey pulled away and moved around the bed to a side table drawer. "I wonder if someone thought to restock our fun drawer." He pulled it open and found it empty. "Ah, this sucks."

Brian and Sed had been the ones who replenished their stock of sex toys, condoms, and lubricants. Now that the two were in committed relationships, Eric supposed they had less need for the usual supplies.

"I'll be right back," Trey said. "Keep her warm while I'm gone, Eric." He tucked his cock into his shorts and left the bedroom.

Rebekah's eyes met Eric's. "Did you like watching me touch myself in my bunk?" she whispered, an adorable blush staining her cheeks.

"It was the hottest fucking thing I've ever seen in my life." He collapsed onto his back beside her and clung to the covers so he wouldn't be tempted to jack off until Trey got back.

She chuckled. "I doubt that."

"I mean it."

"Which part did you like the best?"

"All of it."

"Did you like when I played with my nipples?"

Eric swallowed and nodded.

"And when I took off my panties?"

He'd thought his heart would leap out of his chest when she'd thrown them at him. And when he'd caught the scent of her pussy. Damn. "Yeah." Eric squeezed his eyes shut and banged the back of his head repeatedly on the mattress. He obviously needed something a bit harder than a bed to knock some sense into himself. He could still feel the silky texture of her panties on his fingertips. His hands remembered every caress against her warm, soft skin. He remembered the taste of her pussy. Its smell. He shuddered as the recollection of each erotic sensation merged to fuel his excitement.

Rebekah crawled closer until her body partially covered his. Her bare breast against his naked chest had him on the verge of orgasm. Why couldn't he be like the other Sinners and fuck for hours without coming? Oh no. A girl touches him, and he's ruining another pair of jeans. Fuck. It so wasn't fair. He gulped air and tried to curtail his arousal before he started spurting all over his belly. She grabbed a handful of Eric's hair in each fist and forced him to look at her.

She was so beautiful, he could hardly stand to keep his eyes open.

"What else did you like?" she demanded.

"Everything," he insisted. "Especially when you came." Oh dear God. Her entire body had quaked, and her fingers had been buried inside her pussy. And. And... Eric squeezed his eyes shut and tried not to think of that beautiful sight. Or her scent. Or the little sighs of pleasure she made. Or her taste. Ah God. He was gonna come. The first pulsations of release were already causing pleasure spasms deep inside.

"Did you think that was sexy?" she whispered. "When I came for you?"

She came for *him*? Eric grabbed the head of his cock and squeezed. Hoping the pain would calm his excitement a bit.

"Everything about you is sexy, Rebekah," he gasped.

"Really?" Her voice cracked. She looked like she was going to cry again.

Eric's heart panged, and he released his punishing hold on his cock to touch her face with his fingertips. "What's wrong? I can't stand it when you're sad."

He hadn't noticed the traces of pre-cum on his palm, but she did. She turned her head and licked it from his hand. "Mmm. Is that for me?"

"Ah, shit," he groaned. *Don't come. Don't come. Don't come,* he repeated to himself silently.

"Are you okay?" she asked.

He bit his bottom lip and shook his head. "Not exactly. If you do one more sexy thing, I'm going to embarrass myself even more than usual."

"What do you mean?" she asked.

He couldn't tell her he had control issues.

She turned her head and looked down his body. "You're still really hard," she noted. She released his hair and reached for…

Eric moved sideways along the bed until his feet found the floor. She still had a handful of his hair clutched in one fist, but she released it when he winced in pain.

"I'm going to see where Trey went. He should have been back by now," Eric said.

"But…"

Eric hurried out of the bedroom and closed the door behind him. He banged the back of his head against the door until he could remember how to breathe again.

"What are you doing?" Trey whispered loudly from the open bathroom to Eric's left. From the look of things, Trey had just rubbed one out himself. Hadn't he left the bedroom to get anal lube or something? Why was he jerking it in the bathroom? "And you're still hard." Trey came into the hall to smack Eric in the arm. "Get back in there and fuck her, you idiot."

Eric stared at him. "What?"

"You like her, don't you?"

"N-no. You can—"

Trey punched him in the shoulder. "No. I didn't give up a sweet piece of ass so you can chicken out. Get back in there. How are you not fucking her right now? I was sure she was excited enough before I left."

Trey yanked Eric away from the door so he could open it and shove Eric inside. The door closed behind him, and for a panicked second, Eric pushed against the door trying to escape. Apparently, Trey was leaning against it from the outside.

"What's going on?" Rebekah asked.

The sound of her voice made his overexcited cock twitch.

He turned to face her. Might as well spell it all out no matter how embarrassing it was. "Just looking at you excites me to orgasm."

"Really?"

"Yeah. It's pathetic, isn't it?"

She shook her head. "I'm glad."

She was lying on her back. While he watched, she spread her thighs. Using her fingers, she spread her labia to reveal her opening. He took his cock in his hand and closed his eyes. "If you don't stop showing me things like that, I'm going to come."

"Come closer, Eric," she murmured. "Will you do something for me?"

"Anything." He meant it.

"Will you come on my clit?"

He nodded.

"And then lick it off until I come too?"

Eric's mouth went dry. He approached the bed as if his dick were a dousing wire and Rebekah's pussy was the deepest, purist artesian well ever discovered. He pulled her to the end of the bed and stood between her wide-open thighs.

She sat up so she could see what was happening.

Eric bent over her so that the head of his cock was perfectly aligned with her clit. He could feel her moist heat and knew that if he shifted down a couple of inches and surged forward he'd be inside her sweet pussy. Possessing her. Fucking her. He sucked a breath through his teeth. Just the thought of entering her was too much. He imagined what that hot, slick sheath would feel like around him. He collected her slick fluids with his fingertips and stroked them over the surface of his cock slowly. He repeated the motion until his entire length was wet with her juices. He was careful to keep his cock in line so that he would spurt on her clit as she'd requested. He fought orgasm as long as he could, wanting her anticipation to build.

"Oh God, Eric. Hurry. Hurry. I want your cum on me now." She shifted forward a couple inches and rubbed her clit over the head of his cock. "I want to watch it come out."

Eric cried out as the pulsations of pleasure gripped the base of his cock. Spurt after spurt of cum erupted from his body. They watched it bathe her clit. Both held their breath. Both shuddered with excitement.

"Oh God, Eric, that is so hot. Lick it now. Please."

Eric really just wanted to collapse on the bed and catch his breath, but he couldn't let her down. He wanted to give her what excited her. What she wanted. Needed. Even if that meant he had to lap up his own cum. He dropped to his knees on the floor and tentatively protruded his tongue, trying to get over his uneasiness. His first taste was not pleasant, not sweet like her fluids, but her excited crooning got him over his hesitation quickly. He licked her clean, swallowing their mingled fluids, and continued to lick her until her thighs clamped over his ears, and she came against his face with a startled cry. He blew cool breaths over her hot pussy until she eventually released him. She fell back on the bed, her body quaking sporadically.

Eric staggered to his feet. He stood at the foot of the bed gazing at her. Her beauty stole all coherent thought and made his cock stir with renewed excitement. Eric might not last for hours, but he had no problem getting it up a dozen times in a row. Not that it mattered. Now that Rebekah was satisfied, it was time to return to his bunk and try to get some sleep.

"Good night," Eric said.

She rolled onto her side and curled into fetal position, looking all vulnerable and irresistible. "Good night," she whispered.

He hesitated, his heart thudding. He didn't really want to leave. "Can I stay?"

She glanced at him and nodded. "If you want to."

"I do."

He switched off the light and stumbled around in the dark until he found the bed. He climbed between the covers. He heard her move a moment later. She joined him between the sheets, but he forced himself not to reach for her. He knew he'd just get excited again, and then he'd end up trying to fuck her, and ultimately disappoint her with his lack of control.

Rebekah's warmth moved closer. His heart thudded faster. Her cool hand touched his belly, and he was instantly hard again. Damn. She was going to think he was some horny loser who only wanted one thing. And maybe he was.

"I'm sorry I made you do that," she whispered.

"What?"

"Lick your cum off me."

Eric chuckled. "You didn't make me. If I didn't want to, I would have refused."

"I'm glad you didn't refuse. I've fantasized about it for years. It was really hot." She moved closer. "You. You're really hot."

"You have no idea." Another inch, and she'd discover he was already turned on again. He rolled on to his belly and squashed the evidence into the mattress. Her hand slid across his lower back and he tensed. She cuddled up against his arm, her bare breast pressing into his flesh.

Why had Trey left him alone with her? He couldn't possibly be expected to keep his hands to himself under these conditions. She was naked. And he was still horny. He was always horny. Why was he so fucking horny all the time? Rebekah snuggled closer, pressing her cheek to his shoulder. Ah God, he was so hard again. He wanted to fuck every inch of her. So not romantic. Not what she deserved.

"I should go," he murmured.

"Is Trey coming back?" she asked quietly.

Eric's heart gave an unpleasant lurch. "I don't think so."

"I guess he changed his mind."

"I can go get him if you want him."

"He's not interested."

"Sure he is. He just stepped aside because he knows…" *I want you.* Eric bit his lip to stop himself from revealing too much.

"Knows what?"

"Nothing."

Her hand slid lower on his back. He sucked a breath through his teeth. He was so going to lose control in like five seconds.

"Tell me." Her hand slid lower over his ass. "Eric?"

He grabbed her around the waist and pulled her beneath him. His cock brushed the inside of her thigh, and he shuddered. "He knows how much I want you."

"You do?"

"I don't think I've ever wanted anyone more." Not even when Brian's wife, Myrna, had toured with the band and he'd walked around with perpetual blue balls for months.

Rebekah's mouth found his in the darkness. She kissed him as if he needed to be taught a lesson. He couldn't get enough of her.

"I can't tell you how much I need to hear that," she whispered.

"Then I'll tell you a million times."

"But I can't have sex with you."

"Oh." He supposed he shouldn't be surprised that she didn't return his attraction.

"I want to do other things with you though."

"Other things?"

"I really like it when you watch me."

"You do?"

"I do."

His heart thudded with a mix of anxiety and anticipation. "Can I watch you again, right now?"

"If you promise you'll be okay with no sex."

He didn't have a problem with that, but he wondered why she was reluctant. "Why don't you want to have sex? Are you a virgin or something?" He covered his mouth with one hand. Why did things fly out of his mouth like that?

"Something."

"What kind of something?"

"I don't want to say."

"You can tell me."

Her body was all stiff beneath him now. She sighed in exasperation. "I'm totally out of the mood now."

"I'm sorry. I'll be quiet."

She chuckled. "Too late for that."

"I should leave, I suppose."

"Or you can get me excited again."

"I'm not sure I'm the right man for the job."

"What do you mean?" Her fingers brushed his hair in the darkness, and he shuddered.

"I'm not good at it. Not like the other guys. I get too excited too easily."

"I like that about you."

"You do? I always come way too fast."

"Lots of guys do."

Maybe, but none of the guys in Sinners did. They were all fucking studs, and Eric felt like more of a dud. He remembered how happy he'd been when Jace had joined the band. Vertically challenged guys were supposed to be lacking in the package department. When Eric had seen the size of Jace's massive cock for the first time, he had contemplated suicide.

"Maybe we can help each other out," she whispered.

"Help each other? How?"

She took a deep breath. "Maybe you can help me relax

and get comfortable with my body again, and I can help you last longer."

"What's wrong with your body?" Looked perfect to him. Felt perfect too.

"I don't want to say. If I disgust you—"

"Are you fucking kidding me? You're the hottest woman I've ever seen in my life."

She giggled. "So do we have a deal?"

Seemed like a strange arrangement, but if it meant he got to spend more time with Rebekah in a sexual capacity, then he was all for it.

"How do I help you?" he asked.

"Touch me. Just not there."

"Where?"

"You can touch me anywhere. Just not inside… not inside my… *p-pussy*." She said that last word in a rush, as if it turned her on just to say it.

He wanted to touch her inside her *p-pussy*. So much. "Why?"

"I'm not ready to tell you yet." He could feel her heart thudding like a jackhammer in her chest.

"Okay. I'll touch you. I think I can handle that." He chuckled. Oh yes, he could definitely handle that. "But how are you going to help me?"

She was quiet for a long moment. He was beginning to think she'd decided that he was beyond help when she said, "What makes you come the fastest?"

"Certified Grade A pussy." A second too late, he realized he shouldn't have said that. *Ugh, I'm a fucking idiot!* He winced, waiting for her to cuss him out. She just laughed.

"Well, I can't help you with that. My pussy is off limits. What about oral? Do you like that?"

Was there a man in existence who wouldn't want her plump lips wrapped around his cock? If there was, he wasn't one of them. "Oh yeah, I like oral."

"So you touch me, and I'll suck you."

"You're going to suck my cock?" Just the thought made him shudder with excitement.

"Would you like that?"

He moaned in torment. He couldn't form an intelligible sound, though he wanted to tell her exactly how much he'd like that.

"Okay, lesson one." She squirmed. "Roll onto your back."

"What? Now?" His balls tightened.

"Why not? Do you have something better to do?"

Oh. My. God. He loved this woman's spontaneity so much. "No."

He rolled onto his back. When her delicate hand slid over his belly, he cried out. Damn. He was already so fucking excited, the second her lips touched his cock he'd be coming.

"You are really sensitive, aren't you?" she murmured.

Every inch of him, but eight inches in particular.

She slid down his body and kissed his belly. He squirmed sideways along the bed. At this rate, she wouldn't even have to touch his cock to make him come.

She chuckled. "Hold still."

"God, I want you, Rebekah."

"Do I really excite you that much?"

He nodded vigorously. "Yeah. I can't take it. I want to fuck every inch of you." He bit his lip, wishing she'd gag him so he'd stop blurting inappropriate shit.

Her hand slid down his hip bone. He sucked a deep breath through his teeth.

"Try to think about something else," she advised, before directing his cock into the warm confines of her mouth.

Think of something else? Was she fucking kidding him? How could he possibly think of anything but the feel of his cock head lodged in her throat? Her tongue stroking the underside of his shaft? Her tiny hand lodged against the base of his cock to hold him steady while she pulled back with strong suction?

"Ah fuck, Reb. I'm gonna come. Like right now."

She kept drawing back until he popped free of her mouth. "No, you aren't. The longer you hold back, the sooner we'll do this again."

"What?" He couldn't think well enough to reason through her statement.

"If you last five minutes, we'll try lesson two tomorrow. If you last ten minutes, we'll move on to lesson two as soon as you can get it up again."

"What's lesson two?"

"I'm not sure yet, but I guarantee you'll like it." He could hear the smile in her voice.

"What if I last ten seconds?" Because honestly, he'd be surprised to last that long.

"No lesson two."

"None?"

"Nope. I'm timing you with the clock there. Fight release as long as you can."

She took his cock into her mouth again, and he cried out. But he didn't come. He bit his lip and tried to think of the least sexy thing he could. He settled on solving complex mathematical equations in his mind. It kept his big head occupied (sorta), but his little head's attention was one hundred percent on the pleasurable tug of Rebekah's lips as she sucked him. The writhing of her tongue. The moisture. The heat.

Rebekah was sucking his cock.

Sucking him. Rebekah.

Sucking. In her mouth. His cock was in her fucking mouth.

Thank God it was dark, so he couldn't see it happening. He shuddered hard and clenched muscles, fighting orgasm. No good. Too excited. Felt too good.

Rebekah…

"Okay, I'm done," he gasped. "I'm gonna…"

She sucked harder. Oh God. He was going to come in her mouth. With no condom. Would she swallow it? Or spit it out? Shit.

"Stop. You have to stop. Reb."

Her soft hand slid over his balls. He lost all semblance of control. Gave himself to the blinding pleasure. To the spasms of ecstasy that gripped his entire body. He flooded her mouth with his fluids. Instead of the startled or disgusted reaction he expected, she swallowed him and stroked his balls with her fingertips until he was shouting in triumph.

Unfortunately, that feeling was short-lived. She lifted her head and he slipped from her warm mouth. "Three minutes."

He flushed in embarrassment. Damn it. He hadn't even lasted five. Did that mean no more lessons? He couldn't really blame her if she never wanted to touch him again. What woman wanted to be with a man who had absolutely no control?

"Did I really excite you that much?" Her voice had a hint of pride and happiness.

He lifted his head, but couldn't see her expression in the darkness. "Fuck, woman. I'm surprised I lasted that long. The second your lips touched my dick, I thought I was going to blow."

She giggled, and his heart warmed. If it made her happy to make him come quickly, he was certain to make her the happiest woman in existence.

"Well, the deal was a minimum of five minutes, though I was really hoping for ten, so I could start lesson two tonight. That was fun."

Fun? It had been fan-fucking-tastic.

She slid up his body and kissed him. He could taste himself on her lips. On her tongue. His cock twitched with renewed excitement. She tugged her lips from his. "You taste good, huh?"

"Not as good as you do. Are you sure I only lasted three minutes? Maybe you read the clock wrong."

"I'm sure."

"Does that mean no more lessons?" He felt like crying. "Ever?"

"I didn't say that. You lasted longer than ten seconds. Because you didn't make it five minutes, there will be no lesson tomorrow. You'll have to wait until the next day."

He was smiling with relief and happiness, but he said, "There is no way in hell I can wait that long."

"You don't have a choice. That was our deal. And now it's your turn to live up to our bargain."

Yeah, it was. "Just tell me what you want me to do."

———

This arrangement between herself and Eric was perfect. He might be able to help her get over her fear of intercourse, and then she could go back to seducing Trey. Except Rebekah wasn't sure if she was really interested in Trey anymore. He'd obviously left because she'd freaked out when she'd felt his cock against the opening of her vagina, and she had made him stop. Again. As hot and sexy as Trey was, she was feeling something more substantial for Eric. She wasn't sure what it was yet. His excitement and enthusiasm made her feel beautiful. Wanted. Irresistible. And he was fun. And generous. And almost as spontaneous as she was. She liked him. It would probably wear off quickly—the topsy-turvy happiness he brought bubbling to the surface. This kind of overwhelming emotion never lasted. But while it did, they could certainly have a lot of fun together. And help each other with their sexual inadequacies at the same time.

"Touch me, Eric," she urged.

"Where?"

"Everywhere."

He used those wonderful, strong hands to awaken every inch of her skin.

"Kiss me, Eric."

"Where?"

"Everywhere."

"Can I turn on the light?" he asked, his lips against a sensitive spot just beneath her ear. "I want to look at you."

"If you want to."

He found the lamp on the side table and switched it on. They blinked at each other as their eyes adjusted to the glare. He smiled and touched her face. She turned her head slightly to kiss his bandaged thumb. "How's your cut?'

"It's fine."

He didn't move for a long moment. Just stared at her. Made her feel like the most beautiful woman in the world.

"Is this real?" he murmured.

"It feels real."

She lifted a hand and toyed with the long lock of blue hair curling around his throat. "Are you really okay with this? I don't want you to feel used."

"Why would I feel used?"

"I make you touch me—"

He covered her lips with his fingertips. "You're not *making* me do anything. I want to touch you."

"But what do you get out of it?"

"I get to be with you. That's all I want."

Her heart melted. She didn't know he had a sweet side. She added it to the growing list of things she adored about him.

He grinned crookedly. "Plus, I already got one fantastic blow job and only have to wait two days for another."

She chuckled. Didn't take long for him to cover up that sweet side. "I feel like I'm manipulating you, Eric."

"If that's what you want to call it, fine with me. Please continue to manipulate me. I get off on it."

She hugged him and rubbed her nose against his collarbone. "If you ever want out of this bargain, promise you'll tell me."

"I promise. You'll do the same for me?"

She nodded.

"Good. Now stop worrying about this and tell me what you want me to do."

"I already told you. Kiss me."

"Everywhere?"

She nodded.

"Do you mind if I tell you how beautiful you are the entire time?"

"I think I can live with that."

He kissed her lips, delighting them with a gentle suction. "These are the most succulent lips I've ever tasted," he whispered. He stroked her hair with both hands as he kissed her again. "And they feel even better wrapped around my cock." He dipped his tongue between them.

She laughed. "You're like Mr. Romance and Mr. Porn Star wrapped in one."

"Sorry. I have this bad habit of saying everything that pops into my head. I know it's a total turnoff. I'll try harder to stay quiet."

"Actually, I kinda like it."

He quirked an eyebrow at her. "You do?"

She nodded.

"You're weird."

"You're weird too," she said defensively.

"I guess that means we're perfect for each other." He stared into her eyes, challenging her to deny it.

"I guess so," she said.

He smiled. She could feel his heart thudding against her chest. "Where was I?" He trailed kisses over her cheek. "This is the cutest face I've ever laid eyes on." He kissed her eyelids. "These are the prettiest blue eyes." His fingers, tangled in her hair, kneaded her scalp. "The silkiest hair with the most awesome color that matches mine."

She giggled. He slid down to kiss her neck. He suckled gently and explored the tender flesh there until she gasped in delight when he found that most sensitive spot below her ear. She moaned when his suction intensified, and his tongue lavished that spot until her nipples tightened unbearably and a flood of heat rushed between her thighs.

"Eric."

"I love it when you say my name." He breathed into her ear. "It's so sexy." His lips returned to her sweet spot to work her into a frenzy.

"Eric," she gasped again. "Oh please. Suck my tits." His entire body shuddered and he lifted his head.

"Fuck, woman, don't say things like that." He shifted his hips and she felt the head of his cock against her throbbing pussy.

She tensed. "No. Don't."

"I won't put it in," he promised. "Not until you ask me to. You can trust me, Rebekah."

She nodded, her stomach in knots, but she did trust him. Even though all he had to do was thrust forward and he'd be buried inside her, she trusted that he wouldn't do it. Her pussy clenched at the thought of him inside her. It wanted to be filled with him, but emotionally, she wasn't ready yet.

He eased down, his cock head losing contact with her wet and swollen flesh. She was seconds from asking him to do it. To just put it in and get it over with. His hands moved from her hair to her breasts. He cupped them and stared at them, as if in awe.

"You have such perfect breasts, Rebekah. I love how your pretty, pink nipples get hard when I look at them." They were straining for his attention even now. He lowered his head and drew the flat of his tongue over one nipple and then the other. He then blew a cool breath over their wet surfaces and she shuddered.

"Suck them, Eric," she whispered. "Please."

He huffed several excited breaths and then lowered his head to suck one eager nipple into his hot mouth. She cried out and grabbed his hair. Her back arched, and she held him to her breast, mewing in delight as the pleasurable sensations of his hard suction swirled from her breast to her belly to her throbbing pussy and clit. "Oh yes. Like that," she panted. He sucked until she was sure she couldn't take any more pleasure, and then he switched to her other breast. She cried out and panted his name. "Eric. Eric."

He yanked his mouth away. "Ah shit, I'm about to come again," he groaned, his eyes squeezed tightly shut.

"Come on my tits. I want you to."

He moved so fast, he left her disoriented. He straddled her rib cage and slid his hard cock up her chest. He pressed her breasts together, so that they surrounded his cock, and began to thrust. Rebekah's eyes opened wide. She'd never had a man fuck her tits before. She wasn't sure how to respond. His cock head looked incredibly inviting as it disappeared and reappeared from the top of her cleavage. She bent her neck and extended her tongue to lick it. Eric groaned. Fucked her faster. His excitement fueled hers. She clung to his ass, suddenly wanting him to pump like that into her pussy. She flicked her tongue over his cock whenever it came within reach. He cried out and drew back. His hand released her breasts and grabbed his cock to spurt that first pulse of cum over one breast and a second pulse over the other.

His free hand moved to the headboard to steady himself as his body quaked with release.

"Ah, Reb," he gasped brokenly. "You are too good to me."

"That was fuckin' hot," she said. "I need to come. I'm so turned on right now."

He climbed off her belly and laid down beside her. He rested his head on her shoulder, still breathing hard from his exertions. His hand moved between her thighs and slid over her wet folds before finding her clit. He rubbed her slowly with firm pressure at first. She closed her eyes and concentrated on the sensation. Nothing else. Just the pleasure throbbing through her clit. His fingers moved faster. Faster. Her pleasure built and built. When it burst, she cried out and shuddered in ecstasy. He rubbed her hard and fast the entire time she came, prolonging her pleasure. Her pussy clenched in delighted spasms, but felt so hopelessly empty. She slid two fingers inside to alleviate its ache. Eric lifted his head unexpectedly and moved to investigate.

"That is so beautiful," he whispered. "You have no idea how much I want to slide my cock inside there."

She slid her fingers in and out of her slick passage, and Eric shuddered. His motions on her clit intensified again.

"Come for me again," he urged. It took her awhile, but his relentless rub on her clit and her own thrusting fingers brought her to orgasm again.

"Damn, I'm so hard again," he muttered. "Woman, you're driving me crazy."

He fell onto his back and took his cock in both hands, stroking its length slowly. Rebekah had never had such gratifying sex in her life, and technically they hadn't even had sex. She lifted her body from the bed and kissed a trail down his hard chest and washboard belly. The man didn't have an ounce of fat on him. She supposed all that drumming kept him in good shape. He sucked a breath through his teeth when she planted a kiss just beneath his navel. When she moved between his legs, he released his cock and lay there in trembling anticipation.

"You don't think I'm going to suck your cock, do you?" she teased.

"No?"

"You wouldn't want me to go against our deal, would you?"

He grinned down at her. "Actually, yeah, I would."

"Keep stroking it," she said.

He started to rub himself again. She lowered her head to suck on the loose skin covering his balls.

"Ahhh," he cried out in protest and moved away.

"You don't like that?" she asked.

"Fuck yeah, I like that," he said.

"Then hold still." She loved his exaggerated response as she sucked and licked his sac. He was jacking off so hard that he was sure to spurt again in seconds. She drew one nut carefully into her mouth and sucked gently. He stroked himself faster, groaning in torment. She repeated the treatment on his other nut. It took him quite awhile to come, even though he obviously enjoyed every minute. When he finally erupted, she pulled back to watch him spurt over his belly. Even after he was completely spent, he continued to groan and tremble in delight. When she moved to collect his cum with her tongue, he released his cock and stroked her hair.

"Oh, baby, that felt so good."

"Then why did it take you so long to come that time?" she asked, finding his delightful juices in the middle of his belly and lapping them up.

He hesitated, pausing in reflection of what had just happened. "I don't know."

She thought maybe she did. Helping him with his problem was going to be a hell of a lot easier than she'd first anticipated. And as much as she wanted him inside her already, hers might be just as easy a fix.

Chapter 9

THE NEXT AFTERNOON, THE band caught up with the equipment truck and the other tour bus at the venue. The crew had arrived several hours earlier and were already setting up the stage. Rebekah picked up Dave's notebook and headed off the bus to help with assembly.

"You'd better get busy on those drums," one of the roadies said to her. "You're late."

"Late?" She followed the man up the ramp onto the truck.

"Yeah, late," he said. "Dave doesn't put the stage and lighting together, but he does set up the drum kit to get the mics right and that takes quite awhile. You'd better get busy."

Rebekah didn't know how to set up a drum kit. She had Dave's instructions on how to set up mics in strategic locations *around* a drum kit, but she had no idea how to assemble Eric's instrument. "I'm not sure if I'm the right person for the job. And I didn't catch your name." Rebekah judged the man to be in his mid-forties. A bit soft in the middle, he had a receding hairline and a few flecks of gray in his otherwise dark hair. He had a mean look about him, but probably because he was scowling at her.

"Marcus," he said.

Rebekah smiled brightly. "Oh, you're the other soundboard operator, right? Dave told me all about you. He said I could count on you if I needed help. I'm Rebekah." She extended a hand in his direction, but he ignored it.

Marcus snorted and pushed an equipment case toward the ramp. "We don't have time for a chat. Get busy, girl."

Girl?

Rebekah would have loved to help, but she honestly had no idea where to begin. "Just tell me what to do, and I'll get to work."

"I'm just the monitor engineer, boss. You're in charge. Figure it out yourself." His nose crinkled in displeasure, he pushed the case down the ramp, leaving Rebekah to stand bewildered in the back of the truck.

She had never expected this to be easy, but she had no idea that she'd be in charge of setting up the drum kit. She thought about calling Dave and asking him for advice, but decided against it. She needed to take responsibility and do her job. It was the job she wanted, after all. She set Dave's notebook on top of an amplifier and reached for the nearest equipment case. Putting her weight behind it, it creaked forward an inch after much exertion and grunting. The roadie with the blond mohawk, Jake, entered the truck. He chuckled at her.

"You know, the wheels actually roll if you unlock them." He bent over and flipped the locks on the wheels.

Rebekah almost fell on her face as the case rolled forward with no resistance.

"Let me help," Jake offered.

Together they directed the rolling case down the ramp. Jake held most of the weight, but Rebekah worked hard to help keep it on track. "Marcus says I'm supposed to assemble the drum kit," Rebekah said, "but I don't know how. Can you show me?"

"Ask Eric. He's really pissy about everything being in exactly the right spot."

Rebekah couldn't stop heat from rising into her face. "He does know exactly the right spot," she murmured. And apparently, Eric's propensity to say exactly what he was thinking, no matter how inappropriate, was already wearing off on her.

"You and Eric?" Jake said. "Really?"

"Don't get the wrong idea," Rebekah said sternly. She attempted to hide a grin but wasn't able to keep a straight face. "We totally got it on last night."

Jake's grin spread ear-to-ear. "Right on!"

Once they had the equipment case in the building, Rebekah went in search of Eric. She found him laughing with Jace outside the bus. As soon as Jace spotted her, he turned beet red. He offered Rebekah a slight wave and headed for the bus steps. "Later, Eric."

Eric gifted Rebekah with a brilliant smile. "Hey, gorgeous, what's up?"

She flushed with pleasure. "I was wondering if you have time to show me how to set up your drum kit properly."

He glanced at his wrist. He wasn't wearing a watch, but said, "I think I have the next hour open. If you don't mind listening to me sing the chorus of 'Sever' over and over the entire time. I need to practice."

"Is that the new single?" she asked eagerly.

"Yep. Have you heard it yet?"

She shook her head.

"Don't listen to the radio much, do you?"

"Since Dave's accident, I haven't been keeping up with the outside world much. Do they play it a lot?"

"It's number one on the rock charts."

She hugged him. "That's awesome. Congratulations! We've got to make the song sound amazing tonight." Just the thought of putting her little stamp on a Sinners' song had her euphoric.

Eric stopped walking to keep her securely in his arms. Just as he had all last night while they'd slept and touched. It had taken every shred of her willpower not to engage him in lesson two. Watching him pleasure himself every time he got too excited to hold back had really turned her on. Not that she'd come away from the experience unsatisfied. On the contrary, he'd made sure she received more than her fair share of pleasure.

"We really need to rehearse." His hands gently massaged her lower back as he kept her near. She melted against him, relishing his touch. He was so free with his affection. How could she not respond with complete surrender? And even more perplexing, how was he still single? "Is Jon here yet?" he asked.

He switched from one topic to another so quickly it made her head spin.

"Jon? Jon Mallory?" Dave had mentioned that Jon had been on tour with Sinners when they'd done the Canadian leg of the tour, but Dave had said something about Sed never wanting Jon near the band again.

"Yeah, Jon is supposed to play thirty seconds of Jace's bass line while Jace plays piano for 'Sever's' intro."

"I haven't seen him." She would have remembered seeing Jon. He was even better looking than Trey. At least in Sinners' old music videos he had been. She'd never seen him in person. He had piercing gray eyes and thick black hair that hung in loose curls around his perfectly proportioned face.

"He had better show up," Eric said. "This is his last chance. I won't stick my neck out for him again." Eric squeezed her. "I need to kiss you now."

She chuckled at his mind-boggling change of subject and tilted her head to offer her mouth. "If you insist."

"I do." He kissed her until her head was spinning, and she was clinging to his hard body for support. "Now I'm all hard and excited," he murmured into her ear. "Is it time for lesson two yet?"

"Not until tomorrow."

"Damn it. Well, let's go set up a drum kit. Maybe it will allow me to think of something besides rubbing my cum all over your sweet little ass." His hands slid down to grip her butt.

Maybe she should be offended by his crass compliment, but it made her heart sing. She couldn't help but smile when he took her hand and led her into the venue through the back entrance.

The stage had already been assembled by a combination of temporary workers and Sinners' regular roadies. Marcus was barking orders like a general. He scowled when he noticed Rebekah. That scowl deepened when he saw that Eric was holding her hand.

"Your drums are behind the stage," Marcus said, before turning to find some other temp to bellow at.

"He doesn't like me," Rebekah told Eric.

"Do I need to kick his ass?"

She rolled her eyes and shook her head.

"I'll do it. I will. Say the word."

"Stop it, Eric. Let's get your drum kit set up."

They started with the bass drums. He explained how important it was to get the three of them in the proper order. "Or I'll sound like shit."

"I seriously doubt that."

They worked on the toms next and then the cymbals. He placed his stool in the center of the kit and took a seat. "Something's missing," he said. "Something that usually sits between my legs here." He pointed to the empty space between his thighs with both hands.

"Your snare?"

He tugged her body in front of him. "Nope, it's you."

He retrieved a set of drumsticks from the inner pocket of his black leather vest and tapped a cymbal to his left before entering into an amazing drum solo. She wasn't sure how he managed to keep a beat and try to remove her shirt with his teeth at the same time, but she was laughing so hard by the time he finished that her stomach ached. He had a couple inches of her belly exposed and blew a loud raspberry on her skin. She laughed even harder.

"My snare sounds a little off. I think a few adjustments are necessary," he said.

She straddled his lap and wrapped her arms around his lower back. "Is that better?"

"Yeah," he said breathlessly. "Maybe move it a bit closer so I can reach it properly."

She snuggled against him, pressing her breasts into his hard chest, her face into his neck. She inhaled his scent and couldn't seem to stop herself from sucking gentle kisses over his throat.

"Gah! Boner time," he said and wrapped both arms around her to shift her closer. He wasn't just saying that to make her giggle until her cheeks hurt. He really was hard. She felt him against her mound.

She wrapped her legs around his waist, pressing the heat between her thighs against him. He groaned and kissed her forehead. "If you don't stop encouraging me, I'm going to tell you all the things I want to do to your hot little body and embarrass the hell out of you."

"Try me," she murmured, kissing the sexy cleft in his chin and then sucking his lower lip into her mouth.

"Are you going to fuck her right here in front of everyone?" an unfamiliar voice said from the other side of the drum kit.

Rebekah swiveled her head and caught a glimpse of Jon Mallory before Eric and the stool toppled backward, taking her with it. A cymbal clanged.

"Ow," Eric protested.

His body had cushioned her fall.

"Are you okay, Reb?" Eric asked.

She grinned at his concern. "Me? You're the one who hit the floor."

"Who's the girl?" Jon asked, circling the drum kit and offering a hand to Eric. Rebekah tried not to stare. Jon had aged twenty years since she'd seen him on TV last and that had only been five years ago.

"Our new FOH," Eric said, climbing to his feet and helping Rebekah scrape herself off the floor.

"No shit? What's your name, sweetheart?"

She offered Jon a friendly smile. "Rebekah."

"Jon."

"Well, yeah. I think I know who you are."

He grinned, his gray eyes sweeping up her body. "I suppose this is the reason Marcus has his panties all in a bunch. He about took my head off when I asked him where my bass was."

"He best be getting over it," Eric grumbled.

Rebekah understood why Marcus was upset, but she wasn't going to relent and give up her position as FOH, even if he did have seniority. She had to live up to Dave's expectations, and the band's, and most importantly, her own. "I suppose I should get to work on the mics," she said. "You guys ready to rehearse?"

"I'd rather keep you as my snare," Eric said and wrapped both arms around her back.

"Sounds pretty violent," Jon said.

"Keeps her between my legs."

"Wouldn't you rather be between hers?"

"Maybe someday," she said and wriggled out of Eric's grasp.

She shuffled through equipment cases and found the microphones she'd read about in Dave's notes the day before. She set them up from memory, making sure they were in the right location and the perfect distance from the drumheads.

"You sure you haven't done this before?" Eric asked as he watched her set things up.

"I *have* done this before. In college and on-the-job training. I just never got paid before. Besides, Dave gave great instructions." Speaking of, she'd left the notebook in the equipment truck. She'd probably need it to figure out the wiring configuration. "I'll be right back." She headed out of the venue and into the truck, which was now empty. The amplifier she'd left her notebook on was gone. The notebook, also gone. Rebekah's heart sank. She raced back into the building and found Jake changing the strings on one of Trey's guitars.

"Hey, Jake, have you seen a wire-bound notebook with a black cover? I left it on an amp in the truck, and it's gone."

"Sorry, sweetie, haven't seen it. Maybe Marcus or Travis know where it is."

Rebekah asked Travis next. She really hoped Marcus hadn't been the one to find it. He'd probably give her a hard time for needing it. Travis was helping someone she hadn't met set up a light panel behind the drums. "Hey, Travis!" she called. "Have you seen a notebook around here? I left in the truck."

"Sorry, sugar, haven't seen it."

"I think Marcus might have it," the temporary roadie said.

Great.

"What's the matter, Reb?" Eric asked. He had his snare in place now and was shifting his drums and cymbals around slightly to get them lined up to his preferred specifications.

"Nothing," she assured him. Her heart was thudding as she approached Marcus, who was connecting wires to a soundboard next to the stage. She really didn't want a confrontation with the guy.

"Um, Marcus?" she asked.

He glanced at her and then turned his attention back to his work. "What?"

"I seem to have misplaced my brother's notebook. Have you seen it?"

"Nope."

He plugged in another wire, and she could tell their conversation was over. She wasn't sure if she believed him or not. He probably knew exactly where her notebook was, but she wasn't going to accuse him. The guy already hated her enough.

"Okay, thanks," she said.

She could probably hook up most of the sound equipment from memory. It was the nuances of Dave's specific configuration that concerned her. She wanted everything to be perfect for this show. She wanted to make a good impression on the band. She wanted to prove to them that she could do this job and prove to herself that she wasn't destined to be a failure in everything she tried.

She got to work. Since Eric was already at his drum kit, she did his sound check first. Within two minutes, Marcus headed over to bitch at her. "You need to get the guitar amps hooked up before you start the drum sound check."

Even though he was standing way too close to emphasize his height, she didn't back down. Not an inch. "You do things your way, and I do things mine."

Marcus stared with his mouth hanging open. She turned back to her soundboard, ignoring him as he stood gawking after her. By the time she had Eric sounding awesome, the crew had the white baby grand piano set up stage right. She worked out a few different mic setups. Eventually, Jace wandered in to help her get the piano acoustics right by playing the intro to "Sever" over and over until she was satisfied with his sound.

"Sounds great, Reb!" Travis called from the stage rigging high above. He was doing something with a laser light and trying to get it lined up with the piano. The shiny white paint would pick up the colors of the light show. Rebekah couldn't wait to see it in action.

"Don't blind me while I'm playing," Jace called up to him.

"Do you mind playing it one more time?" Rebekah said. "I think I've got it, but I want to make sure."

Jace grinned and nodded. The guy was so freakin' cute with his bleached blond spikes and dark beard stubble. His sweet little smile coupled with the downward cast of his dark eyes had her momentarily befuddled. When Jace's fingers swept across the keyboard, she snapped out of it.

"That piano intro is awesome, Jace," Rebekah said as he finished the piece again. "Did you write it?"

Jace flushed and shook his head. "Brian wrote the original as a guitar solo, and Eric adapted it to the piano. I just play it."

"Does the new album have a lot of piano segments?"

Jace shook his head again. "Just a couple. We weren't sure how the fans would respond. So far, they seem to like it."

Eric appeared next to Rebekah. "Understatement. The single is doing better than any in our past. Tripod, you rule!" Eric knuckle-bumped Jace, who beamed at his compliment.

Jon Mallory wrinkled his nose and kept trying to get the bass line of the song right. Since it wasn't one of the songs he'd written when he'd been part of the band, Jon had never played it before. Which was quite obvious by the chaotic sounds coming from his instrument.

"Damn it. I cannot get this triplet thing," Jon complained. "Why the fuck did you have to make it so complicated?"

"Because Tripod is awesome," Eric said. "I inspired him to become a bassist, you know."

Rebekah smiled at his obvious pride. "I did not know that."

"I wish I'd never told him," Jace said. He slid from the piano bench. "I'm never going to live it down."

"A man's got to brag when he has a reason to," Eric said and pounded Jace on the back enthusiastically.

Rebekah laughed. "I think you're supposed to be humble about stuff like that."

"Psssh, fuck that. Always take credit where credit is due. Especially when you're solely responsible for inspiring the best bassist who ever lived."

Jace flushed.

"Whatever," Jon grumbled.

"Come on, Jon," Jace said. "I'll work on the bass line with you." He strode over to the side of the stage and picked up his shiny black bass guitar.

Jon looked torn between offense and gratitude. He sighed loudly and nodded. "I don't want to fuck it up. Sed's looking for a reason to hire a studio musician and send me packing."

"You could always play a recorded track," Rebekah suggested.

Eric looked at her as if she'd just called his mama a fat whore.

"No?" she said.

"No fucking way. I can't believe that you'd even suggest it. What do you think we are? Fucking cop-outs?"

"Sorry."

"I don't think I can ever forgive you." He turned his back and strode off.

She watched his retreating back for a scant minute before chasing after him. She must have pushed the wrong button. She hadn't meant to. When she caught up with him in the middle of the stage, she grabbed his arm and hurried to get in front of him. "I'm sorry, Eric. I didn't know—"

His attempts to keep a serious expression failed, and his scowl faltered into a grin. "Gotcha."

Rebekah poked him in the belly, and he laughed. "You were teasing me?"

"Not really. We're known for our live performance. We really wouldn't consider using a recorded track, but I'm not really offended that you suggested it."

"Then why—"

"So you'd pay attention to me."

"I don't know if I'll ever get used to your in-your-face honesty."

His brow crinkled with concentration. "Is it a bad thing?"

"No, just not normal." She bit her lip. That had come out entirely wrong. He just laughed.

"Normal is boring. I thought we were in agreement on that."

Well, yeah, but while she struggled to be different, it came naturally to him. In a strange way, she envied his freedom to be himself.

"You are definitely not boring," she told him. "I can't keep up with you."

"I think you're doing a great job, actually. Most girls would have given up on me by now."

She found that hard to believe. "Well, I'm not most girls."

"That's what I like about you most."

And there he was just blurting it all out in the open, giving her no time to reflect or ponder or wonder. She knew exactly where he stood. She found it strangely refreshing after all the head games her mother and Isaac had put her through over the past several years.

"I haven't decided what I like about you most," she said with a teasing grin. "There's just so much to like."

Eric's breath caught, and she found herself wrapped in his long arms and crushed against his hard chest. "Where have you been all my life?" He kissed the top of her head, his heart thudding like a bass drum against her ear.

Someone cleared his throat behind them.

"Go away," Eric insisted and squeezed Rebekah more tightly.

"We need to rehearse, Sticks," Sed said in an amused tone. "You can cuddle with your new girl later."

Eric eased away slightly, and she craned her neck to look up at him.

"Can I cuddle with you later?" he asked her.

"I'd rather you watch me shower," she whispered.

His entire body stiffened. Yes, his *entire* body. "Uh." He squeezed her tightly again. "Are you serious?"

"Shhh. Go rehearse. I've got work to do."

Once she got the guitar amps in sync with the soundboard—Trey and Brian were phenomenal—she returned to the stage to hook up Eric's vocal mic.

"I think we'll have to go with a headset model," she told him. "You can't flail around like you normally do, or it will fly off." He held still while she slipped a headset into place and adjusted it. "Is that comfortable?"

"Do I look like a fighter pilot?" he asked, looking up at her from his stool with flashing blue eyes.

She grinned. "I don't think that haircut is regulation, soldier." She leaned closer to whisper in his ear. "Do you like to play dress-up in the bedroom?" She'd always thought it would be fun to pretend she was someone else while making love, and him asking if he looked like a fighter pilot had her envisioning multiple scenarios. Isaac had thought she was ridiculous when she'd mentioned wearing costumes. Isaac had thought most of her ideas were ridiculous. He was a very straitlaced individual. Very proper. A good man. He deserved a good wife. One who could give him children.

"What—you mean like you'd be an Amazonian woman and I'd be a fallen fighter pilot whose plane went down in the jungle? And because you saved my life, I must serve your every sexual fantasy to repay you?" he gushed.

Every guy in the crew and band laughed. Eric's mic was on. He glanced around nervously, his face flushed.

"Yeah, exactly like that," Rebekah murmured into his mic.

The laughter changed into tortured mutterings.

"Fuck, yeah. Let's go."

She pecked him on the lips and then stared into his eyes. "That was a rhetorical question."

He slapped himself in the forehead. "You are very hard on my anatomy, baby."

"You are really going to enjoy lesson two tomorrow," she whispered into his ear and stepped away.

He growled and then entered into a spontaneous drum solo that had both arms and legs moving at a blur.

With Eric's microphone, the final piece, in place, Sinners rehearsed their new song from beginning to end. Rebekah forgot her job duties for a moment as she watched in utter awe. Jace's piano intro dropped her jaw. Jon had gotten the hang of the new bass line, and it was hard and heavy. Brian and Trey's guitar riffs sounded sensational. Sed's vocals unparalleled. When they reached the chorus, Eric's voice came through the speakers, and Rebekah's knees went weak. She didn't think anything could top the combined vocals of Sed's roars and Eric's melody until Brian and Trey entered their dueling guitar solo in the middle of the song. Over a minute of six-stringed perfection, topped off by a short solo at the hand of Jace, who took over bass after he finished his piano intro. Eric's drum line tied it together with a perfect rhythm, and Rebekah remembered why she'd fallen in love with this band's music. They were perfect. It wasn't until the song ended that she realized she should be making adjustments with the equalizer. She didn't know if it was possible to improve what was already *that* exceptional. She put on her headset and spoke into her mic, which fed into the earpieces of the band members on stage and a few of the crew who needed to hear instructions.

"That was amazing, guys. Can we do that again from the top so I can make a few adjustments?"

"Reb, you sound so sexy," Eric's voice came through the loudspeaker.

"And I thought Brian was the romantic retard of the group," Sed teased, but he was grinning from ear to ear.

"Well, she does, doesn't she?" Eric persisted.

"I am in total agreement," Trey said. "I'd much rather listen to Rebekah's sexy voice than Dave and Marcus."

Rebekah's heart thudded in her chest. What was it about Trey Mills that worked a girl up so quickly? It was as if the timbre of his voice linked to some seduction center in the brain and demanded instant submission to his will. He didn't even have to try.

They worked through the afternoon. The guys didn't seem to mind Rebekah's nitpickiness at all. Apparently, it was as important to them that they got the song perfect as it was to her. She'd never felt as blessed as she felt working with such a professional and talented group of musicians as Sinners. They'd worked straight through lunch, and the opening bands wanted their turn at a rehearsal before the show, so they adjourned backstage for a meal. The venue had provided snack trays of lunch meat and cheese and crackers. Veggies and dips. Fruit and snack foods. Nothing worthy of feeding hardworking men. Rebekah wished she had time to cook them a great meal. She'd be sure to make it up to them the following night. While she filled her own tiny plate with bits of roast beef and cheddar cheese and miniature pieces of bread, Eric cut in line to stand beside her.

"You're doing a great job," he said.

She glanced at him and smiled. "You sound surprised."

"I think we were all kind of worried that Dave wanted you to take his place just to make you happy, but you're actually great. I'd hire you even if you weren't related to Dave."

She rolled her eyes. "I'm glad you approve."

His breath stirred her hair as he leaned close to her ear. "Are you ready for that shower now?"

She chuckled. "After the show. Okay?"

"No, not okay. I need to see you naked as soon as possible. You've been driving me crazy all day."

Goose bumps rose along the nape of her neck. And that wasn't the only thing rising. Her nipples hardened. Heat and moisture flooded her suddenly throbbing pussy. She pressed her arm against Eric's, consumed by the need to touch him, and she wanted to touch so much more than his arm.

"Who's holding up the line?" someone hollered from the opposite end of the long table.

Rebekah snapped back to her senses and added things to her plate again. "Later," she whispered. "Though I can't say I'm not tempted."

A portable picnic table had been set up for their utilization, and Eric squeezed next to Rebekah on the bench.

"This isn't enough to feed a sparrow," Sed complained. "I'm freakin' starving."

Rebekah supposed muscle-bound hunks required more calories than she did. "I'll cook a huge batch of chicken enchiladas tomorrow," Rebekah said. "How does that sound?"

Sed glowered at his tiny plate. "Tomorrow-Sed says that sounds fabulous, but right-now-Sed is considering barbecuing an event planner."

"I'll order something for you guys," Rebekah said and started to get up.

Eric wrapped an arm around her waist to keep her where she was sitting. "Not your job."

"But—"

Eric grabbed a passing stranger. "Go order twenty pizzas, and get us some cold beer."

"Uh—"

"Now. And make sure you get a pizza with anchovies and onions for Tripod."

"And pickles and pineapple for Sticks," Jace countered.

"Okay, I've got to ask," Rebekah said. "Why do you call him Tripod?"

Jace flushed to the roots of his bleached blond hair.

"Because he practically has three legs," Eric said. "Two actual legs and the hugest dick I have ever seen."

"Me too," Trey agreed and bit into a particularly juicy strawberry.

"And Trey has seen a lot of dicks," Eric teased.

Trey met Rebekah's astonished gaze unflinchingly. "That I have. But I've been in the mood for something more feminine since Rebekah joined the crew."

Eric's arm slid around her back and pulled her body securely against his side. "Look elsewhere, Mills," he said.

Trey just laughed.

Eventually the pizzas arrived, which inspired the opening bands to join the backstage festivities. It was so noisy that Rebekah went back out to her soundboard to get away from the crowd and to check her programming for the twentieth time. Her first clue that something wasn't right was the fact that the monitor in the middle of the panel of sliders and switches was dark. She hit the power switch, but nothing happened. She hunted down the power cord next and found that it had been unplugged. She took a deep breath, forcing back her panic, and plugged it in. Who would unplug her soundboard? Now she'd have to reload all her programs back into working memory. Good thing she'd caught it before the show started or she would have been seriously crunched for time. She reloaded all of the programs but one. The one just entered and saved for "Sever" was gone. She knew she'd saved it. She knew it. Someone had deleted it.

She could think of only one person who would have the know-how, much less the motivation, to do something like that. Marcus. She was so pissed her vision blurred with tears. Had it been possible to shoot forty-foot plumes of fire from her nostrils, she'd have done a very good impression of a fire-breathing dragon. Someone stepped up behind her, and she whipped around to confront the person stupid enough to enter her personal space. She opened her mouth to yell, but snapped her jaws shut when she recognized Eric. No sense in taking it out on him. She blocked Eric's stunned expression by turning back to her soundboard.

"I brought you a beer," he said.

"I think I'm going to need something stronger than beer," she bellowed.

He handed her a silver flask. She took a swig of tequila that singed her nose hairs. Maybe she was breathing fire after all. She shoved the flask in his direction, and he took it from her.

"What's wrong?" he asked.

"Someone deleted the program for 'Sever.' The one I *just* perfected after hours of work. My work. The band's work. Argh!"

"Someone deleted it? Why would someone delete it? Maybe you've just misplaced it."

The look she gave him over her shoulder made him take a step back.

"Okay, scratch that. Is there a way to recover it?"

"Maybe." She did have some experience in computer hacking. She wasn't sure if it was enough. Eric stood watching the tiny monitor as she keyed in DOS codes. She found the file. Deleted. About an hour before. When she'd been backstage.

"You see," she spat. "Someone purposely deleted it about an hour ago."

"That's when we were eating dinner."

"Well, most of us were. Who was missing?"

Eric shook his head. "No one that I remember."

She couldn't remember if anyone had been missing from the crew either. She hadn't been paying close attention. "I know it was Marcus. I know it was."

"But he was backstage with us the entire time. I saw him."

In her gut, she knew it had been him, but she was sure Eric wouldn't lie about seeing Marcus backstage. Eric didn't lie about anything.

"Can you recover the file?" he asked.

"Yeah. It will be damaged and I'll have to do some repair, but I think I remember the program and can fill in the missing code."

She had worked up a sweat by the time she was satisfied that the file was not corrupted and would work as it was supposed to when the time came for Sinners to play the song.

"Got it?" Eric asked. He'd stood there patiently the entire time, tolerating her swearing tirade without protest.

"Yeah. I'm not moving from this spot until the concert is over," she said.

Eric turned her to face him and brushed her hair from her face. "I was already impressed with your work this morning when you set up the sound equipment. Now I'm utterly amazed."

He sought her lips and kissed her deeply.

"You're incredible," he said into her mouth. He drew her closer. Kissed her more deeply, stroking her tongue with his and sucking her lips with tender abandon. His hand cupped her breast and squeezed. This was totally the wrong place, but she wanted him fiercely. And she wanted to be straight with him. To tell him about herself. If he was going to keep coming back for more, she felt she owed it to him.

"Eric," she gasped and pulled away. He bent to nibble on her earlobe. She shuddered violently, her fingers digging into his hard chest. "Eric, not here."

"This is what I want to do to your clit right now," he whispered. He sucked on her earlobe and stroked it rapidly with the tip of his tongue.

"Oh God," she panted, her clit swelling in response.

"And your pussy." His tongue dipped into her ear.

Her pussy pulsed in response. "I need…" *Oh, wow.* "I need to tell you."

"Tell me?" The husky timbre of his voice had swollen, pulsing parts throbbing incessantly.

She nodded, still clinging to him and not really wanting him to stop his glorious assault on her ear, though he really should. They were standing in the middle of a stadium making out on a soundboard.

"About my s-sexual problem," she said.

"I don't see any problem. I sure as hell don't feel a problem."

"L-listen. O-okay?" On the verge of tears, she took a deep

shuddering breath. "T-this is h-hard for me." Damn it. Why did she always stutter when she was upset? She hated it.

Eric stopped and gazed into her eyes. She really did feel like she could tell him anything. They'd known each other for less than two days, and yet…

"I have cancer," she blurted.

The blood drained from his face, and he swayed against her. "What?"

"I'm in remission now. Maybe it won't come back. Maybe it will. I can't know for sure."

"I think I need to sit down."

She pressed on. "I went t-through treatment. I'm not sick anymore. I fought it. I won. But…"

"Are you going to die?" he asked, his voice cracking.

"No. No! That's not why I'm telling you this. I'm fine. Really. I… The reason…" She took a deep breath and forced herself to push on. "I don't feel comfortable having sex because… I'm missing things. Inside."

"I don't understand."

"I had a hysterectomy."

"To save you from cancer?"

"Y-yes."

He hugged her until she feared her ribs would crack. "Good."

Good? There was nothing good about it. "I can never have children."

"So? As long as you're here, who cares about that stuff?"

A tear slipped down her cheek. She had to tell him all of it, because she knew for certainty that she wanted him—Eric—in her life. "It feels weird inside. For a guy, I mean. Isaac said…"

"Who's Isaac?"

"My boyfriend. *Ex*-boyfriend," she clarified quickly. "He wanted me to marry him, but I made him wait to propose until the cancer was gone. He stayed by my side the entire time. Through the treatments and the surgery. The radiation and the healing process. He waited for me to get better, and then afterward, when we tried to, you know…" She blushed. Talking about ex-boyfriend sex with your hopefully new boyfriend was beyond weird.

"Do the horizontal mamba."

She laughed. "Yeah."

"But it was horrible, right?" he asked hopefully.

"Appalling," she said truthfully. "He said it felt weird when he was inside. It was so unsettling for him that he couldn't even keep an erection. He said he couldn't bring himself to do it with me anymore. Ever again."

"Well, he's obviously a limp dick and a moron."

"Actually, he's a doctor."

"Doctors can be limp-dicked morons."

She laughed and hugged him. "Sometimes. They told me I was going to die, and I didn't. Anyway, Isaac wanted a family and I can't give him that, so we broke up and he left. It was for the best, I suppose. But it still hurt that he found me so unappealing. I didn't think I'd ever want to have sex again after that."

He rubbed her back and held her for a long moment. His strength was so comforting, her eyes drifted shut and she melted into him.

"So you can't get pregnant?" he asked, a soothing hand on her hair.

She shook her head. "I'm not supposed to have much of a sex drive either, but you definitely have my thoughts for sex in drive."

"You have my thoughts for sex in warp drive," he murmured.

"Even now that you know about… m-my deformity?"

"When you're ready, I'd like to feel if it's weird for myself. Like everything else about you, I have no doubt that being inside you will be perfect."

She sniffed, trying to keep the tears in check, but they fell anyway. "Thank you," she whispered, "even if you don't really mean it."

He pressed her head against his thudding heart. "Have you ever known me to lie?" he asked.

She shook her head.

"Well, there you have it. Just let me know when you're ready. You know I'm willing and able. My dick is *never* limp."

She laughed and lifted her head to look at him. "You promise not to lie if it feels weird? I don't want you to lie about that either. Even to save my feelings."

"I promise."

And when he kissed her with incomparable tenderness, she knew he was the one to make her feel whole again.

Chapter 10

AFTER THE CONCERT—WHICH had been utterly phenomenal—Eric ducked behind the low, tiled wall in the shower room and peeked at Rebekah. She glanced at him briefly and winked before she turned her back and started to remove her clothes. She'd found him backstage after the show and asked if he really wanted to watch her in the shower. Well, duh, of course he did. She told him she wanted to pretend she didn't know he was there until he couldn't keep his hands off her and had to join her. She didn't really need to instruct him on what she wanted him to do. That's exactly how he would have responded to watching her shower.

Rebekah pulled her T-shirt over her head. She looked so sexy in her lacy white bra and blue jeans. Eric licked his lip and tried to keep his excitement contained. She unbuttoned her jeans and slid them slowly down her thighs. She wriggled her hips as she bent at the waist to release one leg from her pants and then the other. She folded her clothes and put them on a bench, before reaching behind her back to unfasten her bra. Eric held his breath, waiting for a glimpse of her beautiful breasts. Would her nipples be hard? Would it excite her to know he was watching? She kept her back to him when she removed her bra. She was so good at pretending he wasn't there, he could almost believe that she was unaware of his presence.

She turned slightly, and he caught a brief glimpse of one pert breast and her flat belly. She twisted her shoulder-length hair and clipped it to the back of her head. Every movement was mesmerizing.

Exposing her neck like that? Somewhat cruel. Her panties joined her pile of clothes on the bench, and then she approached one of the heads in the community shower. When the first blast of water struck her skin, she emitted a shriek of surprise. "C-cold!" She danced away from the water, and Eric chuckled.

She paused and turned in his direction. "Is someone there?"

Well, duh, she knew he was there, but he ducked behind the wall and pretended to hide.

"Guess not." She reentered the stream of steaming water and sighed in contentment. She had one of those poofy things to spread liquid soap lather over her body. She dumped a healthy amount of soap on her poof and drew it slowly over her skin. Her arms. Her breasts. Her belly. Her breasts again. Transfixed, Eric watched, his hand pressed against his already bulging fly. He had to practice making himself last so she would teach him lessons on a regular basis. No matter how much he wanted to pull his throbbing cock free and stroke it while she soaped her body, he wouldn't. Not yet. *Must. Maintain. Control.*

Damn, she sure didn't make it easy.

Rebekah turned her back and bent to wash her shapely legs. He strained his neck to see the mysteries between her thighs. Still bending forward, she spread her labia with one hand and soaped her tender flesh with her poof. He could see everything, and though he knew no woman washed herself like that unless she wanted someone to see what she had to offer, it didn't make it any less sexy.

Eric unfastened his pants and slid his hand into his underwear. He tugged his cock free and ran his hand gently up and down its length. What he really wanted was to plunge into the slick hole that Rebekah was washing quite thoroughly. He prayed she was ready for his possession soon. He wanted her more now that she'd told him about her problems than he'd ever wanted anyone. That she trusted him with such personal information meant the world to him.

Masses of suds gathered at her mound and dripped down both thighs. Eric wished that white froth was his cum. Wished that finger she'd slipped inside her pussy was his cock. Wished—

"Are you really standing here jerking it?" Trey said. "What the fuck is wrong with you?"

His fantasy shattered, Eric scowled and forced his cock into his pants. "Go away."

"She knows you're watching her."

"Yeah. So?"

"If you're too lame to accept that open invitation, I'll have to crash her party in your place."

Eric reached to grab Trey's shirt, but Trey was already striding toward Rebekah with a sexual confidence Eric knew he'd never match. Trey kicked off his shoes and socks and peeled his T-shirt over his head. He joined Rebekah in the shower still wearing his jeans.

Rebekah gasped in surprise and turned to look at him. "Trey?"

His arms slid around her back, and he drew her against his length, her breasts pressed against his naked chest. "You look lonely," he murmured. And then he kissed her. That son of a bitch.

Normally, when Eric watched one of his bandmates engage with a woman, it excited him. But watching Trey kiss Rebekah didn't excite him. It pissed him off. He was stalking toward them before he knew what he was doing. He grabbed Trey's arm and yanked him away from Rebekah's submissive form. What the fuck? After she'd opened her heart to him, she still wanted Trey?

"Get your goddamned hands off her," Eric said.

With an impish gleam in his eye, Trey grinned at him crookedly. "Why should I?"

"Because I don't want you to touch her. If you touch her again, I'll… I'll…"

"You'll what?"

Eric's hands balled into fists. "I'll kick your ass."

"I don't mind if he kisses me," Rebekah said.

Eric felt as if someone had taken a branding iron to his heart.

"But Eric and I have a deal," she added.

"A deal?" Trey questioned.

"So if he doesn't want me to kiss you, or touch you—" Rebekah ran a hand down Trey's belly and over the bulge in his jeans, "—or suck your cock while he watches, then I won't."

Eric faltered between being really pissed off at Trey for infringing on what he already considered his territory, and being really turned on by the thought of Rebekah on her knees sucking his cock in the shower. Not Trey's cock. His.

"I'd rather Trey leave and you kiss me. Touch me. Suck…"

"You?"

He nodded.

She grinned. "No can do. Your next lesson isn't until tomorrow."

"Lesson?" Trey questioned. He was still holding her loosely. Water from the shower poured between their naked torsos.

"Part of our agreement," Rebekah said. "Sorry, Trey. I'm going to have to ask you to leave."

Eric stifled a relieved sigh. He would rather her have ask Trey to leave because she wasn't interested in him, but Eric would take what he could get.

"Since when would you rather participate than watch?" Trey asked Eric.

"I still like to watch. Just not with you," Eric said. "Or anyone else for that matter."

Trey surprised him by smiling. "Good. My work here is finished." He released Rebekah and sloshed out of the shower in his wet jeans. "Make me proud, buddy."

Huh?

Trey retrieved his discarded clothes and shoes and left the locker room.

"Where were we?" Rebekah asked.

"I believe you were washing yourself, and I was touching myself."

"You were touching yourself?"

Her hand slid into the front of his jeans and brushed against his cock. His underwear separated their skin, but that didn't stop him from drawing a breath through his teeth.

"Show me, Eric. I want to see."

Knowing he wouldn't be able to keep his hands to himself with her this close, he went to the bench where she'd stowed her clothes and sat down. "Make me want you, Rebekah," Eric murmured.

"How?"

"You really don't have to do anything but stand there."

So she stood there, hands on both hips, water coursing over her gorgeous body, and it was more than enough to make him want her.

"Take your clothes off," she said. "I want to see all of you."

She approached him and pulled his sweaty T-shirt over his head. If anyone needed a shower after a live show, it was him.

"Now your pants," she said, her fingertips trailing down one side of his chest to his rib cage. She snagged his nipple ring on the way down and tugged it just hard enough to make his belly tighten.

Eric kicked off his shoes and lifted his hips from the bench to remove his jeans and underwear.

She leaned over him, her fingertips skimming the length of his cock. His entire body jerked at her attention. "I know I said you weren't going to get lesson two until tomorrow, but I'm going to be proven a liar. I am so going to suck your cock tonight. Probably more than once. I want your cum in my mouth. To taste it. To feel it hit the back of my throat. To swallow it."

He groaned.

"Do you want that?"

He nodded.

She glanced over his shoulder. "Is there a lock on that door?"

Her words took awhile to register. Her close proximity and promises of coming in her mouth had all rational thought scattered with the wind.

"I'll go check," he said finally. He forced himself from the bench and staggered toward the door. It did have a deadbolt. After he locked it, he turned to find Rebekah back in the shower soaping her beautiful breasts. He watched her from across the room, completely transfixed by her motions and the way she pretended he wasn't there. She was so perfect for him. Everything about her. Perfect. He'd never believed one person was tailor-made specifically for him until now. He was starting to think like Brian von Romantic de Retard. Pretty lame. Yet so totally not. Now that he knew what it felt like, it wasn't lame at all. Eric approached the low wall slowly, never taking his eyes off Rebekah. He stood there for several minutes, watching her pluck her nipples impatiently until he couldn't stand it and went to join her.

Rebekah gasped, as if surprised by Eric's presence, and covered her soapy, wet breasts with her hands. "Oh, monsieur," she said in a poor attempt at a French accent. "I apologize for my trespass in your private bathroom. How long have you been watching me enjoy the flow of water?"

"Far too long. I couldn't stay away another minute."

"I pray you will not punish me too harshly, monsieur. How will I ever escape such a devilishly handsome rake?"

Eric hesitated. "*Rake?* Like for leaves and junk?"

Rebekah tossed her head back and laughed until Eric thought she would pass out from lack of air. When she finally stopped howling with laughter, she wiped the tears from her eyes and dropped her teasing French accent. "I thought we could play one of those pretend games we talked about," she whispered.

He instantly imagined her in a slutty nurse outfit in his mind's eye. She could test his reflexes all night long as far as he was concerned. "Will this require thinking on my part? I'm way too turned on to think right now."

"Well then, my handsome, devilish rake—meaning scoundrel, not leaf-gathering tool—maybe you should demand certain *favors* in return for this innocent young maiden's safe release. She was trespassing in your private bathroom, after all. The least she can do is please you."

"That's pretty sleazy, even for me," Eric said.

"It's a game. Just go with it."

"Okay, but don't get mad at me for being more devil than rake." He grinned, hoping he looked more devilish than sleazy. "Mademoiselle, there are consequences for trespassing in this part of... *France*?"

Rebekah nodded, grinning and totally out of character. "Please do not turn me in to the authorities, monsieur. I will do anything."

"*Anything*?"

"Yes, yes, anything."

"I require but one kiss," he murmured and wrapped his arms around her to draw her near.

"That's *it*?" she said, losing her accent again.

"It is more than any leaf-gathering tool deserves." He lowered his head and kissed her. She tasted like pure heaven. Her soft curves pressed against his hard chest. He filled his hands with her slick flesh and allowed himself to sample every inch of her mouth. Something had changed between them. There was a mutual trust. A bond. It had spawned from her confession about her brush with cancer and her limp-dicked ex-boyfriend. Eric vowed to never do anything to upset that trust. He didn't want to move too fast and scare her away. He planned to keep her around for a while. Like an eternity, or something a bit longer.

She tugged her mouth away. "Monsieur, what is that poking me in the belly?" She batted her eyelashes.

Well, okay, if she insisted on moving faster and making his every fantasy a reality, he wasn't going to resist. Much. "That is what happens to a man when he has a naked chick in his arms."

"Chick?"

"I mean innocent… What did you call it?"

"Innocent young maiden," she whispered.

"Right." He cleared his throat. He was having an exceedingly difficult time concentrating. "That is what happens to a man when he has an innocent young maiden in his arms. Especially a fucking gorgeous, naked one named Rebekah Blake."

"I've never seen such a thing, monsieur," she said, her eyes wide with wonder. "Might I examine your wondrous protrusion?"

"Wondrous protrusion?" Now it was Eric's turn to laugh. "Sure, baby, you can examine my wondrous protrusion as much as you want."

Her small hand circled his cock and stroked its length. "It's so hard and hot. The skin so smooth." She rubbed her thumb over the expanded head, and he drew a shaky breath through his teeth. "Does that feel good, monsieur?"

"Yes, that feels really good."

She rubbed his cock head gently. Already his excitement was near the breaking point. She touched the bead of pre-cum with her fingertips. "What is this?" she questioned. She collected the tiny sample of fluid with her thumb and rubbed it on her tongue. "Oh, monsieur, the taste is delicious. Is there more for me to sample?"

Eric tried to think of something to continue their little game, but the best he could come up with was a breathless, "Yeah."

She slid down his body and licked the head of his cock tentatively. "How do I get more to come out?" she asked.

"S-suck."

She sucked. His fingers tangled in her silky hair as she sucked hard and bobbed her head to rub her lips over his sensitive rim. He watched her suck him, his cock disappearing into her sweet mouth. His breaths came in excited huffs. His pleasure built. And built. *Oh God.* He fought orgasm, but as usual his body didn't cooperate with his will. He clung to her scalp and thrust deep into the back of her throat as he came with a hoarse cry. She swallowed his cum, her throat muscles working around the head of his cock, and it was almost too much to bear.

"Oh God, Reb. Stop. It feels too good. I can't—"

She sucked him dry and then pulled back to release him from her mouth. "Oh, monsieur, that was so delicious. I would like more please."

"Give me five minutes," he said breathlessly.

She stood and snuggled against his chest. "I have such strange feelings between my legs, monsieur. What does it mean?"

"Strange feelings?"

"Yes, there is a wetness there, and it throbs and aches."

"Perhaps I should take a look."

Rebekah chuckled. "Yeah, I really think you should."

Eric turned off the water and led her to the bench. He spread several towels over its surface, knowing his beautiful Rebekah deserved better. "Lie here, mademoiselle. I will try to help you with your strange feelings between your legs."

"Thank you, monsieur. It is most perplexing."

He sat on a towel on the floor and pulled her to the end of the bench. He stroked her slippery folds with two fingers. "I see the wetness you were talking about," he said.

"What is it?"

He touched his tongue to her flesh, and she jerked in response. "My favorite flavor," he murmured and licked the rim of her opening until she was clinging to his hair, and her juices were flowing freely.

"Oh, monsieur. A little higher up there is a spot that needs examining, I think."

Eric grinned. He leaned away and drew his fingers through the curls at the apex of her thighs. "Here?"

"Close," she panted.

He brushed his fingertips over her clit. "Here?"

She sucked a breath through her teeth. "Yes. Yes. Right there."

He rubbed her clit in a circular motion. "Does that help?"

"Oh yes."

He leaned forward to replace his fingers with the suction of his lips and the flick of his tongue. "Oh Eric," she gasped. "I'm so close. Slide your fingers inside me."

He knew she was worried about her body being weird inside. He hesitated. "Are you sure?"

"P-please."

He slid the tip of one finger into her hot, slick flesh. His cock grew hard within seconds. He inserted a second finger and slowly pushed inward while he continued to suck and flick her clit.

"Oh, yes, Eric. That feels so good. Does it feel weird inside?"

It felt like pure heaven. Smooth. Warm. Silky. He wanted to bury his cock inside that slick, swollen passage. "It feels perfect, Rebekah. Perfect. Not weird at all."

He pressed his fingers into her as deeply as he could and then slowly withdrew before thrusting inside again. He continued to take her deeply with his fingers while he suckled her clit. She cried out, and her pussy gripped his fingers in rhythmic spasms as she came. Nothing weird about that either. He only wished her muscles were gripping his cock and he was joining her in bliss. When her body stilled, he carefully removed his fingers from her body.

"I'm ready," she whispered. "Put it in."

"What?"

"Put it in, Eric. I want to know what it feels like for you."

"You're asking me to make love to you? All the way. For real?"

"Yes."

"Not here," he said.

He climbed to his feet, stricken by her beauty. Flushed skin, dazed expression, heavy eyelids. She gnawed on the side of her finger, and he forgot the thread of their conversation.

"What do you mean, not here?" she asked, a hitch in her voice. If she started that stuttering, he would totally lose it. "Don't you want to?"

"Our first time will be someplace nice. Get dressed. We're going to the most expensive hotel I can find."

"But—"

"No arguments, mademoiselle. I'm going to make love to you in a nice comfortable bed, not on a bench in a men's locker room."

"Why Eric Sticks, I never knew you were the considerate, romantic type."

"I was mostly thinking about how hard it would be on my back." He clutched his lower back and grimaced in pain.

"Sure you were."

⁓

Eric found Jon in a dressing room playing a drinking game with the vocalist and drummer of the opening band, Kickstart.

"Eric!" Jon said in his outside voice. "What's going on? Grab a chair. These dudes know how to party."

"I can't stay. I just want to borrow your car."

"For what?"

"For a while."

"Sit down. We have tequila. Good stuff. Not that rotgut you carry around in your flask."

"I've got other things to do," Eric insisted. He glanced over his shoulder and caught sight of Rebekah waiting near the door. She was twisting her hands in the hem of her T-shirt and looking entirely adorable as usual.

"Such as?" Jon pressed.

Eric forced his attention to the man he had once considered his best friend. "Important stuff. Look, can I borrow your car? If not, I'll call a cab or something."

Jon fiddled in his pocket and produced a set of keys. He held them in Eric's direction suspended on one finger. When Eric reached for them, Jon closed his hand. "You can borrow it, but you owe me one."

Eric stifled an angry retort. It was always like this with Jon. The guy could never do someone a favor out of the goodness of his heart. He always kept a running tab. And there was one thing he'd been holding over Eric's head for almost three years. If Eric hadn't wanted to take Rebekah someplace nice, he would have told Jon to forget it. He really did not want to owe the guy another debt, but taking Rebekah to a hotel where he could treat her right was totally worth it.

"Fine. I owe you one. Give me the keys."

"You're going to party with that hot little roadie, aren't you? Re-bek-kah." Jon chuckled. "She's going to take everything she can from you and leave you high and dry like the others."

Eric scowled. "She's not like the others."

"That's what you always say."

"Just give me the keys." He yanked them out of Jon's hand and stalked away.

"You're welcome," Jon called after him.

Eric flipped him off.

Rebekah wasn't just using him for her own gain. Eric refused to let what Jon said get to him. Just because all his other relationships had been sham and he'd been a sucker didn't mean this one was a repeat performance. He trusted Rebekah. Just like he automatically trusted any member of the female persuasion. Damn it.

He paused in front of Rebekah and she looked up at him, all

beautiful and sweet and delicate. No way could she have some ulterior motive. Right?

"Before I do something all stupid like fall in love with you, tell me exactly why you're with me tonight," he blurted.

Her eyes widened as if she'd been caught doing something wrong, and Eric's heart plummeted into his belly. Great. Just fucking wonderful. She did have some scheme planned. Did she want his money? Someone in the band wrapped around her finger as job security? A way to get closer to Trey? What?

"You're going to make me say it?" she asked uneasily.

"Yeah. I've been nothing but honest with you. I think you should be just as honest with me."

She flushed and struggled to maintain eye contact. "Okay. You… you make me feel special."

"And?" he pressed. "What else?"

"That's it."

"That's *it*?"

"Well, that, and I like to be with you." She placed a hand on his abdomen and leaned closer. "I like you, period."

He couldn't help but grin. "*Yeah?*"

She smiled crookedly and nodded. "Yeah."

He wrapped her in both arms and kissed the top of her head. "I like you, exclamation point."

She laughed and squeezed him. "Why are you acting suspicious all of a sudden?" she said against his chest.

"Stupid Jon. Putting doubts in my head. Sorry to be such a dick."

"You're not being a dick. I've just never been in a brutally honest relationship before. It's a little intimidating," she said.

He did throw it all out there most of the time. "I'll try to tone it down."

"Don't," she said and slid her hand to the center of his chest to push him back far enough that she could look at him. "I like it. No head games. Better to be a little intimidated than royally confused. I spent my last relationship confused. I'm still pretty confused about it, actually."

"I'd pry, but the last thing I want to talk about is one of your ex-boyfriends. Let's go make love now. I need to bury myself in your sweet pussy."

Her eyes widened, and he bit his lip.

"Sorry." He was bound and determined to fuck this up with his big mouth.

"Don't apologize. I need you buried inside my sweet..." She swallowed. "...pussy." That last word came out in an excited whisper.

He grinned. "Yeah, you do."

They headed out of the stadium and hurried toward the buses, equipment trucks, and Jon's Jeep. Jon was not allowed on the tour bus, so he had to meet them at the venues in his own vehicle.

Eric loved how Rebekah held his hand as if they were an actual couple while they crossed the parking lot.

"Are you free of STDs?" she asked.

Eric tripped over both feet. "What? Why would you ask me something like that?"

"Just tell me the truth."

"Yes, I'm clean. I always wear a condom. Sometimes two to decrease my sensitivity."

"Always?"

"Yes, always."

"Would you be against not wearing one tonight? I want you to feel everything inside me. Intimately." She ducked her head. "I swear to you that I'm clean too."

"You want me inside you without a condom?"

"Well, it's not like I can get pregnant." She sounded so sad when she said it that Eric's heart shattered.

He released her hand so he could wrap his arm around her shoulders and draw her closer.

"Does it bother you? Knowing that?" she whispered.

"Of course not. Just the thought of being inside you without a condom has me hard as stone."

Her hand slid over his fly and she discovered he wasn't lying about that either.

"Are you sure you can get it up more than once in a night?" she asked.

He chuckled. That would be absolutely no problem whatsoever. Especially not with Rebekah. He'd had a perpetual stiffy since he'd gotten his first glimpse of her. "I'm sure."

She grinned. "I'm counting on that, you know."

She was? He wondered what she meant. When they reached Jon's Jeep, Eric opened the door for Rebekah and helped her into the passenger side. When he climbed into the driver's side, he pushed the seat all the way back to accommodate his long legs. Rebekah's hand landed in his lap. At first, he thought she had her hand on his cock by mistake, but then she unfastened his fly.

"What are you—"

"Shh," she said. "Turn on the overhead light."

"What? Why?"

"It's dark in here. Don't you want to watch?"

"Watch?"

Her hand slid into his underwear and against his cock. He almost jumped out of the seat. He fumbled with the controls until the light came on. He looked at his lap and watched her slide his cock into her mouth. Watching his flesh disappear into her mouth coupled with the exquisite pleasure had his breath hitching immediately. He tenderly stroked her soft hair from her face and discovered more than the pleasure she gave as he watched. Emotions welled up in his tight chest. He'd never felt anything like this. Well, yeah, he'd had innumerable fantastic blow jobs in his life, but the other side of this was entirely new. The feeling that he'd do anything to make this woman happy, anything to be with her. That was unique and a bit scary. Not scary enough for him to back off though. His dreams of a perfect woman didn't even come close to how wonderful Rebekah was. He knew he'd never done anything to deserve her, but that would not stop him from claiming her as his. Whatever it took.

He lost the thread of his thoughts as her suction intensified. He gasped, and his eyelids fluttered. The steering wheel was in her way, so she couldn't pull back very far. She made up for it by writhing the back of her tongue against the head of his cock.

"You're so beautiful," he whispered as he watched her. "I've never wanted a woman as much as I want you."

She sucked harder.

"God, that feels good," he gasped. She sucked harder. She was going to make him come. Should he even try to fight it? She was unusual in that she didn't expect him to. She liked him to get carried away in his own excitement. "Rebekah. Rebekah? Rebekah!" His fingers clutched her hair. She pulled back at the last moment and held her mouth open. He watched his cum spurt into her mouth and bathe her tongue. She shifted slightly so the second spurt hit her lower lip. Her chin. Into her mouth again.

"Fuck." He gasped and forced himself not to squeeze his eyes shut in tormented bliss. That was the sexiest fucking thing he'd ever seen in his life. She wrapped her lips around the head of his cock and sucked long after he'd stopped spurting.

"Okay. Okay. Okay," he gasped, his entire body shuddering with the aftereffects of release.

She released him from his blissful torture and sat upright. Her tongue slid from between her lips and she licked at the cum just under her lower lip. Eric grabbed her and pulled her onto his lap. The horn blared, and she started before laughing. He placed open-mouthed kisses on her chin, collecting his fluids from her skin before kissing her smiling lips. She returned his kisses hungrily. By the time she tugged away, his excitement was already getting the better of him again.

"If you don't stop doing sexy stuff like that, you're going to give me a heart attack," he said.

"I think your heart can take it," she challenged. "You're young and healthy. And you lasted at least ten minutes that time."

"I did?"

"I have this theory about you," Rebekah said. She reached for his softening cock, which twitched excitedly in her hand as soon as she cradled it in her palm. She carefully tucked it into his boxer briefs.

"What kind of theory?"

She looked at him, her beguiling blue eyes half-hidden by thick lashes. "The more often I make you come, the longer you'll last."

His heart thudded. Did that mean what he thought it meant? "Are you planning on testing that theory?"

She grinned. "Heck yeah, I am."

"You are the smartest woman I've ever met."

She laughed. "I'm more into hands-on learning, if you know what I mean. Are we going to the hotel now? I want to try more experiments."

He started the ignition, checked over his shoulder, popped the clutch, and punched the accelerator. The Jeep shot backward out of the parking space. He shifted into first and the tires squealed as they sped out of the lot.

Eyes wide, Rebekah fastened her seat belt and clung to the dashboard with her fingernails. "Eric, slow down."

He grinned, and the tires barked as he downshifted and slid around a corner. "I always drive like this."

"Then I absolutely refuse to help you fix your Corvette. You'll end up killing yourself with that much power in a little car!"

He eased off the accelerator slightly. For her sake, not his. He loved to go fast. There were few things that got his blood pumping as quickly. He spotted a neon sign ahead flashing XXX. And that would be another one.

"Pit stop," he said and hit the brakes.

Skidding sideways, he stopped directly in the center of a parking spot in front of the entrance of the adult store.

"I'm driving the rest of the way," Rebekah said. "As soon as my knees stop knocking together and I can get my fingernails pried out of the dashboard."

"I'm a good driver," Eric insisted. "Never had an accident."

"How many speeding tickets have you had?"

"They have to catch you to give you a ticket." He winked before opening his door and darting around the car to her side.

Her eyes were as wide as saucers when he helped her out of the car. "W-what are we d-doing here?"

Oh God, the stuttering thing. He kissed her trembling lips. Couldn't help it. "Supplies," he said and grasped her hand.

"I've n-never been in an adult s-store before." Her stuttering was so fucking cute. He wondered if she had any idea how endearing she was when she was unsettled.

"Do you want to wait in the car?" he asked.

She shook her head. "I didn't say that."

She clung to his hand with both of hers as they entered the store. She attempted to use his body as a human shield, which made everyone notice her more, not less. They started in the adult toys section. Even more adorable than the stuttering, Rebekah blushed a shade redder than her T-shirt. He couldn't wait to get her alone and just bask in her sweetness. When she pulled a huge vibrating dildo off the shelf, his thoughts took a sudden turn south. Oh God, she was going to let him fuck her. Accept his cock inside her body. Without a condom.

"What is all this stuff?" she whispered, her eyes wide as she ogled the package in her hands.

"For your pleasure, my lady."

He stole a kiss and selected several things he figured she'd enjoy. He handed them to her in quick succession. Her arms were overflowing with dildos and vibrators, butt plugs and clit stimulators within minutes.

"We better get lots of batteries," he told her.

She blushed a shade deeper and then busted out laughing, dropping several packages in the process. "They have costumes," she said, nodding toward the back of the store.

Eric dropped off a load of purchases on the counter. If the clerk was surprised, she didn't show it. "Is there anything I can help you two find?" she asked.

"Just start ringing it up. We're in a hurry," he said.

Eric grabbed Rebekah's hand and tugged her to the back of the store. He reached for a nurse's outfit first. He still wanted her to test his reflexes. He held up the little white dress in front of her. "Is this the right size?" he asked.

She checked the tag. "It should fit. I don't think it will cover my ass though." She tugged at the hem.

"Then it's exactly the right size." It was about the length of a long T-shirt and cut low in the front. Ah man. He was getting hard just picturing her in it. Maybe she'd wear white thigh-high stockings and heels. And a little hat. And stick a thermometer in his...

Eric forced his attention back to the merchandise. Unable to decide if he'd rather her dress as a cat or a pirate wench or a devil girl or a French maid or a teacher or a naughty schoolgirl or any other fantasy a man could possibly have, he grabbed one of every costume available and all the accessories that matched.

"If you think I'm the only one dressing up, you have another thing comin', Eric Sticks."

"What did you have in mind?"

"Get the chaps and the cowboy hat."

"Yes, ma'am." He rifled through a rack of fringed, suede chaps, looking for his size. Tall.

"Oh, and the vampire cape and the baseball player and the camouflage with the dog tags." She paused and looked up. "And the rock star leather."

He laughed. "That's not a fantasy, baby."

"Maybe not for you, but it is for me." Arms overloaded with purchases, she tilted her head back and offered her lips. "We need to go. It's getting late."

He kissed her. "Yeah, we've both had a long day. We'll probably just fall asleep as soon as we find a bed." He glanced at her sidelong, giving her a chance to back out if she wanted to.

She chuckled in the back of her throat. "You'll be lucky if I let you sleep at all. I'm ready to have fun. I hope you're ready to be up all night."

He smiled. She still wanted him, even knowing he was far more Mr. Porn Star than Mr. Romance. His arms full, he nudged her toward the checkout. While Rebekah oversaw the process, Eric browsed an aisle for various oils. He caught Rebekah sneaking things into their pile of purchases when she thought he wasn't looking.

Standing at the counter beside Rebekah, a display caught his eye. He lifted the package and read its contents. "They have numbing condoms I could try," he whispered into Rebekah's ear.

She looked at him with a wrinkled brow. "Why would you suggest that?"

He bent close to her ear again. "So I can't feel anything. I'll last a lot longer."

"No," she said. "I told you that's not important to me."

He sighed. "You say that now." He put the condoms back in a display on the counter.

"And I want you to feel everything," she whispered.

Her words punched him in the gut and left him breathless. Well, if she insisted.

"Did you find everything you needed?" the cashier asked.

Rebekah chuckled. "I think so."

"Wait," Eric said. "Do you have any camouflaged condoms?"

"Camouflaged?" The cashier's forehead crinkled in concentration. "I don't think so. We have every flavor and color imaginable, but I don't think we have any camouflaged."

"Why would you need a camouflaged condom?" Rebekah asked.

"So you won't see me coming."

Rebekah snorted and then burst into delighted laughter. The cashier rolled her eyes and shook her head as she stuffed a large dildo into a sack.

Eric kissed Rebekah's temple, his heart thrumming with adulation. "I love that you laugh at my corny jokes."

"They're funny."

Well, if she insisted.

When Rebekah and Eric finally got out of the adult store, they had multiple bags overflowing with their purchases.

"I think we'll need to check into a hotel for a week to try all this stuff," Rebekah said as they loaded the trunk.

"I don't have a problem with that. Do you have a problem with that?"

"We sorta have a job to do. What time does the bus leave tomorrow?"

"Sed mentioned hiring a driver so he could get some fucking sleep. That should give us a little more time. We need to be in Austin in two days."

She held a hand out. "Keys."

"You're not going to let me drive? For real?"

"For real."

There was one good thing about letting Rebekah drive. Eric could watch her the entire time and dream up things they could do once they reached the hotel. Also, there was something undeniably hot about a woman who could handle a stick shift.

Chapter 11

THE DESK CLERK LEERED at Rebekah as Eric tucked his credit card back into his wallet. Rebekah didn't care that the world knew exactly why she was checking into a hotel room with a rock star and five bulging sacks of sex toys and kinky costumes. She couldn't wait to continue what she and Eric had started back in the locker room. He was exactly what she needed. She was ready to forget the hurt Isaac had caused and move forward. Besides, they had all that stuff they'd bought at the store to keep them entertained for hours. The night clerk's opinion of her would be the furthest thing from her mind in no time.

Their suite was spectacular, and while she'd been hoping that Eric would pounce on her the moment they stepped over the threshold, he didn't. He set several bags of their purchases on the bed and retrieved his flask of tequila from the inside of his leather vest. He took a swig, glanced at her, and took another. The easy passion that had existed back at the stadium was lacking now. The fun camaraderie at the store had also vanished. She set her bags next to the bed and moved closer.

She still wanted him, but was starting to suspect that he'd changed his mind. "What's wrong?"

"Nothing."

She approached him. When she tried to wrap her arms around him, he stepped away. "Something's wrong. You haven't lied to me since we met. Why would you start now?"

They stared at each other for a long moment. He finally broke the silence. "I'm afraid I'll disappoint you. You think I come fast when you suck me, wait until I'm inside you."

"It's okay, Eric."

He shook his head vehemently. "No, it's not."

"I still want to be with you. I don't care how long you last."

This time when she hugged him, he didn't move away.

"Kiss me," she urged. He obeyed. She worked at removing his clothes, separating their mouths only long enough to pull his T-shirt over his head. She unfastened his pants and pushed them and his underwear to his knees. He kicked off his Converse tennis shoes and helped her complete the task. When he was naked, she kept right on kissing him and waited for him to take the initiative in removing her clothes. It took him awhile to oblige. She let her hands wander over his back, his firm butt, and the backs of his thighs.

Eric's hands trembled as he slowly undressed her. They kissed long after they were both naked. It seemed they were both a bit reluctant to get started.

Rebekah eventually got up the nerve to ease over to the bed. She tossed the covers back with one hand and held Eric with the other so he'd follow her onto the mattress. They tumbled to the bed together. Settling between her open thighs, Eric held his weight off her by propping himself on his elbows. He stroked her hair gently and stared into her eyes.

"I know we haven't known each other long," he murmured, "but I already care about you, Rebekah. Deeply."

He kissed her before she could respond. She cared about him too. Maybe even loved him. She wasn't sure yet. Whatever words applied to her feelings for this man, she knew for certain that those feelings were substantial and amazing and true. If they hadn't been, she never would have trusted him with her body. Even knowing what was about to happen, she wasn't nearly as nervous as she'd thought she'd be. She knew he would be honest. She needed that.

Eric's kiss moved from her mouth, to her jaw, to her neck, just beneath her ear. She shuddered.

"I'm so afraid that I'll mess this up for you," he said. "Maybe you should pleasure yourself, and I'll just watch."

"No," she said firmly. "You're going to make love to me, Eric. And I'm going to thoroughly enjoy it. I'm more worried that it will be weird for you."

"I know it won't be. It will be too wonderful for words." He kissed her gently and stroked her hair soothingly.

"So let's stop talking about how great it's going to be and start experiencing it for real."

"Right," he agreed breathlessly.

He took his time with her, using those magnificent hands of his to bring every inch of her body to life. When she was sure she couldn't take more of his touch, he massaged both breasts, then sucked one hard nipple into his mouth. He then sucked her other nipple before kissing a trail of fire down the center of her belly. His mouth found her clit. His fingers found her pussy. He sucked and licked her clit while slowly driving two fingers deep into her body. He quickly brought her to the brink of orgasm. Just before she went crashing over the edge, he pulled away abruptly. He slid up her body and looked her in the eyes.

"Are you ready?"

"Yeah," she said breathlessly.

He rose up slightly and reached between their bodies. She felt the head of his cock against her as he sought her throbbing passage. She forced herself not to jerk away, but she was far from relaxed. When he found her, he sank into her slightly and then grabbed her hip to steady himself. They stared at each other.

"You okay?" he whispered. "You're tense."

She nodded and allowed her taut muscles to relax.

His head tilted back as he slid a few inches deeper. His body twitched, and his face contorted in ecstasy.

"Does it feel weird?" she asked, her voice wavering with emotion.

He shook his head, gulping air. "Oh God, Rebekah. This is the best pussy I've ever had in my life."

She giggled. "Do you mean that?"

"Fuck yeah, I mean it. It feels so good, I don't think I can move."

She wriggled her hips and he slid several inches deeper. They gasped in unison.

"You still okay?" he asked breathlessly. "Does it hurt?"

"No, it's the best dick I've ever had in my life," she said. And though she was giggling, she meant it.

"Please don't laugh at me, sweetheart."

Her heart panged when she realized she'd hurt him. She cupped his face. "I'm not laughing at you, Eric. I'm happy. So happy to be with you like this. Happy that it feels good for you. And for me."

He smiled crookedly. "It definitely feels good for me. Do you think you can take it all? I'm only in about halfway."

"I'll try."

He backed up slightly and thrust forward gently. And again, each time possessing her a little deeper, until his balls pressed against her. He rocked against her then. She had all of him. All.

"Oh, baby, I'm so about to blow it. I'm sorry. I wanted it to be good for you."

"It will be good for me. Go ahead and come. As soon as you're hard again, you're going to do this again. And again and again, until I'm finally satisfied. I don't care if you have to come twenty times to get me there."

He grinned and began to move inside her. "That I can do," he murmured.

He thrust into her slowly. She couldn't take her eyes off his face.

His pleasure and excitement were apparent in his expression. Both eyes squeezed tightly shut, he bit his lip, and his back arched a bit more with each steady thrust. He made this little sound of bliss each time he plunged into her body. It felt amazing to be filled with him, but the pleasure he found within her body delighted her to near tears. Rebekah rocked with him, meeting his slow, steady strokes, wondering why he refused to open his eyes.

"Look at me," she whispered.

He struggled to open one eye and immediately closed it again. "You're too beautiful," he groaned. "I'm having a hard enough time not getting overexcited from being buried in your soft heat."

But she wanted him excited. She wanted to make him come, even though it was such an easy thing to do and no real challenge. She slid her hands over his sides, loving the way his corded muscles bunched beneath her fingertips. Her hands moved to his back and then to his ass, fingers digging into his flesh to urge him deeper.

"Ah." He gasped and thrust into her hard and deep as his body shook with release. "Rebekah?" Her name was a tortured question. He trembled for several minutes, before he gathered her close in his arms, and thrust in and out of her gently until his cock went soft. "You feel so good. And I came so hard." He kissed her jaw. "Sorry. I should have warned you not to touch me."

"I like touching you." She kissed his shoulder. "That was wonderful."

He looked down, his eyes wide with surprise.

"But I think it could be better."

He chuckled. "This brutal honesty thing is... brutal."

"It's my turn to come hard now, so you'd better get busy. You have a lot of work to do."

He smiled and slid down her body. He used his mouth and fingers to bring her close to orgasm. She sighed with impatience, wanting his cock buried inside her again. Knowing how good it felt to be filled with him. "Oh Eric. I need it again. Need it inside."

"Damn," he muttered. "Woman, you're driving me crazy."

"Sit," she insisted.

"Huh?"

She urged him to sit on the bed with his back against the headboard. Finding him hard again, as if it were a constant state, she straddled his lap, facing him. She grabbed his cock and directed it into the emptiness inside her, taking it deep in one stroke. Her eyelids fluttered, and she gasped brokenly. "Yeah, that's what I want." She leaned back as she rose and fell over him. He supported her back, but let her carry the rhythm.

"Can you see it, Eric?" she murmured. "Your cock entering my body?"

She leaned back farther to give him an unobstructed view. He glanced to where their bodies were joined and made a tormented sound in the back of his throat. "That is so beautiful."

One of his hands moved between their bodies and stroked her flesh as it ebbed and flowed with his rhythmic possession. His fingers then shifted to her clit. He held two fingers curled upward near his pelvis so that every time she pressed downward to take his cock deep, his fingertips rubbed against her just right.

"Ah God, that feels good." She gasped, her head falling back as she rode him and rubbed her clit against his perfectly placed fingers. Her pleasure built slowly. She was nearing her peak when Eric grabbed her hips to hold her down on his shaft as he shuddered in bliss.

"Fuck," he cried. When his trembling stilled, he whispered, "Sorry." Eric forced his unfocused eyes open.

She leaned forward and kissed him. "It's okay," she assured him. "Stop apologizing."

"Did you come?"

She was tempted to lie and tell him that she had, but they'd started this relationship with honesty, and she wasn't about to lie now. "Not yet."

"I really am sorry. You just feel so good. I can't focus on anything but your Certified Grade A pussy."

"My *what?*"

He closed one eye and winced. "Certified… Grade A… pussy…"

She chuckled and shook her head. "I'll take that as a compliment."

"You should," he insisted. "Few pussies get that distinction."

"I was close, Eric. I just needed another minute, and I would have come."

He wrapped his arms around her and held her against his chest. "I'll get you there next time," he promised. "Just let me catch my breath."

Placing a hand on his hard chest, she pushed away and shook her head. "You'll get me there now."

He grinned. "Only fair." She squeaked in surprise when he wrapped his long-fingered hands around her hips and pulled her off his lap. He pushed her on her back and surprised her by climbing from the bed.

"Where are you going?" She watched him circle the bed.

He lifted one of the sacks they'd purchased at the adult store and began searching for something. Within minutes, he was ripping open packages, inserting batteries, and washing things in the sink. Her eyes were blinking drowsily by the time he rejoined her.

"I'm about asleep," she murmured.

"I think this will wake you up."

Chapter 12

ERIC STARED AT REBEKAH, spread across the bed, her thighs wide open, his come trickling from inside her body and down her ass. It was all he could do not to jump on top of her again. He felt guilty for wanting to find his pleasure again when he'd already so utterly disappointed her the last time. Correction, the last *two* times. Fuck, he was such a loser. He slipped her feet through the straps of one of her new toys and slid the butterfly-shaped vibrator over her clit. He adjusted it and then pressed the button on the controller in his hand to turn it on. When her body jerked, he decided it was in the right spot. He turned it off.

"Feel good?"

She nodded. "Do it again."

He grinned. "I'm in control of this." He handed her a vibrating phallus. "You're in control of this."

"What am I supposed to do with it?"

"I think you'll figure it out."

She lifted the vibrator in front of her face and found the on button. When it started vibrating in her hand, she dropped it. She laughed and retrieved it. "It surprised me."

He switched on the butterfly. Her back arched, and she gasped. He turned it off again.

"Wow, that thing is awesome," she said.

"Try yours now," he encouraged.

"Do I just slide it inside?" she asked, looking for his genuine opinion.

He wondered if she'd ever experimented with toys before. He was probably a bit too fond of them. "Whatever feels right."

He held his breath while he watched her slide the vibrator into her swollen pussy. Her flesh swallowed the thick black phallus slowly, and when it was fully inserted, her lips tightened around the device. "Oh," she gasped.

He buzzed her clit again. This time he prolonged the stimulation until her entire body went taut before turning it off.

"Don't turn it off," she moaned. "I'm so close to coming."

She pulled the vibrator out before thrusting it deep again.

"That's it," he whispered. "Show me how you like to be fucked." It wasn't quite as beautiful as watching her use her fingers to bring herself pleasure, but she obviously enjoyed her new toy. She was thrusting it into her body faster and harder now. He switched on the butterfly and sent her over the edge. She cried out, and her legs clamped over her hand as she shuddered in ecstasy. He turned off the stimulation to her clit and stroked her thighs until they relaxed.

"Let's switch now," he murmured.

Still breathing hard, she lifted her head to look at him. "So what, we put the butterfly thingie on your cock, and the vibrator goes up your ass?"

He laughed. "Nothing that big is ever going up my ass. I meant you control the butterfly, and I've got the shaft."

"I don't think I can handle…"

He handed her the controller for the butterfly and took the vibrator from her fingertips. He had another surprise but kept that hidden as they worked together to build her back toward orgasm. Plunging the vibrator into her body with a steady rhythm, he leaned closer to inhale her scent. Damn, he was hard already and wanted to be inside her again, but he wouldn't rob her of her orgasm this time.

"Eric. Eric! Eric!" she cried.

When her body convulsed, he pressed a plug into her ass and watched her body writhe involuntarily on the mattress. Damn. Giving her pleasure made him want her so fucking much. He pulled the vibrator from her pussy and slid his hips between her trembling thighs. He thrust into her hard. Her pussy gripped him tightly as he pumped into her as fast as he could.

"Yes, yes, yes," she screamed as her body continued to jerk uncontrollably.

The vibrating butterfly was still stimulating her clit, and she'd somehow lost the controller. She was getting off so hard, he didn't have the heart to shut it off. He continued to plunge into her body and ride her orgasm. Her nails dug into his chest. Her back arched off the mattress. "Oh God," she screamed. "Fuck me, Eric. Harder, harder!"

If he hadn't already come four times that night, he would have erupted at the sound of her pleading demand. He'd watched women get off this hard with Sed, but never with him. Eric wanted to make her come this hard over and over again. Her hand fumbled on the mattress until she found the controller for the vibrator still buzzing against her clit. She shut it off and shuddered.

"What did you put in my ass?" she asked him, rocking her hips to meet his hard thrusts.

"Do you want me to take it out?"

"Fuck no, I love it. I think I'm going to come again. Oh, oh…"

He bent so he could suck her nipple into his mouth.

"Oh Eric, that feels so good. Your cock. Your mouth." She switched on her butterfly, and her pussy tightened around him as she came again. She was screaming so loud, the person in the next room banged on the wall in protest. Eric thrust into her harder, wanting her to scream louder, wanting the world to know that he was fucking Rebekah Blake, and she was totally getting off on him. He didn't care if he had needed a few props to get her there. Rebekah was having one mind-blowing orgasm after another, and Eric knew he was responsible.

She'd managed five or six orgasms by the time he let go at least twenty minutes later. As his cum burst free and pulsed into her trembling and exhausted little body, Eric held onto her for dear life. He'd never experienced such an intensely satisfying sexual encounter, and something told him things would get even better as they learned to give each other pleasure.

When he collapsed on top of her, she entangled him in her arms and legs and held him just as hard as he was holding her.

"Eric?" she whispered.

"Hmm?" He doubted he was capable of forming actual words.

"Can I be brutally honest with you?"

He almost wanted to say no. *Lie to me and tell me it was as good for you as it was for me.* Somewhere, he found the courage to say, "Of course."

"I didn't know sex could be this great." She squeezed him closer. "If I had, I'd be the biggest slut on the planet and would want to fuck constantly. Dear God, that was amazing."

He wished he had the energy to lift his head and look into her eyes. "Amazing," he agreed breathlessly.

"Is it too soon to tell you I love you?" She snuggled her face into his chest so her words were muffled. "If it's too soon, I won't say it."

His heart swelled to bursting. He was pretty sure he was going to start crying if he said more than a few words, so he said only three. "I love you."

She pinched his ass.

"Ow!"

"I wanted to say it first," she said.

"Fine, I take it back," he said and moved his hand to rub at the pain she'd inflicted on his ass.

"Don't you dare." She pushed against his chest and squirmed

until he relented and rolled onto his back. She crawled up his body and looked into his eyes. "I love you."

Ah, damn it, it was far too soon to be spouting this kind of sentiment. It didn't stop him from feeling them. Or from saying them. "I love you. A lot. Like way more than my car." Damn, that sounded stupid now that he'd said it.

She grinned and kissed him. "Way more?"

"Yeah."

"I'll let you take a short nap, but then I want you to show me exactly how much you love me."

"Didn't I just do that?" he murmured. He was almost asleep already. He hadn't known it was possible, but his limitless energy supply had dwindled to nothing.

"I think I'll need a lot of reminders."

He smiled. "If you insist." Rebekah's beautiful face was the last thing he saw before he closed his heavy eyelids and nodded off to sleep. The last thing he heard was the hum of Rebekah's vibrating butterfly as she switched it on and cuddled against his side with a soft sigh. The last thing he felt was her tiny hand against his abdomen. He had the feeling he'd be waking up with a major hard-on and a horny girlfriend to contend with. His drowsy smile widened.

Chapter 13

REBEKAH SNUGGLED CLOSER TO the warm body beside her. A large hand splayed over her lower back and drew her closer. "Isaac," she murmured.

"Isaac?" Eric growled.

Her heart dropped. It sank even deeper when Eric pushed her away and climbed from the bed. "Wait. Where are you going?" she asked, her thoughts still thick with sleep.

"Last night you tell me you love me. This morning you're calling me by another man's name. Where the fuck do you think I'm going?"

He put on his underwear and scooped his jeans off the floor. She jumped out of bed and grabbed one leg of his pants. They engaged in a tug-of-war over his jeans, which he would undoubtedly win, but she wasn't going to let him walk away mad.

"I was still asleep," she said defensively.

"So you were dreaming about him. Is that it?"

He wrenched his pants out of her hands and bent to put one foot into a leg hole. While he was teetering off balance, she shoved him with both hands, and he toppled onto the bed.

"No, that's not it, damn it. Isaac is the only man I've ever slept with before you, okay?"

He paused, absorbing her words. "You've only had sex with one other person?"

"Not exactly. I just didn't wake up with them beside me. Isaac and I were together for three years. I'm not accustomed to waking up next to anyone but him. Saying his name was a... a habit."

Eric sat on the edge of the bed and folded his hands on his lap. He stared at his thumbs and asked, "Do you still love him?"

Her heart froze in her chest. "I left him, didn't I?"

Eric lifted his gaze. "You didn't answer my question."

It wasn't one she could easily answer. She would probably always love Isaac. Not in the crazy way she loved Eric, but Isaac had seen her at her worst and had stood beside her regardless. Isaac had never let her give up, not when she had been bald and looked like an eighty-four-pound skeleton with a perpetual case of nausea.

"Isaac is in my past, Eric. I'm with you now. Being with you feels right. I never felt this way when I was with him. This happy. You make me feel... alive. Happy to be alive." She moved to stand between Eric's knees, not sure if she could handle his rejection. Not when she'd given her absolute trust so easily. "You can call me by an old girlfriend's name if it will make you feel better. I really didn't mean to call you Isa—"

He covered her lips with one long finger. "I'd appreciate it if you wouldn't say his name again."

She pantomimed locking her lips with a key and throwing it over her shoulder.

He wrapped his arms around her back and tugged her closer. He pressed his face between her naked breasts and took a deep breath. "Things always look different in the morning," he said.

She stroked his hair with both hands. "What do you mean? You aren't having second thoughts, are you?" She could feel him slipping through her fingers already. It wasn't fair. She knew they should have taken things more slowly. She shouldn't have spouted her feelings so carelessly. She wished she could take the words back.

"No one has ever loved me before. Not really. Not for who I am. Maybe for what I could give them, but not for me."

Her breath caught. She was so glad she couldn't take the words back, because she meant them. "I love you for who you are, Eric." She hugged him closer. "I do."

"Last night when I was delirious with pleasure it was easy to believe. Now…" He looked up at her. The loneliness in his blue eyes stole her breath. "I'm sorry. I should learn to keep my mouth shut."

"So when you were delirious with pleasure you believed that I love you, but now that your head's clear, you don't?"

"I don't know. I want to believe it."

"I guess there's only one thing to do in a situation like this."

He swallowed hard and grimaced. "Slow down?"

She quirked an eyebrow. "Fuck no. I need to make you delirious with pleasure again."

He chuckled and hugged her enthusiastically. "That should take you all of three minutes."

"Give me ten." She kissed his forehead and pulled out of his grasp. Grabbing several bags of their purchases from the night before, she hurried to the bathroom and locked the door behind her. She found what she was looking for in one of the bags and began to dress. She wished she had some cosmetics with her, but he was going to have to live with a naughty nurse without makeup. She was smoothing her thigh-high stockings when he knocked on the door.

"Reb, I can't wait anymore."

She grinned at his enthusiasm. "Almost ready."

"I have to pee so bad I can taste it."

Oh, that's why he was eager to get into the bathroom.

She slid into her shoes and crammed the little white hat onto her bed hair before opening the door. His jaw dropped when he saw her.

"Mercy, baby," he whispered.

"Mr. Sticks, hurry up and go. Then get back into bed. It's time for your sponge bath."

"I can hold it," he assured her.

She shoved him into the bathroom. "Just go. I don't want you having an accident."

"I can't go when I'm hard, and seeing you like that definitely has me hard."

"Try," she said and closed him in the bathroom.

She heard something bang on the inside of the bathroom door repeatedly. Concerned, she pulled open the door and caught Eric banging his head against the solid surface.

"What are you doing?"

"Trying to calm down. I was about halfway there before you opened the door." His eyes raked over her body. The skirt of her uniform was so short it didn't cover the tops of her stockings. He could probably tell that she wasn't wearing panties without her having to bend over. Her breasts were pushed up and together by strategically located underwires. She looked like she had significant cleavage. There was barely enough material to cover her nipples. "Oh fuck, Rebekah, you look so hot. Can I please get back in bed?"

"Stop banging your head on the door, and go pee." She closed the door in his face and went to the mirror over the dresser to see if she could get her flyaway hair under control and secured under the little hat she wore.

She was starting to worry about Eric when he finally opened the door. He was entirely naked and looking sexier in his self-confidence than she could ever hope to look in her nurse's attire. His cock was soft when he exited the bathroom, but already hard when he moved behind her and cupped her breasts.

"Into bed with you, Mr. Sticks," she said. "And keep your hands to yourself."

"Huh?" Far from complying with her demands, his hands skimmed down her belly and hip bones. "Are you wearing panties?" he breathed into her ear. His hand found the inside of her thigh and pushed her skirt up.

She pulled away and faced him. She wagged her finger.

"What's under my skirt, sir, is none of your business. Get into bed. I must start your personal care immediately. You wouldn't want me to get fired, would you?"

His lips brushed her neck just beneath her ear, which sent a thrill of excitement coursing down her spine. "No, ma'am. I would not want that. Exceptional nurses like you are impossible to find."

She looped his arm around her shoulders and encouraged him to lean on her. "I'll help you back to bed now. You are in desperate need of my attention."

"I *am* on my last limb. Luckily, it's the inflatable one."

Rebekah bit her lip so she didn't bust out laughing and ended up snorting through her nose. She recovered her composure quickly, trying to be sexy. Snorting was so not sexy.

Hand splayed over his waist, it was all she could do not to bury her face in his side and inhale his scent. She decided it was going to be very difficult to stay in character, especially when his hand reached down to cup her breast. Her nipple strained toward his palm immediately. She considered slapping him across the face as if offended, but couldn't bring herself to do it. Since the nurse's outfit was the first one he'd grabbed when they'd looked at costumes, she assumed it was his favorite. She was going to pretend to be a *very* naughty nurse and encourage his attention. She hoped it didn't ruin the fantasy for him. She twisted slightly so that his fondling hand shifted her nipple right out of the cup of her uniform. She pretended not to notice. Like that was possible with Eric's rush of breath and wayward thumb. When they reached the bed, she lifted his arm over her head and urged him onto the mattress. He grabbed her on the way down, and she found herself sprawled across his hard body.

"Mr. Sticks," she said, lifting her head to look into his desire-glazed eyes, "this is highly inappropriate."

"Dear lord, woman, I'm so turned on right now. You can drop the act and get naked immediately."

She grinned and kissed him. "You always say exactly what I want to hear."

"You're kidding, right?"

She shook her head.

"Most women would slap me for saying that."

"Do you want me to slap you?"

"No, I want you to fuck me."

She laughed. He was so fun to tease though. "You are in no condition for that kind of activity, Mr. Sticks."

He shifted so that his rock-hard cock was pressed against her hip. "I beg to differ, nurse."

"It's time for your sponge bath."

He huffed in feigned exasperation. "Well, if you insist."

She extracted her body from his tight embrace and climbed from the bed. She could feel his eyes on her as she walked away. She made sure there was plenty of sway in each calculated step. He groaned and began to bang his head on his pillow. Since it wasn't a solid object, she didn't chastise him. She recognized that he did that when he was so excited he was about to do something he knew he shouldn't. She took the ice bucket to the bathroom and filled it half full with warm water. There were no sponges, so she'd use a washcloth, but she fully intended to clean every inch of Eric's body. *Every* inch. Some inches more than once.

"Nurse!" he called from the bedroom. "I'm in desperate need of assistance in here."

She held the container of water against her chest and returned to his bedside. She stopped abruptly so water sloshed over her cleavage and trickled between her breasts. "Whoops!"

Eric produced a sound very close to a growl. It made goose bumps rise all over her body.

"Are you ready for your bath?"

"You know what I'm ready for." He nodded pointedly at his straining cock.

"Oh my," she said and set the water on the nightstand. "That does need my immediate attention. It's so swollen. Does it hurt?"

"Only when you *don't* touch it."

She soaked the washcloth in warm water and rung out the excess before climbing onto the bed. She used two fingers wrapped in the cloth to clean his belly button. He chuckled. "A little lower," he said.

She drew the washcloth along the narrow strip of black hair that ran from his navel downward. His cock twitched when she stopped an inch from touching it. She moved her cloth to the left slightly and drew it back up his belly, away from his straining cock.

"U-turn. U-turn," he demanded breathlessly.

Down again. Stop. Over and up.

"You keep missing the dirty spot," he panted.

"I don't see it," she insisted, trying not to laugh and partially succeeding.

"Then get closer."

She shifted to her hands and knees. Careful not to run one of her spiked heels through his skin, she straddled his body, one knee on each side of his chest, palms on the bed on either side of his thighs. "Is it down here?" She used her cloth to wash his knee with vigorous circular motions.

"Mercy, that's beautiful," he gasped.

She looked over her shoulder to find him gazing up her short skirt. His hands slid over the backs of her thighs to push her skirt up the two remaining inches that covered her butt. While she scrubbed his other knee, he traced her swollen folds with two fingers. Finding her already wet with excitement, he plunged both fingers inside her. She gasped.

"Mr. Sticks," she whispered, "what are you doing?"

"Enjoying the view."

"You look with your eyes, not with your hands."

"I'm also enjoying the feel and the smell and the sound. Pretty soon I want to enjoy the taste, too."

She bent her elbows so that the head of his cock lodged into her cleavage.

"Whoa…" Eric's fingers moved inside her. Thrusting deep. Twisting. Withdrawing slowly. Rebekah tried to concentrate on her task, but his fingers felt so good that she just held still and took it. His free hand stroked her thighs above her stockings. Her ass. He pulled his fingers free to lick them and then thrust them deep inside again.

"Eric," she groaned. "Rub me, please."

"I thought that's what I was doing."

"Oh, my clit. Please, Eric."

"Show me what you want, Rebekah."

She supported her upper body on one hand and reached between her legs to stroke her clit.

"That's it, baby," he murmured. "Make yourself come."

She cried out when the first waves of release gripped her. Eric swore under his breath and slid from beneath her body to kneel behind her. He pulled his fingers free of her clenching pussy and replaced them with his cock. Still stroking her clit, still coming, Rebekah rubbed her face over the mattress and rocked back to meet his hard, deep thrusts.

"You are the sexiest woman in existence," he said in a low growl, and for once, she believed him.

He leaned over her back and pushed the bodice of her outfit down to free her breasts. He kneaded them roughly as he pounded and pinched her nipples between his fingers. She moved her hand to gently stroke his balls as he thrust into her. He straightened again and leaned back slightly so she could reach him better. She glanced over her shoulder to catch him watching the action between their bodies. "Your pussy is so beautiful as it swallows my cock," he whispered. "Can you hear how wet it is?"

Hear it? Yeah, she could hear the squish of her fluids each time their bodies came together.

"It's wet for you, Eric. You fill it so well."

He rewarded her compliment by dipping the tip of one finger into her ass.

"Mmmm," she purred.

"You're such a naughty nurse," he said. "Do you like my finger in your ass?"

"Oh yes."

He pressed his finger deeper. She massaged his nuts more vigorously. Eric's breath hitched, and he grabbed her hips to hold her still while he let go inside her. They still needed to work on timing their orgasms to coincide. He pulled out and collapsed on the bed. "Thank you, nurse. That was a wonderful treatment."

She grinned. She was just getting started.

Chapter 14

"Are you sure we have to go back?" Eric murmured and tugged Rebekah closer. They were both sticky with cum and sweat and saliva. He doubted he could get it up again, but he was far from ready to share her with the rest of the world. The sex was phenomenal, but just being with her was enough to make him giddy.

"We have to be in Austin in two days."

"So we stay in bed for another twenty-four hours, and we'll take off then. It won't take me long to drive from Phoenix to Austin."

She laughed. "No way in *hell* am I letting you drive that far, Eric Sticks."

"Then we'll get on a plane."

"I think Jon will want his car back."

"Like I care."

"This isn't the end of our relationship, sweetheart. Just the beginning. We'll have other nights together."

He was that transparent, was he? She was right. They would have other nights. Days. Evenings. Mornings. Afternoons. Hopefully, a lifetime full of them.

"Let's go take a shower," she said.

Eric lifted his head about an inch off the pillow but couldn't muster the strength to open his eyes and look at her. "Together?"

"Unless you have a better idea."

"It's a great idea. I just don't think I can stand." He dropped his head back on the pillow. "You wore me out, woman."

"Awww, poor baby. Did I ride my cowboy too long?" she asked, grabbing the cowboy hat from the bed and squashing it on his head.

He grinned. "I'm not complaining."

"Perhaps if you hadn't insisted that you had a six-shooter." She giggled and ran a finger down his limp cock. Eric doubted it would ever work again.

"I should have stopped after three."

"You lasted over half an hour that last time." She rose on one arm, knocked his hat back, and looked at him. "Seems my theory was correct."

"I'm surprised I came that last time. I don't think there's anything left in my balls but dust."

"I'm a little tender down there too," she admitted.

"Do you need me to kiss it and make it feel better?" His kiss landed on the tip of her nose as it was the only place he could reach with no effort.

"Don't tempt me." She kissed his chest and extracted her body from his feeble embrace. "I'm going to shower. I hope you'll find the energy to join me."

He groaned but stayed sprawled across the center of the bed. A moment later, he heard the spray of the shower. Rebekah's off-key rendition of Sinners' newest song, "Sever," brought a smile to Eric's lips. He drifted on the edge of consciousness until Rebekah's shriek of terror pulled him directly to his feet. He crashed into the bathroom and found Rebekah, soaking wet and soapy, standing on the toilet lid clinging to the towel bar.

"What's wrong?"

She pointed at the shower with a shaky hand. The water was still running behind the shower curtain. He tossed the curtain back, expecting to see a dead body, or at the very least, Norman Bates in drag. There was nothing there.

"Why did you scream?"

"Sp-spider!"

Eric searched the shower, looking for the huge, hairy tarantula that had her hyperventilating. Nope. Nothing.

"I don't see anything."

"It's right there!" she screeched, clinging to his shoulder as she pointed into the far corner.

Eric climbed into the tub, the water hitting him in the back, and found the tiny arachnid hiding behind the bottle of complementary shampoo.

"This little thing?"

Eric scooped the spider into his hand, and it skittered up his wrist. This sent Rebekah into a fit of hysterics. She leapt off the toilet and scrambled into the bedroom, making sounds of heebie-jeebiness and rubbing her hands all over her body while she high-stepped across the carpet.

Eric captured the spider and held it in a loose fist. Its little legs scurried about on his palm as it tried to escape. Watching Rebekah freak out in the nude was far too great a temptation for him to resist.

"Got him," Eric announced as he joined her in the bedroom.

"Did you *kill* it?" she wanted to know, skirting a wide berth around him.

"He's fine," Eric assured her and opened his hand. The spider dashed to the end of his finger, about to kamikaze itself onto the floor, when Rebekah's shriek and acrobatic leap onto the bed startled it into cowering on Eric's fingertip. Chuckling, Eric secured the creature in his hand again.

"It's just a little spider, Reb. It won't hurt you."

"I *hate* spiders."

"I think that goes without saying."

"Get rid of it!"

He opened the door to the balcony and set the spider free

outside. He turned to find Rebekah still standing in the middle of the bed with one hand over the center of her chest.

"It's gone."

"You should have squashed it."

"Awww, what did the little guy ever do to you?"

"Tried to give me a heart attack, that's what."

She hopped off the bed and headed back toward the bathroom, scanning her surroundings.

Eric followed her. "I think I should join you, in case another murderous creature tries to attack."

"I agree!" She climbed into the still running shower and pulled him into the tub with her.

Instead of washing, she wrapped him in both arms and kissed him hungrily. "Mmmm," he murmured. "I should save you from man-eating spiders more often."

"My hero."

He chuckled. "So I'm assuming it wouldn't turn you on if I dressed up like Spider-Man and spurted my magic web all over you."

She grinned. "I'm not sure. I might get over my arachnophobia if you did. We'll have to try."

Chapter 15

ERIC AND REBEKAH STOPPED by the stadium to pick up Jon. He was sitting on the curb poking a rock with a stick when they arrived. He looked up when the Jeep stopped and stared daggers at Eric.

"About fucking time," he grumbled. "That's the last time I let you borrow my car, Sticks."

"Sorry it took us so long. We had a lot of fucking to do," Eric said. He hesitated, still not sure how much he should censor those inappropriate thoughts.

"Yeah, we did," Rebekah agreed.

Ah God, he loved this woman.

"Who's driving?" Jon asked.

"You are," Eric said.

"He's not a maniac like you are, is he?" Rebekah asked.

"He's an entirely different kind of maniac. You're sober, I hope," Eric said to Jon.

"Un-fucking-fortunately."

Rebekah slid from the driver's seat to Eric's lap. She wrapped her arms around his neck and kissed him. "Keep me company in the backseat?" she whispered into his ear.

Eric's cock instantly hardened. "I hope you don't mind if we take a little nap in the backseat while you drive. We had a long night."

"Of fucking," Jon said. "Yeah, so you said. You really owe me now, Sticks. Making me wait here for three hours after the buses left. Sed absolutely refused to let me even ride in the equipment truck."

"He told you if he caught you doing drugs, you weren't allowed near the tour vehicles again. You're a liability."

"It was just a little cocaine."

"I thought it was crack."

"Oh yeah. But I'm clean now."

Eric wasn't so sure. Jon's eyes looked a bit bloodshot, but probably because he'd been drinking the night before. They weren't glassy though. Maybe Jon was finally clean. Eric hoped so. He wanted that for him.

Eric joined Rebekah in the backseat, and Jon climbed into the driver's seat. They headed east out of Phoenix toward Austin. Rebekah cuddled up against Eric, her face pressed against his side, and promptly fell asleep. Eric was exhausted too, but there was no way he would sleep while Jon was driving, so he just held her while she slept and stroked the smooth skin of her arm.

After nearly an hour of silence, Jon said, "You know, maybe you could say something to Sed about letting me back on the bus." He looked at Eric through the rearview mirror.

"Forget it, Jon. You've had too many chances already. You never learn."

"But you—"

"Owe you. Yeah, I think I'm aware of that. You bring it up every time I see you."

"You know, if I hadn't taken the fall for you, you'd be the one watching a replacement play your music. You have no idea how much that sucks."

"That wasn't the only reason Sed told you to get lost. It was just the last straw."

"I took the fall for you, Eric. Don't forget that."

How could Eric possibly forget when Jon rubbed it in his face constantly? He was half-tempted to tell Sed that he'd been the one to take the band's last five hundred dollars, leaving them without enough money to fix the transmission on the tour bus. *Shit.* Eric couldn't help that he was a sucker for a pretty face. Speaking of pretty faces. He pressed a kiss to Rebekah's soft hair. She shifted in her sleep, and her hand landed in his lap. Her fingers curled, cupping his balls, while her palm pressed against his suddenly attentive cock.

Eric shifted her hand to his thigh before he contemplated molesting her in her sleep. "I don't know how I'm supposed to repay you, Jon. No matter what I do, it's never enough for you."

Rebekah moved her hand back to his crotch. While she rested against him with her body limp and yielding, as if she were still asleep, she slowly unzipped his pants. Apparently, their talking had woken her.

"You know what I want, Eric," Jon said.

"I tried to get you what you want. Even succeeded once."

Rebekah eased Eric's cock out of his underwear.

"Just because Jace was injured," Jon griped. "That's the only reason they used me. They didn't really want me back in the band."

"Why is it my responsibility to get you back in? You have to earn it. Besides, why would we ever give up Jace? He's fucking awesome, and you know it."

Rebekah curled her hand around Eric's hardening length and stroked him slowly. She turned her head and nipped his nipple through his T-shirt, catching his nipple ring with her teeth and tugging gently. Perhaps she thought he was ignoring her. As if that was possible.

"He's not that great," Jon grumbled. "I'm just out of practice."

"Whatever."

Rebekah slid down Eric's side and leaned over his lap. Eric bit his lip when she drew the head of his cock into her mouth. He tried to stay quiet so he didn't draw Jon's attention to the backseat.

"I can play the new bass riff, can't I?"

"Barely. Jace worked with you for h-h-hourssss…" Eric's eyes rolled into the back of his head as Rebekah sucked and licked the head of his cock. Ripples of delight coursed up and down his length. His balls tightened. She slipped her hand into his underwear to hold them, and he groaned.

"What the fuck? Is she giving you head back there?" Jon met Eric's eyes in the rearview mirror.

"Almost finished," Eric gasped.

She worked him until he erupted into her mouth. She swallowed, sucking until he was spent, and then drew away. She tucked his slackening cock back into his underwear and then zipped his fly. She cuddled against his side again and closed her eyes.

"She wakes up to suck you off then goes back to sleep. Where the fuck do I get a chick like that?" Jon asked.

"She's one of a kind."

"I'm experimenting," Rebekah explained quietly. "He needs to come every couple hours for it to work."

"It's working really well so far," Eric said with a grin. He stroked her hair lovingly.

Jon burst out laughing. "You're fucking kidding me! How did you trick her into that arrangement, Sticks? I need to take notes."

"He didn't trick me," Rebekah said. "It was my idea. Sorry if it bothered you, Jon. I'll try to be more discreet in the future. Can I borrow your jacket to cover his lap next time?"

"What? You're going to make him come inside my jacket! Fuckin' sick."

Eric got to chuckling, and he couldn't stop for several minutes. "I should have brought Brian's lucky hat."

Rebekah pressed a hand against his belly so she could move far enough away to look at him. "Brian's lucky hat?"

"Yeah. Myrna gave Brian a hand job on Jace's motorcycle one night. Apparently, she used his lucky hat to cover the evidence, and he came all over the inside."

"And *you* have it?" Rebekah asked, looking perplexed.

"He gave it to me. Tricked me into wearing it as a joke. I didn't know what was in it at first, but Jace is weak to purple nurples. And I had sticky stuff in my hair." He laughed again.

"Didn't it piss you off that he made you wear it?" Rebekah asked.

"Nah. All in good fun. I fuck with those guys all the time. Only fair that they get me back on occasion."

"That's sick, man," Jon said. "You had Sinclair's cum in your hair?"

"What? You jealous? You've been subjected to worse, Mallory. Remember that time Sed gave you a brown bottle of some roadie's chew spit? You took a big ol' drink thinking it was beer."

"How can I forget? I puked for like two hours straight."

"Into a garbage can behind a stadium." Eric snorted. "Fucking hilarious!"

"The good ol' days," Jon said, grinning broadly. "I tried to get Sed back by filling his water bottle in the toilet, but he never fell for it. Bought his own bottle of water out of a vending machine that night. Like he fucking knew what I was up to."

"I have never had a prank work on Sed," Eric said. "I don't even bother to try anymore."

"It would be awesome to get him. Just once," Jon said.

"Yeah," Eric agreed. "He's too fucking cool for his own good."

"You guys are so bad," Rebekah said, shaking her head at them.

"You could help us get him, Rebekah. Sed would never suspect you," Jon said.

"No way. In case you forgot, Sed's my boss."

"I'm your boss too," Eric said.

"So you're fucking Eric in the hopes that you'll get a raise?" Jon laughed. "I knew she had some ulterior motive."

"Nope. I'm fucking him because he gives me fantastic orgasms."

She looked at Eric and smiled. Eric's heart turned into a big puddle of mush. "I'm going to make you come so hard later," he whispered.

"Why not right now?" she whispered back.

She reached into her pocket and pulled out a little controller. The slender plastic wire disappeared down the front of her pants. He examined the controller. It was the one that went to the butterfly-shaped clit stimulator he'd bought her the night before. Eric flushed and leaned closer to her ear. "You're wearing it right now?"

She grinned crookedly. "Not telling."

He switched on the remote, and her body jerked. A faint hum came from inside the crotch of her jeans. He switched it off again. Her body relaxed.

"It's a long ride to Austin," he murmured.

"That's why I wore it," she whispered.

He kissed her passionately, wondering why they had ever left the hotel room.

Eric switched on the butterfly again, and he felt its vibration against his thigh where her hip was pressed against him. "I don't think you have it in the right spot. It's supposed to buzz your clit."

She laughed. "That's my cell phone."

She pulled her phone out of her pocket and wrinkled her adorable little nose as she read the display screen. "It's my mother."

Eric shut off Rebekah's clit stimulator so fast that he feared it would never work properly again.

Rebekah answered her phone. "Hey, Mom. What's up?"

Eric caught snatches of the woman's tirade. "...saw what kind of sleazy individuals you're working for... no place for a decent woman... come home right now... your father... blah, blah, blah..."

"Things are going really well," Rebekah cut in.

"...think you're some sort of harlot... filthy rock star... bunch of beasts... sex and drugs... blah, blah, blah... Dave said..."

"How is Dave?" Rebekah blurted.

"Don't change the subject."

"I'm not coming home, Mom. I have a job."

"…wrong kind of job for a nice young lady… dirty minds and devil music… going to hell… what would your father say… blah, blah, blah…"

Rebekah rubbed her forehead and rolled her eyes. Eric just stared at her in horror.

"I've gotta go, Mom."

"…head home right now if you know what's good for you… blah, blah, blah…"

"Mom! I have to go," Rebekah annunciated slowly. "Tell Dad and Dave hello."

"…can't believe my own daughter…"

"Bye, Mom."

Rebekah disconnected the call and slumped back in the seat.

"What was that all about?" Eric asked.

"Trust me, you don't want to know."

She tossed her phone on the seat beside her and covered his hand with hers. She stroked the power switch on the clit stimulator remote still in his hand. "Turn it on," she whispered. "Make me feel dirty."

He couldn't even pretend to understand that request, but he did what she asked. Her back arched, thrusting both breasts forward. She moaned and writhed, her hand clinging to Eric's thigh.

"Jesus, I'm trying to pay attention to the road here," Jon bitched.

That fueled Rebekah to moan louder. "Oh, it feels good, Eric. I'm about to come. Turn it off. Make me suffer."

Eric switched off the stimulator, and she squirmed in her seat, her eyes on the rearview mirror to check if Jon was paying attention. She totally loved that he was listening. She wanted him to watch her get off. The little minx.

Eric sucked gently on the flesh just under her ear. "I bet Jon's dick is as hard as a rock after hearing how sexy you are."

"You think?" she whispered.

"Yeah."

"Turn it on again."

She vocalized louder and louder as she approached orgasm again. "Turn it off," she cried at the last second. She squirmed again. "That drives me crazy," she gasped. "My pussy is so fucking wet right now."

"Knock it off, you two," Jon grumbled and adjusted his fly with a wince.

Rebekah grinned at Eric and reached for his belt buckle. "Do you want a blow job or a hand job this time?"

Oh yeah. He totally loved this woman.

Chapter 16

THEY MET THE TOUR buses at a rest stop outside El Paso, Texas. Rebekah grabbed Eric's hand and tugged him up the bus steps. She needed him inside her. Like immediately.

"There you are," Sed said as they rushed past on their way to the bedroom.

"Are you going to cook those enchiladas you promised?" Brian asked.

She'd forgotten that she was supposed to cook for them. "Uh, I need to do something with Eric in the bedroom, and then I'll cook."

Eric had an ear-to-ear grin plastered on his face.

"I'm starving," Brian complained.

"It's Eric," Trey said. "He'll be done in like two minutes."

Rebekah hoped Trey was wrong. She'd been helping Eric through-out the entire day, and he'd been teasing her clit off and on for seven hours. If she didn't get some dick soon, she was going to die.

As soon as they were in the bedroom, she pulled off her shirt and tossed it aside. Her bra followed. He watched her shuck her jeans, his eyes off her only long enough to pull his shirt over his head. She removed her sopping wet panties and the delightful little butterfly that had no battery power left. When she was naked, she bent forward over the bed and spread her legs.

"Hurry, Eric. Put it in."

"Hold on. I'm not hard yet."

He squatted behind her and licked at her wetness. "You smell so good," he groaned.

She made mewing sounds of desperation as he sucked her slick flesh. "Please, baby. Fuck me. I'm so hot and achy, I can't stand it anymore. I need you inside me."

He stood and slid his now hard cock into her with one deep thrust.

"Oh yes," she gasped. She rocked back into him. "Harder. Harder." He fucked her hard, his balls slapping against her with each vigorous thrust. Within seconds she was shuddering with an intense orgasm. She cried out in ecstasy and collapsed on her face. His cock slipped out, and he grunted in protest. Eric pushed her body up the bed, so she was lying flat on her belly, and suspended himself over her back. He sank between her legs and entered her again, pressing his lower belly against her ass. Buried deep, he rotated his hips and ground himself inside her, stretching her in all directions and rubbing her clit with his balls.

"Oh, that feels good," she gasped, lifting her hips off the bed slightly to ease his access. He began to thrust then, maintaining a hard, steady rhythm until she convulsed with another orgasm.

He took her from the side next, experimenting with angles of penetration until he found a position that stimulated her clit with each thrust and made her chant in excitement. Another orgasm left her delirious. She rolled onto her back to face him and found him drenched in sweat.

"This is fucking awesome," he said, eyes sparkling with delight.

She smiled and cupped his sweaty face. "You're such a stud."

"Yeah," he agreed with a happy little laugh and wrapped his arms around the backs of her thighs to press her knees into her shoulders. He thrust into her, his hard shaft rubbing her with a perfect friction. When her legs got tired, he released them and rubbed her hips while he thrust into her gently. "This is so cool," he whispered and kissed her gently. "I think I can go all night."

"And I think I've created a monster," she said and chuckled.

"Do you want me to try to come now?" he asked, sucking on her jaw.

There was a loud knock at the door. "Will you two hurry up? We're starving out here!" It was Brian. "You've been going at it for over an hour."

"Over an hour?"

"Sounds like I owe you a bunch of lessons," she whispered.

He laughed. "I love you so much right now," he murmured, still thrusting into her. "I should probably hurry."

He pulled out and tugged her down the mattress until her crotch was even with the end of the bed. He slipped inside her again and watched his cock slide in and out of her body. "Damn, that's hot," he whispered. He moved faster. Faster. Still watching their bodies come together and separate. Breath hitching with excitement, he rubbed her clit to help her reach her pinnacle. When her pussy clenched with release and she cried out, he thrust deep and let go. His face contorted in ecstasy as his seed pumped into her, and she writhed before him, delirious with pleasure.

When his breathing slowed, he pulled out with a groan. He collapsed on the bed beside her, and she cuddled against his side. "That was fantastic," she said. "Even better than last night with the toys."

"Really?"

"Definitely."

"I thought so too," he said breathlessly. "We came together that time."

"You were perfect." She planted a row of kisses along his rib cage. "Do I really have to get up and make the guys dinner? I just want to lay here with you."

"I say let them starve."

"Are you two finished yet?" Brian called from the hallway. "Sheesh!"

Rebekah chuckled. "I'll go cook. They'll be busting down the door soon if I don't."

He kissed the top of her head. "I'll be out to help you in a minute. I just need to catch my breath."

"I could use some help. My legs are a little wobbly. They might collapse from under me."

His giddy grin made her heart swell with happiness.

Dragging herself from the bed, she located her discarded clothes.

She got dressed, found fresh panties in her suitcase, and headed to the bathroom to clean up. All five guys on the bus watched her go into the bathroom. Flushed, she avoided their heavy stares and closed the bathroom door.

While she was washing up at the sink, the bedroom door opened ,and the guys erupted into cheers in the living area. Were they watching a football game on TV or something?

"I never thought I'd live to see the day," Brian said.

"Eric finally fucked a girl properly," Trey shouted. "Woot! Woot!"

"And all by himself, too," Sed added, sounding like a proud father.

Rebekah could hear them high-fiving each other through the door.

"You owe me twenty bucks, Sinclair," Trey said.

"Damn it!"

Rebekah chuckled. They were cheering Eric for that? What a bunch of goofballs. Trey was right, though. Eric had definitely fucked his girl properly.

Chapter 17

EVERY GOTH WORLD IN every suburban mall in America looked exactly the same. Almost all the merchandise was black, and much of it had silver studs or spikes imbedded in leather. T-shirts and hoodies of the most popular alternative, rock, and metal bands hung from floor to ceiling. The overall effect was claustrophobic, but this was where many of Sinners' fans shopped, so Jerry sometimes scheduled them to do meet-and-greets at these stores. Eric took off his leather jacket and hung it over the back of his folding chair before sitting down. On the table before him there were stacks of Sinners' CDs and posters, T-shirts, and other memorabilia. Merchandising is the key to success, Jerry liked to say. Eric believed the key to success was turning out one awesome album after another, but there was no arguing with Jerry.

Trey sat in the chair beside Eric, locked his fingers together, and stretched them in preparation for a long afternoon of signing. "How did we get stuck doing this?"

"Brian didn't make it back from Kansas City in time. His flight was delayed due to snow." He'd flown back to visit Myrna for one night when she'd proclaimed her temperature was just right. Whatever the fuck that meant.

"Yeah, that's how *you* got stuck doing this, but why did I have to come?"

"Because if it was just me, no one would show up."

Trey laughed. "How embarrassing for you."

The store manager paused before their folding table. "Are you two ready for this? There's been a line through the mall all day. They started lining up outside the doors last night even though the temps are subzero."

Sinners' fans were awesome and more than a little crazy. Eric glanced over his shoulder, relieved to see their head of security, Mitch, watching in case some awesome fan got a little overexcited.

"Let them in," Trey said. "Let's hope they don't kill us when they realize Master Sinclair isn't here."

"Or Sed," Eric added.

"How did he get out of this?" Trey asked.

"Hell if I know."

There was an ear-shattering cacophony of excited squeals overlaid with roars of masculine approval. The first of their fans hit the table with enough force to send CDs scattering.

"Oh my God, oh my God, oh my God, oh my God," the first pair of girls in line screamed in unison. They looked like they spent all their parents' money at Goth World.

"What's your name, sweetheart?" Trey asked to the blonder of the two as he reached for one of the small posters they were signing for free.

"Trey Mills just called me sweetheart!" she sputtered at her girl-friend. "My name is H-H-Heather."

"Where's Master Sinclair?" the less blond girlfriend asked Eric.

"Something suddenly came up," Eric told her.

"Yeah, his dick." Trey sniggered.

The teens turned to stare at each other with wide eyes and then screamed in unison. "Oh my God! Just imagine Master Sinclair's dick!"

Eric busted up laughing. Two signed posters, two signed CDs, four signed T-shirts, a signed hoodie, beanie hat, music score book, several exuberant hugs, a few exploring hands, and camera phone pictures later, Heather and Lauren had finally spent enough of their parents' money to let the next person in line have a chance to interact with Eric and Trey.

"I'm Tony," a young man in his late teens said. His hair was star-tlingly similar in style to Eric's, right down to the blue lock of hair resting against his collarbone. Tony grabbed Eric's hand to pump it up and down excitedly. "I couldn't wait to meet Sinclair, but to get the chance to meet Eric fuckin' Sticks? Amazing. I wish I would have brought my drumheads for you to sign."

"You play drums?" Eric asked as he signed a poster for Tony.

He nodded and then shook his head slightly. "I try, but I'm not very good."

"Keep practicing."

"You're my idol. The best drummer who ever lived. I fuckin' worship you."

Eric couldn't help but smile. He really liked this kid. Eric reached into his inside vest pocket and pulled out a spare drumstick. He always carried a few. He signed it for Tony and handed it to him. "Take this, and when you don't feel like practicing, my drumstick will be there to remind you not to slack off."

Tony held the drumstick in his outstretched palms as if it were blessed by God and crafted from solid gold. Dumbfounded, he started to shuffle away.

"Don't forget your poster," Eric called after him.

The next person in line grabbed the poster and thrust it in Tony's direction. After he claimed it from her, she leaned over the table to give Eric and Trey a spectacular view of her immense cleav-age. She flopped both firm tits out of the neck of her tank top and said, "Sign my tits. I'm going to get your signatures permanently inked on them."

Trey palmed one beautiful breast and rubbed his thumb over her nipple while he signed his name with sensually slow marks across her right breast. Eric did his best to sign the left one without touching her at all. Seeing bare tits reminded him of Rebekah. He wondered what she was doing at the moment.

It was hours before the line finally dwindled, and Eric and Trey got up to leave.

"I need a nap after all that excitement," Trey said.

"I want to get something for Rebekah," Eric said, glancing around the store for a suitable gift.

"Like what?"

"A bracelet maybe. She wears bracelets."

Trey chuckled. "You're in over your head, buddy."

Eric scanned the row of cheap leather jewelry on the far wall. There was nothing there that he felt compelled to give her.

"Just give her a hug, and tell her she looks pretty," Trey suggested.

Eric's shoulders slumped. The need to buy her something was almost overwhelming, but he didn't want to give her something that had no meaning behind it.

They left the store, Mitch keeping a watchful eye for potential confrontations. As they walked past a jewelry store, a necklace caught Eric's eye. He stopped abruptly, and Trey slammed into his back.

Trey followed his line of vision to the display case. "Eric, don't even think about it."

"I have to get it. It's perfect."

"Butterflies?"

"It reminds me of things she keeps in her panties on occasion." Eric dashed into the store.

Trey grabbed Eric's arm before he could locate a salesperson. "Eric, it's much too expensive. You're going to make her feel uncomfortable. Like she owes you something."

"The cost doesn't matter. It reminds me of her. I need to get it."

"Eric, this is a bad idea. Think about how it will make her feel if you drape forty thousand dollars worth of diamonds around her neck."

"Beautiful?" That's all he wanted for her. A constant reminder that he thought she was beautiful.

"She doesn't need a necklace to feel beautiful."

Eric took a steadying breath. Maybe Trey was right.

"Can I help you?" a saleslady asked, looking as if she thought he, Trey, and Mitch were about to rob the place.

"Maybe."

―――

Rebekah glanced up from her video monitor to find Marcus leaning against her soundboard with his arms crossed over his chest.

"Mind sharing that 'Sever' program with me?" He didn't look at her when he asked. She was tempted to tell him no, but knew refusing would hurt Sinners and their fans, not Marcus.

"Do you have a thumb drive?" she asked.

He handed it to her and waited while she replaced her drive with his and saved her file to his device.

"You'll probably want to turn up rhythm and bass for the playback," she suggested. "Eric needs to hear it over the drums when he sings the chorus. He gets his cues fr—"

"Don't fuckin' tell me how to do my job," Marcus grumbled.

She handed him the drive, and he stalked away. He offered her no "thank you." No "kiss my ass." Nothing. She understood why Marcus was angry, but taking it out on her wasn't benefiting him, unless his goal was to look like an asshole. She wasn't sure how to get him to understand that. The tension between them was affecting the entire crew as Marcus prodded them into picking sides. Because she rode on the bus with the band instead of the roadies, Marcus had plenty of opportunity to badmouth her.

"Sound check," Rebekah announced to the sound crew.

When they had Sinners' equipment sounding perfect, she assisted with the opening bands' sound checks as well. The three bands played in succession. The first band's equipment was at the front of the stage, with the second's setup behind theirs, and Kickstart's equipment behind theirs. Sinners' equipment was at the far back. By setting up the stage this way, after each band played, their equipment could be removed from the stage to reveal the next band's setup. It saved a lot of time in switching between bands during the concert, but there was a lot of prep work before a show.

Near the end of the final sound check someone moved behind her and slid something cool around her throat. She started and jerked to the side. Eric grinned at her, fastening a clasp at the back of her neck. Her hand flew to the cool, slender object around her throat. It felt suspiciously like a necklace. She strained her neck to look at the strand of sapphires in butterfly-shaped settings. Each sapphire butterfly was spaced from the next with large, round, clear stones—she hoped they were cubic zirconium, not real diamonds.

"What's this?" she asked, her heart hammering.

"A present for you," Eric said. "The blue stones reminded me of your hair, so I had to get it. The jewelry lady said they were sapphires. And the butterflies… well, you can probably guess why butterflies remind me of you. Do you like it?"

"It's beautiful, baby, but I can't accept this. It must have cost you a fortune."

She reached for the clasp to remove it, but hesitated when she saw the devastated look on his face. He looked like a little kid who had just been told his crayon-drawn stick figures sucked. How was she supposed to refuse his thoughtful gift when he looked at her like that?

"I mean, I love it!" she screamed and jumped into his arms, kissing him excitedly. She burrowed her fingers into his hair and clung to his scalp as she deepened their kiss. His arms wrapped around her to draw her securely against his chest. Her feet were suspended at least a foot off the ground.

When they drew apart at last, he laughed. "Do you really like it?"

"Of course I like it. It's beautiful."

"Like you." Eric pecked her on the lips and set her on her feet. He dug around in the pocket of his jeans until he pulled out a matching bracelet and took her arm to fasten it around her wrist.

"Please tell me these are fakes," she whispered. She had a sinking sensation that he'd spent more on these two items of jewelry than she'd paid for her college education.

"Fake?" Now he looked offended. "Of course I wouldn't buy you fake jewelry."

"Sweetheart, you don't have to buy me anything."

"But I wanted to."

"Why?"

His brow furrowed. "I don't know. When I saw it in the window it reminded me of you, and I thought you would like it, so I bought it."

"You don't have to buy my affection," she said.

"That's not why…" The crease in his brow deepened.

"Don't frown, baby. I really do love it."

"Are you sure?"

She grinned. "It's the most beautiful gift I've ever received."

He released a breath of relief.

"But you know what means more?"

He pointed at her with a figurative lightbulb glowing over his head. "A ring?"

She chuckled and hugged him. "No, not a ring. That you thought of me."

"Well, I do that all the time," he said.

She tilted her head to look up at him. "And that's enough. I don't need jewelry, Eric. Just you."

"Oh." He grinned. "But you already have me."

"It's hard to buy for a girl who has everything, isn't it?"

His grin widened. "I do love you, woman. Are you almost done with your work?"

"I think I can take a little break."

She turned back to the soundboard and removed her thumb drive. She wasn't going to risk someone deleting an important file again. She never did find out who had done it before the last show. Better safe than sorry.

As they walked, Eric draped an arm around her shoulders. His strong fingers massaged her shoulder with that perfect touch. Her body was already responding to his on an instinctual level, her nerves humming in anticipation of the delights to come.

"Where are we going?" she asked.

"I suppose we don't have time to fly to a tropical beach and make love in the surf."

"No, but I do have that mermaid costume. And you can be my lost pirate, seduced by my magnificent singing voice." She winked at him suggestively.

"You have a magnificent singing voice?"

She realized she couldn't lie because he'd heard her sing in the shower. "No, actually, but you do."

"I don't think I'd look good in a coconut bra." Eric ran his hands down his chest. "I'm sorely lacking in cleavage."

"Pirates don't wear coconut bras. They have eye patches and hooks and peg legs."

"Hooks, peg legs, and no depth perception. Sounds dangerous."

"You just need to focus on your booty and leave the moves to me."

"I'd rather focus on your booty as it moves against me."

She groaned at his corny joke. She'd walked right into that one.

"So how am I supposed to get between your legs if you have a tail, little mermaid?"

She stroked her new bracelet and watched the gemstones sparkle in the light while she contemplated his question. "Good point. Maybe mermaids just give blow jobs to the pirates they seduce."

"Lucky pirates."

Rebekah scowled. "Wait a minute. You won't even be able to reciprocate if I'm with tail."

"Okay, forget the mermaid. I've got a better idea."

Ten minutes later, Rebekah was wearing a French maid's uniform and had Eric naked with his wrists tied to the headboard with silk scarves. She took her feather duster and lightly flicked it over his chest. He laughed and tried to escape her tickling by sliding sideways across the mattress. And he'd wondered why she'd insisted on tying him down.

"Monsieur, you are so dirty. Hold still, please."

She feather dusted under his arm, and he tried to climb the headboard with his back. "No, no, stop," he gasped. "Tickles."

"My, my, such dirty ribs." When she tickled his rib cage, he tried to push her away with one large foot but was laughing too hard to follow her evasive moves.

"Don't hurt your arms," she said. "Do you want me to untie you?"

He shook his head, trying to catch his breath.

"Then hold still."

He bit his lip and watched her through half-closed eyelids. Damn, he looked so sexy when he did that. She flicked her feather duster over his belly. He tried to hold still and not laugh, but managed it for only about ten seconds.

There was a knock at the door. Rebekah opened it to find Trey standing in the hall with a towel wrapped around his narrow hips. His wet hair dripped water down his face and naked chest. A few days ago, Rebekah would have had to pick her jaw up off the floor if she'd seen Trey Mills in such a state of undress. Not that he was any less gorgeous than he'd always been, but she had a singular obsession now, and he just so happened to be tied to the bed and at her mercy.

"Do you mind if I get dressed?" Trey asked, sultry green eyes zeroing in on the lacy black garter at the top of Rebekah's thigh-high, fishnet stocking. "All my clothes are in the closet. I could perform naked tonight, I suppose, but I'm not sure that's a good idea."

"I'm sure your fangirls would think it's a wonderful idea." She stepped back in the room. "Come in."

Trey wandered into the bedroom, took one look at Eric, and grinned. "How is it possible for two people to have that much fun in the bedroom?" Trey asked. "I could hear him laughing all the way in the bathroom. I really don't see anything funny about Rebekah's sexy little outfit, Eric. I mean…. *damn,* girl."

Rebekah demonstrated by tickling Eric's belly.

Trey chuckled. "I see. You're torturing him. I guess his bribe worked."

"His bribe?"

"The jewelry I tried to talk him out of."

"I tried to talk him out of it too," she said.

Eric nodded. "She did."

She flicked her feather duster over the head of Eric's rigid cock. He sucked a breath through his teeth.

"So this kinky little game isn't to repay him for the gift?" Trey opened the closet and pulled out some clothes.

"He doesn't have to buy me gifts to encourage me to get my kink on."

Trey shook his head. "And I practically gave you to him."

Rebekah dusted Eric's balls gently.

"Thank you!" Eric gasped, his muscles tightening, flesh quivering.

"Who are you thanking?" Trey asked, removing his towel from around his hips so he could use it to dry his hair.

"Both of you," Eric said.

Rebekah caught one inspiring glance of Trey's perfect, naked ass before forcing her attention to Eric. At least Trey's back was to her. Mercy. Okay, one more glimpse, and she'd be set for life. She didn't mean to stare, but the colorful tattoo on Trey's butt cheek could not be ignored.

"What the fuck is that?" Rebekah asked, leaning closer for a better inspection.

Trey glanced over his shoulder and followed her line of vision to his ass. Upon that perfect, firm cheek, a tattoo of a racing unicorn surrounded by rainbows decorated his skin. The calico kitten perched upon the unicorn's back could only be described as nauseatingly cute. "Hmm. Why don't you ask your boyfriend?"

Rebekah dragged her gaze from the monstrosity of a tattoo and glared at Eric. "You had something to do with that?"

Eric chuckled. "I designed it. Well, Jace helped a little. Isn't it awesome?"

"That isn't the word I'd use, no."

"A bet's a bet," Eric said. "Brian has one too."

"Eric! That thing is permanent."

"So?"

"It is a great conversation starter at parties," Trey admitted.

Rebekah's head whipped around. Trey tilted his head forward and ran a hand through his long bangs, looking his absolute orneriest. And his most naked.

"At p-parties?" she sputtered. "*Trey!* It's on your ass."

He chuckled and cocked an eyebrow. "Exactly."

Rebekah gaped. What kind of parties did this guy go to? And how did she get an invitation?

Trey nodded in Eric's direction. "I think he needs to be tortured some more."

Her entire body jerked as she forced her attention away from wayward thoughts of Trey partying—*naked*—and shifted her attention to her prankster boyfriend currently tied to the bed. "I agree."

"Um, Reb…" Eric said, his eyes wide.

Rebekah lifted a bottle of chocolate syrup from the nightstand

and climbed on the bed to kneel next to him. She poured a line of chocolate from the center of Eric's chest to his belly button.

"Oh, monsieur," she said. "I've made a mess of you."

She lowered her head to lick and suck the chocolate from his body while teasing his cock mercilessly with the feather duster. Eric twitched and groaned. When she was working at removing the syrup from between Eric's washboard abs, Trey took the bottle from her hand and dotted a trail up Eric's side.

"What are you doing, Mills?" Eric asked.

"Helping out a friend in need," he said with a sly grin and dotted syrup on Eric's left nipple.

Rebekah followed the chocolate trail, dropping a sucking kiss at each spot, and then licking to make sure she'd retrieved all the sticky syrup. She spent extra time at his nipple, flicking the ring there with her tongue, while Trey dripped a trail up the side of Eric's throat to his lips and then down the other side of his chest.

"If you were a true friend, you'd put some of that on a more sensitive location," Eric said.

"Sensitive?" Trey chuckled and walked to the end of the bed. "Oh right. She's supposed to be torturing you."

He grabbed Eric's ankle and got a kick in the stomach for his efforts.

"Not the feet!" Eric protested.

"Yeah, not the feet," Rebekah agreed.

"And I said *sensitive*, not ticklish," Eric said.

Trey squirted syrup over the base of Eric's cock and completely drenched his balls. "Don't say I never did anything for you, buddy," Trey said and set the bottle on the nightstand. "Have fun. I'm all horny now. Better go find me a little tail of my own before the show." Slipping a black T-shirt over his head, he let himself out of the room and closed the door.

Rebekah kissed and licked her way up Eric's neck to his lips. She kissed him leisurely. Deeply. When she drew away and looked into his eyes, he made a weird face. She chuckled. "What's that look for?"

"That feels so weird."

"What? Me kissing you?"

"No. The chocolate syrup dripping off my balls." He wriggled his hips and winced.

"I suppose you'd like your maid to clean that up."

"If she would, please."

Rebekah kissed him again. "Are your arms getting tired?" she asked, moving her lips to the sexy cleft in his chin. His jaw now. "You have a show tonight."

"Not really." He inched upward impatiently. She found chocolate on his collarbone and licked it off. "Baby, please."

"You have chocolate all over your chest, monsieur."

"Save that for later."

"But monsieur..." Her tongue darted out to collect chocolate from his side.

"I am so going to get you back for this," he said breathlessly.

"Are you going to make me get a hideous tattoo on my ass?"

"Yeah," he said. "A tattoo of my face."

She laughed. "Your face isn't hideous, but why would you want it on my ass?"

"So even when I'm not around, you'll still be sitting on my face." He flicked his tongue at her suggestively.

She rolled her eyes.

His teasing grin faded, and he squirmed uncomfortably. "Please, Rebekah. I can't stand that sticky, drippy feeling down there."

"You are not satisfied with my work, monsieur?" she said, trying to look horrified as she licked his belly. "You know I only desire to please you."

"I'd like you to work on your priorities a little."

"Clean the parts with the most syrup first?"

"Exactly."

She moved to the end of the bed and slid up between his legs. With her tongue, she traced the chocolate-coated crease between his balls and then sucked at his scrotum, slowly removing the traces of syrup one square inch at a time.

Between his curses and moans, he started to beg. "Reb. Reb. I need to come. Please."

"I'm working here," she said and sucked one nut into her mouth.

"Ahhh." He banged his head against the headboard and lifted his hips off the bed. "Reb. Reb."

She released his flesh from her mouth. She kind of liked this torturing stuff. "Shhh. One more to go."

She scratched her nails over his belly and hips gently as she methodically sucked chocolate from his other nut. He gyrated his hips with her motions. Damn, she wanted to climb on that straining cock, bury it deep, and gyrate with him. But driving him insane was so much fun. She lifted her head and licked the syrup from the base of his cock.

"Clean now?" he asked breathlessly.

"I'm not sure. Better check it one more time. I want to do a thorough job."

She licked his balls with the flat of her tongue, going over the skin several times. There wasn't a trace of chocolate anywhere, but she so enjoyed making him jerk and twitch and shudder.

"You're killing me, baby," he groaned.

"I think you'll live." She discreetly peeled her panties off and kicked them aside. She moved up his body again, finding traces of chocolate on the side of his abdomen. She licked it off and moved a leg over his body so that she straddled his lower belly. Looking into his glazed eyes, she rubbed her dripping pussy against his abdomen. "I'm so wet right now. Do you feel it?"

He jerked, pulling against the scarves.

She lifted her hips and shifted backward. She grabbed his cock and rubbed its head against her, coating it with her juices. "You didn't answer me. Can you feel how wet you make me?"

He gritted his teeth and stared up at her, his expression twisted with a mixture of bliss and agony.

She slipped his cock an inch into her throbbing pussy. "Is it hot?"

He slammed his head against the headboard and whimpered. She rubbed the back of his head with her free hand. "Careful. Did you hurt yourself?"

"Untie me," he said in a low growl.

She ignored his request and plunged down on his cock, burying him deep in one thrust. His back arched, and he cried out. Wow, he was really turned on. She rode him slowly, watching him twitch in excitement. Lord, she loved him like this. She wondered if she could push him further.

She lifted her hips until his cock slipped from her body. He sucked a breath through his teeth.

"I want to *fuck* you so hard," he growled.

"Oh yeah?"

He nodded vigorously.

She pushed the bodice of her dress down to reveal her breasts. "Don't you want to play with these a little first?"

She rubbed the curves of both breasts. She lifted them, pushed them together, and plucked at her nipples until they were hard. She then slid up his body and pressed one nipple into his mouth. He sucked. Hard. Pleasure coursed through her overexcited body. She clung to Eric's hair and crooned.

"Untie me," he requested again.

She rubbed her neglected nipple against his lips and reached for the scarf. He'd pulled on it so much, the knot was impossibly tight.

"I can't get it," she said.

"You're kidding!"

She shook her head. "I'll go get something to cut you free."

"Don't leave me like this, Reb," he pleaded. "Just ride me then."

"But I want your hands on me. I'll hurry."

She pulled up her bodice to cover her breasts and her skirt down before hurrying to the door. She opened it and checked the corridor. Finding it empty, she hurried to the kitchenette and opened a drawer, looking for a knife.

A solid body slid up behind her and breathed into her ear. "What do we have here?" Jon whispered in her ear.

—⁓—

Eric jerked on the scarves cutting into his wrists. Next time Rebekah wanted to tie him up, he'd insist on borrowing restraints from Jace. His skin was raw.

"Get your hands off me," Rebekah shouted in the corridor.

"Rebekah?" Eric called.

"Oh fuck, baby. You aren't wearing any panties," Jon said.

"This is your final warning," she said.

Eric yanked harder on the scarves. "You better not be touching her, Jon!"

"Watcha gonna do about it, Eric?"

There was a loud thud. "Rebekah?" Eric called, his heart thumping with panic.

She appeared a moment later carrying a huge chef's knife. Eric's heart skipped a beat. "Did you kill him?"

She closed the door and smiled. "Do you see any blood?" she asked, holding up her clean knife. She approached the bed and started sawing on one scarf. "Jon messed with the wrong girl. My brother taught me how to defend myself."

As soon as she freed one arm, Eric grabbed Rebekah around the waist and pulled her onto his lap. He squirmed, trying to find her slick heat with his throbbing cock. He was on the verge of spontaneous combustion. Her fault. All her fault. Had to be inside her. Had to.

"Just a minute, baby," she said breathlessly. "Let me get your other arm loose."

She hadn't finished sawing through the scarf when he finally managed to slip inside her. With a groan, he wrapped his free arm around her waist to pull her down to engulf him. Oh yes.

The knife slipped from her grip and fell behind the headboard. Still tied to the headboard with one arm, Eric shifted her sideways across the bed and moved her onto her back beneath him. He thrust between her thighs, driving into her delightful warmth as hard as he could, needing her to feel how excited she'd made him. She clung to his back, meeting his thrusts and encouraging his mindless possession with excited vocalizations. He continued to pull at his trapped arm as he plunged into her. The need to wrap her securely in both arms overwhelmed him. Eric yanked repeatedly at the scarf until the fabric ripped, freeing him at last. He gathered Rebekah in his arms and held her close, his feelings for this woman so overpowering, he wasn't quite sure how to express them. He trailed kisses along her neck, catching the necklace he'd given her between his lips and her heated skin. When she arched against him and cried out with release, he slowed the rate of his thrusts, letting her drift back to her senses. Eric brushed his lips against her forehead. "I love you," he whispered.

Before she could return the sentiment, the bedroom door opened. Eric glanced over his shoulder to find Jon standing there, fuming.

Rebekah trembled beneath him. "Oh baby," she moaned, "fill me with your huge cock. Fuck me, Eric! Make me come."

Eric looked at her, one eyebrow arched in question, wondering if she realized Jon was watching them. "Jon," he whispered into her ear.

"I want him to see," she whispered back.

"Why?"

"It makes me feel sexy."

And he wanted that for her. Knew she needed it, though he'd never understand how she could possibly think she *wasn't* sexy. Everything about her was sexy.

"Show him my tits," she whispered.

He yanked the bodice of her French maid costume down to release her breasts. Watching them bounce with each thrust obliterated his concentration for a long moment. He pounded into her harder to make them bounce more delightfully. Bending over her, he licked the taut nipple of one perfect breast with the flat of his tongue. She clung to his hair, vocalizing her excitement with so much enthusiasm, he feared she'd explode.

"Oh Eric. Eric!" And if she kept saying his name like that, he *knew* he would explode.

"Isn't she sexy, Jon?" he murmured. "Sexy, beautiful Rebekah…"

"When I tried to show her I thought she was sexy, she flipped me over her back and onto the floor," Jon said. "What is it about me that makes Sinners' chicks kick my ass?"

"Look, don't touch," she said.

Jon snorted. "That's more Eric's thing."

"Not with Rebekah," he said, blowing a breath over her wet nipple. "I can't get enough of this woman."

Rebekah put a thumb under Eric's chin and tilted his face upward so she could kiss him. "You can leave anytime, Jon," she said, glancing out of the corner of her eye.

Eric heard Jon close the door behind him. "I thought you wanted him to watch."

She smiled. "You're enough for me. You always make me feel like the sexiest woman in the world."

"Well, you are. It's not like I have to work at it."

Chapter 18

WAITING FOR THE SIGNAL to go onstage, Eric stood behind his drum kit twirling his drumsticks. Rebekah's soft, yet confident, voice filtered instructions through his earpiece and made him smile. The woman was too good to be true. It was as if she'd been made especially for him. Things were almost too perfect. He kept waiting for a meteor to fall from the sky and pulverize him to ash. His life had been one train wreck after another. Something this wonderful had to end badly. And when it did, he knew it would destroy him.

"Eric. Eric? Eric!" His name echoed through his head. Rebekah was shouting into his earpiece to gain his attention.

Eric realized the lights had come up, the band was onstage, and he was supposed to be tapping out the intro to "Sever," but he wasn't even seated yet. *Shit!* Daydreaming on the job. Eric rushed to sit on his throne, aka small stool, and tapped a beat on his snare.

A spotlight hit the surface of the white baby grand piano. The piano reflected various colors—blue to red to yellow to green—in time with Jace's playing. The rest of the band entered the song, and Sed roared that first note over the shouts of a chaotic crowd. Eric got sucked into his zone, letting the music, the beat, sweep him into a place where nothing existed but sound. Arms flailing, legs pumping, he put everything he had into the rhythm. He almost forgot he was supposed to sing the chorus until the time was upon him. While Sed roared, "Sever," in increasingly loud and lengthy tones, Eric entered with his softer melody. He concentrated on his breathing, his arms and legs carrying the beat with little thought. He loved this song, but it was a bitch to sing live and play the drums simultaneously. Not enough air. By the time the first chorus ended, he was panting and trying to regain his breath. He hoped he'd sounded okay and not like an obscene phone caller. He was glad Rebekah decreased the volume on his mic when he wasn't actually singing. She did it so it didn't pick up the drums, but he was gasping for air, and his mic was sure to pick it up.

The playback in his ear suddenly sounded off to his drumming. Eric stumbled over a beat as he slowed to match the track. Sed entered the song several beats off, while the three guitarists struggled to keep up with Eric's attempts to regain control of the song.

"Marcus." He heard Rebekah's panicked voice in his ear. "Marcus, the playback is off. Marcus!"

She was right. That was the problem. The band was hearing the echo of the stadium sound rather than what they were actually playing.

"You're the one who programmed the damned song," Marcus said. "It's your fuckup, not mine."

Sed stopped singing and lowered his microphone, glancing to the side of the stage where Marcus stood with his arms crossed over his chest. The band followed Sed's cue and stopped playing with a discordant ring of notes. Eric went still, sweating and panting, wondering what the fuck was going on. They'd never had this problem before. Had Rebekah really fucked up? His first instinct was to speak in her defense, but he honestly didn't know who was at fault.

"That's bullshit, Marcus," Rebekah said into the crew's feed. "You're the monitor engineer. You're supposed to control the playback to the band. It has nothing to do with my program. That's to control what the crowd hears, not what the band hears. You don't even use my program."

"Excuse us, folks," Sed said to the crowd. "Technical difficulties.

Bear with us until we get it straightened out." His voice echoed through their feed a half-second later.

"Or you could *bare* with us," Trey said, his voice also echoing strangely. Trey lifted the hem of his T-shirt and showed off his belly to a group of fangirls near the front of the stage.

Because of the echo in his earpiece, Eric could tell for sure that this was a monitor engineer mistake. Rebekah didn't have anything to do with the band's feed from the amplifiers. That was Marcus's job. Did he think they were too stupid to realize that?

"So explain the echo in my ear when Sed and Trey just spoke," Rebekah said, her voice breathless with anger. "How can you blame that on my program, Marcus? They might not know how this works, but I do. You're trying to make it look like *your* intentional error is my fault, so they'll fire me."

"Bullshit, little girl," Marcus growled. "You're paranoid."

"This isn't about us, you jerk. This is about the band, the music, and the ten thousand people who paid to be entertained," Rebekah continued. "Get your self-important head out of your ass, and do your fucking job. If you have a problem with me, we'll take it up after the show."

"Damn, baby," Eric said to himself, "I love it when you exert your authority. Makes me all hard."

The crowd broke into raucous laughter. Sed turned and quirked an eyebrow. Eric's face fell.

"Shit, I forgot I have a live mic," Eric said.

The crowd laughed again.

"I see the problem," Marcus said into the feed going through everyone's earpieces. At least the crowd couldn't hear him or Rebekah's hot little tirade. Marcus's voice was significantly more humble when he asked, "Do you want to start from the top?"

"They've got it fixed now," Sed told the crowd.

Jace struggled to remove his bass and get back to the piano. Jon was beaming when he returned to the stage with his bass. He got to play twice tonight instead of just once.

"Whenever you're ready," Rebekah said into their feed. "'Sever' from the top."

The rest of the show went over without a hitch. Afterward, Eric grabbed a bottle of water and waited for the crowd to clear out of the arena before going in search of Rebekah. She was probably still upset about what had happened at the beginning of the show, and he had the powerful need to comfort her. And then to dress her up like a naughty cop so she could exert her authority over him.

He finally found her backstage cringing beside Marcus. Sed had them both cornered and was in berate mode. Eric had suffered under Sed's wrath more than once. It wasn't fun.

When Rebekah tried to speak in her own defense, Sed raised a hand. "I don't give a shit whose fault it is. This isn't going to happen again. Do you understand?"

Rebekah bit her lip, struggling to maintain her composure.

"Don't yell at her," Eric said to Sed.

Sed glanced over his shoulder. "I'm not yelling."

Eric lifted an eyebrow. "Sounds like yelling to me."

"Touring is hard enough without a feud going on between my soundboard operators."

"It won't happen again," Marcus said. "I found the problem and fixed it."

"If the two of you break into an argument during a show again, you're both fired. *Capisce?*" Sed continued.

Rebekah nodded sullenly.

Marcus flung his hands out, his palms at chest level facing the ceiling. "Sed, I've been with this crew for four years. You can't—"

"Marcus, I wouldn't care if you were my own father. You fuck up another Sinners' show, by neglect or on purpose, you're out of here. End of story. No argument. Out of here."

"This is fucking bullshit." Marcus glared at Rebekah before storming off.

"Way to defuse a bomb, Sed," Eric said.

"Do you have a better idea?" he asked.

"Yeah, don't drag Rebekah into this when you know she had nothing to do with it." Eric wrapped an arm around her back and tugged her closer.

"Then Marcus would think I was singling him out, and he'd get even more pissed at her."

Eric glanced at Rebekah, and she nodded in agreement. "Sed's right."

Eric sighed loudly and shook his head. "Sed's always right."

Sed grinned like a shark. "Well, we're all in agreement on that."

"I've got to tear down the equipment," Rebekah said, squirming out of Eric's sweaty grasp.

"Will you dress up as a cop for me later?" he asked.

She glanced at Sed and flushed, then turned her gaze to Eric and said, "You have the right to remain silent."

He chuckled. "I think I want to waive that right."

"I know a great soon-to-be attorney," Sed said. His fiancée Jessica was in her final year of law school.

"If Jessica wants to participate in our scenario, I would not object," Eric quipped. It earned him a thump in the forehead from Sed.

Rebekah tilted her head back for a kiss, which Eric gave eagerly. When they drew apart, she patted his butt before returning to work. He watched her until she was out of sight and then turned to find Sed grinning.

"What?"

"Nothing. Just happy for you." Sed clapped him on the shoulder and directed him toward the tour bus.

Eric was happy for himself as well. There was still one thing that continually ate away at him though. It was past time that he spilled his guts to Sed. Sure, Sed would be pissed for a while. He might even hit him, but it had to be better than this constant cloud of darkness hanging over his subconscious for almost three years.

"Sed?"

"Yeah?"

"Sed, there's something I need to tell you about me and Jon."

Sed's head swiveled, and his eyes were the size of saucers. "You and Jon? No fucking way."

It took Eric a few seconds to realize why Sed was so shocked. "Ew. No, not that. Shit, where did that come from?"

Sed released a long breath through pursed lips. "Sorry. Now that I'm not getting it on with three or four different girls a night, I've been noticing Trey's activities more. That guy will fuck anyone."

Eric laughed. "You're just now noticing that? He actually has excellent taste and a lot to choose from on both teams."

They paused in the corridor that led to the stadium exit. "So now that my mind is out of the gutter, what were you actually trying to tell me?" Sed asked.

"Do you remember when the old bus broke down outside Phoenix and the cash that we kept in the lockbox for emergencies was sort of missing?"

"How can I fucking forget that? Jon used every penny we had to buy drugs. That was the last straw. We had no choice but to fire him."

Eric winced. "Well…" Eric was starting to reconsider this confession. Maybe it was better to let Jon take the blame.

"Well, what?"

"There was this lady at a gas station near Tucson. She laid this sob story on me about running out of gas and having no food for her two little kids. They were in her van all sweaty and hot because it was frickin' almost a hundred degrees that day. Crying that they were thirsty and hungry. So…" Eric sighed. "I didn't have much cash on me. So I gave her the money out of our lockbox."

"All of it?"

"Yeah. I figured she needed it more than we did. We were almost home. We had some great gigs lined up. I knew we'd make the money back in no time. And then the bus broke down, and we were stuck without a dime. I was going to tell you, but Jon said you were already pissed at him, a little more wouldn't hurt. Next thing I knew, Jon was out of the band, and we were stuck without a tour bus. We had to cancel a bunch of shows. Lay off some of the crew. It kept snowballing from there."

"Jessica dumped me."

Eric winced. "Yeah."

"At least, I thought that's why she dumped me. Turned out it was really because I was a conceited ass, but at the time, I blamed Jon for wasting all our money, so I couldn't pay her law school tuition."

"I'm really sorry. If I'd have known, I wouldn't have given that lady the whole five hundred dollars. I just felt bad for her, and her kids were so cute." Eric peeked at Sed through one eye. "Did I mention they were hungry and thirsty?"

"You gave some stranger five hundred dollars?"

"Yeah, I know. She could have gotten gas and food and stuff for a lot less. I probably should have given her a hundred bucks or so. I'm just…"

"A generous sucker. Yeah, I realize that." Sed wiped a hand over his face. "There wasn't five hundred dollars in that lockbox, Eric. There was eight thousand."

Eric stuck his finger in his ear and wiggled it around. "I don't think I heard you right. I know there was only five hundred in there. I took it. Emptied the whole thing."

"Which was a fuckin' bonehead move." Sed slapped him in the arm. Not even hard enough to hurt. Shouldn't he be more pissed?

Maybe it was because so much time had passed, and everything had turned out all right. Eventually. "Ever wonder why Jon was so willing to take the fall for you?"

"He was my best friend."

Sed shook his head. "He didn't want you to know that he'd spent seventy-five hundred dollars on his drug habit. He'd just gotten out of rehab, remember?"

Eric nodded.

"Remember what landed him there?"

"He took the band's ATM card and cleared out the checking account to pay for one of his weekend benders."

"And all of the crew's paychecks bounced."

"Yeah, that was a mess."

"So I had to start paying everyone with cash."

Eric glanced at Sed, trying to reconstruct past events with this new information. "He took all the payroll money?"

"Good morning, Eric. Glad you're finally waking up."

"So all this time, he's been making me feel like shit to hide what he did and—"

"Keep you under his thumb."

"That asshole!"

"I've been trying to make you see what he's really like for years. You're so blind when it comes to those you care about. You've always been as faithful as an abused dog."

It was true. Eric couldn't deny it. He wasn't sure he appreciated being compared to a dog, but he'd been called worse. "So why did you let Jon fill in for Jace? Why is he on tour with us now?"

"Because you wanted him to be."

"Since when does anyone listen to me?"

Sed chuckled. "All the time, Eric. Where would Sinners be without you? Not where we are today, that's for sure."

Eric stared at him. What did he mean? Most of the time the

other guys tolerated his eccentricities, but he was unquestionably the least celebrated member of this band.

"You're the creative genius behind our music, Eric. That little bit of gray matter floating around in your skull is what makes us great. Always has been. Always will be."

"So why do you always boss me around? And take charge? And act like the leader of this band? And take all the credit for our success?"

"Do you think I like all of this responsibility?" Sed paused and grinned sheepishly, both dimples showing. "Okay, I do. But you'd hate it. Your heart's too big, Eric. People would take advantage of you. You'd have to deal with a whole lot of logistical bullshit, and it would stifle your creative energy."

Eric snarled. "Why are you always fucking right about everything? Do you know how annoying that is?"

"Nope." Sed wrapped an arm around Eric's shoulders and walked him toward the tour bus. "Do you feel better now that you got that big secret off your chest?"

"Sorta." Eric sighed remorsefully. "So what do we do about Jon?"

"I'm going to leave that up to you."

Oh sure, the one time Eric actually wanted Sed to be in command, he hands over the controls. When they passed one of the open dressing rooms backstage, Eric caught sight of Jon sniffing something off the side of his hand. Jon's eyelids fluttered as he held one nostril shut and then he covertly handed something to one of their temporary roadies. Very temporary. Sed shook his head in disgust and followed the guy back to the stage area where he was supposed to help with teardown. Eric was glad he didn't have to fire him. He hated to admit it, but Sed did make a better bandleader than he ever would.

Jon spotted Eric standing in the doorway. He beamed a bright smile and hurried over to Eric. "I have this great idea on how to prank Sed,"

Jon said. "We can tie a stuffed rat to a string and hide it inside the refrigerator. When Sed opens it to get a beer, the rat will fly out and scare the piss out of him. What do you think? It will work. I know it will. We just have to make sure he's the one who opens the refrigerator."

Eric had really wanted to wait to collect his thoughts before he confronted Jon. But if he did that, Eric knew he'd start to feel sorry for Jon and make excuses for him again. Enable him. "I know about the lockbox."

"I didn't take anything," Jon said nervously. "I don't even know the new combination."

Eric shook his head. "But you tried, didn't you?"

"Prove it."

Dealing with this guy made Eric tired. He knew his life would be a whole lot easier without Jon in it. "I wasn't talking about the *current* lockbox. I was talking about the old one. The one I supposedly emptied out, and you claimed to take the fall for me. The incident you've been holding over my head for years. Ringing any bells?"

"I did take the fall for you."

"Sed told me that there was eight thousand dollars in there, not five hundred. You took the rest of that money for what? For drugs?"

"I have no idea what you're talking about," Jon said. "I didn't take any money out of the lockbox."

Eric hesitated. "You didn't?"

"No. You should get your facts straight before you start accusing people of things."

Jon shook his head and stormed away, his hands shoved deep in the pockets of his jeans.

Eric watched Jon stalk off down the corridor. Maybe Jon hadn't taken the money. Maybe Sed was wrong.

Or maybe Jon was lying.

"Fuck my life," Eric muttered under his breath.

Chapter 19

OVER TWO WEEKS LATER, somewhere between Buffalo and Detroit, Rebekah squirmed onto the dining table to sit next to Trey as they waited for dinner to finish cooking. Both booths were full, so she didn't have many seating options to choose from. Jace sat next to Brian on one side of the table, and Sed next to Eric on the other. She might have squeezed onto Eric's lap, but he was trapped against the wall, and Sed took up more than his fair share of the booth with his broad shoulders.

Eric had been pensive since their Austin show. She knew why. He'd told her about his situation with Jon. She'd advised him to cut all ties with the guy, but Eric was big on second chances and third chances and twenty-seventh chances. So Jon still played the shows, following the tour buses in his Jeep, and Eric avoided him as much as possible. Rebekah patiently waited for Eric to get his head out of his ass, and Sed held his tongue.

"This tour schedule is killing me," Trey complained, rubbing his face with both hands. "The venues are scattered all over the fucking place."

"Rescheduling canceled shows is a bitch," Sed said. "They never align properly. Just be glad we're putting off the canceled shows in Canada until the spring."

"My blood's not hot enough to survive a Canadian winter," Trey said.

"Your blood's hot enough to melt the polar ice caps," Brian

teased and gave Trey a playful shove. Trey ricocheted into Rebekah, who burst out laughing.

Rebekah's laughter died when Brian's cell phone beeped in his pocket.

"Myrna?" Sed asked. They all knew Brian was waiting to hear the results of her latest pregnancy test. He'd managed to fly in to visit her for one night during her fertile time, and she'd yet to call crying that she'd started her period again.

Brain read the screen and nodded. He looked a bit ill. "Text message."

"Well, what did she say?" Eric asked.

A look of confusion spread across Brian's handsome features. "Uh? It says the rabbit died. The *rabbit* died?"

"Did she hit a rabbit with her car or what?" Trey asked around the cherry sucker in his mouth.

Rebekah chuckled. "They used to inject rabbits with women's urine to determine pregnancy."

"Ugh," Trey said, "that's fucking disgusting. Are you serious?"

Rebekah tousled his hair and nodded. "Completely."

"So what does it mean when the rabbit dies?" The look of concern on Brian's face made Rebekah's heart twang.

"Nothing bad, sweetie. It means she's pregnant."

Brian's jaw dropped. "I'm going to be a daddy?"

Rebekah smiled and nodded. "I'd say that's what she's trying to tell you."

"I'm going to be a daddy!" Brian grabbed the nearest person, who just happened to be Jace, and gave him a bone-crunching hug. "I'm going to be a daddy," he told him.

"Congratulations," Jace gasped.

Sed reached across the table and gathered half the band in a huge hug with Brian in the middle. His large biceps pressed Rebekah's head firmly against Trey's shoulder. "That is *fucking* awesome, dude,"

Sed's deep baritone rumbled through his chest. Rebekah could hear the emotion in his words. She didn't know Sed could get emotional.

"I've got to see Myrna," Brian said, fighting his way out of the group hug. "I should be there with her."

"We have a show tomorrow," Sed reminded him.

"This is more important."

Brian climbed to his feet. Standing in the aisle, he dialed his wife and fidgeted with a chain hanging from his belt loop as he waited for her to answer. His features softened the second he heard her voice.

"Does this mean…" he said. His bright smile could only mean she'd affirmed their suspicions. "When?" He bit his lip. "July? I can't wait that long." He shook his head and chuckled. "God, I want to hold you right now." He swallowed hard and noticed that the entire band and Rebekah were staring. He pressed on one eyelid with his fingertips, turned on his heel, and disappeared into the back bedroom. As soon as the door closed, Rebekah turned to look at Eric.

He smiled slightly and mouthed, "Are you okay?"

She nodded. Sure, she'd never know the joy of telling the man she loved that he was going to be a father, but she was happy for Brian. She knew how much he wanted a baby.

"This sucks balls," Trey grumbled. He slid off the table and shut himself in the bathroom.

Rebekah figured Trey would be happier for Brian than anyone. He was his best friend.

Sed shook his head. "Spoiled brat."

Rebekah stared at the floor, wondering how this new development was going to affect the band. They wouldn't break up over something like this, would they? Or tour less? She loved this job.

Without warning, Eric reached out, grabbed Rebekah around the waist, and dragged her across the table. He growled and gobbled against her neck until she was laughing and squealing at the top of her lungs. She kicked her feet, trying to escape his assault, but Eric held tight. On the opposite side of the table, Jace grabbed her ankle to avoid getting kicked in the face. When Eric decided she'd laughed enough, he tucked her head under his chin and held her gently. She wasn't in the most comfortable position, stretched across the dining table on her side, wedged against Eric's shoulder as he sat in the booth, but she let him hold her. She knew he needed to provide comfort as much as she needed to receive it. He couldn't stand it when she was melancholy.

A moment later, the bedroom door opened, and Brian wandered out.

"How's she doing?" Sed asked.

"She's fine. Cussed me out when I told her I wanted to cancel tomorrow night's show to see her."

"That sounds like her," Sed said and chuckled. "Is she going to fly in to see you then?"

Brian shook his head. "She said we'll see each other at Thanksgiving."

"That's only two weeks," Rebekah said, hoping he'd stop looking so fucking miserable. The man was intense in every imaginable way. He played his guitar intensely. Loved his wife intensely. Experienced emotions intensely. Rebekah bet he was one hell of an intense lover. She flushed at her thoughts and cuddled closer to Eric, who wasn't exactly intense, but definitely enthusiastic.

"It's sure to be the longest two weeks of my life," Brian murmured. He glanced around. "Where's Trey?"

"Sulking in the bathroom," Sed told him. "We have got to find that guy someone to love."

"He has a different someone to love every night," Eric said with a chuckle.

"And that's his problem."

No, his problem was that he already had someone to love, and that someone didn't return the sentiment. Rebekah didn't say it, but she was pretty sure everyone except Brian was thinking it.

Brian sighed. "I'll go talk to him."

"Hey, Brian," Rebekah said and eased out of Eric's embrace to sit up on the table again.

Brian turned to look at her, one eyebrow raised in question.

She smiled brightly and met his intense gaze. "You're going to be a daddy."

He beamed, all his troubles flowing away in an instant. "I'm going to be a daddy!" He tossed the bathroom door open. "Hey, Trey! I'm going to be a daddy!"

"Fuck off."

"That is not the appropriate response."

Brian yanked Trey into the corridor by one arm and forced him into a headlock. Trey poked Brian in the ribs, hooked his leg around Brian's ankle, and took him to the floor. Rebekah giggled as they wrestled, not sure why watching them go at it made her hungry for sex. Eventually, they stopped wrestling and lay in a tangled heap on the floor laughing.

"What's the appropriate response, Trey?" Brain asked.

His head pinned to Brian's chest, Trey wrapped an arm around Brian's abdomen and gave him a squeeze. "Congratulations," Trey said breathlessly. "Daddy."

Brian placed a hand on Trey's head and pressed him closer to his chest. "I hope my son's smart like his mother and not a knucklehead like the two of us."

Trey squeezed his eyes shut and clung to Brian as if he planned to never let him go.

Chapter 20

REBEKAH HAD NEVER BEEN more exhausted in her life. Tonight was their last show before a six-week break centered around Thanksgiving and Christmas. She was pretty sure she would need every day of those six weeks just to recover from their grueling tour schedule. Carefully winding a power cord so the soundboard could be put on the truck, she paused when she felt someone's presence behind her.

"Uh, Rebekah?"

Rebekah spun around to look at Marcus, her eyes wide in question.

"I sort of owe you an apology," he murmured, his eyes downcast. "I found this a few weeks ago and forgot to return it."

He pulled a spiral-bound notebook from under his sweatshirt and held it out to her. It was Dave's collection of notes that she'd misplaced her first night on the job.

"That would have come in handy when I had no idea what I was doing," she said, "but I don't need it now."

"Dave's a genius," Marcus said, still not meeting her eyes. "I thought I would be the best choice to take his place, but…"

She waited for him to continue. He looked up, and his pug-like eyes met hers steadily. "But…" he said, "you're good at what you do. The band sounds awesome. I'm not sure if Dave could have done any better."

Rebekah couldn't hide her smile. "You really think so?" she said eagerly.

Marcus chuckled and got a sappy look on his face. "Yeah. You've proven yourself over and over. I'm sorry I misjudged you. It's just really hard to take someone as fucking adorable as you are seriously."

Rebekah's smile faltered.

"Uh, uh, uhnnnn," Eric said as he moved to stand between them. "You will not be teaching Marcus any lessons for mistaking you as adorable."

Marcus flushed and did an about-face. "Later."

Eric wrapped an arm around Rebekah's waist. "Are you about finished?"

"Not even close. We have to get this stuff put away properly tonight so everything is easy to find when we go back on the road in January. Did you talk to Jon yet?"

"Sorta."

"Eric, you promised!"

"I told him we wouldn't need him when we went back on tour in January."

"You did?"

"Yeah."

"How did he respond?"

"Made me feel as if I betrayed him. Told me to go fuck myself. Took off in his Jeep."

"Do you think he's gone for good?"

Eric shook his head. "I have no doubt he'll try to manipulate me again. I'm not going to cave next time though."

"I'll make sure of it. This has been eating you alive for weeks. You need to stop being his martyr."

He rubbed the spot between his eyebrows with one finger. "I know… I just… He was the first real friend I ever had. Turned out he wasn't my friend after all." He grinned unexpectedly. "I got you something."

There he went again, changing the subject without warning. "Eric, we discussed this. No more expensive gifts."

"It wasn't expensive." He pulled a little white teddy bear out of his vest. It was wearing a tiny blue T-shirt that read I ♥ Sinners. "It reminded me of you because..." He leaned closer to her ear. "It's adorable."

"Eric Sticks, I'm not adorable!" She tossed the teddy bear at him, and he caught it in one hand.

"Prove it," he teased and jogged backward. He cuddled the bear against his chest. "Oh, look at adorable little Rebekah," he said, squeezing the stuffed toy until its head threatened to pop off. "Cutest girl in the world."

She knew he just wanted to play, and she was tempted to chase him around the stadium, corner him, and tickle him into submission, but sometimes work had to come first. "I'll deal with you later."

His eyebrows lifted, and his smile of anticipation almost convinced her to forgo work. "Promise?"

If he wanted to act like a naughty boy, she was going to treat him like a naughty boy. "I do not tolerate that kind of misbehavior in my class, Mr. Sticks."

The excited little huff he produced was almost more than she could bear.

"As your first punishment, you will write an essay that describes all the ways you plan to repent for your disobedience," she added.

He scowled. "Essay? I'm not writing a fucking essay."

Rebekah yanked a blank piece of paper out of the notebook Marcus had returned. She took a pen from a cup sitting next to her soundboard and handed it to Eric.

"Rebekah..."

"Write: I am sorry I upset Ms. Blake."

He stared at her for a minute, trying to figure out her game. When he put the paper on the edge of the soundboard and started to write, she smiled.

Looking over his shoulder to check his progress, she said, "Now write: To make it up to her, I will suck on her clit until she comes."

His head snapped up, and he pinned her with a look that made her toes curl in her sneakers. She knew how Eric's mind worked. Half of his excitement, maybe more, came from thinking about sex, and this would definitely make him think about it.

"I expect you to write down a lot of ways you plan to make this up to me, Eric. A lot. You've been a very naughty boy." She turned her body to block the view of her cupping the crotch of his jeans. She knew he'd be hard, and he didn't disappoint her. Stroking the length of his cock, she looked up at him with a teasing smile. "The second part of your essay will describe all the things you think Ms. Blake does to naughty boys. When you're finished, turn in your paper to me, and then go wait on the bus until I come to punish you. Have I made myself clear?"

"Yes, ma'am," he said breathlessly.

"It will be a couple hours before I can get to you, so you might as well take your time on that essay." She released his cock, took the teddy bear out of his hand, and set her new mascot on her soundboard.

"Ms. Blake?" he said.

"Get to work," she said harshly.

"I think I'm going to need more paper."

She grinned and ripped out several additional sheets. The kiss he planted behind her ear as he snatched the papers was all the motivation she needed to finish her work as quickly as possible.

Eric handed his seven-page essay to Ms. Blake as respectfully as a guy with a raging hard-on could manage. He wasn't sure what excited him more, writing it, or knowing she would read it. Maybe it was knowing she might do the things he'd written on the page. And let him do things to her.

Ms. Blake glanced at the top sheet. The sternness in her

expression did strange things to him. He wanted her approval. Her praise. "This looks acceptable," she said.

Acceptable? He'd poured himself into that essay. Admitted fantasies he'd never admitted to anyone. He tried to snatch the papers back, but she held them out of reach behind her back.

"I'm almost finished here," she said. Her gaze locked with his, and he knew he'd do anything she asked. "Go wait in my office, and don't touch anything. Especially not your cock. I see how hard it is. That is very naughty, Mr. Sticks."

"Where's your office?"

She lifted an eyebrow at him. "Where do you think it is?"

"The bedroom on the tour bus."

She shrugged. "That will do. Go now." She continued with her work, organizing color-coded cords in a large case.

He backed away slowly, wondering if he could wait without dying. He could see the headline now. *Rock Drummer Killed By Lack of Blood Flow to Brain*. And it would all be Rebekah's fault for making him so damned hard. Then how would she feel about tormenting him ceaselessly? She'd feel really guilty for sending him to an early grave by keeping all his blood sequestered in his cock, instead of serving his vital organs. Not that he actually minded the torment. He loved every minute of it.

She glanced at him over her shoulder. "Are you still here?"

He turned and tried to walk casually to the back of the stadium where the bus was parked. It wasn't easy in his condition. Especially when some fangirl spotted him and hurdled a barrier fence to hug him excitedly.

"Oh Eric, I've been waiting forever to see you," she crooned. "I didn't think you'd ever come outside."

"Um, okay, sorry," he said, trying to untangle her arms from around his neck. He remembered a time when the occasional lust-crazed fan made his entire week. Now he just wanted to get the fuck away from her before she discovered his arousal. She rubbed up against him and chuckled. Too late. Now he'd never convince her to leave him alone.

"Is that for me?" she asked, her hand sliding down his belly to his crotch.

"No, actually, it's not. Could you—" He grabbed her wrist to move her hand.

"Let me suck you off," she said huskily. "I want a picture of me with your cock down my throat." She handed him her camera phone and reached for the top button of his jeans.

"Whoa, no!" he gasped and jerked away. "Here." He shoved her phone into her hand and pounded on the side of the bus so they'd open the door and let him in. Besides, it was fucking cold outside, and he didn't have his jacket.

"Don't be shy," the girl said, plastering herself to his back and rubbing his cock through his pants. "You're super hard, baby. I know you want me."

"Stop touching me like that," he demanded, grateful when the bus door finally opened. He climbed onboard and found the entire band was already inside. When the girl tried to follow, Sed came to stand at the head of the stairs. The girl took one look at him, went white as a sheet, and ran off. Eric didn't bother to ask why. He was glad to be rid of her.

"Where've you been, Sticks?" Sed asked. "We've been waiting for you so we can leave."

"Rebekah's not ready yet. She's still packing up equipment."

"She can ride on the pigsty bus with the other roadies," Sed said. "We need to get home. I know *you* get laid every two hours, but I'm about to explode."

Brian nodded in agreement. Jace was blushing and texting on his cell phone feverishly, which meant he and Aggie were sexting each other again.

"I'm good," Trey said around his lollipop. Undoubtedly, he'd gotten a little action after the show.

"I'll go tell her to hurry," Eric said and sprinted off the bus. No way in hell was he riding on a bus for fourteen hours without her. He didn't know how the other guys handled being away from their respective ladies for days and weeks at a time.

He almost bumped into Rebekah as she hurried out of the building carrying a case. He scooped it out of her hands. "Let me get that."

"You are supposed to be wait—"

"Eric, come on or we're leaving without you!" Sed yelled from the tour bus.

"Are you almost finished?" he asked her. "If you don't hurry, we'll be forced to ride on the pigsty bus."

"The guys are going to load all the stuff. I was on my way to deliver your punishment and thought I could drop off that case on my way."

He slid the case into the back of the moving van, lifted her onto his shoulder, and headed for the bus.

"Eric, this is no way to treat your teacher. You are in big trouble." He heard the laughter in her voice and couldn't wait to see how much trouble he could get into before they made it to the bus.

He paddled her rump playfully. "I'm guessing the naughtier I behave, the more I'm going to enjoy this."

"I don't know about that. Maybe I'll make you wait for it."

"You wouldn't! You make me write all that kinky stuff, get me all worked up, and then you're going to let me suffer?"

"I haven't gotten the chance to read it all yet."

He set her down on the bottom step. "Can I have a kiss before you start abusing me?"

She wrapped her arms around his neck. "It's cold out here," she said, staring into his eyes. For once he wasn't looking down at her; they were eye to eye. And despite the chill in the air, he felt himself melting under her heated gaze. "I love you."

He wondered if she'd like a new wristwatch or perfume or a yacht or a private island in the Caribbean or something. She kissed him before he could say he loved her back, but she knew how he felt. How could she not? Their tender kiss quickly turned heated.

He was tugging on her clothes.

She was tugging on his hair.

He pressed her against him so he could feel her soft breasts against his chest. His hands slid down to her luscious little ass. He found his paper in her back pocket. Maybe he should take it back before she got the chance to read it. Somewhere in that essay, he'd admitted some pretty embarrassing desires he had for a certain bandmate's college professor wife. Rebekah had pushed that button by bringing up the naughty schoolboy scenario. Myrna Sinclair always made Eric feel like a naughty schoolboy. He just hadn't recognized how much he'd wanted her to exert her authority over him until he'd started writing his essay to Rebekah. He no longer had an interest in Myrna fulfilling that fantasy. Not when he had Rebekah. She didn't fulfill one of his fantasies. She fulfilled them all.

Someone cleared his throat somewhere above them. Eric forced his lips from Rebekah's and glanced at Sed, who looked ready to strangle him. "Are you saying good-bye or what?" Sed asked gruffly.

"Nope, we were making out," Rebekah said. "His sexiness overwhelms me sometimes, and I have to kiss him." Eric would have thought she was joking, but she maintained a completely straight face. Rebekah turned and trotted up the steps. Eric followed, knowing he was a slave to his desire for this woman, but not much caring at the moment.

He followed her to the bedroom. When they reached the door, she turned to look at him. "Wait here," she said sternly. "I'll come get you after I read your essay."

She let herself in the bedroom and closed the door in his face. She was totally going to leave him hanging. He just knew it. He sighed resolutely and went to sit at the dining table across from Jace, preparing for a horrible case of blue balls.

"You texting Aggie?" Eric asked and shifted uncomfortably on the bench.

Jace jumped as if he'd shot him. And the guy knew what that felt like from experience. Jace flushed and then tucked his cell phone under the table. "She misses me." He grinned.

Eric reached across the table and slugged him in the shoulder. "We should hang out over the break."

Jace grinned even more widely. "Yeah, sure." He glanced over his shoulder at the closed bedroom door. "Shouldn't you be in there?"

"I'm not sure. Maybe she wants me to burst in there, throw her on the bed, rip her clothes off, and fuck her. Or maybe she really does want me to obey her and wait out here until my balls explode."

They stared at each other in complete befuddlement. Trey hopped up to sit on the kitchen counter across from the dining table. He pulled his sucker out of his mouth. "What signals was she giving off?"

"Signals?" Was Trey speaking a foreign language? Eric had no idea what he was talking about.

"Yeah, signals. Women talk more with their bodies than their mouths."

"Damn. That's a whole lot of body yapping," Sed said with a wide grin.

"You don't listen to their bodies either. That's why it took you so long to understand Jessica," Trey said.

Sed scowled. "I listen to her body just fine."

"But only during sex," Brian interjected.

"How did she look at you? Like this?" Trey produced a come-hither look that made Eric decidedly uncomfortable.

"Uh… no." Eric would have remembered Rebekah looking at him like that. He wanted to forever wipe the memory of Trey looking at him like that, however. It was bad enough that he'd kissed the guy one lust-fueled night.

"Then you better wait," Trey advised.

"Maybe I'm tired of waiting." He grabbed the edge of the table to heft himself to his feet. He paused when the bedroom door opened. Rebekah emerged in an outfit he'd never seen. His jaw dropped.

Rebekah strode confidently in his direction. She wore her hair in a severe twist, the blond strands arranged to cover most of the blue. A pair of thick-rimmed glasses sat perched on the end of her nose. Her propriety stopped there. Her tweed suit could only be described as revealing. The jacket had elbow-length, tight sleeves and buttoned under her breasts, drawing attention to her cleavage, and the plain white blouse unbuttoned low enough to reveal the edge of her lacy, white bra. A couple inches of her midriff showed above her tiny skirt, which was so short he could see her garters and the skin of her thighs above her flesh-toned stockings. Her wide-heeled, three-inch shoes made her legs look hot as hell. *Damn.* Eric stared. He couldn't think well enough to do anything else. Not even the most basic things like breathing and blinking.

She stopped in front of him, her expression tight with displeasure, and touched the center of his chest with a ruler. "Mr. Sticks, I need to see you in my office." The ruler caught him under the chin, encouraging his eyes to settle on hers. "*Now*, Mr. Sticks."

She spun around and strode back to the bedroom. He got a flash of her bare ass before her flippy little skirt settled in place.

"Oh God," Trey said, slamming his head against the upper bank of kitchen cabinets. "I practically gave her to you."

Eric tripped over his feet as he raced after Rebekah. Heart hammering, he entered the bedroom and closed the door, leaning against it for support. She was pacing the room, his essay in one hand, the ruler in the other. Was she going to hit him with that ruler? God, he hoped so. He wished he could take his paper away and add that new fantasy to his list: *spank me with ruler*. His heart thudded harder and harder as he watched her read his essay, using the end of her ruler to keep her place as she paced back and forth near the foot of the bed. He couldn't read her expression. He'd written pretty kinky stuff on those pages. Did it freak her out?

"This, Mr. Sticks, is a monstrosity," she said.

Oh shit.

She read his words from the page. "I want your fingers up my ass while you suck my cock, rubbing some spot in there like that one time when Myrna sucked off Brian in the hotel bathroom."

Eric was simultaneously appalled and excited to hear her read it aloud.

"That is a run-on sentence, Eric. It will never do."

She was grading his sentence structure? *Seriously?*

"I've never seen a guy come so hard," she read. She shook her head. "Pathetic grammar."

"I never *saw* a guy come so hard?" he attempted to correct himself.

She smiled at him. "That's better. Unbutton your pants. Show me what you want me to suck."

He couldn't get his cock out of his pants fast enough. She ran her ruler gently down his sensitive length, and he shuddered.

"Why are you so hard, Eric?" she asked.

He gasped excitedly and closed his eyes so he could concentrate well enough to speak. "Because you're so hot, Rebekah." He opened his eyes and reached for her, but she stopped him by poking him in the chest with her ruler.

"Ms. Blake," she corrected. "Take off all your clothes. I want to see if the rest of you is as fine-looking as that long, hard cock."

She watched him appraisingly as he stripped. When he stood before her naked, she ran her palm over his flesh, as if inspecting him for flaws. His belly quivered beneath her touch.

"Yes," she purred. "Perfect. Looking at your body makes my

pussy sopping wet, Mr. Sticks. How naughty of you. You should try to be less sexy. It's not proper to make your teacher want to fuck you."

She'd probably read about how much he liked her to talk dirty. She leaned over, her face inches from his straining cock. "Is this for me?" Her tongue slid out between her soft pink lips and collected the bead of pre-cum glistening at the tip of his cock.

His abs contracted involuntarily.

"Yes," he gasped. "For you. It's hard for you."

Her tongue slid around the rim of his cock head, causing thousands of pleasurable sensations to ripple up his spine. She squatted and tilted her head back so he could watch his cock sink into her sweet little mouth. She sucked him deep until she couldn't swallow any more of his length and then drew back until he popped free of her lips. She rose and sauntered toward the bed. When he moved to follow her, she held a hand in his direction.

"Stay where you are," she said. "I'm not finished with you yet, naughty boy."

He froze and leaned against the surface of the closed door.

"You want my fingers up your ass?" she asked.

He bit his lip and nodded.

"While I do what?"

"Suck my cock."

She collected a pillow from the bed, bending unnecessarily across the mattress as she reached for it. She somehow managed to flip up her skirt to give him a glimpse of her rounded bottom and the white string of her thong. He clutched his hands into tight fists to keep himself put. She hugged the pillow to her chest and opened the drawer next to the bed. She retrieved a tube of lubricant. Was that for him? Was she going to shove her fingers up his ass like he'd mentioned? By the time she tossed the pillow at his feet and knelt on it before him, he was a tangle of nerves and anticipation.

"I've never done this before," she said, looking so beautiful on her knees that he was tempted to take a picture, blow it up to poster-size, and hang it on the underside of the bunk above his. "You'll have to let me know if I find the spot or if I hurt you."

He closed his eyes and nodded. Oh God, she was really going to do it. He'd fantasized about it for months. It probably wouldn't live up to his expectations, but he was eager to find out.

His cock entered the warmth of her mouth. The gentle tug of her suction as she bobbed her head made his balls tighten. Her hand touched the inside of his thigh, and he almost leapt out of his skin. His entire body taut, he breathed heavily to calm himself. Maybe the fantasy was better than reality. Maybe he should stop her now.

She cupped his balls and gently massaged the loose skin, driving him insane with desire. When he relaxed again, her hand moved from his balls, and he heard her squirt lubricant onto her fingers. She urged him to spread his legs wider by pressing on the inside of his thigh with the back of her wrist. He loosened his stance, but tensed when her cool, slippery fingers pressed against his ass.

"Wait," he gasped. Too late. She pressed upward and slid a finger inside him. It felt weird. And somehow satisfying. He relaxed after he became accustomed to the sexy invasion. He grunted in protest when she pulled her finger free. Was she finished?

"I liked it," he admitted, getting caught up in the tug of her lips on his cock as she sucked him. He looked down and found her applying more lube. So she wasn't done.

She slid two fingers inside him this time, filling him in a way he'd never been filled before. When she slid her fingers in and out of him—driving deeper, deeper—he began to tremble uncontrollably. "Oh God, Rebekah," he groaned.

Her fingers moved inside him. Seeking. Pressing forward. He shuddered hard when she found it. "Right there," he sputtered.

She sucked him hard then, rubbing against something inside

him that made him come so hard he could scarcely stay on his feet. His vision blurred as she bobbed her head faster, sucked harder, rubbed and rubbed against a perfect little place she'd discovered. He couldn't stop coming. Excited beyond comprehension, he grabbed the back of her head to hold her still while he spurt into her throat. After his fluids were spent, the pleasurable waves pulsated through the base of his cock, up his ass, and deep inside.

"You have to stop," he panted. "Oh please, oh please." With one hard shudder, he found he was coming again. Not ejaculating, but coming. "*Rebekah?*" His fingers tightened in her hair, and his back arched until the back of his head slammed into the door. And she kept him there, suspended in ecstasy for so long he thought he'd pass out. When his body stilled, she pulled her fingers free, leaving a strange, wet, inside-out feeling in their wake.

She released his cock from her mouth, and he forced his eyes open to look at her.

"Are you okay?" she asked.

His response in the affirmative was no more than the flutter of his lashes as his eyes tried to roll into the back of his head.

"Did I do it right?"

He slid down the door, his feet sliding out from under him, and collected her in a tight hug when she came within reach. "Mmmm," he murmured, his thoughts languid and body exhausted. "Love you," he managed and landed a kiss somewhere on her head.

"Love you too. Are you finished for the night?"

He shook his head. "Give me a minute. That was fucking incredible."

He held her as he caught his breath. After a long while, she pulled away and climbed to her feet. Looking at her in that hot little outfit, with those geeky glasses and her hair coming loose from its knot, had his cock stirring with renewed interest.

"Get up, stand at the end of the bed, and don't move," she said. "I'm going to wash my hands, and then I'm going to show you how hot and wet my pussy is for you right now. You are going to watch me make myself come as punishment for making me want you."

Oh, hell yeah. She really had read his essay. Eric climbed to his feet and stood facing the end of the bed to wait. He squirmed. Still wet with lubricant, his ass felt really weird. That anal probe had totally lived up to his expectations. Wow. No wonder Brian had married Myrna.

Rebekah left the room. It felt like an eternity before she finally returned. Jace was with her. Eric's heart skipped a beat. He'd participated in threesomes with Aggie and Jace. He'd mentioned them in his essay. Described how good it felt to have Jace's cock sliding against his while they'd both been buried inside Aggie. Shit. He wished he hadn't mentioned that. Eric hoped Rebekah didn't plan on hooking up with Jace. Eric didn't care how hot threesomes were or how much pleasure a woman might receive when stuffed with two cocks. Eric was not sharing Rebekah with anyone. Not even his best friend.

Jace crouched at Eric's feet and fastened a thick leather cuff around his ankle. Jace secured the cuff to the leg of the bed with a chain.

Eric scowled. "What are you—"

Rebekah cracked him on the ass with her ruler. "Quiet," she demanded. "He's helping me make sure you don't participate while I pleasure myself."

After both of Eric's ankles were secured to opposite legs of the bed, Jace bound Eric's wrists together behind his back. He secured Eric's ankles together with a short chain and then fastened another chain behind Eric's back to connect his wrists to the chain between his ankles.

"He won't be able to bend forward," Jace said.

Eric tried it. Just an inch of bending, and Eric's shoulders and hamstrings protested in pain. "He's right."

"If he tries to squat, he'll lose his balance and fall," Jace said. "His knees and ankles will hurt like a son of a bitch."

Eric would take his word on that one.

"And if he stands there like a good boy?" Rebekah asked.

Jace grinned, his typical cuteness overshadowed by the wicked gleam in his eyes. "He doesn't have a choice." He handed something to Rebekah. "Use these if you really want to drive him insane."

Eric tried to see what they were doing behind him.

"How does this work?" she asked.

Jace leaned close to whisper into her ear. Eric could see him demonstrating something, but he couldn't turn his head far enough to see much.

"Thanks, Jace," she said.

Jace shook his head as he inspected his handiwork. "Damn, I miss Aggie." He let himself out of the room.

Eric glanced behind his back at Rebekah. "What did he give you?"

She moved to stand beside him and leaned against his side. "Things for punishing naughty boys."

He felt something against his ass. "What?"

With one motion, she filled his ass with something hard and cold and just thick enough to keep him aware of its possession.

She massaged the plug she'd inserted in his ass until he squirmed, and his cock was as hard as granite.

"You like that, don't you? Admit it. It feels good to have that inside."

"Yeah. I like it."

She stepped behind him, her skirt brushing against his restrained hands. She slid a cock ring in place, moving it all the way to the base of his erection and then fastened some leather harness around his balls and connected it to the cock ring.

She stroked his cock until it was so swollen it ached. The butt plug, the harness around his nuts, and the cock ring took him to that instant right before climax and held him there. He groaned in torment.

Rebekah crawled onto the bed in front of him. She stretched out on her back and spread her legs. Unfortunately, he couldn't see under her skirt, and when he bent slightly to catch a glimpse, his restraints had him straightening in an instant. Still fully clothed, if you considered her revealing outfit clothes, Rebekah massaged both breasts.

Her hand slid down her belly and under her skirt. She rubbed her clit through her panties. The sound of her juicy pussy begging to be filled made Eric's cock throb painfully. Her hand disappeared into her panties, and he knew she was sliding her fingers into her body, but his view was obstructed.

"Show me, Rebekah," he pleaded. "I want to see."

"Do you want to see my fingers sliding in and out of my slick pussy?"

"Yes."

"They feel good in there," she whispered, her panties moving with the movement of her hand. "I'm so turned on by my naughty boy that I think I might come soon."

"I wanna see when you come."

"Oh, I'm so wet and swollen and hot, Eric. You make me that way."

"Take your panties off," he requested. This was driving him crazy.

"I'm gonna come," she gasped. "Oh. Oh."

She shuddered hard, her body writhing across the mattress, and he couldn't see a damned thing. "Rebekah," he gasped. He understood now why she'd restrained him. She wanted to torture him until he died from lack of gratification.

"I want your cock inside me," she said. She moved to her

hands and knees and backed up to the end of the bed where he stood. She tugged her panties to one side and rocked backward, seeking his cock. He watched in torturous bliss as she missed continually. The fact that he couldn't do anything but watch and wait for her to find him drove him to distraction. She didn't seem to improve her aim at all. She kept bumping her hot slit against his oversensitized cock head, not letting him sink into her body.

"I can't take much more of this," he growled.

He slid into her an inch. He gasped, his head dropping back in bliss. She rocked back and forth, taking him shallow. He wanted to plunge forward, but couldn't without risking injury, so he had to stand still and let her have her way. His balance was already compromised by the restraints, and the movement of the bus as it climbed a hill put him in further jeopardy of falling.

She crawled forward after a moment and turned around. "I bet I taste good," she said. "What do you think?"

"I know you taste good."

She sucked her cum off the head of his cock. He could feel the beginning pulsations of orgasm at the base of his dick, but he couldn't attain the release he so desperately needed.

"You're right. I do taste good," she said. "Would you like to watch me eat out another girl?"

He thought about his answer carefully, because he, like most any guy, had fantasized about watching two sexy girls get it on. But he, unlike most guys, had witnessed it more times than he could count. He'd loved the experience every time but had no desire to see Rebekah's sweet mouth on anyone but him. Not even another girl. "No," he said after a moment.

She seemed surprised by his answer. "I thought that would be your ultimate fantasy."

"You and me alone. That's my ultimate fantasy."

She smiled. "Oh, naughty boy, when you say things like that, I want to fuck you even more."

"Have I been punished enough?" he asked breathlessly.

"No."

She peeled her panties off and spread out before him on her back again. This time he could watch her fingers rub her clit and disappear inside her silky pussy over and over and over again. It took her forever to come, and when she finally did, he figured she'd let him off the hook. Nope. She kept right on pleasing herself as if he didn't exist, and his needs didn't matter.

"Rebekah!"

She lifted her head. "What?"

"Can I come now?"

She glanced at his cock and licked her lips. "Damn, you're swollen," she said, "but no, not yet."

She retrieved one of her vibrators from the side table drawer. When she plunged it inside her pussy, Eric's entire body went taut. "This is too cruel," he muttered.

"You didn't think punishment would be fun, did you?"

"Yeah, actually."

"So this isn't turning you on? I thought you liked to watch."

"Yes, it does, and I do, but I'd rather participate."

"I don't remember reading that in your essay."

"I don't remember writing anything about restraints and butt plugs and cock rings either."

"That's true. Okay, I'll remove one thing. You choose."

"Arm restraints. My shoulders are starting to ache."

He breathed a sigh of relief when she climbed from the bed and started unfastening the restraint on his left arm. His shoulders weren't really aching, but if his arms were free, he could put an end to this ceaseless torment. When his arm came free, he resisted the urge to grab her. She surprised him by removing his other wrist cuff and then squatting down to free his ankles too.

"Why are you releasing me?" he asked as the last restraint fell free.

"Because your naughty teacher can't wait any longer. She wants you to fuck her now."

He picked her up and tossed her in the center of the bed. She laughed until she saw the intense expression on his face. He climbed on top of her and plunged deep with one hard thrust. Her pussy had never felt hotter or tighter. He thrust into her hard and deep, finding that if he ground his hips, it moved that plug in his ass in ways that made him quiver inside.

"Oh God," he groaned, having never experienced this level of pleasure. It felt like he was coming, but the feeling never abated. Instead, each gyrating thrust intensified it. Made him feel like he was coming harder. And harder. How?

Still thrusting, Eric unbuttoned Rebekah's sexy little suit jacket and shoved it open. Finding his progress impeded by a white blouse, he ripped it open and grabbed her breasts. Pushing them together, he tried to fit them both in his seeking mouth, bra and all. Rebekah arched her back and reached behind to unclasp the garment. She fought with her clothes, trying to get naked. Watching her thrash around impatiently fueled him to thrust faster.

"Oh God, Eric. Your cock is so huge." She managed to get one arm out of her suit jacket and blouse. She grabbed his hair and pulled.

He winced in pain. Fucked her harder.

"Pull my hair, Eric."

When he complied, her body buckled, and she came. He shuddered as he tried to come with her, but the cock ring held his release back. His vision blurred as pleasure coursed through him and then receded enough to let him keep going. "Oh dear God, thank you for inventing the orgasm."

Rebekah chuckled. "I second that."

"And the cock ring."

"Hallelujah!"

He continued to plunge into Rebekah's spent body until his next orgasm gripped him. This one was hard enough to make him spurt despite the tight ring around the base of his cock. He almost passed out, it was so intense. He clung to his woman, crying out in bliss, and then collapsed on top of her, breathing hard from his exertions.

She trailed a lazy hand up and down the sweat-drenched skin of his back. "Has my naughty boy been sufficiently punished?" she asked, kissing his shoulder tenderly.

"Ask me that again in an hour." He snuggled his face against her neck. "Right now, I can't even move."

Luckily, she didn't seem to mind that he was squashing her beneath him. "Eric?"

"Yeah?"

"We're going to keep seeing each other even when we're not on tour, right?"

"Of course."

"Do you live in LA?"

"I'm kind of out in the country actually."

"Really? Can I come visit you?"

He was almost asleep, so he spoke without thinking, "I'd prefer if you just stayed with me the entire six weeks."

"Okay," she agreed immediately.

"*Okay?*" He lifted his head to look at her. He figured she'd protest. At least a little.

She smiled and nodded. "Make sure you bring all our costumes. I plan on working through your entire essay and then giving you some new things to fantasize about."

Chapter 21

Eric pushed the button to open the garage and waited for the door to lift. He glanced at Rebekah, unable to wipe the smile off his face. He'd always believed in luck, just not his own. And now, with this woman in his life, he felt like the luckiest man in the world.

"I've got to ask," she said, straining to look at the house through the window. "What's with the Pollyanna house and the white picket fence?"

His heart sank. "You don't like it?"

"It's great. For someone's grandmother. But you're a young, hot, very hot, single-but-taken, hot, did I mention hot, man."

He laughed at her description and then shrugged. "I liked it, so I bought it." He'd always wanted to live in a big Victorian-styled house with intricate woodwork, a huge porch, a picket fence, and a tire swing in a big oak tree, so when he'd found this place, he had to buy it. Not that he was home often. Not that it didn't remind him that he had no one to share it with. Not that it wasn't frivolous and huge and expensive. But he had hoped Rebekah would like it as much as he did. He wasn't sure why that was important to him.

When they pulled into the garage, she gasped. He followed her gaze over his shoulder. "Is that a '68 Camaro?" she squealed.

She didn't like his showcase house, but liked the rusted out, beat-up muscle car that wouldn't start. He had to chuckle. "Yeah. That's my next project. After I finish the Corvette."

"Let's get to work!"

She climbed out of the car and went to inspect his tools and the spare Corvette parts scattered across the bench along one wall of the garage. "You have every part imaginable here!"

"Yeah, I wasn't sure what I needed, so anytime I find parts for this model, I buy them automatically."

Rebekah opened the Corvette's hood and peered at the engine. "I can't wait to get started, but the engine's too hot."

Was it possible for this woman to be any more perfect? He didn't think so. "Let's take your stuff into the house," he said, dropping a kiss on the back of her neck. "Are you hungry?"

She looked up. "Not really."

"Horny?"

Her grin made his heart stutter. "Getting that way."

Eric grabbed his duffel bag and Rebekah's overnight bag out of his trunk and unlocked the door between the garage and the kitchen.

She stepped inside and looked around the huge kitchen with its white cabinetry and chef-sized appliances.

"You don't cook, do you?"

He shook his head.

She smiled. "How many bedrooms does this place have?"

"Why don't we try them all, and you can count them?"

"Six?"

"Seven," he admitted.

"There's something I'm missing here," she said, wandering farther into the kitchen and setting her purse on the pristine slate countertop at the breakfast bar. "It looks like Martha Stewart lives here." She examined the bowl of fruit on the counter.

"You don't like it?"

"I didn't say that. It's a spectacular house. Just not what I was expecting."

"What were you expecting?"

She laughed. "I dunno. That you live in your mother's basement?"

Eric grimaced.

She misinterpreted his pain for insult. "I'm sorry. You're probably a millionaire or something." Rebekah snapped her fingers. "I've got it. You inherited it from your great-aunt Edna."

He shook his head, unexpectedly sad that he didn't have a great-aunt Edna to inherit from. Rebekah crossed the room and snuggled against him, craning her neck to look at him. "What's the matter?"

He shook his head again. He'd never felt lonely in this house until now. And for once, he wasn't even alone.

"Why don't you give me a tour?"

He guided her through all three floors, showing her his storybook house with its perfect furnishings and its perfect decor, and for the first time, recognizing his house for the fantasy it was.

She was sufficiently impressed and even insisted that she loved the place. They ended up in the huge family room filled with the musical instruments he owned.

"Can you play all these?" she asked.

"Yeah."

"Really? Why so many?"

"I like them all."

"Eric?"

He looked up but stared over her head.

"I thought we weren't going to lie to each other," she pressed.

"It's not a lie. I do like them all."

When she didn't say anything for several minutes, he lowered his gaze to meet her eyes.

"I just realized I don't know anything about you," she said.

"You know all the important stuff."

"I don't think so. This house, it's perfect—like a fairy tale—but there's nothing personal here. Where are the pictures of your family? Your memories?"

"I don't have any."

"What do you mean? Do you have amnesia?"

He'd have laughed if he had any air in his lungs. Eric clenched his teeth, flexing a muscle in his jaw until it ached. "I mean, I don't have a family."

"No one?"

He shook his head.

"Did they die?"

"What's with the third degree all of a sudden, Reb?"

"When we're on tour with the band, it's easy to think of you as Eric Sticks, the famous and sensationally talented drummer of Sinners, but here, you're just a man."

He scoffed. "Just a man, huh?"

"Just the man I love. I want to know more about you, Eric. Tell me."

He sat on a piano bench and leaned his forearms on his thighs. He clasped his hands and stared at his thumbs as he considered how much he should tell her.

She sat beside him and nudged his knee with hers.

"No one knows who my father was. My mom was a junkie. She left me when I was four. She's probably dead."

"She left you?"

"Yeah, left me. I was put into foster care."

"So you're adopted?"

He shook his head. "No one wanted to adopt me. I got into a lot of trouble. They moved me around a lot—one home after another. And if they didn't move me, I ran away."

Rebekah slid a hand along his lower back. "That explains this house."

"I guess."

"But not the music."

He glanced around at the various instruments he cherished. "I had an inspiring music teacher in elementary school. Music came naturally to me. I think I'm hardwired for it. She saw that talent and encouraged me. I'd have done anything for her praise. She doted on me when I played music, so I became obsessed with it. I was only in her class for a few months, but after that, I sought music. Each time I started a new music class at a new school, I lied about what instrument I knew how to play and picked a new one until I could play everything I got my hands on. Most schools loan instruments to poor kids. Did you know that?"

"They used to. I think a lot of schools are cutting their music programs for lack of funds."

Eric made a mental note to check on the programs at local schools and offer a huge donation of musical instruments if they needed them. "I don't think I'd be alive today if it weren't for those programs."

"So music was the only constant in your life?"

He contemplated her question. "Yeah, I guess so. Even now, with Sinners."

She reached up to touch his face. He expected pity when he looked into her eyes, but saw only tenderness. "I want to be a constant in your life, Eric."

"Are you sure?" He grinned. "I'm kind of a pain in the ass."

"I don't think so. Everything you've ever done to my ass has felt really good."

He laughed. Rebekah accepted him. His past. Relief hit him suddenly, and he laughed some more. Eric fell off the piano bench, gripping his stomach with both arms, and tried to catch his breath between laughs. Eventually, he rolled onto his back and looked at the tray ceiling. "This house is pretty ridiculous, isn't it?"

Rebekah climbed off the bench, snuggled against his side, and laid her head on his heaving chest. "No. It fills a hole inside you. And the car does too. Are you sure you want to finish fixing it?"

"Of course. I can't wait to see you covered with grease."

"It won't make you sad to see it complete?"

"Maybe a little, but that's where the Camaro comes in."

"And after that?"

"You pick our next project."

"I want you to meet my parents," she said unexpectedly.

Eric's heart skipped several beats. "That's a bad idea, Reb. Parents don't like me. Not even my own."

"You're important to me, Eric. I want to show you off."

"Trying to get back at your father for repressing you as a teen?" he teased.

"Well, my dad is a minister, but he's never been repressive. My mother, on the other hand…" She laughed. "That's not why though. I love you, and I want them to love you too."

Was she seriously offering the one thing he thought he'd never have? A family?

"Okay," he said.

"Yeah?"

He nodded.

"What are you doing for Thanksgiving?" she asked.

He shrugged. "Nothing that I know of." Thanksgiving was a week away. It would give him time to get used to the idea of meeting her parents. Between now and then, Reb could teach him which fork he was supposed to use for salad.

"We always get together and help serve at the local homeless shelter before our family dinner. Will you come?"

He smiled. He actually enjoyed doing community service. He'd gotten into enough trouble as a youth that it had been required of him several times. Even though he kept out of trouble most of the time in his old age, he still liked to help.

"Sounds fun."

"We'll stop by the shelter and sign up tomorrow."

"I should sign up the guys too. I'm sure they aren't doing anything important for Thanksgiving." And they could protect him from Rebekah's parents, if necessary.

"Perfect. I'll call my mom right now and let her know we'll be over for dinner."

She took her cell phone out of her pocket and dialed her parent's house.

"Dave!" she said when someone picked up on the other end. "How are you?"

Eric could hear a bit of Dave's voice, but not his words. "I can't wait to see you," she said. "Can you let Mom know I'll be over for dinner Saturday evening?"

Eric stiffened. Saturday? Saturday wasn't Thanksgiving.

"Yeah, and tell her I'm bringing someone special." She paused. "Yeah, it's a guy. No, I'm not telling you who. You'll have to wait and see."

She shifted her body to hold Eric down when he tried to get up.

"I've got to go. Don't forget to tell Mom." She paused. "I love you too."

"Saturday?" Eric said. "I thought I was going to meet them on Thanksgiving."

"You'll see them again on Thanksgiving. You'll probably see a lot of them. They're my family, and you're my guy."

Oh no, she was using that smile he couldn't resist. *Stick to your guns, Eric. You can do it. Tell her you're busy Saturday.* "I've got stuff… to do… on Saturday."

"What kind of stuff?"

"Work on the car!" he said as he fabricated his excuse.

"We'll work on the car tonight and tomorrow. Eric, this is important. Please say you'll come with me."

He sighed heavily. "Okay. I'll go. But I'm warning you again. Parents do not like me."

"Doesn't matter. I like you."

She smiled and slid up his body to kiss him. Soon her tender kiss turned deep and passionate. "Did you bring any costumes in the house?"

"Just the rock star one."

Her breath caught, and he could practically see her inventing a naughty scenario. Dear lord, he loved this woman. He'd never let anything take her away from him.

"Will you play your drums for me?" she asked.

"Why?" He chuckled. "You hear me play them practically every night."

"Yeah, from the middle of a stadium as part of my job. I want to show you what I want to do to you when you're onstage playing before a crowd of thousands."

"You want to do stuff to me when I'm onstage?" He shifted his head to look at her.

"You're not the only one with fantasies, you know."

"Tell me."

"How about you start playing and I'll show you."

As if he could say no to that. He climbed to his feet and sat behind his ancient drum kit. The one he'd found in a junkyard in the eighth grade and hid in an abandoned warehouse because his foster family at the time had insisted rock 'n' roll was the devil's music. He hadn't lasted long in that house, but he'd held onto the drums for over fourteen years.

"Did you say your dad was a minister?" Eric reached for his drumsticks.

"You did not just ask me about my dad when I'm thinking about jumping your bones, did you?"

He glanced over his shoulder sheepishly to find her scowling. "Sorry."

"Yes, he's a minister."

Eric cringed.

Rebekah lifted an eyebrow. "You better start looking sexy, or I'm going in the garage to start tearing an engine apart."

He shed his leather vest and peeled off his white T-shirt. "How's that?"

"It's a start."

He found the bass drum pedal with one foot and the high-hat pedal with his other. It had been awhile since he'd only used one bass drum. He used three when he played onstage. "What should I play?"

"Something slow and sexy."

"You know I don't do slow, sweetheart."

"Try."

Since there was only one Sinners' song that was remotely slow, their ballad "Goodbye Is Not Forever," he started with that. When Rebekah pressed against his back and let her hands roam over his chest and belly, he closed his eyes and concentrated on the mixture of rhythm and sensation. He soon abandoned the song and let her touch dictate how he thumped the bass, tapped his cymbals, hit the snare, or followed a progression around the various tom-toms in his kit. He usually wailed on the skins as hard as possible, but he kept his pounding to a minimum so it wasn't uncomfortably loud. Just rhythmic.

Sensual.

Rebekah's lips pressed against his shoulder. She kissed a path to his ear, matching his tempo with each sucking press of her lips.

Eric shuddered. Mixing his three loves—music, sex, and this woman—stole his ability to think beyond the moment. The rhythm consumed him. He allowed it to rule his current existence.

Rebekah's fingers found the tiny hoop in his left nipple. She rubbed her thumb over it, tugging it gently with the beat he set.

His cock began to rise, hardening in pulsations that matched the rhythm. When Rebekah drew away, he gasped in protest.

Her T-shirt landed on one cymbal, her bra on his cowbell. Then she was against his back again, the hardened tips of her naked breasts pressing into his flesh. She rocked against him, rubbing her nipples into his back. "I love the tattoo on your back," she said.

She probably wouldn't if she knew what the fiery crack in the earth and the demon hand emerging from it symbolized.

Her lips returned to his neck. Her left thumb to his piercing. Her right hand slid south. She released the top button of his fly on one beat, the next button on the next beat. When his fly was open, she slid her hand into his underwear and freed his cock.

He'd already lost himself to the beat, didn't think it was possible to feel it more than he already did, but her hand circled him and began to move along his length. Up on one beat, down on the next. There wasn't a solitary cell in his body that wasn't consumed by the rhythm.

"Rebekah," he gasped.

"Shhhhh. Just feel it. What your rhythm does to me. What I want to do to you every time you play."

Man, he would never play without a boner again.

He increased his tempo slightly, so she'd stroke his cock faster. She followed his lead without hesitation.

Faster.

Faster.

Oh. She moved away abruptly, and his entire body shuddered with unfulfilled desire. He heard her release the zipper of her jeans behind him and the rustle of fabric as she removed the rest of her clothes. He turned his head when she appeared beside him and stumbled over a beat. She ducked under his arm and climbed over one leg to stand before him, beautiful and naked.

He slowed his tempo again and stared into her eyes, wondering what she'd do next. Knowing no matter what it was, he would like it. Her fingers slid into his hair, and she tugged him to her breast. He latched on with his mouth and sucked in time with the beat.

"That's it," she whispered. She released his hair and lowered her hands, her fingertips resting against the head of his cock. When she tapped her fingers against his sensitive flesh, his belly tightened with excitement.

"Mmm." He sucked harder on her nipple.

He released her nipple and looked at her, his eyelids heavy, his breathing ragged. She bent and grabbed his shaft in both hands. Her thumbs bumped over the rim repeatedly, still keeping time with his beat.

"I want you inside me, Eric Sticks."

"What are you waiting for?" he murmured.

"Can you keep your balance?"

He grinned. "Only one way to find out."

He paused in his drumming while she climbed onto his lap, facing him. She wrapped both arms around his neck and kissed him hungrily. He shifted his, drumsticks to one hand and then grabbed his cock to seek her slick heat. When he found her, she sank down, taking him deep. He wobbled on the little stool, then tightened the muscles of his thighs, back, and stomach to maintain balance. Good thing he was in great shape from all that drumming, or he wouldn't have been able to hold his position. He shifted forward on his stool a few inches, and she sank deeper.

They gasped into each other's mouths.

His jeans cut into his flesh, but somehow, that discomfort made him crave the pleasure offered by her body all the more.

Rebekah deepened her kiss, her fingers digging into his scalp. Feet on the floor, she began to rise and fall over him.

His toe found his bass drum pedal, and he matched her rhythm with a low, steady beat. Instead of hammering out a beat with his arms, he wrapped them around her, drumsticks caught in his fist against her back.

She drew away, staring into his eyes while she made love to him. He couldn't look away. Even as he increased their tempo by speeding up the bass drum beat and his release approached, he couldn't tear his gaze from the love shining from her baby blue eyes.

How had he lived a single day without her? What would he do

if he ever lost her? Overcome by emotions, he squeezed his eyes shut and concentrated on the pleasure building inside.

"Oh," she gasped and arched backward as her body shuddered with release.

He held onto her for dear life, partly because he didn't want to fall off the stool, and partly because he let himself follow her in bliss. As his fluids pumped into her, he rubbed his open mouth against her collarbone, lost in ecstasy. She went limp against him, and he stiffened his leg just in time to stop them from tumbling to the floor. A cymbal crashed as the drum kit slid forward and hit a boom.

"Wow," she breathed. "That was hot."

He made some incoherent sound of agreement.

"One fantasy down. Five million to go."

He chuckled. "Only five million?"

"For now." She kissed his jaw. "Ready to work on the car?"

"Can't I take a nap first?" he whispered drowsily.

"If you need to. I can work on it myself for a while."

He shook his head. "I want to help. Just give me an hour or two to catch my breath, woman."

She tried to climb off his lap, but he held her in place. She relented and snuggled against him again. It was much easier to maintain his balance when she held still, and he wasn't ready to let her go just yet.

"Eric?" she said after a long moment.

"Yeah."

"I have to get an MRI the first week of December to… see if I'm still healthy. Will you come with me? Isaa—um, that *other* guy used to go with me. I don't like to go by myself. Waiting for the results is really…" she sniffed, "…hard."

Eric held his breath and nodded. He bit his bottom lip to stop its trembling, his heart clogging his throat. His hand moved to the back of her head to press her closer, so she wouldn't see the tears blurring his vision. He wanted to be there for her, but all he could think when confronted by her mortality was no. *No!* Rebekah didn't really need an MRI. Her body wouldn't betray her again. It couldn't. He wouldn't let it. Wouldn't even accept the possibility that she could get sick again. She could not leave him. He would not lose her before she turned a hundred and twenty-three. Or ever. He needed her. *Needed* her. Not just now. Always. She couldn't go. She just couldn't.

"Thank you," she whispered. "I'm not strong enough to face this alone."

And he wasn't strong enough to face it at all. "Let's go work on the car."

Chapter 22

REBEKAH SQUEEZED ERIC'S HAND and opened the front door of her parents' house. The guy looked like he was about to ralph all over his shoes, and Rebekah couldn't really blame him. Her father was laid-back and easygoing, but her mother? She wouldn't wish that woman on anyone. Rebekah smiled at Eric reassuringly and squeezed his hand again.

"Anybody home?" she called into the foyer.

Her mouth fell open when Dave wheeled himself through the dining room door. "Hey, little sis!"

"Dave!" she released Eric's hand and squeezed Dave's neck excitedly as she hugged him. "You look great!" She planted a big wet kiss on his temple. "How's your recovery going?"

"I've got about seventy-five percent usage in my left arm. Ninety percent in the right." He wriggled his fingers and made a fist. "They still say I'm not going to walk again."

"I say they're full of shit," Eric said with a grin.

Dave grinned back. "Sticks? When Rebekah said she was bringing a guy home, I was sure it would be Mills."

"I managed to snag the best one," Rebekah said. She sauntered over to Eric and grabbed him around the neck to draw him to her waiting lips.

Someone cleared her throat in the dining room. "Not only do you bring riffraff into my home," Mom said, "but you engage in inappropriate behavior with it right before my eyes."

Rebekah rolled her eyes for Eric's benefit and then turned to face her mother. "And he gave me a little tongue too," she said.

She glanced at Eric, expecting him to participate in her teasing, but he looked entirely shell-shocked.

"Mom, this is Eric Sticks, the drummer of Sinners," Dave said.

"Sinners. The band who practically kidnapped my daughter and exposed her to only God knows what? The band who paralyzed my only son?"

"The man who saved Dave's life with CPR," Rebekah said.

Mom snorted. "I guess he can stay since he's already here." She turned her back and returned to the kitchen.

"She's a little prickly tonight," Dave whispered.

"A *little*?" Rebekah squeezed Eric's elbow. "Don't let her get to you."

Eric shook his head slightly.

"So how are things going with the tour, Reb?" Dave asked nonchalantly.

"As good as can be expected, considering you're not there," Rebekah said.

"She's being modest," Eric said. "She's absolutely amazing."

Dave grinned with pride.

"Not as good as Dave is though," Rebekah said, ruffling her brother's hair and bending to smother him with another hug.

"It's okay that you're great, Reb," Dave said. "You don't have to feel guilty. I'm proud of you."

She didn't know why her eyes were suddenly leaky. Maybe because she did feel guilty. She was off having the time of her life, making a career for herself, finding love, while Dave was stuck here in a wheelchair with their oppressive mother.

"Is that my little girl I hear?" her dad called from the living room.

She released Dave and grabbed Eric's hand. "Come on," she said. "I want you to meet my dad."

"The minister?" Eric said.

"No, the poodle trainer." She shook her head. "Yes, the minister. I only have one dad, you know."

Eric followed her with heavy feet.

"I thought I heard your voice," her dad said, a huge smile on his jovial face. His smile faltered when he caught sight of Eric.

Eric's palm grew damp against Rebekah's hand, but she held it tightly.

"Who's this?"

"This is Eric," she said. "My new boyfriend."

Her father pressed his recliner's footrest down and climbed to his feet. He craned his neck to appraise Eric carefully. "Don't you think he's a bit... *tall* for you, sweetheart?"

"Nope. He's perfect for me." She hugged Eric's arm and smiled happily.

Her dad's eyes roamed her face, and then he smiled. "I trust he takes good care of you and treats you well?"

"Like a princess."

Dad extended his hand toward Eric, who for once was speechless. He took Dad's hand and shook it firmly. "Nice to meet you, Father Blake."

"Likewise, Eric. Have a seat." He waved at the empty recliner situated next to his. "Tell me about yourself."

Eric glanced at Rebekah uncertainly. Her heart melted into a puddle. She released his hand and patted him on the back reassuringly. "You can talk to my dad about anything. He doesn't judge."

"I leave the judging to God," her dad said and returned to his recliner.

Eric looked like he was about to bolt.

"Sit," Rebekah insisted. She knew her dad would love Eric once they got to talking. Her father would appreciate Eric's open honesty and quirky sense of humor.

Dave wheeled himself into the room and arranged his

wheelchair next to the unoccupied recliner. "Rebekah, Mom's got a surprise for you in the kitchen."

"What kind of surprise?"

"Go see. Dad and I will keep Eric company."

Rebekah nodded. She'd never once in her life liked any surprise her mother had for her. She was fairly certain she wasn't going to like this one either. She gave Eric's hand a squeeze of encouragement and then turned to head for the kitchen. Before she was even back in the foyer, Eric already had Dave and her father laughing.

She smiled as she walked to the kitchen. She knew it would take awhile for her mother to get used to the idea of her dating Eric. Her mother had been completely enamored with the idea of Isaac becoming her son-in-law. Rebekah doubted her mother would give any man an easy time, but one in a rock band who had tattoos, his nipple pierced, and a strange haircut? Rebekah didn't have her heart set on her mom ever accepting Eric. She didn't care though. She loved Eric with all her heart. If her mother couldn't see what a wonderful man he was, that was her loss, not Rebekah's. Not Eric's.

Rebekah bumped open the swinging door to the kitchen with her hip. "Mom, Dave said you had a surprise for me."

Isaac turned from the counter where he was helping her mother prepare dinner. Rebekah's heart skipped several beats and began to race. "You're back?" she gasped.

Isaac dashed across the kitchen and wrapped both arms around her. He planted a tender kiss on her temple and squeezed her until she was breathless. "Oh Rebekah," he murmured. "I missed you so much."

She caught her mother's expression of glee just before she went into the pantry.

"Isaac," Rebekah said. She tugged away from him to look into his gentle gray eyes. "What are you doing here?"

He was still the handsomest man she'd ever encountered. Wide eyes, straight nose, perfectly sculpted lips, even features, and thick, brown wavy hair framed his face. And his recently acquired tan contrasted nicely with his white dress shirt. The sleeves were rolled up to reveal strong forearms. As attractive as he was, he didn't make her heart race when she looked at him. She didn't experience even a twinge of lust.

"Your mother invited me. You know I can't turn down her homemade biscuits." Isaac searched Rebekah's face and then cupped it with both hands. "You look fantastic, angel."

"I feel great."

"Have you been getting all your medical screenings?" he asked, looking at her with concern.

Touched, she brushed a wavy lock of hair from his forehead. "I have. So far, no signs of it. I have another appointment in December."

She didn't have to say what *it* was. They'd lived through *it* together and come out stronger people on the other side. That bond between them would always exist.

He hugged her again. "I missed you. Did I tell you that yet?"

"Yeah. I missed you too." It wasn't a lie. She had missed him. But as he held her, she realized she'd never really loved him. At least not romantically. Her feelings were the same as they'd always been. That of a really close friend. A friend she could count on to be there for her no matter what. Isaac was her best friend, but they weren't meant to be lovers. She knew that now. Now that she had Eric, she could tell the difference.

Rebekah pulled away from Isaac's embrace and smiled, knowing everything was as it should be. They weren't meant to be together as a couple, but they meant too much to each other to be kept apart. She was really glad to see him, and that was okay. It wasn't a betrayal of her feelings for Eric, because they weren't the same feelings she had for Isaac. Realizing that was such a huge relief, she couldn't help but beam at Isaac. "Tell me all about Africa," she said and took a seat at the counter to listen to him talk about his adventures while he chopped vegetables for their salad. Her admiration grew as he told her about all the people he'd helped while living under abysmal conditions in the bush.

"So the baby survived?" she asked, her eyes wide with wonder.

Isaac nodded. "There was another woman in the village who had lost her baby to cholera, so she took the newborn as her own. I wish I could have saved the mother too, but the crocodile had done too much damage to her spine, and I lost her on the table."

Rebekah's vision blurred with tears. "That's so horrible," she said. "And you. You are absolutely wonderful, Isaac."

A sudden intake of breath alerted her to Eric's presence. He looked like someone had punched him in the stomach. "Eric," she said. "Come here. There's someone I want you to meet."

Eric had wondered who the too-attractive-to-be-believed man was. Rebekah was hanging on his every word like she'd been struck dumb by his charm and charisma. When she'd said his name—*Isaac*—and called him absolutely wonderful, Eric was certain his soul had been sucked from his body. And now Rebekah wanted Eric to meet the guy? No, thank you.

"I was looking for the can," Eric said. A lie, but he in no way wanted to be anywhere near Dr. Perfect over there.

"I'm sure you can hold it for a minute," Rebekah said. She hopped off the stool and took his hand before he could flee the kitchen.

"Eric, this is Isaac. A dear, dear friend."

Isaac looked none too happy to be called her friend. Eric extended his hand. "I'm Eric, Rebekah's very possessive boyfriend."

Isaac's eyes widened.

"And lover," Eric added. "We get it on constantly."

Isaac's tan face paled several shades, but he took Eric's hand and shook it cordially.

"*Eric*," Rebekah chastised. "There is such a thing as need-to-know information, and that definitely wasn't it." She giggled, but didn't deny his claim. Eric felt marginally better.

Rebekah's mother bustled into the kitchen. "Rebekah, help me mash those potatoes," she said. "Isaac, would you get the roast out of the oven? I need to get the biscuits in."

"Sure." Isaac put on a pair of oven mitts and headed for the oven.

"Can I do anything to help?" Eric asked, his heart thudding. Rebekah's mother scared the shit out of him.

"Don't be silly. You're a guest. Go sit down with Bill and Dave until dinner is ready."

"Isaac's a guest too," Rebekah reminded her mother.

Mrs. B offered Isaac a one-armed hug as he struggled not to drop the roast. "Don't be ridiculous, Rebekah. Isaac is family. Just set that on the stove, dear."

Isaac set the roast on the stove.

Eric watched Rebekah drain the potatoes and start whipping them with a mixer. Mrs. B cut biscuits from dough and arranged them on a baking sheet. Isaac took it upon himself to carve the roast. They did look like a family. Something Eric had never had, but had always wanted. He wouldn't be getting one now either it seemed.

Dave bumped the door open with his wheelchair. "Come on, Sticks. I need help setting the table." Dave pulled plates and bowls from a china cabinet and set them on his immobile legs.

Eric smiled, grateful for a task.

"David Adam Blake, don't ask Rebekah's guest to do your work," Mrs. B said.

"I don't mind," Eric insisted.

"Go sit down in the living room," Mrs. B said.

Eric had no choice but to obey.

Father Blake, or Bill, as he insisted Eric call him, looked up from his war movie when Eric sat in the empty recliner beside him. "Did you get shooed out of the kitchen?"

Eric nodded. "Apparently I'm a guest, but Isaac is family."

Bill chuckled. "Isaac *is* family." He patted Eric's forearm. "Great kid. He's a doctor, you know."

"Yeah, Reb mentioned that."

"He just got back from Africa. He said taking over his father's practice could wait a year. Wanted to go where people needed him most. You don't come across many men as selfless as Isaac in this day and age."

True, but Eric still hated him.

"Dinner's ready!" Mrs. B called.

Eric rose to his feet. Mrs. B steered him to the end of the table. "Guests get the seat of honor," she said.

Eric sat at the far end of the long table, and Bill sat at the opposite end. A chair had been removed from the side of the table to accommodate Dave's wheelchair, and his mother sat beside him. That left Rebekah and Isaac to sit next to each other. The dinner was delicious, but though Eric ate everything on his plate, he scarcely tasted it.

Everyone was so enthusiastic for Isaac's tales of Africa, which were amusing and heroic. Eric couldn't deny it. He felt like an unwanted outsider. Rebekah scarcely glanced at him the entire meal. She was too busy laughing with and fawning over Isaac, who was so fucking charming, it was nauseating. When Isaac started passing around pictures of himself treating the sick and wounded in some village in the Congo, Eric said all the appropriate things, but his heart sank. How could he compete with that? He'd never done anything remotely honorable. After dinner, Mrs. B brought out a cheesecake smothered in cherries.

"I know it's your favorite," she said, beaming at Isaac as she served him a huge slice.

"You're spoiling me," he said, his knockout smile charming even Eric.

Fuck. The guy could at least have the decency to be ugly or stupid or boring. Something!

"It's the least I can do for our heroic, life-saving physician."

"Seems to me Isaac isn't the only lifesaver at this table," Dave said. He grinned at Eric, who shook his head slightly, not wanting to bring up his little attempts at CPR.

"Oh yeah?" Isaac questioned, looking genuinely interested in what Dave had to say, the bastard. It was really difficult for Eric to maintain his hatred for the guy. "What happened?"

"Eric saved two lives this year alone," Dave said. "One of them mine."

Eric stared at the slice of cheesecake in front of him and speared a cherry repeatedly. "It was nothing. Anyone would have done the same."

"That's not true," Isaac said. "Most people look the other way when someone is in trouble, even if they're capable of helping. They just… don't."

Eric poked at his cheesecake, trying hard not to feel pride due to Isaac's words.

"Who else did you save, Eric?" Rebekah asked.

"It was nothing," he said again.

"Trey," Dave said. "He had a seizure, and Eric kept him breathing until the ambulance arrived."

"How have I not heard this story?" Rebekah said, glancing from Eric to Dave, then back to Eric.

Eric shrugged. "Trey doesn't like us to talk about it."

Rebekah leaned closer and whispered, "And I thought I was witness to the first time you locked lips with Trey." She giggled and squeezed his knee under the table.

Eric stared at her with wide eyes. He prayed no one had heard her little aside.

"Who's Trey?" Isaac asked.

"Sinners' rhythm guitarist," Rebekah said.

"Sinners?"

"Yeah, Eric's band. Sinners."

"So you're in a band? Like a local band or what?" Isaac asked in all seriousness and took another bite of cheesecake.

Rebekah laughed and hugged Isaac's arm. "You're so sheltered! One of the most famous drummers in the world is having dessert with you, and you're totally clueless."

"This guy's famous?" Isaac asked, eyes wide with wonder. "Should I be asking him for his autograph or something?"

This caused Rebekah to laugh even harder. She released Isaac's arm to hold her stomach. "Stop. You're killing me."

Eric thought he was the only one capable of making her laugh that hard. Apparently not.

"So you're a rock star? For real?" Isaac asked. "How'd you meet him, Rebekah?"

"Dave was Sinners' soundboard operator. When he got hurt, they let me fill in until he's back on his feet." She realized her slip a second too late. Her eyes widened, and she whipped her head around to look at her brother. "Oh Dave, I'm sorry I said that. I didn't mean…"

Dave just smiled. "It's okay. I'm hoping they might take me back before I'm literally back on my feet."

"Are you up for touring again?" Eric asked. "You know how grueling it can be."

Dave nodded. "I'm hoping when you go back out in January that I'll be ready to take over most of my duties. Well, those I can do in my chair. I don't think I'll be walking that soon and won't be all that helpful at assembly and teardown. I'll do as much as I'm able to though."

"Don't rush yourself, son," Bill said. "You can stay here with your mother and me for as long as necessary."

Dave and Rebekah exchanged glances and then smiled at their mother.

"I like to work," Dave insisted. "I really miss it. And the guys. I miss them too. How are they all doing?"

"Great!" Eric said. "Me and Reb signed them all up to volunteer this Thanksgiving at the homeless shelter. I can't wait to tell them."

"Awesome. I'll be there," Dave said. "I can't wait to see them again. And I really can't wait to go back on tour."

"Whenever you think you can handle it," Eric said with a smile. It was great to see Dave doing so well.

"But… what about me?" Rebekah asked.

"Reb, you knew your work with the band was temporary from the beginning," Dave said.

She ducked her head, looking entirely defeated. Eric didn't want her to leave, but when Dave was ready to return to work, she'd have to. And then she'd be here with Isaac all the time, while Eric was on the road.

This entire situation sucked.

"I don't like the idea of you on the road with all those sinful, dirty rock stars in the first place, Rebekah," Mrs. B said.

Eric's hackles rose. He had the sudden urge to hit someone.

"As you've told me every other day on the phone, Mother," Rebekah said. "Give it a rest."

"Is it safe?" Isaac asked, glancing at Eric out of the corner of his eye. "They wouldn't hurt you, would they?"

Rebekah rolled her eyes. "The guys are great. All of them. I had a bit of a rocky start with Marcus, but things are going perfectly now."

"Did Marcus give you a hard time?" Dave asked.

"At first," Rebekah admitted. "We're good now. We've come to an understanding. He's stopped trying to sabotage my soundboard, and he even gave your notebook back to me."

"*What?* I'm so going to kick his ass," Dave said. He chuckled.

"Well, maybe I'll have Eric knock him down so I can roll over his fuckin' ass."

"David Adam, watch your language!" Mrs. B said.

"Sorry, Mom," Dave said sheepishly.

"Is everyone finished?" Mrs. B asked.

Eric was so ready to leave it wasn't funny. He stood and picked up his plate. "I've got dishes."

"Don't be ridiculous. Guests don't do dishes," Mrs. B said. "Rebekah, get the dishes."

Rebekah stood to obey her mother, scraping plates and stacking them.

"Why don't you help her, Isaac?" Mrs. B smiled fondly.

"Yes, ma'am."

Eric watched Isaac and Rebekah clear the table, his heart aching. They were so comfortable with each other, sharing quiet words and laughs. He had no doubt it was common for them to be domestic. Like a couple.

"Can I help?" Eric grabbed Rebekah's hand as she collected his empty wineglass. He ran his finger over the butterfly bracelet he'd given her.

She smiled. "Isaac and I have a routine. We'll be done in no time." She leaned close to his ear. "Then we can go home. You look like you're ready to climb out of your skin."

How very observant of her.

"Where's the bathroom?" he asked her.

"There's a powder room off the kitchen."

"I don't need powder," he said.

She laughed and poked him in the ribs. "Joker." She kissed his lips eagerly. The metallic clang of silverware interrupted their exchange. Isaac crouched to retrieve all the silverware he'd just spilled across the floor.

Eric climbed to his feet to find the powder room, whatever the fuck that was. It turned out to be a half-bathroom, though there was a wooden placard on the door denoting it as a powder room.

He took his time using the facilities, needing to collect himself. He was a jumble of conflicting emotions, his stomach tied in knots. His hands were shaking, for fuck's sake. He took several deep breaths to try to calm his nerves. This was all too much, too soon. Sometimes he was glad he didn't have a family to call his own. His interactions with families always left him bewildered. Even Sed's family, pretty much the most awesome people Eric had ever met, became too much to handle after a few hours. It was all so... busy. And close. When he finally came out of the bathroom, Mrs. B accosted him immediately.

"What exactly do you think you're doing?" she hissed.

"Uh, taking a piss." He bit his lip. "I mean, going pee."

The woman made a sound of exasperation. "That's not what I mean, You're bound and determined to corrupt my daughter, aren't you?"

"Huh?" He honestly had no idea what she was talking about.

"I mean look at her. Her hair is blue, for crying out loud."

He smiled. "Her hair was blue before I met her."

"You have nothing to offer her. Traveling all over God's creation with a bunch of no-good musicians. What kind of life is that for a young woman?"

"She seems to enjoy it."

"She needs a stable home. With strong support. Did she even tell you that she has cancer?" Mrs. B said, as if it were scandalous.

"She told me. I can support her just fine."

Mrs. B released another exasperated sigh. "She does these things to get back at me, you know," Mrs. B said. "She broke up with poor Isaac just because I like him."

"Uh..." He decided it wasn't his place to set her straight on that issue.

"Will you look at them?" she said, waving a hand toward

Rebekah and Isaac, who were side by side at the sink washing dishes and sharing the tender camaraderie that flowed between them so easily. "Have you ever seen a more perfect couple?"

No, actually, he hadn't, but Eric and Rebekah were great together. Her mother just didn't get it.

"I know you don't like me," Eric said, "but I love your daughter. I'm not stepping aside for Isaac. Forget it."

"You *love* her?" The skepticism in her question frayed Eric's already raw nerves.

"Yeah, I love her. What? You think because I'm not like Dr. Perfect over there, I'm not capable of loving her?"

"If you really loved her, you'd let her go. She can't possibly be happy with you. I mean, look at you!"

Eric's brow crinkled. He was well aware of what he looked like. He knew he didn't fit the image of a mother's dream man for her daughter, but he wasn't so hideous that he scared babies or anything. "What does the way I look have to do with anything?"

The woman apparently thought it best to change tactics. "Isaac stood beside her while she was sick. What have you ever done for her?"

"Maybe you should ask her that." He stepped around her and headed into the kitchen. Eric had to admit the woman was right. Isaac had done a lot more for Rebekah than Eric had. Was it Eric's fault he hadn't met her sooner? He could have been there—*would* have been there—had he known her when she'd been sick.

Isaac dabbed suds on Rebekah's nose, a loving smile on his lips. She laughed and squirted him with water, wetting his crisp, white dress shirt. They really did make a cute couple. Nauseatingly cute.

Eric stopped behind Rebekah and wrapped his arms around her waist. "You ready to go?" he murmured into her ear. "I need a blow job."

The look on Isaac's face was priceless.

"She sucks good dick, doesn't she?" Eric said to egg Isaac on. He really wanted the guy to take a swing at him, so he had a legitimate reason to punch him in his perfect nose.

"I don't think that's an appropriate thing to say in front of a lady," Isaac said, lowering his gaze to the dish he was scrubbing.

"I'm not in front of a lady. I'm behind her. She likes it from behind. Did you know that, Isaac? Or is that too kinky for you? I take you for a missionary position only kind of guy, limp dick."

Eric was too busy trying to piss off Isaac to notice he'd missed his target and pissed off Rebekah instead.

She jerked the long yellow latex gloves from her hands and tossed them on the back of the sink. "It was great to see you, Isaac," she said and kissed his cheek. "I'll call you. Let's go," she bellowed at Eric.

She jerked from his grasp and stomped out of the kitchen.

"If you hurt her, I will make you regret it," Isaac said calmly and placed a sparkling clean dish in the drain board.

That sounded like a threat. Eric was half-tempted to provoke him, but Rebekah was already heading for the front door. "Thanks for dinner, Mom," she said and gave her mom a peck on the cheek. "Bye, Dad. Dave," she called into the dining room and opened the front door. "I'll see you all Thursday, if not before."

"Nice to meet you all," Eric said and dashed after her.

Rebekah didn't know it was possible to be this pissed off at someone you loved. She could not believe Eric would say those things in front of Isaac. She headed for the car, not much caring if Eric had followed her or not.

He caught up with her halfway down the walk and tried to take her hand. She jerked away. "Don't touch me."

"What's wrong, baby?"

"What's wrong? What's *wrong*?"

He looked at her, genuinely confused by her tirade.

"Why did you bring up our sex life in front of Isaac?"

Eric shrugged. "I dunno."

"You don't *know*?"

He shook his head. She growled in frustration and continued to the car. She opened the door and climbed inside before he could assist her. A moment later, he climbed in beside her and closed the door, but he didn't start the car. After a long silence, she turned to look at him. He was staring at her. "Are you mad at me?" he asked.

"Wow, Eric. How did you ever come to that brilliant conclusion?"

"I really don't know why I said that," he said quietly. "He just… gets on my nerves."

"Isaac?" How could Isaac get on anyone's nerves? The man was wonderful.

"Yeah. I don't like him. I don't want you around him."

She couldn't believe what she was hearing. "Why not?"

"You used to be lovers!"

"So what? We can still be friends."

Eric scoffed. "Let me tell you something about guys. Once they've fucked you, they can never just be your friend. They might say it and pretend, but every time they look at you they're thinking about how great your pussy feels around their dick."

She shook her head and rolled her eyes. "That's probably true for someone like you, but Isaac's different."

"Someone like me? Your perfect pansy of a doctor is better than me, is that what you're saying?"

"I didn't say that."

"But you implied it. Get out of my car."

She was too stunned to move. "What?" she breathed.

"You fuckin' heard me. Go back to him if you want him so much." He leaned across her body and opened the door. "Get out!"

"Eric?" She'd never known him to behave this way. It made

absolutely no sense. She wasn't even mad anymore. Just confused. "I don't want him that way. Why are you being like this?"

Staring out the dark windshield, he said, "Because I don't want to be with you anymore."

Her heart caught in her throat until she thought she'd suffocate. He started the car and gunned the perfectly tuned engine.

"Well? What are you waiting for?" he asked, still not looking at her.

Her heart was breaking, and he was being an insufferable asshole. If he didn't want her, fine. It wasn't like she didn't know how to be alone. She climbed out of the car and slammed the door. He took off so fast, the Corvette was nothing but an emerald green blur. She knew she shouldn't have helped him fix it. He was going to kill himself in the damned thing. At the moment, she wasn't sure she cared.

Chapter 23

ERIC'S CHEST WAS SO tight he was going to suffocate. He punched the accelerator and drifted around a corner with skidding tires. From nowhere, a little black dog darted in front of his car. Gritting his teeth, Eric slammed on his brakes and slid to a screeching halt. Heart hammering, he peered over the hood, afraid of what he'd see. The dog trotted unharmed onto the sidewalk with its tail between its legs and ears drawn back, eyeing the car warily.

Eric released a breath of relief and eased forward at a speed more reasonable for a residential area. Why was he so pissed off? And so hurt? And why had he kicked Rebekah out of his car? Had he really broken up with her? Ten minutes ago, he'd told her mother that he wasn't stepping aside for Isaac. Isn't that what he'd just done? Stepped aside for Isaac?

"Fuck," he growled. He had to go back. Eric drove around the block and headed to the house. Rebekah was still standing in front, but she wasn't alone. Isaac was holding her securely in his arms, one hand smoothing her silky hair. Isaac caught sight of Eric and grinned. He tilted Rebekah's head back and kissed her deeply. The middle finger Isaac extended in Eric's direction behind Rebekah's back was more provocation than Eric could handle.

Eric was out of the car and crossing the yard in a heartbeat. He wrenched Rebekah away from Isaac's lips. Her tear-streaked, startled face scarcely had time to register before Eric's fist was flying. It connected with Isaac's nose, knocking him flat on his ass. Eric's satisfaction was short-lived. Rebekah dropped to her knees beside Isaac, who had both hands cupped over his nose, trying to clear his vision by forcing his eyes open and closed several times.

"Oh my God," Rebekah cried. "Are you okay, Isaac?"

"Get up, you fucking pansy," Eric said. "I'm not done kicking your ass yet."

Isaac didn't get up, but Rebekah leapt to her feet and turned on Eric, spitting mad. "What in the fuck do you think you're doing?"

"He was kissing you."

"So that gives you a right to punch him?"

Uh, duh. "Well… yeah."

She rolled her eyes and shook her head. "You need to leave."

"But I came back for you."

"Leave!"

"Call the cops," Isaac said, climbing to his feet and brushing off the seat of his slacks. His perfect nose was still perfect, though swollen. Not even bleeding. "He's obviously unstable."

"I'll fuckin' show you unstable," Eric said. Before he could throw another punch, Rebekah stepped between them.

She squeezed her eyes shut, as if expecting him to actually hit her.

After a tense moment, she opened her eyes and took a deep breath. "I asked you to leave, Eric. I'm not sure who you are right now, and you're scaring me."

Scaring her? Eric immediately relaxed his stance. "Rebekah?" He'd never hurt her. Not for anything. She had to know that.

"Good-bye, Eric. You need to cool off before you do something you regret." She grabbed Isaac by the sleeve and pulled him into the house, leaving Eric alone on the front lawn.

Eric stood there, oscillating between anger and anguish. It took him several minutes to notice that his unattended car was rolling down the street.

Rebekah watched Eric chase his car down the road. He caught it, climbed inside, and sped off.

"Is he gone?" Isaac asked.

She nodded, the tears she'd been holding in check flowing freely now.

"Good riddance."

"Why did you kiss me, Isaac?"

"I think that's fairly obvious, angel," he murmured. He cupped her face and brushed her tears away with his thumbs. "I love you."

That was the last thing she wanted to hear at the moment. "Isaac."

"Will you marry me?"

She stared at him in disbelief. *Marry* him? Was he serious?

Chapter 24

Eric had been driving on autopilot for almost an hour. He didn't even know where he was going until he turned into Jace's driveway. He parked beneath the portico and sat there trying to collect his scattered thoughts.

Maybe he should just go home. The thought of being in that big fairy-tale house by himself was intolerable. He climbed out of the car and rang the doorbell. Aggie answered in full dominatrix regalia. Had he not been so distraught, he'd have probably gotten a stiffy and started panting. Thing was, he was already panting. His only other option seemed to be crying, and that wasn't going to happen.

"Eric?" Aggie said. "I thought you were a client. I was about to hit you for not going to the back door."

There was probably a quip he should be spouting, but nothing came to mind. "Is Jace here?"

"Yeah, come in." Aggie ushered him inside. She appraised him in the lighted entryway. "Sweetie, you look like shit. Is something wrong?"

"Had a little fight."

"With Reb?"

He nodded.

She patted his back. "It will all work out."

Eric wasn't so sure about that, but he nodded again. The doorbell rang. A chime that sounded like a doomsday theme.

"That's for me," Aggie said. "Jace!" Aggie called into the house. "Eric's here!"

Jace came into the foyer carrying his black tuxedo cat, Brownie, on one shoulder. His smile of greeting faded when his gaze landed on Eric's face. "Dude, you look like shit. Is something wrong?"

"I don't know."

Jace patted Aggie's butt as she sauntered by. "Do you have your panic button, babe?"

She cupped his cheek and gifted him with a lingering kiss. "Yeah. I told you subs aren't a threat. I don't know why you worry about me so much."

"Yes you do."

She smiled and slapped Jace's ass with a resounding crack. He tensed, his lip curling with primal desire.

"Get Eric a drink," she said. "He looks like he can use one."

Jace approached Eric and handed the cat to him. Eric held the creature at arm's length and stared into her appraising amber eyes. She batted a beckoning paw at him and he drew her closer. She sank a set of claws into his shirt and pulled herself closer. For a second, Eric thought the cat was going to bite him, but she rubbed her face against his jaw and purred. "Browww wwwooownnnn," she meowed. Eric chuckled and cuddled her against his chest like a baby. He followed Jace deeper into the house, while Brownie batted at the lock of blue hair that rested against his collarbone.

Eric expected Jace to lead him to the family room, which had a well-stocked bar, but he led him into his home gym.

"Do you have a secret stash of booze in here?" Eric asked.

"You don't need booze."

"I beg to differ."

"You need to hit something."

"Or someone." Though he'd already hit a certain someone, and it hadn't solved his problems, only made them worse.

"Sit," Jace said, indicating a bench along the wall. He picked up a roll of white tape and grabbed Eric's free hand to tape Eric's knuckles. "Talk."

Eric released Brownie, who went to stare at herself in a floor-to-ceiling mirror along one wall. Eric allowed Jace to tape his hands and wrists while he told him what had happened at the Blake residence.

"Do you think she still cares about him?" Jace asked when Eric reached the end of his story.

"Looked like it."

"I'd have hit him too."

"You would have?"

Jace nodded. "But not in front of her."

"Too late to fix that part."

"Yeah. So now you've got to play it cool. Get the aggression out of your system so you don't do it again." Jace walked over to a large punching bag suspended from the ceiling. "What's his name again?"

"Isaac."

Jace used the tape to make a letter *I* on the punching bag. "I'll leave you two alone," Jace said. "I'll be in the family room. Come find me after you kick his ass."

Eric felt a little foolish beating the shit out of a punching bag. First of all, punching bags didn't shit. Second, they didn't fight back. While Eric loved to engage in a good brawl, he wasn't into doling out unchallenged beatings. Sometime during his attempts to beat that tape letter off the punching bag while imagining Isaac's perfect face, he realized that the guy would never fight back. Hitting Isaac was like beating up the punching bag and even less satisfying.

Drenched in sweat, Eric appraised what was left of the tape. "Fuck." He shoved the bag with both palms, sending it rocking back and forth.

Eric had learned to get what he wanted by fighting a long time ago, but he would have to change tactics in this case. Beating Isaac to pulp might be fun, but it wouldn't bring Rebekah back, and that's all he really wanted. He raked his fingers through his hair, trying to figure out what would win her over again. He knew jewelry wasn't the answer. Maybe Jace had an idea.

Eric unwrapped the tape from his hands as he wandered through the house on his way to the family room. Jace nodded toward the empty recliner beside him. There was already a shot of tequila waiting for Eric on the side table. He sat on the edge of the chair and downed the shot.

"Feel better?" Jace asked.

"Not necessarily. I've come to the conclusion that I can't beat the shit out of Limp Dick if I want Rebekah back."

"So you officially broke up?"

"I don't know. I hope not. She was so pissed."

"Maybe you should call her. Talk to her."

Eric pulled out his cell phone and stared at the screen saver of himself and Rebekah kissing and smiling. She had a smudge of grease on her cheek. He'd snapped that picture the day before. A memento of them getting the Corvette running perfectly. How could he have fucked things up between them so quickly?

Eric decided he had no clue what to say and was afraid they'd get into another argument if he talked to her then. "I'm not sure that's a good idea. I'll probably say something I'll regret."

"Then text her," Jace said.

Yeah, text her. He couldn't put his foot in his mouth in a text message.

I'm really sorry, baby. I'll call tomorrow when I have my head on straight. Love you. He sent the message and sank back into the recliner, holding the phone loosely. Within a minute, his phone beeped with a message.

His heart dropped when he read it. *Fuck you, asshole. I never want to see you again. Isaac asked me to marry him, and I said yes.*

"What?" he sputtered. They have one fight, are out of each other's sight for two hours, and she's already agreed to marry Isaac? "No fucking way."

He dialed her number. The call connected, then disconnected.

"She hung up on me," Eric grumbled. He dialed her again.

"Hello?" a man answered her phone.

"Who is this?" Eric growled.

"This is Rebekah's fiancé, Isaac."

"Bullshit. Put her on the phone."

"Look, loser," Isaac said. "She doesn't want to talk to you. Don't call her again."

"Put her on the fucking phone."

"Take a hint. She doesn't want to be with you." Isaac hung up.

"Son of a bitch."

Eric dialed her number again. This time it rang, but no one picked up.

"What's going on?" Jace asked.

"Rebekah is marrying Isaac."

Chapter 25

Rebekah came out of the bathroom drying her hair with a towel. A shower had made her feel almost human again after an hour-long crying jag. She found Isaac sitting at the end of her bed fiddling with her phone.

"Did Eric call?" she asked hopefully.

Isaac shook his head. "Nope."

Her heart sank, and the tears she'd finally managed to suppress filled her eyes again. "He must be really upset. I thought he'd be cooled down by now. I hope nothing happened to him. He drives like a maniac."

She sat on the bed next to Isaac, and he wrapped a comforting arm around her shoulders. "I'm sure he'll call, angel. Give him time to realize he was in the wrong."

"Maybe I should call him." When she reached for her phone, Isaac hid it behind his back.

"He's the one who needs to apologize, not you."

"We both need to apologize. Actually, you need to apologize too. Why did you kiss me like that?"

"I'm not going to apologize for kissing the woman I love."

"But I'm in love with Eric, Isaac. Why can't you understand that?"

Isaac brushed her hair back and tucked it behind her ear. "Look me in the eye and tell me you don't love me."

She looked into his gentle gray eyes, opened her mouth, but couldn't say it. She did love Isaac, but she wasn't attracted to him.

With Eric, she had both. Her love for Eric was still growing, but her attraction was there in full bloom. Her love for Isaac was strong, but she would never be attracted. It wasn't the kind of love you had for the man you want to spend the rest of your life with. Was it? She felt like crying again. Why did Isaac insist on confusing her?

"You know we're good together," he said.

"Eric and I are good together too," she insisted. "I've never been happier. Every minute with him is exciting and fun."

"But how long will that last? He's a rock star. You're not stupid, Rebekah. It's only a matter of time before he falls to temptation and breaks your heart."

"He would never break my—"

"*I* would never."

"But you did, Isaac. I was devastated."

His brow crinkled with confusion. "You broke up with me."

"Because you couldn't stand to have sex with me. I disgusted you."

"I told you I was sorry about that." His hand slid across her back. "Your body has had more time to heal. We can try again."

"No, Isaac. I love Eric. Why is it so hard for you to understand that?"

"I love you too much to watch you throw your life away," he said emphatically. "He's not right for you, Rebekah."

"He's perfect for me, Isaac. You just don't know him."

"I don't think I want to know him. He's crass. Low class. Violent. I worry for your safety. He punched me without provocation."

She shook her head at him. "Without provocation? You kissed me, Isaac. I'm his girlfriend. I don't approve of him punching you, but I understand why he reacted that way."

"Like a mindless thug?"

"I'm not going to sit here and listen to you insult him. I think it's time for you to leave."

Isaac hugged her tightly, reminding her how safe he always made her feel. "I don't want to leave. I've missed you so much. Let's talk about something else. Tell me about your new job."

Rebekah really didn't want to sit by herself while she waited for Eric to call. But she didn't want to be alone with Isaac either. He was confusing her. Nothing new about that.

"Yeah, okay." She climbed from the bed and headed toward the door. "Let's go hang out with Dave. He could probably use the company."

Chapter 26

ERIC HAD LURED THE guys to his house with promises of a huge turkey dinner and football, so they weren't too pleased to find out they were actually being put to work.

"Did you seriously sign us up for kitchen duty?" Trey grumbled.

"Yeah," Eric said. "It'll be fun."

"Fun?" Brian said. "What's fun about shoveling food on the plates of homeless guys?"

"You'll see," Eric promised.

"It's great publicity," Sed said in his deep voice. "Jerry is getting a news crew to cover it."

"Aggie wants to join us. Is that okay?" Jace asked.

"Yeah, I signed up the ladies too," Eric said.

"And Rebekah?" Trey asked.

"I don't know if she'll show up or not." Eric secretly hoped so. "She's the one who suggested it originally. Her family does it every year. I kind of got carried away on the sign-up list and volunteered everyone."

"So we're supposed to give up our Thanksgiving dinner and football because you were trying to impress a girl?" Trey said.

"I wasn't trying to impress a girl," Eric said. "I thought it would be good for us." Impressing the girl was just an added bonus. And she hated him now, so it didn't really matter anyway. He'd called her like a thousand times, and she never answered. When he drove past her parents' house, her car was never there. He checked his messages every twenty seconds. She was obviously avoiding him. Probably busy planning her wedding with Dr. Perfect. *Fuck!*

God, he wanted to see her. He hadn't slept all week.

"Dave was excited when he heard we were all going to be there," Eric added, trying to get the guys to cooperate. "I think he wants to show us that he's willing and able to get back to work."

"We're going," Sed said, and that was the end of all arguments.

Eric rode with Aggie, Jace, and Trey in Aggie's brand-new Mustang. Brian and Myrna rode with Sed and Jessica in Sed's Mercedes. It was great to have everyone together again. Everyone got busy with their own thing when they were home on break, and he didn't get to see them. At times, Eric longed for the good ol' days when they'd all been bachelors, but then he saw how happy his bandmates were with their significant others and decided he'd been just as happy when he'd had Rebekah. Home wasn't supposed to be hell.

When they arrived at the shelter, the news crew started hounding them before they were even inside the building. Sed—bless him—stopped to talk to the reporter about "Sinners' new Thanksgiving tradition," while the rest were directed into the kitchen and given sharp utensils.

While most volunteers were too intimidated to boss them around, Myrna had no such reservations. She had Jace and Aggie peeling potatoes, Jessica putting ice in cups, and Trey spraying whipped topping onto pieces of pie. An entire flock of women watched him the entire time, probably because he got a lot of cream on his fingers and kept licking it off in a most Trey-like fashion. Brian mostly followed Myrna around trying to talk her into taking it easy due to her pregnancy and insisting on lifting anything that weighed more than two ounces.

Eric looked around for something he could do.

"You can help me with the cinnamon rolls," a familiar voice said behind him.

Eric's heart was already pounding before he even turned around. Rebekah offered him a timid smile and lowered her gaze. She'd dyed her hair all one mousy brown color and was wearing a plain white blouse and trim black pants that accentuated the gentle flair of her hips. His eyes automatically went to her throat. Instead of the sapphire butterfly necklace he'd given her, she wore a slender silver chain. Her wrist was completely unadorned. He took her lack of jewelry as an obvious sign of rejection. She hated him. And she looked so abysmally normal and sedate. What had happened to the vibrant, quirky girl who'd captured his heart? Had that all been an act? Or was this girl-next-door persona an act?

"I don't know how to make cinnamon rolls," he admitted.

"But no one shakes spices like you do." She glanced at her mother who was staring at her with stern disapproval.

"I do have good wrist action," Eric said and simulated jacking off vigorously.

Rebekah laughed, her eyes lighting up with delight. Mrs. B cleared her throat, and Rebekah's smile faded. "Do you want to help?" she asked the middle of Eric's chest.

"Sure."

Eric followed Rebekah to a large mixer. Isaac, who was mixing one hell of a huge ball of dough, smiled warmly at Rebekah. "It's almost ready, angel."

Eric closed his eyes and took several deep breaths. The man just had to breathe and it pissed him off.

"What are you doing here?" Isaac asked Eric.

"Helping the less fortunate," Eric said, forcing himself to meet Isaac's displeased gaze.

"Which would be me," Rebekah said. "I need help sprinkling the cinnamon."

"I was going to help you with that," Isaac said. He dumped the mountain of dough onto the silver countertop that had a coating of flour over its surface.

"I think my dad needs help carving turkeys."

Isaac located Father Blake carving one of dozens of turkeys. "Looks like it." When Isaac turned to walk away, Eric almost cheered. He'd never been happier to be considered inept with a knife. There would be no turkey carving in his immediate future.

Rebekah handed Eric a big silver shaker. "I'll let you know when to start shaking," she said.

Truthfully, he was already shaking. He wanted to draw her into his arms so badly he had to grip the shaker with both hands to control the impulse. He watched her roll out the dough with a big wooden pin.

"How have you been?" she asked, concentrating on her task. She was probably avoiding looking at him.

"Okay. You?"

"Okay."

She rolled the dough into a big rectangle. An awkward silence stretched between them. She reached for a tub of softened butter and spread it over the dough with her hands. He was imagining buttering up her breasts until they were slippery, pressing the succulent globes together, and sliding his cock...

"Eric?"

Rebekah's inquiry pulled him out of his delicious fantasy. A fantasy he could have made a reality less than a week ago. "Huh?"

"You can start shaking the cinnamon and sugar now."

"Okay," he said breathlessly.

He moved to stand beside her. She worked her way down the dough, still spreading it with a thick layer of melty, slippery butter, and he followed, shaking the cinnamon and sugar mixture over the butter. He was soon lost in fantasyland again. Rebekah was rubbing that butter all over her breasts, her nipples standing erect and begging to be licked. Instead of shaking sweet powder over the dough, he was stroking his cock and spurting cum all over her chest. His attention riveted to her chest.

The first signs of her arousal produced two small bumps on the front of her blouse. He was showing off his own arousal as a bulge in his pants. They had both stopped working and were staring at each other's hard evidence.

"What are you thinking about?" she whispered.

"Watching you spread butter on your breasts until they're all slippery, while I jack off and come all over your tits," he whispered back.

"I want it in my mouth," she whispered.

Eric groaned. It wasn't nice to tease him like that. Wasn't she going to marry Isaac? He opened his mouth to ask her just that when Mrs. B appeared on Rebekah's opposite side.

"Are you two about finished?" Mrs. B said. "We've got to get those in the oven."

Mrs. B helped herself to Rebekah's butter and spread it over the dough. Eric's erection withered to nothingness. He was no longer entertaining fantasies of slippery breasts.

"I've got it, Mom," Rebekah said, spreading butter faster now.

Eric shook his shaker more vigorously to coat the buttered dough.

"Go get the baking sheet," Mrs. B said to Rebekah.

Rebekah glanced at Eric and then went to retrieve a baking sheet, her buttery hands in the air.

"Don't think I don't know what you're doing," Mrs. B said to Eric as soon as Rebekah was out of earshot. "Trying to interfere with her relationship with Isaac. It won't work. She will marry that young man, and you will not mess things up."

Wow, this woman hated him. It wasn't the first time someone had hated Eric, but it didn't usually bother him this much.

"Why are you busting my balls, lady?"

Mrs. B's eyebrows attempted to disappear into her hairline. "Didn't your mother ever teach you any manners?"

"No, actually, she deserted me when I was four years old."

"I can understand why," Mrs. B huffed.

Eric set his jaw in a harsh line and dropped the shaker on the counter. He felt like he'd had the wind knocked out of him. He didn't often think about the mother who had left him behind. He sure as hell didn't agonize over his situation or let it bother him, but that... *that* hurt. Stomach in knots, heart aching, eyes stinging, Eric turned and strode away before he called Rebekah's mother a fucking bitch to her face.

"What did you say to him?" he heard Rebekah ask her mother as she returned with the baking sheet.

"Nothing," Mrs. B said in a saccharine sweet voice. "Isaac," she called. "Would you mind helping Rebekah cut the dough into strips? She was never any good at it."

"Sure thing, Mrs. B," Isaac said eagerly.

Aggie snagged Eric around the waist as he stalked by. "We could use some help," she said. Eric found himself wedged between Jace and Aggie. They continued to peel potatoes. Eric stood there and gulped air.

"You okay?" Jace asked.

"I was until Mrs. Bitch showed up."

Jace sniggered. "She makes a guy miss his mama not at all."

"I think she's even worse than my mother," Aggie said, "and that's saying something."

"She gets along with Isaac fine. She just hates me."

Aggie bumped Eric's leg with her hip. "She doesn't know you, doll. If she got to know you—"

"She'd hate me even more. Maybe I should get a haircut and wear something nice and be more careful about what I say and—"

"Don't go there, dude," Jace said.

"Who cares what Mrs. Blake thinks about you?" Aggie said. "Rebekah loves you. What her mother thinks doesn't matter."

The three turned to watch Mrs. B chatter animatedly with Isaac, who was cutting dough into strips, while Rebekah coiled them and placed them on the baking sheet. Rebekah glanced at Eric and offered him a miserable smile before turning her attention back to her dough arranging.

"Rebekah would obviously rather be over here with you," Aggie said.

"Yeah? So what's stopping her?"

Aggie shoved the pot of peeled potatoes into Eric's chest. "Go rinse these in the sink over there, and bring them back so we can cut them up."

Eric did as he was told. While he was washing the potatoes, Rebekah appeared at his side. "Do you mind if I wash my hands?" she asked. She held her greasy fingers up for inspection. "I'm all buttery."

Eric stepped aside. "Go right ahead."

"Did my mother say something to you?" she asked as she scrubbed her hands with dish soap.

"No."

She sighed heavily. "Liar."

She rinsed her hands and was gone before he could find his tongue. He was starting to wish he'd never come. The heartache wasn't worth viewing Rebekah from afar.

Eric did his best to avoid Rebekah and crew while they were in the kitchen. When it came time to serve, he found himself in charge of serving mashed potatoes. Rebekah was to his right with the gravy, and Isaac to his left with the stuffing. Hell. On. Earth.

What made it worse was that Trey was at the end of the line. Being the social creature that he was, he kept slowing up the line as he chatted with and teased every person who wanted dessert. And everyone wanted dessert when Trey Mills was offering it.

"Can I get some extra stuffing?" a legless man in a wheelchair asked Isaac as they waited for the line to start moving again.

"Of course. Just don't tell my boss," Isaac said and scooped more stuffing onto the man's plate.

"You can have extra potatoes too, if you want," Eric said.

"I would like more potatoes. Thanks."

Eric added potatoes to his plate.

"The stuffing is excellent," Isaac said and scooped more onto the man's plate.

"But not as good as the potatoes," Eric insisted and added to the heap already on his plate.

The man looked relieved when the line started moving, and he could get some gravy for his mountains of stuffing and mashed potatoes.

Isaac scooped larger and larger servings of stuffing onto each plate. Not to be one-upped by a twerp, Eric made sure each person's serving of potatoes was larger than their pile of stuffing.

"What are you trying to prove, rock star?" Isaac growled out of the corner of his mouth.

"Not a thing, doc."

Rebekah shook her head. "Will you two take it easy? We're going to run out of food. I know you're both generous, but—"

"I'm way more generous than he is," Isaac said.

"Not!" Eric added.

The news crew flitted about, zooming in on the band members as they served people they would never encounter on a regular day. Despite Isaac's constant presence as a thorn in his side, Eric started to remember why he was there in the first place.

It wasn't to ogle Rebekah. It wasn't to wonder if he'd ever win over Mrs. B. It wasn't for good publicity. It wasn't even to hang out with his best friends. It was to make a small difference in a stranger's life. Instead of stuffing visitors with potatoes, he shifted his focus to talking to them while they waited for Trey to stop yakking at the end of the line.

When a mother with two young daughters made their way through the line, Eric's heart melted. The two girls stared at him with wide eyes, uncertain what to make of the tall, thin guy with the crazy hair.

"How come your hair is blue right there?" one of the girls asked. Eric estimated her to be about seven.

"I wanted it to match your eyes."

"Mah eyes is brown."

He leaned over the counter for a better look. "I guess they are. Should I change the color to brown then?"

She shook her head. "I like blue. I never saw blue hair afore."

"Don't frequent West Hollywood much then, do you?"

Rebekah snorted.

Her younger sister stared at him, but was apparently too shy or too scared to initiate conversation. "Do you like blue too?" Eric asked.

She nodded.

"It's about time for me to change colors again. What color do you think I should do next?"

"Purple!" the older girl said.

The younger nodded again.

"Purple?" Eric pretended to be perplexed. "Isn't that a girl color?"

"No, pink is a girl color," the girl insisted. "Boys can have purple."

"Alright, purple it is. I trust you wouldn't steer me wrong and make my hair a girl color."

The younger girl laughed. "Pink. Pink. You should have pink hair!"

"Now I know you're trying to make me look silly."

"You've already succeeded in that on your own," Isaac mumbled. Eric refused to take his bait.

The mother offered Isaac a scathing look and then smiled at Eric. "Thank you," she said quietly and helped her girls push their trays further down the line. Eric caught Rebekah smiling sadly as she offered gravy to the two little girls. He placed a gentle hand in the center of Rebekah's back, and she leaned against his arm. When she looked up, his throat closed off, and all he could think about was how much he wanted to kiss her.

"Yo, Eric," Sed called from the beginning of the chow line. "Gather the rest of the guys and come down here for an interview."

Eric knew Sed could do a fine job with the interview on his own, but he did his bidding anyway. Something about Sed made Eric always want to do his bidding. "Bring Dave with you. And Rebekah too." Especially when Sed made requests such as those.

Eric gathered his bandmates and Dave. They went to sit at one of the picnic tables. Trey sat on the table with his feet on the bench, while the rest lined up in a row. Dave maneuvered his wheelchair into the space at the end of the table next to Sed. The only one not present was Rebekah. Eric made a return trip to retrieve her.

"Sed wants us all to have an interview with the news crew."

"Why me?"

Eric shrugged. "I dunno. He specifically requested you join us though."

She handed her gravy ladle to a volunteer and wiped her hands on her black pants. Eric noticed the flour handprints on her ass and wondered if they belonged to Isaac. He wished he could say that they belonged to him.

"Where are you going?" Isaac asked.

"I'll be back," she assured him and headed toward the group.

Eric hung behind her so he didn't take her hand. He sure wanted to hold it, but that would bring Mrs. B running for sure.

"Okay, everyone's here now. You can start," Sed said to the reporter.

The reporter spoke into her microphone, "It's been awhile since you gave an update on the state of the band. It's obvious that Trey's hands are better." Trey wriggled his fingers to demonstrate. "But how's your voice, Sedric?"

"Perfectly fine," he said.

Which wasn't exactly true. His throat specialist harped on him constantly about screaming in live shows. He was getting better at keeping his volume down and allowing the soundboard operator to increase it electronically. Rebekah made a lot of adjustments for him. Eric glanced at her. She looked a bit shell-shocked to be sitting amongst them in an interview.

"A lot of fans were upset when the new single had less of your signature screaming and more singing. Was singing a decision or necessity?"

A little of both, but Sed chose to sugarcoat it.

"Well, as a band we wanted the new album to show our growth as musicians," Sed said. "When I first started out, I screamed because that's what I knew how to do best. As my singing voice evolved, I wanted to sing more, but the fans have come to expect screaming."

"We're taking a lot of chances on this album," Brian said. "We hope our fans stand beside us as we stretch our creativity to its limits."

"So there are more surprises in store for fans?" the reporter asked.

"You might say that," Eric said.

"You're the main composer, right?" the reporter asked Eric.

"More of an arranger," Eric said. "Brian writes the guitar music. Sed writes most of the lyrics. I pick out the pieces that work well together and arrange them into songs. Then I add drum tracks, and on this album, Jace worked out the bass lines."

"What does Trey do?"

"I just look pretty for the camera," Trey said.

Everyone laughed.

"You don't compose at all?" the reporter pressed.

"Brian writes the guitar music," Trey reiterated. "No way could I ever come up with the amazing stuff he composes. I'm just along for the ride."

"Trey has written the lyrics for a couple songs," Sed entered.

"I did write 'Goodbye Is Not Forever,' our only ballad," Trey said. "And I wrote one of the new songs."

"'Sever'?"

"No, Sed wrote that one. We're not finished recording yet. My song might not end up on the album, so I don't want to say much about it."

"It will end up on the album," Sed said. He squeezed Trey's forearm, and some connection between them solidified.

Eric decided it had something to do with Trey's addiction to painkillers and Sed's involvement in getting him off them.

"What's it called?" the reporter asked. Eric could tell she was hanging on Trey's every word.

"'Fall.'"

"Like the season?"

Trey shook his head and stared at his hands, which clutched the fabric of his jeans.

Sed patted him on the back. "It's a great song," Sed said.

Trey smiled a little but didn't raise his head. The reporter seemed to realize she should change the subject.

"You've added a couple new instruments to the mix too. Will you play violin on the album, Sed?"

"I mostly used the violin to fill in for my screaming when my throat was injured, but yeah, there are a couple songs where I use the violin on purpose." Sed chuckled.

"Can't wait to hear that. The piano piece sounds amazing on 'Sever.' Did you write that, Jace?"

Jace flushed and shook his head. "It was originally one of Brian's guitar solos. Eric modified it into piano music."

Eric caught Rebekah staring at him with something that might have been adulation. He wasn't sure what had brought it on all of a sudden.

"So when can we expect the new album to hit the shelves?"

"This spring. We still have some tour dates to make up in January, and then we'll hit the studio hard and heavy in February. After that, we'll take a little break and start a tour next summer to promote the new album."

"Sounds busy."

Sed chuckled. "We're always busy."

"And we're all happy about that." The reporter turned to Dave. "You're the soundboard operator who was injured in the bus crash in Canada, right?"

"Yeah. David Blake. I've been working with Sinners for several years now."

"Are you still part of the crew?"

"No, I—"

"Yes," Sed interrupted. "That's why I called you over here. We want you to come on the road with us in January, if you're up for it."

Dave smiled. "Yeah, of course. Sinners is the greatest bunch of musicians I've ever worked with. They're just… great." The tears in Dave's eyes were unmistakable. "They've given me hope. They also gave up their Thanksgiving to be here and help at the shelter."

"Myrna said she'd cook for us all tomorrow," Brian said. "It's no big deal."

Dave shook his head. "You're all coming over to my house for dinner tonight. Mom is a wonderful cook, and she always makes enough for fifteen people."

"We couldn't possibly impose," Sed said. His stomach growled a protest, and he covered his belly with one hand.

"It's not imposing. I want you to come. I'm sure the folks would be more than happy for you to join us, right, Reb?"

Rebekah started. She'd been staring at her hands clenched in her lap. "What?"

"I just invited the guys over for Thanksgiving dinner."

"You should probably ask Mom," Rebekah said.

"Ask Mom what?" Mrs. B said.

"The band's coming over for dinner tonight," Dave said.

Mrs. B's jaw dropped.

"Please, Mom. They let me keep my job. Even though I'm stuck in this wheelchair."

Mrs. B smiled gently and smoothed Dave's hair with one hand. "Of course they can come. It's the least we can do to repay them for that smile on your face, David."

Dave's smile widened. "Awesome! We have dinner late," he told them. "Around eight."

"I guess I better head home and get the turkey in the oven then," Mrs. B said.

Which would finally get Rebekah out of her ever-watchful eye, and maybe Eric could get her alone so they could talk. She was obviously torn up about Dave replacing her as soundboard operator. Even if she solidified his fears that their relationship was over, at least it was better than being ignored and wondering if they'd ever make amends.

Rebekah glanced up and met Eric's eyes. She looked like she wanted to talk too. Even though she hadn't answered his calls, he still hadn't given up hope. Maybe, if he could get her to listen to him, she'd give him a second chance.

"Rebekah, grab Isaac and your father, and meet me at the car," Mrs. B said. "I'm going to need lots of help."

"We could all help," Eric offered.

"Don't be ridiculous," Mrs. B said. She grabbed the back of Dave's chair and directed him toward the exit.

"Did you have any more questions?" Sed asked the reporter.

"Thousands," the reporter insisted.

Eric watched Rebekah and Isaac leave the kitchen. He tried to pay attention to the rest of the interview, but it was hard when his thoughts were following the woman he loved out the door.

Chapter 27

TREY WATCHED THE INTERPLAY between Eric and Rebekah, Rebekah and Isaac, Eric and Isaac, and his anger increased with each passing minute. It took a lot to piss him off, but he was livid. Rebekah was a complete idiot. How could she choose a homosexual man over Eric? And how could Eric just let her? She and Eric worked great together. They'd been so happy. How could they just let that go? And then there was Isaac, who was in total denial, pretending he loved Rebekah to hide what he really was. Fucking idiots. All three.

When Isaac excused himself from the table to use the restroom, Trey followed a moment later. Maybe it was wrong to stick his nose in their business, but it wasn't every day Eric found a girl crazy and stupid enough to love him. And she did love him. Otherwise, she wouldn't appear so heartsick every time she looked at him.

Which happened to be pretty much constantly since they'd sat down to eat at the Blakes' dinner table.

Eric seemed to believe he was thinking of Rebekah's happiness by giving her the time and space she needed. What a tool. If he'd really been thinking of her happiness, he would have told Isaac to get lost by now.

Trey waited outside the bathroom door. He listened to the sounds of water running as Isaac washed his hands. When the door opened, Trey blocked his exit. Isaac stopped short. Trey was an inch taller than him, if that, but one intense look sent in the guy's direction had him instantly in the submissive role. Just where Trey wanted him.

And Trey did want him. Wanted to show him that accepting who he was would bring him far more contentment than pretending to be something he wasn't. Trey knew these good boys often had a hard time coming to terms with their homosexual nature. That they thought it was wrong. Trey would show him different.

"Ex-excuse me," Isaac said, his eyes drifting downward.

"I need to talk to you," Trey said.

Isaac straightened his spine and lifted his gray-eyed gaze. He really was a looker. Pretty, but not effeminate. Strong, but not too strong. Cherry. Yes, very cherry. Exactly Trey's type. "About?"

"Privately."

Isaac took a step back. Trey took two steps forward. When they'd both crossed the threshold, Trey closed the door behind him and locked it.

"What are you do—"

Trey moved forward until he had Isaac against a wall.

"I don't believe in violence," Isaac said, trembling.

Trey laughed. Did he think he was here to beat him up? Hardly. "Me neither. As the saying goes, I'm a lover, not a fighter."

Isaac chanced a glance at him and then lowered his gaze to Trey's chest. "What do you want from me then?"

Trey placed both hands on the wall on either side of Isaac's body to further assert his dominant role. Trey could go either way, but nothing got his blood pumping like a confused virgin.

Isaac's trembling intensified.

"You really don't know?" Trey took another step forward. Inches separated the length of their bodies. Trey's nose brushed Isaac's jaw as he whispered, "I want you to admit who you are, that's all."

"You're making me very uncomfortable," Isaac said.

"Uncomfortable or excited?"

Isaac pressed a hand against Trey's chest. Perhaps his intention had been to push Trey away, but instead, his hand curled and gripped Trey's shirt.

"That's what I thought," Trey murmured. "I'm guessing you've never been this turned on in your entire life, and I haven't even touched you." Trey breathed a hot breath against Isaac's neck, and Isaac shuddered. "Yet."

Isaac's other hand moved to Trey's waist and slid around to his back. He stopped short of pressing his body against Trey's, but he wanted to. Trey knew he did. "This is wrong," Isaac said breathlessly.

Trey rubbed his open mouth along Isaac's jaw. "Doesn't feel wrong though, does it? It feels right. Nothing has ever felt more right."

Isaac made a sound of torment in the back of his throat.

"Do you want me to kiss you?" Trey murmured. Isaac obviously did, but Trey was going to make him admit it.

"No," Isaac panted. "Rebekah…"

"She can't give you what you want, Isaac."

"She and I can…" Isaac took a step forward, pressing his body against Trey's. Trey felt Isaac's excitement against his hip. His cock was hard as stone. "We can adopt children."

"I'm not talking about that. She can't fuck you the way you want to be fucked." Trey leaned closer, resting his forearms on the wall. He brushed his nose against Isaac's jaw and said, "The way *I* can fuck you."

Isaac swallowed hard. "I don't…"

Trey moved a hand to Isaac's ass and shifted him slightly so their hard cocks were pressed together. "If you didn't want it, you wouldn't be hard. If I held a straight man like this, he'd be freaked out, not excited. You want it, Isaac. You can admit it to me. I won't judge. I want it too." Trey leaned back slightly to stare into Isaac's bewildered gray eyes. "Say you want me." Trey took his free hand from the wall and slid it into Isaac's soft, loose curls. Isaac really did have the face of an angel. If he didn't admit it soon, Trey was going to kiss him regardless. "Say it, Isaac."

"I…" He squeezed his eyes shut.

Trey slid his hand over Isaac's ass so that his fingertips pressed against that place Trey so wanted to fuck, though he had no intention of taking it that far. At least, not today. He rubbed Isaac there, and Isaac went limp against Trey's body. Completely submissive in his arms. Maybe Trey would take it that far after all. Fuck Isaac in the bathroom at Rebekah's parents' house. Wouldn't that give Mrs. B a stroke? Knowing the son-in-law she so craved got fucked in the ass by one of those dirty rock stars in her own home while they ate Thanksgiving dinner. The thought made Trey's heart thud with excitement. Hell, even if she never found out, he'd know. Trey grinned wickedly.

"Does that feel good?" Trey whispered, still rubbing Isaac's hole through his pants.

"Mmmmm."

"I can make it feel a whole lot better."

"Please."

"Please, what?"

"Please… f-fuck me. There."

Who could turn down that plea? Not Trey. "If that's what you want."

"Yes." He nodded vigorously. "I've always wanted it. Always."

"How does it feel to admit that?"

Isaac took a shaky breath. "Terrifying."

Trey understood that. "It's okay. I can give you what you want. What you need. You don't ever have to be afraid when you're with me." Trey tightened his hand in Isaac's hair to hold his head still so he could kiss him.

The instant Trey's lips touched Isaac's, Isaac thrust his tongue into Trey's mouth and pulled him closer with surprising strength.

Still kissing Trey with deep enthusiasm, Isaac turned and slammed Trey against the wall. He pulled away and separated their bodies enough to unfasten Trey's belt and open his fly. The soft-spoken guy had gone from zero to a hundred and twenty in three seconds flat. Maybe he was more dominant than Trey had first expected.

Fine with him. Trey liked to get it as much as he liked to give.

Isaac's hand trembled as it touched Trey's cock for the first time. His breath came out in an excited huff when he gripped it in his palm and gently stroked its length. "Forgive me, God," he whispered, "for I am about to sin."

He dropped to his knees, and Trey wasn't sure if he was going to start praying—which would have totally freaked him out—or what. Trey gasped when Isaac directed his cock into his mouth and sucked him deep. Trey leaned heavily into the cool tile wall behind him and stroked Isaac's hair. He watched Isaac struggle not to gag each time his cock bumped into the back of his throat.

Isaac's technique was a little timid, but the guy had no way of knowing how much Trey loved to have a man on his knees sucking his cock. The combination of sensation and the vision of his cock disappearing into Isaac's mouth made Trey's belly quiver. Isaac's hand slid over Trey's heavy balls and between his legs. When he realized Isaac's intention, Trey relaxed his stance and allowed Isaac's finger to slide up his ass. He fleetingly wondered how many times Isaac had fantasized about doing this to another man.

For a virgin, he was very keen to explore. When a second finger slid up Trey's ass, the involuntary need to thrust overtook him and he rocked forward, driving his cock deeper into Isaac's throat.

Isaac somehow managed to suck harder. Mercy.

Trey tilted his head to lean against the wall. His eyes drifted closed as he allowed sensation to carry him away.

Isaac's suction intensified, his fingers curled forward and pressed against Trey's prostate. How had he known... Oh yeah, the guy was a doctor. "That feels amazing," Trey whispered. "You can rub harder."

When he complied, Trey groaned. Close to orgasm, Trey eased Isaac back. Trey sucked a breath of air through his teeth as his cock popped free of Isaac's tight suction. Damn, he loved the power of a man's mouth.

"Did I do it wrong?" Isaac asked. The uncertainty in those trembling words brought a smile to Trey's lips.

"No, baby. You were perfect. I'm seconds from coming, and I want to give you what you want now."

Isaac's fingers slid free of his ass, and Trey urged him to his feet. He turned Isaac to face the wall and moved behind him. He wished they had all the time in the world to explore each other's bodies, but he knew the reality was that they had to hurry. Someone would probably come looking for them soon and Isaac needed time to adjust to what he was discovering about himself before revealing it to others. It was one thing to accept who you were and an entirely different thing to find the acceptance of people you cared about.

Trey unfastened Isaac's pants and pushed down to his knees. He caressed Isaac's hips, his hands traveling down either side of Isaac's erect cock to trail lightly over his balls. Trey palmed them gently, but didn't touch Isaac's cock, just the area around it, above it, and below it, until Isaac was whimpering with excitement. Trey paused to apply a condom and then returned to the gentle caresses that would drive any man insane with need.

"Fuck me, Trey. I can't stand the anticipation."

The problem was Trey didn't have any lubrication, and he sure didn't want to hurt Isaac his first time. Maybe there was something in the medicine cabinet they could use.

"Hold that thought," Trey said.

He opened the medicine cabinet and found a tube of K-Y Jelly.

Jackpot. So Mr. and Mrs. B still liked to roll in the sack. You never could judge a person's sex life by looking at them.

"Hurry," Isaac said, hands on the wall, beautiful virginal ass exposed and begging for penetration.

Trey applied lubricant to his straining cock and then to Isaac's waiting hole. Isaac gasped excitedly and strained against Trey as his fingers pressed inside his silky depths for the first time. Trey withdrew his fingers completely and applied more lube. He slid them deep again and rotated them inside Isaac to prepare him for his first deep penetration.

"Oh," Isaac crooned. "Oh yes. Take me."

Trey was too excited to loosen him up properly. He needed to possess Isaac's tight, eager ass. Like immediately. Trey grabbed his cock in one hand and carefully inserted its head into Isaac's body. It took every shred of his willpower not to surge forward and bury himself balls deep. Trey pressed an inch deeper and then withdrew completely before entering him again. Just an inch. Another. Withdraw. Again. A bit deeper this time.

"Ahhh," Isaac gasped.

"You okay?" Trey whispered.

"No."

"No?" Trey started to pull out, but Isaac pushed against him.

"Deeper. I want you deeper. Fuck me for real! Don't tease."

Can do. Trey began thrusting slowly. Pressing half an inch deeper with each penetration until Isaac was taking all of him with every thrust. When Isaac crooned with excitement and met his thrusts, Trey reached around his body and took Isaac's cock between his palms, stroking his length in time with each plunge.

Isaac tried to keep his cries of pleasure to a minimum, but he was totally getting off and rocking back to take Trey harder and harder. Isaac thrust his cock into Trey's hands at the same time. Trey grinned, loving to give a lover pleasure even more than he liked to receive it. He knew that giving always came back twenty-fold, and Isaac's body was pure bliss. Trey's own pleasure was building him toward orgasm quickly. He stroked Isaac's cock faster, fingers bumping lightly over the crown to bring him quickly to orgasm.

Isaac bit his hand as he cried out, his ass gripping Trey tightly as he came. His hot cum filled Trey's hand and dripped between his fingers. Trey let go in the next instant, still pumping vigorously into Isaac as the spasms of pleasure gripped the base of his cock. He shuddered in the aftermath of bliss for a moment, planting tender kisses on Isaac's nape as his breathing returned to normal. He pulled out with a reluctant sigh.

Trey urged Isaac to face him, knowing all the emotions that went through a guy the first time he realized he enjoyed getting fucked up the ass. To be dominated by another man. To be filled while he came. There was nothing like it. It was humbling and empowering. Trey licked Isaac's cum off his hand as a sign of affection. Isaac watched, his eyes glassy, breathing still irregular.

"That was perfect, Isaac," he said.

Isaac flushed.

"Did you like it? Did getting fucked live up to your expectations?"

He nodded. "Even better than I imagined."

Trey smiled. "Good. Go clean up now."

Isaac reached for the toilet paper. Trey removed the condom and cleaned up in the sink.

"You need to tell Rebekah the truth," Trey pressed as he refastened his pants and secured his belt buckle.

Isaac hesitated. "Is that why you seduced me?"

Trey drew him into his arms. "I seduced you because I wanted you." Maybe that hadn't been his reason when he'd entered the bathroom, but it was true now. Trey kissed him, his tongue brushing Isaac's upper lip. "You're sexy, Isaac. Desirable."

"I am?" He glanced at him shyly.

"Yeah. I'd fuck you again right now if I had the time. I'll give you my number. We can get together again. Maybe I'll let you fuck me next time."

Isaac smiled. "I think I'd like that."

"And then I'll fuck you again. Harder next time, and you can cry out as loud as you want when you come."

"I know I'll like that."

"I'll even wear my tongue piercing for you."

Isaac gasped and fumbled to get his phone out of his pocket. "Here. Program your number in. I'll call you. Like tomorrow."

Trey took his phone and entered his number into its memory while Isaac cleaned up and rearranged his clothes. "Yeah, sure. I have plans for lunch tomorrow, but I'm free around dinnertime."

"Come over to my place. I'll cook for you."

"You cook?" Trey asked.

Isaac nodded vigorously. "What do you like?"

"Cherries…" He grinned wickedly. "But I'll eat anything." Trey kissed Isaac gently and pressed his cell phone back into his hand. "Tell Rebekah the truth. Promise me."

Isaac nodded slightly, and with that, Trey left the bathroom with a huge smile on his face and a spring in his step. He fucking *loved* deflowering virgins.

Chapter 28

ERIC GAVE TREY AN odd look when he returned to the table. Trey had the hugest, self-indulgent grin on his face. He'd obviously been up to something. This was Trey after all. He was always up to something.

"Where've you been?" Sed asked Trey.

"Making room for seconds," Trey said, his smile broadening further. He patted his flat belly with both hands.

Isaac sat down, wincing slightly as his butt settled in the chair. He glanced at Rebekah and blushed to the roots of his carefully arranged curls. Except his hair wasn't immaculate anymore. It looked as if someone had been running their fingers through it. Eric turned his attention back to Trey. Still grinning. And then back to Isaac. Still blushing.

No way. Those two couldn't possibly… Eric shook his head to settle his thoughts somewhere other than the nearest gutter. Dr. Perfect and Trey Mills? It simply wasn't possible. They had been gone for twenty minutes. Odd that they returned at the same time. Eric caught Trey's eye, and he winked at Eric. Eric shot a pointed look in Isaac's direction, and Trey shrugged as if he didn't get what he was asking, but his smile never wavered.

Rebekah took Isaac's hand. "Are you okay? What took you so long? I was starting to worry."

"Oh nothing," he said, avoiding eye contact. "I'm feeling better now."

"Are you sick?"

Isaac glanced at Trey and blushed again. "Probably."

"Do you want to go?" Rebekah asked. "I can take you home."

He shook his head. "No. That would be rude. Your mother worked so hard to put this wonderful meal together, and your friends want to spend time with you."

"Think nothing of it," Mrs. B said. "If you're feeling poorly, you should go lie down, dear."

Eric wondered if she'd ever refer to him as dear. Not likely. Not even if he and Rebekah had still been together. Not that Rebekah would ever dump Dr. Perfect for him. Eric glanced at her, his heart in his throat, and then picked at his mashed potatoes.

"You're a fantastic cook, Mrs. B," Brian said. "Even better than my wife."

It earned him a glare from Myrna, but he hugged her and kissed her temple, and all was forgiven.

"You better eat more than that, Myr. You're eating for two now." With his fork, Brian poked a piece of ham on his plate and shifted it to hers. He then rubbed a hand over her flat stomach. She smiled at him, the love between them tangible.

"Actually, I'm eating for one, plus a little bitty future rock god about the size of the tip of your finger."

"He's that small?"

Eric chuckled at the astonished expression on Brian's face.

"Yep," she said. "For now."

Brian touched Myrna's face tenderly, and Eric diverted his gaze so he didn't have to watch their PDA. "Maybe you'd rather have turkey," Brian said. "Sed, pass the turkey this way."

Sed was eating more than enough for two, while Jessica picked at her food and chatted with Mr. B about something political or lawyerly. Sed grunted an affirmation and passed the platter of turkey in Brian's direction. Brian forked a large piece of turkey onto Myrna's plate.

Myrna chuckled. "You're bound and determined to make me fat, aren't you?"

"I just want you happy and healthy."

Her fingertips resting on Brian's jaw, she kissed her husband tenderly. "Mission accomplished."

Eric's attention turned to Rebekah. She stared at her plate with a sad expression. He knew she was thinking about never being able to have kids. Shouldn't Dr. Perfect be comforting her about now? The jackass. Eric extended his foot beneath the table and touched her instep. She glanced up and he smiled at her. She smiled back, gave Isaac a wistful glance, and lowered her gaze to her plate. Eric wanted to get her alone. Hold her. He didn't care if she didn't return his affections. He simply could not stand to see her gloomy. He missed her smile. He'd do anything to see it again. Even make silly faces at her.

She giggled after he'd made several stupid faces in an attempt to cheer her up. He didn't give a shit if Mrs. B rolled her eyes a hundred times.

After dinner, they retired to the living room to play charades. Eric's favorite of all games. He settled next to Rebekah on the sofa. Dr. Save-the-World sat on her opposite side. Her warmth. Her scent. Her mere presence drove Eric to distraction. He really hoped she was happy with her doctor guy, because Eric was absolutely miserable.

"Do you want to go for a walk?" Rebekah asked.

For a second, he thought she was asking Isaac. He glanced at her, and she smiled hopefully.

She was asking him. Eric's heart leapt into his throat. "Yeah."

She jumped to her feet and headed for the front door. Eric followed at a half-run.

"Rebekah, where are you going?" Mrs. B called after Rebekah with a look of stern disapproval.

"I'll be back soon."

Eric took Rebekah's hand as they walked down the deserted street. It was a little chilly, but he doubted Rebekah would like him to wrap his arm around her shoulders and draw her against his side for warmth.

"I'm not sure where to begin," she said.

He was. "Are you really going to marry Isaac?" he blurted.

She stopped short. "Where did you ever get that idea? Did my mother tell you that?"

"No, *you* told me that."

"I did not. He did ask me, but I told him no. I told him you were my boyfriend. That I loved you. And *you*... You never even bothered to call me after our fight. I thought I meant something to you, Eric." She planted a fist on either hip and glared at him in the light of a nearby street lamp.

"You mean everything to me. And I *did* call you, Rebekah. A thousand times I called you, even after you texted me and told me to fuck off and that you were marrying Isaac."

"What? You liar," she yelled. "I never texted that."

"Yes, you did. And then Isaac answered your phone and told me you didn't want to talk to me and that I should never call you again."

She hesitated. "Isaac answered my phone? When?"

"A couple hours after I saw you kiss him."

"I didn't kiss him! He kissed me."

"Well, you didn't stop him!"

"I didn't get the chance. You punched him before I could retaliate."

Now Eric hesitated. "You didn't want him to kiss you?"

"No. I love you, you fucking idiot. Why would I want to kiss another man?"

Eric panted heavily, a mixture of anger and confusion and joy. She loved him. Sure, she had called him a fucking idiot, but she loved him. He almost believed her, but the hurt of the past few days made him hesitate. "If you love me so much, why did you hang up on me?"

"I would never hang up on you. Never. I *wanted* you to call, so we could work things out."

"Then why didn't you call me?"

"Isaac made me think that you didn't want to talk to me."

Eric's fists clenched. "That little weasel."

"Did you really call me after our fight?"

"Yes. Like I said, I called you around a thousand times."

"I think I would have noticed if you called a thousand times, Eric. You never called me. Not once. I even slept with my phone so I wouldn't miss your call."

"Maybe there's something wrong with your phone. I called you, Rebekah. I did."

"There's nothing wrong with my phone. I've used it several times today." She pulled her cell phone out of her pocket and flipped through her missed calls. "There's nothing from you," she said. "A bunch of calls from an unknown number, but not a single call from you."

"That's weird. Let me try now."

He took out his phone and dialed her number. The screen lit up, but there was no sound. Her display said caller unknown.

"Answer it," he said.

She answered. "Hello."

"That fuckin' jerk," Eric grumbled into his phone.

"What?"

"Don't you get what he did?"

"Who?"

"Isaac—who else?"

"What?"

"He changed my ringtone to silent and my name to caller unknown. Programmed it right into your phone."

Her eyes widened. "What? Why would he do that?"

"To get rid of me."

"I can't believe he'd do something like that!"

"Believe it."

They stared at each other for a long moment.

"I love you, Rebekah."

"I love you too, Eric."

They were standing next to each other talking on their cell phones. "Bye."

He disconnected and then flipped through the messages on his phone. "Did you send me this?"

She read the saved text on his screen: *Fuck you, asshole. I never want to see you again.* She shook her head, her eyes filled with tears. "That's horrible. Don't you know I'd never say anything like that to you? I love you so much. The past five days have been pure hell."

Eric wrapped her in his arms and drew her against the length of his body. "I can't believe how sneaky that guy is. I want to wring his fucking neck."

Rebekah shook her head. "I'll talk to him. He's my best friend. He must have a good reason to do something like that."

"Yeah, he's a selfish prick who wants you for himself. That's his reason."

She shook her head. "I don't want to talk about Isaac anymore. Kiss me," she whispered. "Please, Eric. Kiss me and never stop."

Eric drew her against him and captured her lips in a searing kiss. She clung to him. He could taste her tears as she rubbed her lips against his desperately. "Let's never fight again," she murmured into his mouth.

"Agreed."

"And if we do, we talk about it face-to-face right away. No phone calls."

"Agreed."

"I love you," she said.

"Agreed."

She laughed, and he smiled. He stroked her hair away from her face and kissed the tears from her cheeks.

"Why aren't you wearing the jewelry I gave you?" he asked. It had been another thing that had slashed at his soul every time he looked at her.

"I took it off before we went to the shelter. I thought it would be pretty tacky to wear something that expensive in front of people who have nothing. And then I got so busy helping make dinner when we came home that I forgot to put it back on."

"That's all it was?" he asked.

She nodded.

He kissed her deeply. "I thought it meant we were through."

She shook her head, breaking their kiss, but only for a brief moment. "Let's go back to your place," she said.

"What about your guests?"

"You're the only guest that matters to me."

"Shouldn't we confront Isaac?"

"I'll talk to him later. Right now I don't want to even think about him, much less look at him. I'll probably punch him in the nose."

"I'd like that." Eric lifted her into his arms and continued to kiss her as he carried her to the car. "They'll come looking for us if we don't tell them we're leaving."

"I'll call them while you drive," Rebekah said.

He opened the door to Rebekah's car and slipped her into the passenger seat. "I hope you have keys."

She flipped the visor down, and a set of keys tumbled into her lap. "Drive like a maniac. I want to get you in bed as soon as possible."

He had no problem fulfilling that request. While he navigated the streets, Rebekah called her mother. Eric tried not to let her argument bother him, but it did.

"I didn't call you to discuss this, Mother. I called to let you know that I left with Eric, and I didn't want you to worry."

Eric caught snatches of her mother's tirade. "I raised you better than this... acting like a little slut... I can't believe you'd just leave Isaac here by himself... You'll be lucky if he ever speaks to you again..."

"He'll be lucky if I don't cut his balls off with a rusty knife."

Eric chuckled. He caught the flash of Rebekah's white smile in a streetlight. "I'll be by tomorrow to pick up my stuff. Tell everyone good-bye for me."

"And me!" Eric said enthusiastically.

He swore he heard Mrs. B emit a long line of obscenities just before Rebekah ended the call.

"Are you sure this is what you want?" he asked, reaching across the car to place a comforting hand on the back of her neck. "I don't have much experience with mothers, but I think it's important to keep them happy."

"I wish she'd think of *my* happiness. I think she believes she's doing what's right for me, but Isaac never made me happy. Not the way you do. He did take good care of me, and I feel obligated not to be mean to him—"

"I don't."

Rebekah laughed. "He is being a royal dick, isn't he? I wonder why."

"Like I said, he wants you for himself."

"Well, he isn't going to have me." She squeezed Eric's knee. "I'm yours."

Eric's heart fluttered like a caged bird. "Reb?"

"Yeah."

"Since we're back to being honest with each other."

"Yeah."

"Why did you change your hair color?"

She sighed loudly. "It's just a rinse. Dad asked me to make it look normal for our family Christmas picture. I can't say no to my daddy."

Eric breathed a breath of relief. "I don't know why it bothered me so much. Maybe because the first time I saw you, I knew we were destined to be together because our hair was the same shade of blue."

She laughed. "Really? I thought you were drunk or something. You were tripping over your feet."

"I was knocked silly by your perfection."

She laughed again. "You're such a ham."

"Glazed or cured?"

"Will you drive faster?"

"I don't think that's possible. You need a better car," he said. "How about a '68 Camaro?"

"What?"

"Well, the Corvette is running like a dream, thanks to you, so now we can work on the Camaro. When it's fixed, I want you to have it."

"And I suppose if I say it's too much and decline your gift, you'll get all hurt and act like I've run you through the heart with a spear."

"Something like that."

"Okay. We'll fix up the Camaro. And I'll keep it." She did an excited dance in her seat. "I'll buy the next piece of junk for us to fix. How about that?"

"That sounds perfect. That way I know I'm going to keep you around for a while."

"Try forever."

"Yeah, let's do that," he said. "Let's try forever."

"What do you mean?"

"I think I want to get married."

"Why?"

"To have a family."

"Oh." She went very quiet. "You know I can't give you a family, Eric."

"You'll be my family. And maybe we could adopt some kids, if you want."

"Adopt?"

"There are lots of kids out there who need a good home. I know. I used to be one."

"Let me think about it."

He knew she dreamed of having kids of her own, but it wasn't possible. He'd give her time to adjust to the idea.

"You deserve a woman who can give you kids of your own," she said after a long moment.

"I honestly don't want kids of my own. I want to adopt."

She fell silent again. She still hadn't spoken when he turned into his driveway. He parked the car and turned to her.

"Tell me what you're thinking," he said.

She closed her eyes and shook her head.

"Honesty. Remember? It's the only thing that works between us."

"I feel so selfish."

"Why would you feel selfish?"

"Because I want to say yes. I want to marry you. And I want you to give up having kids of your own to be with me. And I would absolutely love to adopt children and raise them with you."

"How is that selfish?"

"It's all about me."

"Us," he corrected.

"You only say you want to adopt to make me feel better. Don't you think I realize that?"

He shook his head. "Not true. I want to adopt the most troubled kids in existence. The ones who act out and get into trouble. The ones failing at school and in so much pain you can see it in their eyes. The ones so terrible that no one could possibly love them. I want that for a kid, because no one ever did it for me. I was that kid, Rebekah. Now who's selfish?"

She reached across the car and wrapped her arms around him. "I want to adopt that kid too," she said. She kissed him tenderly. "I want to marry the wonderful man he became."

"Yeah?"

"Yeah."

"Glad that's settled. Let's go get naked."

She laughed and let him drag her out of the car through the driver's side door. He carried her through the garage, into the kitchen, and set her on the table.

"Did you really just agree to marry me?" he asked.

"Yeah."

"Your mother is going to kill us both."

"Please don't mention my mother. I'm all horny and still completely dressed."

"Let's remedy that now."

His fingers moved to the buttons of her blouse and he released them one at a time, slowly revealing her flesh to his eager gaze. She loosened his tie and drew it over his head, before working on unfastening the buttons of his shirt.

"Tomorrow we should pick out an engagement ring," he said.

"You're thinking entirely too much," she said. She slipped under his arm and headed toward his bedroom. He followed, the look in her eyes already stealing his thoughts. She dropped her shirt in the hallway, and instead of entering his bedroom, went into the living room.

"I think I'll watch a little TV," she said.

"Huh?"

She unfastened her pants and slipped out of them before sitting on the sofa. When he sat beside her, she looked up and said, "Go sit in the chair over there."

"I thought we were getting ready to have fantastic makeup sex."

"We will. In a little while. I'm not in the mood right now."

She turned on the TV and leaned against the cushions in nothing but her bra and panties. "Go sit over there," she repeated.

He groaned and moved to the chair across from the sofa. "Do you really want to watch TV?"

She grinned wickedly. "Of course."

As soon as he sat in the chair and turned his attention to the TV, she began to rub her mound through her panties. So she didn't really want to watch TV. She wanted to put on a little show. Hell yeah. He was more than ready to watch that.

She propped her feet on the coffee table and slid her hand into her panties. He couldn't see what she was doing to herself inside those panties. Could only imagine her fingers sliding over her slick folds. Disappearing into her tight pussy. Eric was instantly hard and ready to devour her. But he stayed in his chair and just watched.

Rebekah's eyes were closed, but her mouth was open as she continued to give herself pleasure just out of sight. Her nipples strained against the lace of her bra. She moved her free hand to massage her breast and pinch her nipple through the fabric.

"Oh, oh, oh," she gasped. "I'm coming. I'm coming." Her back arched off the sofa, and she shuddered hard.

Eric winced and pressed a hand against his cock, throbbing inside his shorts. He hadn't had sex in almost a week, and watching Rebekah get herself off had him on the verge of orgasm. She would have to help him regain his staying power.

"Take off your panties," he requested breathlessly.

She cracked her eyes open to look at him. "You first."

"I'm not wearing any panties."

She chuckled. "You know what I mean. Show me your cock. Is it hard?"

"Have you ever known it not to be hard?"

She grinned. "Not often."

"Well, it's behaving in its typical manner right now."

"I want to see."

He unzipped his pants and lowered his underwear until his cock sprang free.

"It's definitely hard," she said. "Make yourself come and I'll take off my panties."

"Take off your panties, and I'll make myself come," he countered.

She lifted her hips off the sofa and pulled her panties down. When she removed them, she opened her legs wide so he could see all that she'd kept hidden. He let his mind drift to fantasy. Pictured himself rubbing his cock head in the slick moisture between her thighs, slipping inside her, retreating. His hand began to move over his cock.

"Stroke it faster," she requested.

He obeyed.

"Harder."

Yes, harder.

"Faster, baby, faster."

"I want to be inside you."

She slid a finger into her pussy. "Like this?"

"Yeah."

"Do you want to come inside me?"

He bit his lip and nodded, almost ready to explode.

"Come here."

He moved from the chair and knelt between her open legs.

"Take me," she whispered.

He rubbed his cock over her opening, teasing her. Making her want it.

"Oh," she gasped when he slipped the head into her hot body.

He bit his lip and watched as he fucked her shallow, inserting just the head before withdrawing completely and slipping in just an inch again. She wriggled her hips, tempting him to take her deeper, but he refused. He continued to thrust into her a few inches, knowing if he plunged deep he'd come.

Rebekah moved her hand between her legs and stroked her clit, rotating her hips to stimulate his cock head each time he thrust into her.

"That actually feels really good," she gasped, "but it makes me want you so bad. Ah, God, Eric, just a little deeper. Please."

He gave her another inch, but still pulled out completely with each thrust.

Her excited cries had him by the balls. Lured him deeper. He lost control and thrust deep. She moved her hand out of the way so he could rub his groin against her clit as he drove himself into her over and over and over again. When she cried out and her pussy clenched around him, he let go, still pumping into her body as he came.

He collapsed against her and nuzzled her neck. "I love you," he whispered into her ear. "Rebekah."

Chapter 29

THE NEXT AFTERNOON, REBEKAH kissed Eric and smiled up at him. They had skipped lunch at Brian's house to stay in bed for another six hours. She had been tempted to stay there all day, but she had a few things she needed to take care of. All Eric could talk about was buying her an engagement ring. And she was going to let him.

"Do you want me to pick it out, or do you want to help me?" he asked.

She couldn't even imagine the ginormous ring he'd end up buying. She'd have to walk around with her hand in a vault. "I'm sure you'll go way overboard if you pick it out yourself. I'm going to pack some stuff at my mom's house. How about I meet you at the mall for dinner, and we can go shopping afterward?"

"Okay."

She kissed him again and hugged him for several minutes. She honestly did not want to let him go. Ever. But she'd eventually need clothes. And she missed the weight of her butterfly necklace and bracelet against her skin as a constant reminder that Eric thought she was beautiful.

Rebekah climbed into her car, and after waving good-bye, she headed toward her parents' house. She knew there would be a confrontation with her mother. She was looking forward to it. To standing up to the woman who had tried to rule her life for twenty-seven years. Yet part of her wanted to curl into her protective shell and sneak back to Eric and never confront the woman at all.

When she let herself into the house, her mother was standing in the foyer. "You spent the night with him, didn't you? That dirty rock star."

"Well, yeah. I didn't sleep in my car." She tried to walk around her mother, but she grabbed Rebekah's arm.

"You'll be lucky if Isaac will ever take you back now. You didn't have sex with that man, did you?"

"Multiple times, Mother. We're getting married."

Her mother's pupils dilated. Rebekah's heart thudded with fear. "You are not marrying him. You are marrying Isaac. He told me last night that you said you would marry him."

"I said that over a year ago. Before we broke up."

"He was in tears."

"Tears?"

"Yes, tears. He said he has never loved a woman the way he loves you, and the thought of losing you was tearing him up inside."

Isaac had *cried* in front of her mother? What in the world was his damage?

"I'm sorry I have to hurt him, Mom, but I don't love him. I love Eric."

"I don't care who you love, you're marrying Isaac."

"This isn't the seventeenth century, Mother. I can marry whoever I want. I'm a grown woman. I can make decisions for myself."

"Bad decisions. You always make bad decisions. First you decided you wanted to be a mechanic. A mechanic! Your father said you should be allowed to choose your own career, so we let you go to that vocational college, and after you graduated you worked in a garage for what? A month?"

"Six weeks," she mumbled. "I don't like working on new cars. They have too many electronics."

"So you decided you wanted to go to college to be an audio engineer like your brother. You went to Alaska each summer to work on fishing boats and oil rigs. Why?"

"To get away from you, maybe?"

"That's lovely, Rebekah. Where did you learn to speak to your mother that way?"

"Let go of my arm. I'm leaving."

"And then you got sick during your junior year. You know why you got sick?"

"Because I had cancer?"

"Because God is punishing you."

Her mother's words punched Rebekah in the stomach, and her heart gave an unpleasant lurch. "That's not true."

"It is. I know it is. You're lucky He let you live."

"*He* didn't let me live. Medical treatment let me live." Rebekah yanked on her arm. "Let go."

"He took your ability to have children, Rebekah. God is punishing you. Punishing you for making bad decisions."

"Punishing me? What did I do that you think is so wrong?"

"All those bad decisions, Rebekah. Your whole life. Cancer was your wake-up call."

"It *was* my wake-up call. It showed me that I have to live life to the fullest each day, and the only one who has ever made me feel truly alive is Eric."

Rebekah twisted her arm, not caring that her mother's grip would leave bruises. Mom refused to release her no matter how hard she pulled.

"I'm moving in with Eric. We're going to get married and adopt kids. That's what I want."

"What you want doesn't matter, Rebekah. All that matters is what God wants."

"How do you know what God wants?"

"He talks to me."

"Mom," she said, "I think maybe you need to talk to, not God, but a psychiatrist."

"You think I'm crazy?" Mom shook her head in annoyance. "I want what's best for you. You know Isaac stood by your side the entire time you were sick. He's a good man."

That was true. He also did some pretty sneaky, conniving things to come between her and Eric. "If I promise to talk to him, will that get you off my back?"

"Are you going to marry him?"

"No."

Mom scowled, and then she got a peaceful look on her face. "Yes, talk to Isaac. God will bring you back together. I have faith."

Rebekah did plan to talk to Isaac as soon as she left. She had a few choice words to share. Words her mother would be embarrassed to know her daughter knew, much less used.

Eric sat in the restaurant where he and Rebekah had agreed to meet for dinner. She was over forty minutes late. She wasn't answering her phone. He was starting to worry. He didn't want to leave the restaurant and miss her, but something wasn't right. He wanted to believe that she hadn't gotten cold feet and run for the hills, but that was better than the thought that something bad had happened.

Another ten minutes passed. Another. A petite woman entered the restaurant and his heart stuttered, but it wasn't Rebekah. When he couldn't stand it any longer, he dialed her parents' house.

Mrs. B answered the phone. "What do you want?"

"Rebekah was supposed to meet me for dinner after she stopped by your house. Have you seen her?"

"She's not here."

"Did she make it there?"

"Yes, but she already left."

"How long ago?"

"Almost an hour ago."

"She should have been here by now," he muttered, more to himself than Mrs. B.

"I don't think you'll be seeing her anymore. She's with Isaac now."

He didn't want to feel the jealousy those words inspired, but he couldn't help it.

"With Isaac?" he questioned breathlessly.

"I told you they were meant to be. As written in the good book, *Isaac brought her into the tent of Sarah, his mother, and took Rebekah, and she became his wife, and he loved her.* Isaac loves Rebekah. She will become his wife."

"What?" Was she quoting from the Bible?

"I promised God that if He spared Rebekah's life, I would do His bidding. I promised."

"God's bidding?"

"The book of Genesis speaks of it: *And Isaac prayed to the lord for his wife, because she was barren. And the lord granted his prayer, and Rebekah his wife conceived.*" Mrs. B muttered under her breath. Eric wasn't sure she knew she was still on the phone. "Though barren, Rebekah conceived. Isaac prayed, and Rebekah had two sons. There is still hope for her. My daughter. My Rebekah. Still hope. She must... must be with Isaac. Must be. So she can have babies. And he loves her. Isaac loves her. Loves Rebekah. It is God's will."

Eric was starting to think that Mrs. B was off her rocker. "Where is Rebekah?" he asked.

"When David was paralyzed, I knew God was punishing me again for allowing Isaac and Rebekah to break up. I promised if he spared David that I'd make sure Isaac and Rebekah would end up together. I promised. They must stay together, you see. I cannot live through another tragedy brought upon my children. I cannot."

"You honestly believe that, don't you?" Eric asked, flabbergasted. "That the bad things that happened to Rebekah and Dave are a punishment from God."

"Leave Rebekah alone. I will not let you come between her and Isaac again. Will not."

"Can I speak to Dave?"

The woman's demeanor changed from demonic to angelic in an instant. "Dave is with his physical therapist. Did you know he stood for the first time the other day? I'm so proud. I think he'll be walking soon. God answered my prayers. I must live up to His expectations."

Eric decided Mrs. Blake needed a new jacket. A jacket with sleeves that fastened behind her back.

"Okay, thanks."

Eric hung up and tried to call Rebekah again. He wondered if she had any idea how unbalanced her mother was.

Chapter 30

REBEKAH TOOK A DEEP breath and knocked on Isaac's apartment door. She knew she probably shouldn't show up unannounced. He might not even be home. She wanted to clear the air between them now. She didn't want anything to weigh on her thoughts while she was having dinner with Eric. Or while they picked out her engagement ring.

A minute later the door swung open, and Trey Mills stood in the doorway in nothing but a pair of black satin boxer shorts. "Hey, Rebekah," he said with a devilish grin. "What brings you here?"

"Uh…" Why was Trey in Isaac's apartment? Maybe they'd hit it off after she and Eric had left the evening before. Okay. That made sense. But why was he almost naked? "Is… is I-Isaac h-here?"

"Yeah, he's here. Why don't you come in?"

Trey stepped to the side, and Rebekah entered the apartment. She could smell dinner cooking. Garlic, oregano, parmesan. Isaac had always been an excellent cook. Italian cuisine was only one of his specialties. Trey shut the door behind her and pressed a hand to the small of her back.

"Don't be too hard on him, okay?" he said quietly. "He's happy, but scared."

"About what?"

"I'll let him tell you."

Isaac stepped out of the bedroom, drying his hair with a towel. He was wearing gray lounge pants, but was shirtless and barefoot.

"I was thinking," he said, a huge smile on his face, "maybe I should get my tongue pier—" He noticed Rebekah, and his smile faded. He dropped the towel around his shoulders.

They stared at each other wide-eyed for what seemed like hours.

"Isaac," she said finally. "What's going on?"

Isaac's eyes flicked to Trey. Isaac looked like a caged animal ready to dart as soon as a break presented itself. "What did you tell her?"

Trey shook his head. "Nothing."

"We need to talk," Rebekah said.

Isaac nodded. He turned and went back into his room. She didn't really want to go into his bedroom, but she supposed since Trey was there, they needed someplace private to have their falling out.

Rebekah entered his room and closed the door. The lamp on the bedside table glowed softly. She couldn't help but notice the empty condom wrappers. So he claimed to love her but had slept with some other woman? Not that she cared. It just added to her confusion about how Isaac had been treating her lately.

His back was to her. His head hung low. He was obviously feeling guilty about something.

"I know what you did to my cell phone," she said.

"I'm gay," he blurted.

The words registered, but the implications behind his statement were difficult to grasp. "You're... *what*?"

"Gay. Homosexual."

She blinked and shook her head slightly. "You're... *what*?" she repeated.

"I like guys, okay?" He glanced over his shoulder. "I'm gay. Is it that hard for you to understand?"

Yes, it *was* that hard for her to understand. They'd been in love. Engaged. Had sex. Granted, it had been passionless, sorta icky sex, but it had been sex. Infrequent. Lights off. Boring. Tedious sex. But it had been sex, by God.

Isaac's gay.

The reality struck her so hard that she laughed. "You're gay?"

He nodded, avoiding her gaze.

Her eyes darted to the empty wrappers on the bedside table. "You had sex with Trey?"

He flushed and did this cute eye-rolling thing that not only told her he had done it with Trey, but it had been phenomenal. Not icky. Not boring. Not tedious. It had been full of passion. And the lights had definitely been on.

"I need to sit down," Rebekah said. She sat on the edge of his bed and breathed through her lightheadedness.

He sat beside her. After a moment, he took her hand and gripped it in both of his. "I'm sorry."

"For what?"

"For trying to come between you and Eric. I know you love him, but I needed you to marry me."

"I'd like to say I understand, Isaac, but I honestly don't."

"I need a wife," he said. "For appearance's sake. You know my father will disown me if he finds out I'm gay. I might as well kiss the family practice good-bye. You and I get along so well. You can't have kids anyway, so no one would be suspicious if we adopt. It just makes sense that we stay together."

"So I'm supposed to give up my chance at happiness so you can pretend to be something you're not."

He ran a hand over his face. "It seemed like a good idea at the time. I love you, Rebekah. I do. I always have. I'd be a great husband. Treat you well. Take care of you forever. Give you anything you could ever want or need. It's just the thought of having sex with you makes me physically ill."

As if she could forget how unattractive he'd made her feel. "But that's not because I'm not sexy or because my body feels weird inside, it's because..." For the first time, she realized her body wasn't the problem. It never had been. She jerked her hand out of his and jumped to her feet to glare at him. "How could you do that to me?"

"Do what?"

"Make me feel so sexually unappealing! Talk about a major mind fuck, Isaac. If it weren't for Eric, I'd still think I had nothing to offer a man in the bedroom. I thought there was something *wrong* with me. That my body was disgusting."

"I thought there *must* be something wrong with you. I wanted to be attracted to you, Rebekah. I just... wasn't. And I couldn't... I couldn't force myself to have sex with you after the surgery. I tried. Mentally, I had convinced myself that I needed to. Physically? I couldn't even maintain an erection. I really did think it was because of your surgery."

"It never occurred to you that *I* wasn't the problem?"

"Did that occur to you?" he asked.

She lowered her eyes. "Well, no, actually. You've always been so... so... well, *perfect*."

"That's a pretty hard label to live up to."

The turmoil in his eyes made her cringe. She wasn't even mad at him anymore. She emitted a loud sigh. "You must be struggling to come to terms with this. When did you realize?"

"Last night."

"Thank you for confiding in me. I'm sure that wasn't easy." She sat beside him again and wrapped an arm around his back. He leaned against her for support, and they sat there for a long while, silently offering strength to one another. He'd done this so many times when she'd been sick. Just offered his presence so she never felt alone. She was happy to offer him this bit of comfort in return.

"Rebekah?" he said quietly. "I need to ask you a favor. Will you do something for me?"

She stroked the loose waves from his forehead with one hand. "Of course."

"My father is having a big dinner party next week. All the physicians from the clinic will be there. The entire staff too. He didn't say specifically, but I think he's going to ask me to join the practice full time. In front of everyone." He took her hand and clung to it. "I was hoping… would you go with me? We could pretend…"

"Isaac…"

"We could pretend that we're still a couple, and then after he makes the announcement, I'll tell him about…" He took a deep shuddering breath. "I need time to come to terms with this, and if you're there, I won't get all the regular questions."

"The regular questions?"

"When are you going to settle down, son? Are you ever going to get married? I already had two kids by the time I was your age. Don't you think you need to start having a family?" he said in a pretty good impression of his father's deep voice. "You know. The regular questions."

She understood exactly where he was coming from, and she was tempted to say yes, but she wasn't sure how Eric would feel about her pretending to be Isaac's woman. Even if it was only for one evening. "I have to ask Eric," she said.

Isaac cringed. "He hates me. He'll never go for it."

"You have been acting like an ass lately," she said. "Can you blame him for not understanding how we can be friends?"

"Sorry."

She kissed his temple. "I forgive you. This time."

"You're good to me, Reb. Sometimes I wish… Sometimes I wish you were a guy," he said.

Rebekah laughed. "I've always been sort of a tomboy. Maybe that's why you thought you loved me." She glanced at the clock radio beside the bed and her heart sank. "Oh crap, I was supposed to meet Eric an hour ago. He's probably worried."

She pulled out her phone and found that it was turned off. She tried to turn it on, but the battery was dead. "Shit. He's probably been trying to call me. Can I use your phone?"

"Of course."

She climbed to her feet and kissed him on the temple. "I'm here for you, you know. Just like you were there for me when I needed you during my treatments."

He groaned and fell back on his bed. "Stop being so nice to me. You're making me feel like a complete jerk."

She chuckled. "Good. Maybe you'll remember that the next time you act like a selfish asshole."

He chuckled. "When did you become so blunt?"

"Recently. And I like it."

She let herself out of the bedroom and went into the kitchen to use the phone. Trey was sitting on a stool at the breakfast bar still in nothing but his boxer shorts. He was fiddling with his smart phone. He looked up and grinned. "Did he tell you?"

"Yeah."

He nodded. "Good."

"Are you going to break his heart?" Rebekah asked.

"Who, me?" His look of innocence wasn't fooling her.

"Let him down easy."

"I know what I'm doing," Trey assured her.

Rebekah dialed Eric's number and hoped he'd answer. He probably wouldn't like seeing Isaac's number on his caller ID. He answered after several rings. "Is Rebekah okay?" he asked breathlessly.

"I'm fine," she said. "Sorry I'm late. I'm getting ready to leave now. I'll tell you what's going on when I get to the restaurant. Are you still waiting there?"

"Yeah. I think I've eaten twenty or thirty complimentary breadsticks. I tried to call. You didn't answer."

"My battery is dead. Go ahead and order for us both. I'll hurry."

Rebekah gasped when Trey cuddled against her back. "Come

on back to bed, Rebekah," he said near her ear and phone receiver. "Isaac and I aren't finished with you yet."

Rebekah elbowed him in the stomach, and he chuckled.

"Is that Trey?" Eric asked.

"Yeah, he thinks he's funny."

"There's nothing funny about how hot you look in this deep sea diver getup," Trey said, making sure Eric would hear. His bangs tickled her cheek as he leaned close to the receiver. She giggled. "Have you seen the oxygen tank and flippers on this woman?" he continued. "Lord have mercy. Hot."

"What is he talking about?" Eric asked.

"He's just teasing," Rebekah assured him.

"Isaac, hand me the snorkel. I'm going down," Trey said. "I won't be coming up for air for a while." Isaac leaned against the opposite side of the counter and quirked an eyebrow at Trey.

Rebekah snorted as she tried not to laugh. "Stop it, Trey."

"Yeah, stop it, Trey." Eric sounded out of sorts. "Why are you at Isaac's house? And what is Trey doing there?"

"I'll explain as soon as I get to the restaurant."

"It will probably be at least another hour, Sticks," Trey said and made obnoxious kissing noises against the back of Rebekah's neck.

Shoulders scrunched, she laughed again and slapped Trey until he finally backed off. She lost her train of thought when Trey leaned over the counter, holding Isaac's gaze in a sensual stare and kissed him tenderly. The only thing Rebekah could do was gape, heart thudding with… She couldn't identify the feeling exactly. Curiosity? Excitement? She wasn't sure, but she kind of liked watching them kiss.

"Rebekah?" Eric said into her ear, drawing her attention away from the way-too-hot guys totally trying to out-kiss each other at the moment.

"I'll be there in fifteen minutes," she promised. "Love you."

"Me too," Eric whispered and disconnected.

She hated to interrupt the festivities. It was interesting to see how passionate Isaac could be when he was actually turned on. He'd never kissed *her* the way he was kissing Trey. Um… "Isaac, I'll call you tomorrow about the party after I talk to Eric."

He peeled his lips off Trey's and said, "Thanks, angel. I appreciate it."

"Party?" Trey said. "What party?"

"You wouldn't be interested," Isaac assured him, eyes wide with what Rebekah could only construe as abject horror.

"I'm always interested in a party," Trey said.

"No," Isaac said emphatically.

"I'll see you guys later," Rebekah said.

Trey grabbed her and hugged her. "Thanks for introducing me to your ex-boyfriend," Trey murmured into her ear so Isaac couldn't hear. "He's way fun to fuck with. Mmm, and fuck."

Poor Isaac. He had no idea who he'd gotten himself tangled up with here.

Trey released her and offered a lopsided, ornery grin. He winked. Rebekah's heart skipped a beat. On second thought. Lucky Isaac. He had no idea who he'd gotten himself tangled up with here.

"You should totally mess with Eric when you see him. Make him think you were doing something with me and Isaac. It will drive him insane."

She shook her head. "No way. We're still in the making-up phase."

"He wouldn't hesitate to do it to you, you know."

Probably true, but she'd already kept him waiting for over an hour and needed to put the poor guy out of his misery. "Bye, Isaac." She waved at Trey and let herself out of the apartment.

By the time she arrived at the restaurant, guilt was eating her alive. The scowl on Eric's handsome face didn't make her feel better. She kissed his cheek and slid into the chair across from him. Her salad was already waiting. He'd finished his.

"I'm really sorry I'm so late."

"I think you have some explaining to do."

She stuffed a bite of salad in her mouth and held up one finger while she chewed and swallowed. "I went to Isaac's apartment to confront him about his behavior—reprogramming my phone for one thing—and Trey answered his door. I never did get to tell Isaac off properly. He told me… He told me that he's—" she lowered her voice to a whisper and leaned across the table, "—gay."

Eric didn't look the tiniest bit surprised. "And that makes everything he did okay?"

She had sort of let him off the hook as soon as he'd confided. "It's hard for him. His father will never accept this."

"Like your mother will never accept me."

Rebekah lowered her eyes. "It's different."

"I talked to her on the phone when you didn't answer your cell. She was spouting Bible verses at me."

"Let me guess, the story of Isaac and Rebekah." She stuffed more salad in her mouth and watched him fidget with the stem of his wineglass.

"Yeah, actually."

"Did she tell you the reason I got cancer is because I make bad decisions, and God is punishing me?"

"She said that to you?"

She nodded and closed her eyes to hold in emotions suddenly overwhelming her.

Eric reached across the table and squeezed her hand. "She told me she promised God that you would marry Isaac. Otherwise, she seems to think more horrible shit is going to happen to you and Dave."

Rebekah sighed. "We thought she was better."

"Better?"

"Yeah, she had a mental breakdown when I was going through chemo. That's one reason why I depended on Isaac so much. After my treatments, she seemed to recover. I guess the stress is getting to her again. I'll talk to Dad about it."

Their entrees arrived before Rebekah had finished her salad. She was grateful Eric had ordered for her. That meant they could get out of here sooner. "Are you sure you want to marry me?" she asked him. "I've got a lot of baggage."

"It makes you more interesting."

She laughed. "If that's what you want to call it."

"We could do what Brian and Myrna did and skip the engagement."

"Is that what you want?"

"I don't know. I never thought much about getting married until a couple months ago, when Sinners started falling like dominoes. I figured I'd be the last one standing."

"Technically, Brian is the only one who's married. You could be the second to fall if you want." She winked.

"Don't you want the huge ceremony and the big dress and the pile of Crock-Pots?"

"You mean crackpots."

"Crackpots?"

"Otherwise known as my crazy family."

He laughed and some of the tension drained from his body. Her mother got under his skin too. Another thing they had in common. "I'll do whatever you want, Reb. I don't want to make you feel like you're missing out on anything."

"I want to do something unusual," she said, her heart thudding with excitement.

"Like what?"

"I don't know yet. Let me think about it. We'll brainstorm. Come up with something really fun and unique."

He grinned. "I love you, you know that?"

"Yeah, I know. That's why you're going to let me pretend to be

Isaac's girlfriend at a party next week." She was picking up on Eric's uncanny ability to change the subject without missing a beat.

"What?"

"No matter when we decide to get married, I still want the engagement ring. So don't think you're getting out of that," she said, trying to keep him unbalanced. "Hurry up and eat."

"What party, Rebekah? I thought Isaac was gay. Why would he—"

"Pretend," she said. "It's just a favor. Nothing more. He's not ready to come out publicly yet."

"But—"

"Let's play cops and robbers when we get home. You can pretend I'm a jewel thief and handcuff me. Show me your long arm of the law until I confess to crimes I never committed."

"Stop changing the subject."

She laughed. "Disorienting, isn't it? Do you have handcuffs at home, or do we need to stop by Bonds-R-Us?"

He dropped his fork and grinned. "It's definitely time for another pit stop. Maybe we'll pick up a deep sea diver outfit for you to wear." He nonchalantly took a sip of water, while he watched her closely.

She contemplated the idea, knowing he was trying to find out what she, Trey, and Isaac had really been doing in Isaac's apartment. After a moment, she shook her head. "I don't think so. I don't want to catch crabs."

Eric laughed and sucked water down his windpipe. He was choking so hard, Rebekah stood to whack him on the back.

"Are you okay?" she asked.

He nodded, still choking. "Jeez, woman," he gasped between coughs. "I'm the one who's supposed to crack all the stupid jokes."

"Sorry. I'll try to come up with smarter jokes from now on. The stupid ones are all yours."

"This is why we work," he said, wiping his mouth with a napkin. "Compromise."

"I thought it was the great sex."

Her flippant comment elicited several stares from nearby tables.

"Well, there's that too," Eric said.

After dinner, they walked across the parking lot to the mall. They found the jewelry store, but when they arrived the metal gate was down, and the lights were off.

Rebekah's heart sank with disappointment. "Closed? How can it be closed? What time is it?"

"It's after eight," Eric said.

"Why is it so late?"

Eric lifted his eyebrows.

She made a sound of annoyance. "Of all the days for Isaac to come out of the closet." She gazed into a display window with longing. Not because she really wanted a ring, but because she wanted the world to see proof that she'd given her heart to Eric. "These are all too girly anyway," she said, trying to make herself feel better about having to wait at least another day.

Eric chuckled and wrapped an arm around her back to direct her to the parking lot again.

"There's probably someplace still open that's more suitable to brand you as mine," he whispered into her ear.

"Yeah, a tattoo parlor," she said with an unladylike snort. Once the idea took hold, she grew excited. "Eric!" She grabbed his forearm and stopped walking abruptly. "I want your name as my tramp stamp." She lifted the back of her shirt and pointed to her lower back. "Right there. Your name and music notes on either side. Maybe some little butterflies."

"Are you serious, Reb? That's permanent, you know."

"I know. You don't want me to?" She traced a tattoo on his forearm with one finger. It showed a dagger through a skull. It was a beautiful piece of art, but masculine. "Would you rather I get one that matches yours?"

"I would love my name permanently etched on your sexy little back. I could stare at it while…" He lifted her shirt and took a peek at the area in question. "Damn…" he said breathlessly and gave himself a little shake. "Yeah, okay. Let's go."

He scooped her into his arms, tossed her over his shoulder, and headed toward his car.

"Right now?"

"Yep. And I'm going to get your name tattooed down the length of my cock."

"You are not!"

"Yeah, I am."

She wondered if her name would get bigger when he was hard. She wondered about something else. "How long does it take for a tattoo to heal?"

"Several weeks."

"Then you won't be able to have sex for several weeks."

"You're right. Forget that then. Where do you want your name?"

She thought for a moment. What was the sexiest part of Eric's body, besides his cock? That sweet V-shape at his lower belly that disappeared into the waistband of his underwear. That's where she wanted her name. Then when he held her back against his belly, their names would press together.

"Put me down," she said. "Let me show you where I want it."

He gently set her on her feet, and she lifted his T-shirt in front. She pushed the waistband of his jeans lower and traced a swath of bare skin above his underwear. "I want it right here."

He drew a breath through his teeth. "That is going to hurt."

"More than it would on your cock?"

He chuckled. "Good point." He hurried her to the car and opened the door for her. "I know a great artist. He's done all my ink and the smiley-faced flower on the top of Jace's foot."

"Jace has a flower on his foot?"

"Yeah, I got him really drunk. Let's just say his judgment was impaired. Usually, they won't tattoo someone when they're that inebriated, but I've known Butch for years. And Jace said it was okay before he passed out. We both got our nipples pierced that night too."

"Kind of like when girls get their nails done together."

He looked grievously offended by that comparison. "Uh, no."

She laughed. "If you say so."

Eric headed out of the parking lot and drove toward the coast. "As excited as I was to get you a ring, I'm even more excited by the thought of my name tattooed on your skin."

She smiled. "Me too. My mother is going to *hate* it."

Eric's face fell. "Is that what this is about? Revenge on your mother?"

"Of course not."

The tattoo parlor was in a quaint strip of old stores a few blocks from the ocean. A cool breeze blew onshore. Rebekah wished she'd brought a sweater. Eric fed a parking meter with quarters while Rebekah waited. He grabbed her hand and led her into The Ink Well—a shady establishment at best. A man, tattooed from neck to toe, looked up from the tattoo he was inking on some guy's chest.

"Yo, Sticks. Back for more?" the artist called.

"You know I can't get enough."

"Who's the pretty lady?"

"My girlfriend, em…" He glanced at Rebekah. "Fiancée? Can I call you that?" he whispered.

"Do you see a ring on this finger?" She shook her bare, left hand in front of his face.

He sighed. "Still my girlfriend," he said. "She wants my name tattooed…" He turned her around and lifted her shirt, running a finger along her lower back. "… right there." He then rubbed his lower belly. "And I want hers right here. Can you squeeze us in right now?"

"Yeah, I'm almost done here." Butch dabbed the guy's chest with a towel, removing dots of something red from his skin.

Rebekah winced when she realized the guy under the needle was bleeding.

"Does it hurt?" she whispered to Eric.

"Yeah. In a strange way, it feels good too. Like, you know that itch you can never scratch enough? This scratches it. Do you want me to go first?"

She shook her head. "If I wait, I might chicken out."

"You're sure you want this done?"

She looked at him, her heart fluttery with emotions. "Yeah."

When it was Rebekah's turn to go under the needle, she explained her vision to the artist, Butch.

"Just his first name? Or first and last?" Butch asked.

"Just Eric in fancy lettering. And maybe a music staff and music notes on either end to bracket it, and tiny, multicolored butterflies above it to make it look feminine."

Butch nodded, obviously picturing what she wanted in his mind. "I'll draw up a stencil real quick. See if I can capture what you want. Then we can make adjustments before we make it permanent."

Rebekah's tummy fluttered as if she'd swallowed a few of those feminine little butterflies. "Okay," she croaked.

"I'm going to help him," Eric said. He handed her a book that had photos of the tattoos Butch had done. "Keep yourself occupied."

Nervous, she looked through the pages. Butch really was a talented artist. She could tell she was in good hands. Some portraits he'd inked on people looked so real it was as if she were looking at a photograph taped to their skin. Ten minutes later, Butch and Eric returned.

The stenciled drawing he showed her stole her breath. It was perfect! She imagined brides must feel that way when they tried on the wedding dress they were destined to wear for one special day.

She was trying on a piece of artwork she would wear for the rest of her life.

"Oh… I love it!" She waved at the tears suddenly in her eyes. She was making a lifelong commitment to this piece of art and the man it represented. Or all the guys named Eric in the world.

Eric ran his finger along the notes drawn on the wavy music staff that tapered into pointed curls on either side of his name. "I'll play this for you when we get home," he said.

"Did you write me a real song? I thought it was just for looks."

"Just a little melody." He brushed her hair behind her ear and leaned close to whisper, "It means I love you."

She turned her head to capture his lips in a lingering kiss. "I'm so gonna rock your world when we get home, baby."

"You always do." He patted her butt and directed her to the table where Butch was waiting.

She unfastened her jeans and slid them low on her hips so he had more area to work with. He transferred the stencil to her lower back and made her look in the mirror to make sure it was where she wanted it. It looked even better on her skin than on the paper.

"So sexy," Eric murmured.

Butch laughed. "She'd make any tattoo look sexy. Great-lookin' woman you've got here."

Rebekah beamed. She never tired of compliments.

While the stencil dried on Rebekah's lower back, Butch busied himself changing the needle in the little machine that reminded Rebekah of a small gun, only with a big freaking needle sticking out of the end. She was trying to be brave, but her tummy fluttered with nerves.

"Do you want yours to match hers?" Butch asked Eric.

"Less swirls in the lettering and bats instead of butterflies, but yeah."

Rebekah tensed when Butch dragged the buzzing needle across

her skin. It felt like someone was scratching her repeatedly. It didn't hurt nearly as bad as she'd expected, but adrenaline continuously pumped through her body. Eric held her hand the entire time and kept asking if she was okay.

"Why don't you try taking my mind off it instead of reminding me that someone is jabbing me with a needle eleventy million times?" she asked testily.

"Sorry."

"Do you still have that jagged crack I inked between your shoulder blades?" Butch asked Eric.

"Yeah. I haven't even modified it. Still looks great."

"That's the first tattoo I ever did professionally," Butch said. "How old were you, Eric?"

"Um, fifteen, I think."

"Yeah, he tried to tell me he was eighteen. I figured he was lying, but I needed the experience, so I put him under the needle."

"I like that tattoo," Rebekah said. It looked like a crack in the earth that led to hell. The fingers of a demonic hand protruded from the fiery interior, clinging to the edge of the fissure, as if trying to escape. She sucked a breath through her teeth as the needle passed over bone for the first time. "Ow." Another surge of adrenaline coursed through her body.

Butch paused to let her catch her breath. "Okay to continue?" he asked.

"Yeah."

"Your name wasn't even Sticks back then," Butch said. "What was it again?"

Rebekah strained her neck to look at Eric. He was scowling.

"Anderson," he said finally.

"Sticks isn't your real name?" Rebekah asked. The needle scraped over her spine again. "Ow."

"Yeah. I had it legally changed when I turned eighteen."

"Why?"

"Because I didn't want my mother's fuckin' name anymore, that's why."

Apparently a testy subject.

"And that design he wanted on his back?" Butch said. "He told me it was a crack in his soul to let the pain escape. Pretty profound for a fifteen-year-old kid."

"You have a big mouth, Butch," Eric grumbled.

"You haven't told her any of this stuff? No wonder she's willing to have your name inked across her back."

"The past can't be changed," she said. "The future can't be predicted. All we really have is the present. So none of that matters to me."

"Isn't she perfect?" Eric murmured.

"It's about time you found the perfect girl," Butch teased. "You're practically an old man."

"Twenty-eight next week. I am gettin' up there."

"Your birthday is next week!" Rebekah sputtered. "How come you didn't tell me?"

"Never occurred to me."

"What day?"

"December third."

She didn't have much time to put together a special surprise for him. "Well, happy birthday," she said. "In case I forget." As if.

He took her hand and linked his fingers through hers. "Thanks. I never thought I'd live to see twenty-eight. Live fast, die young."

She squeezed his hand. "Don't say things like that."

"Okay, all finished," Butch said. "Take a look."

While Rebekah admired her new tattoo in a full-length mirror, Eric helped Butch design the tattoo that would be inked on his lower belly. Butch's assistant helped Rebekah put salve and plastic wrap over the new addition to her body, while explaining how to take care of the tattoo until it fully healed. By the time she snuggled against

Eric's back, her adrenaline rush was starting to wan and she was already thinking about where she wanted her next tattoo.

"When we first decided to do this, Eric said he was going to get my name tattooed on his penis," Rebekah said. "Have you ever tattooed a guy's penis before?"

"Yeah, more often than you'd think."

Rebekah eyed Butch's tattoos. Besides his face, and most of his fingers, there wasn't an inch of undecorated skin on him. She wondered...

"Before you ask," Butch said with a chuckle, "no, my cock is not decorated. At least not with ink." He laughed at Rebekah's wide-eyed expression.

"Pierced?" she squeaked.

"Multiple times."

Ouch. She glanced at Eric, who turned pale. "Don't even think it," he said.

She was curious about what a cock piercing would look like, and feel like, but wouldn't admit it in front of Butch. To distract herself, she peeked over Butch's shoulder at the design he was sketching on thin paper. Eric was showing him where to put the last few musical notes. She noticed it wasn't the same melody as hers. "I thought our tattoos were going to match," she said.

"It's a duet. I'll teach you to play it with me on the piano."

Awww, as if he hadn't melted her heart enough times already that day.

Eric didn't even flinch the entire time Butch etched Rebekah's name into his flesh. When Butch worked on the outer edges, he even laughed. "It tickles!" As Butch added the finishing touches, Rebekah leaned close to Eric's ear and whispered, "I like my name there. I can't wait to see it when you're naked, with your cock all hard and thick beneath it. I wonder what it will look like when you're buried inside me. Will I be able to read it when you're balls deep or just on the out-stroke?"

"Oh my God, woman! Don't turn me on when there's a dude that close to my crotch," Eric protested.

Butch chuckled. "Lots of people get sexually excited when they get a tattoo."

"It's her fault. She's saying naughty things in my ear. Are you almost done?" Eric asked with an impatient sigh.

"Yeah, hold still."

By the time they left The Ink Well, it was after dark. To prevent his waistband from irritating his new tattoo, Eric had to drive with his pants unfastened. This prompted Rebekah's hand to wander into his lap frequently. She was so incredibly turned on by what they'd just shared that she couldn't keep her hands off him.

"Who needs weddings when you can get a tattoo together?" he said.

"Much more permanent than a few spoken words," she agreed. Her breath caught. "We could have our vows to each other tattooed on our bodies."

He chuckled. "I'd love that. You know getting tattoos can become addictive. You don't want to end up like Butch, do you?"

"No. I just want one more." She slid her hand into his open pants again and stroked the silky skin of his hard shaft. "Maybe two."

Eric pulled the car into the garage and shut off the engine. He didn't even bother opening his car door, just scrambled out through the convertible top. He took Rebekah's hand, but instead of following him into the house, she pressed him against the hood of the car.

"I can't wait," she said and unfastened her jeans. Shimmying them down her thighs, she pulled them off and kicked them aside.

He yanked her shirt over her head and tossed it on the floor. Her bra followed. When she was naked, he filled his hands with her curves, wanting her, needing her, loving her so much he couldn't breathe. He wanted to see it. The proof that she loved him. His name across her lower back. Symbolic of her commitment. Her devotion. She was his. Just as he was hers. Forever. He wondered if she had any idea how much that tattoo meant to him. He wanted to stare at it as he filled her.

He turned her to face the car, and she bent forward without hesitation. His breath caught. She looked so beautiful leaning over the hood of his treasured car. Her skin caught the low light coming from the fixture near the door. The soft globes of her ass were presented invitingly. Unfortunately, his name was scarcely legible beneath the plastic wrap covering her tattoo. He gently peeled the wrap away so he could see it more clearly and carefully stroked the skin above and below the design. He wanted to kiss it, lick it, bite it, remind her that it was there, but he knew it would be tender for a while. He'd wait until it healed before he showed too much enthusiasm.

Hands splayed on the hood of his car, she rocked backward and squirmed against his thighs impatiently. He shed his clothes and then spread his legs so he could sink low enough to possess her. When he sank into her hot body, they shuddered in unison.

"God," she gasped. "I don't know if I've ever been this hot for you."

He was so turned on, he couldn't even speak his agreement. He held onto her hips and began to thrust into her. He watched his cock slide in and out of her silky depths, the name across her lower back never out of his peripheral vision. She rocked back to meet him, encouraging him to thrust harder. Deeper. His balls slapped against her mound with each stroke, contributing to the ache, the need for release.

"Oh," Rebekah gasped. "Eric!" Her back arched, and her pussy clenched around him as she cried out. Eric gritted his teeth, fighting the urge to follow her over the edge. He didn't want it to end. Never wanted his time with her to end. He bent over her and kissed the center of her back tenderly, thrusting gently until her quaking body relaxed.

"Let's go inside," he whispered. "I want you to see it."

She looked over her shoulder. "See what?"

"Your name."

Her smile made his breath catch. He pulled out and took her hand, hurrying into the house and upstairs to his bedroom. He turned the lights on and laid on his back on the bed. He pulled the wrap covering his tattoo free and waited for her to join him. She crawled onto the bed beside him. Stroking his skin lightly, she trailed tender kisses along his lower belly.

"I never knew my name was so sexy," she murmured. "Must be the surrounding view." She ran a finger down the length of his cock and he shuddered.

Rebekah straddled his hips and took him inside her. Just as he had been, she seemed fascinated by the look of her name on her lover's skin. Her tiny hands pressed against his belly as she rode him, looking down where the action occurred, obviously enamored by his new tattoo.

He let her possess him, consume him, gave himself to her until he was convinced they weren't separate people any longer. When he knew he couldn't hold his release for another second, he reached between their bodies to rub her clit so they could let go together.

She squeezed her eyes shut. Her mouth dropped open. Her body arched back in abandon.

He followed her this time, spasms of pleasure gripping him so hard, so deep, that his vision blurred and he had to cling to the comforter with both hands to keep himself grounded.

She collapsed on top of him, breathing hard. He eventually found the strength to lift his hand and cradle her head against his chest.

"Wow," she gasped. "Why didn't you tell me getting a tattoo was so fucking sexy?"

"It usually isn't." And now that her full weight was on him, the only thing registering in his new tattoo was stinging pain, like that of a bad sunburn. He carefully shifted her onto the bed beside him and then cuddled against her back. Their names were pressed against each other. Even though it was mildly uncomfortable, he liked the reminder that no matter where she happened to be, her name would always be a part of him, and his would be a part of her.

Chapter 31

THE NEXT MORNING REBEKAH woke alone. Her clothes were in a pile on the floor beside the bed. Apparently, Eric had retrieved them from the garage. She applied more salve to her tattoo before slipping into her clothes and going in search of the man who consumed her thoughts, her heart, her body, her soul.

She didn't find him with his musical instruments or in the kitchen or in front of the TV. He wasn't on the porch swing or in the garage. Neither was his car. He'd deserted her without letting her know where he was going. And because her car was still at the restaurant where she'd met him the night before, she was pretty much trapped. The Camaro wasn't even close to running yet.

She returned to the kitchen and found a pot of coffee waiting. Under a clean mug, she found a note.

I'll be back soon. Make yourself at home. Eric

She still didn't know where he'd gone, but she was feeling a little less abandoned. At least he'd thought to leave her a note and make her coffee. She gulped a mug of black java and started thinking of all the things she wanted to do for his birthday. She was determined to make it the most special day of his life. Bored and more than a little lonely, she eventually went to the garage to tinker with the Camaro. The sooner she got it running, the sooner she could drive it. She was quite a mess by the time Eric returned a couple hours later. He climbed out of the car with a huge smile.

"You've got grease all over your face," he told her, stroking her cheek with the pad of his thumb.

She had her hand deep in the engine compartment, tightening a bolt. He eased her T-shirt up and kissed her lower back inches above her new tattoo. "How does it feel?"

"A little sore. But not bad. Yours?"

"It's a constant reminder of you."

She grinned and stood upright to kiss the cleft in his chin. "Then it's perfect. So where have you been all morning?"

He reached into his vest and retrieved a thick piece of paper from the inside of his vest. "I had this printed up," he said and showed her a short music score. It only had two lines of music. One line was labeled as *his* and the other as *hers*.

"Is that from our tattoos?" she asked.

"Yeah. Let's go play it together."

She lifted her greasy hands. "I'm a mess."

"It'll wash." He peeked into the open engine compartment. "Any hope for the Camaro?"

She smiled, bouncing on her heels with excitement. "Yeah. I think it should start now. I switched the plugs, the distributer, and the carburetor. You should have seen the muck in the old one. I think a squirrel died in it or something."

He laughed and opened the creaky driver's side door for her. She climbed behind the wheel. Anticipation killing her, Rebekah pumped the gas pedal twice and turned the key. Though it started, the engine was a bit hesitant from sitting idle so long. Once it got going, it ran strong and loud, with a few knocks and pings beneath the rumble, but it probably just needed to run. Rebekah gunned the gas pedal, and the car emitted a satisfying *vroom*.

"I can't believe you got it started," Eric yelled over the roar of the engine.

She beamed at him. "Hop in, we'll take it for a spin."

"And then you'll play our song with me?"

"Of course. I can't wait."

Eric hit the button to open the garage door as he made his way around to the passenger side. Once he climbed into the car beside her, she backed out of the garage and turned around to take the long, winding drive.

The power of the engine was exhilarating, especially on the loose gravel.

"Yeah!" Eric shouted as Rebekah hit the gas, and the car fishtailed before gripping the road again.

At the end of the driveway, Rebekah spun onto the blacktop and pushed the car faster. She shifted into third, and the engine whirred in neutral before catching with a harsh shudder. "Transmission needs some work," she said.

She turned her head to find him staring at her.

"What?"

He just smiled and shook his head slightly. She turned the car around at the end of someone's driveway and headed back home. She'd just entered their driveway when there was a loud squeal followed by a snap. "I think that was the fan belt." She stopped the car, and it died.

"I guess she's not quite ready for street racing yet," Eric said.

"Not yet. But soon!" They left the car in the driveway and walked hand in hand to the house. He kissed her knuckles when they entered the kitchen. "Wash up, and meet me at the piano," he said.

"Don't I get a good morning kiss?"

"It's almost noon."

"So I'll take a lunchtime kiss too."

He kissed her. Twice. Neither kiss long or deep enough as far as she was concerned, but she could tell he was anxious to play their short duet, and she was anxious to hear it.

She scrubbed as much oil and grime from her hands as she

could with lava soap and examined her nails with a grimace. She really could use a manicure, but she'd just end up breaking them off while working on the car anyway. She wondered if Eric regretted falling for a less-than-feminine woman.

She found him sitting at the piano bench in the family room, staring at the piece of music as if he were trying to set it on fire with his eyes. She slid onto the right half of the bench beside him.

He shifted closer so that her body was against his from calf to shoulder and slid his right arm around her lower back. He placed the fingers of her right hand on the proper keys and showed her the sequence of the notes. There were less than thirty notes in the little piece of music, but it moved her so profoundly she could scarcely breathe. She knew it was weird, but it sounded like *her*. Like who she was on the inside. If she had been a song, this joyous, hopeful little melody would be it. She couldn't believe he could capture it so perfectly in a few notes.

"Do you think you've got it?" he asked as he helped her play it for the tenth time.

"Yeah," she said breathlessly. "How did you do that?"

"What?"

"Capture me in a piece of music."

He shrugged. "I don't know. It just sort of came to me. Keep playing. I'll add mine now."

His left hand moved to a lower octave, and he joined her hesitant playing with a different melody. It sounded entirely different from hers. Still upbeat, but a little darker. It sounded like Eric. And when the two melodies were played together, they complemented each other perfectly.

"This is why we work together," he said. "We're different, but harmonious."

She nodded in agreement, too awed to form words. The man really was a musical genius. He should be writing concertos and symphonies. No, she decided, he was where he belonged. He made Sinners' music phenomenal and rocked millions.

She stopped playing her little string of notes and reached up to cup Eric's cheek. He looked into her eyes. When she didn't do anything but stare, he lifted an eyebrow. "What?"

"Why don't you take more credit?"

"Credit for what?"

"For writing Sinners' music."

"Because I don't write it all. I arrange it."

"What would they do with Brian's disjointed solos and Sed's words if it weren't for you?"

"I'm sure they'd think of something." He laughed. "It would probably sound like shit, but they'd think of something."

"You're a genius, baby, but you act—you act like a goofball most of the time."

"Yeah, well, who wants to hang with a genius? Boring."

"There's nothing boring about you."

"I have written a few things," he said, avoiding her gaze.

"Really? Can I hear them?"

"They're not ready yet."

"Are they for Sinners' new album?" she asked.

He shook his head. "No. They're more alternative rock than metal. Much too soft for Sinners."

"I'd still love to hear them." She grasped his hand.

He looked up and smiled. "Yeah?"

She nodded eagerly. "When they're ready."

He lowered his gaze, suddenly looking nervous. "You're probably going to be mad at me for doing this," he said, "but…"

He reached into the inner pocket of his vest and pulled out a little plastic bubble—the kind they filled with novelty "prizes" (aka junk made in China), so kids could hound their parents for quarters at grocery stores.

"Here."

"What is it?"

"It took me nine tries, but I finally got one I liked," he said. "Open it."

She quirked an eyebrow and popped open the container. A small, black spider dropped into her hand. She shrieked and tossed it into the air before tipping backward and almost falling off the piano bench.

Eric grabbed her to save her from a certain concussion and released her only once she'd regained her balance. He retrieved the plastic spider from the piano keyboard and extended it in her direction. She cringed. Even though she could tell it was fake and part of a cheap plastic Halloween ring, it still gave her the willies.

"You don't like it?" he asked.

"Did you expect me to?"

"It reminded me of the time I rescued you from the spider in the hotel shower. Remember that? It was the morning after our first time. The day I started believing that someone could love me for me. I thought your engagement ring should be significant in some way."

"It significantly freaks me out," she said. And then the enormity of his words sank in. "My engagement ring?"

He dug in his pocket and produced another plastic bubble. He took her hand and folded it around the novelty. "Maybe this one will be more to your liking."

Her heart thudded. She was almost afraid to look. If another plastic spider tumbled into her hand, she was totally going to lose it. She shook the container slightly, and the prize inside rattled loudly. This one had some weight.

She popped the bubble open and a thick, platinum band tumbled into her palm. A full-carat princess-cut diamond seemed to be suspended in the ring's setting by magic. She'd never seen such a unique yet beautiful ring in her life. It wasn't too girly or too strong.

It was just right. She looked at Eric, trembling so hard, she feared she'd need some of that CPR he used so capably.

"Oh…" she whispered.

"Do you like it?"

Unable to form words, she nodded. He released a breath of relief.

"Will you wear it?"

She nodded again.

"And you promise to marry me?"

Nod.

He took the ring from her hand and slid it onto her left ring finger. It felt heavy. And cold. And foreign. And substantial.

And real.

"Tomorrow?"

Tomorrow… She almost nodded, but changed her mind and shook her head. "After my MRI."

"When's that again?"

"In ten more days."

"A ten-day engagement sounds just about right. I guess Brian's record of three days still stands."

Rebekah chuckled. "You guys compete over everything, don't you? If you have your heart set on beating Brian, you can take the ring back and ask me again eight days from today."

"I'd rather not," he murmured and lowered his head to kiss her. "I'm too fuckin' stoked that you accepted it to ever take it back."

She gazed at the sparkling ring on her finger. Its beauty almost drew her attention from the grease under her fingernail. "I need to get my nails done. It's so gorgeous, and my hands look terrible."

"Your hands look perfect," he said. He lifted her knuckles to his lips. "Perfect."

Just beneath his lips, the diamond of her engagement ring sparkled in the light filtering through the curtains.

Her engagement ring. Engagement ring.

Rebekah's vision blurred with tears. She couldn't breathe. Her heart rate accelerated out of control.

"What's wrong?" Eric asked breathlessly. "Why are you crying?"

She was crying? That would explain why her cheeks were wet and her nose was running. Why she couldn't see his face or anything but smears of color. She squeezed her eyes shut.

"Rebekah?"

She needed a minute to collect herself. Putting her head between her knees would probably be her best bet. She flipped forward and banged her head on the keyboard with a discordant *blam!*

She was going to get married! A dream she had all but given up on. She hadn't thought any man in the world would want to marry a woman who could never give him a family, and here she was engaged not to *any* man, but the most wonderful man she'd ever known. The man she loved so much she couldn't imagine a single day without him. The man who probably thought she'd lost her mind.

"Reb?" he whispered as he tried to pry her forehead from the keyboard.

She gulped air.

"Look, if you changed your mind about getting married—"

No! She sat up abruptly and lifted her hand to cover his mouth, but managed to accidentally hit him in the nose. Her hand was shaking so hard, she was surprised it found his face at all.

She shook her head vigorously. "Of course I d-didn't change m-my mind. I'm j-just so… so… h-happy."

Eric hesitated and wrapped a comforting arm around her lower back. "You don't look happy."

She turned to face him on the bench, wrapped both arms around his neck, and sought his mouth. Good thing he had better aim than she did. He kissed her deeply, passionately, lips tugging hers with a gentle suction, tongue brushing her upper lip.

"I love you," she whispered, trailing kisses along his stubble-rough jaw.

"Forever?"

"For the rest of my life," she said breathlessly. And her mortality reared its ugly head again. What if she had to leave him alone before she was ready to go?

He kissed the tears off her cheeks. "Forever," he said, holding her hair in tight fists so he could tilt her head back and kiss her lips. His kiss was hard and deep, almost punishing. "It has to be forever, Rebekah."

"But if the cancer comes back, if I die…" She took a deep, ragged breath. She didn't want to talk about these things, but they couldn't hide from these real possibilities. That's why she wanted to wait to marry him until after her MRI. "I don't want you to be alone, Eric."

"Forever, Rebekah." His resolute stare told her he wasn't backing down on this.

"Forever," she agreed breathlessly.

He cradled her against his chest and held her for all he was worth. "Forever."

She clung to him, sobbing. Tears drenched his shirt, but he didn't let her go. She knew with certainty he never would. Not even if it was best for him. She let the fear find her. She'd been pretending it didn't exist for so long that it felt good to recognize it. Confront it. And even share it with Eric. "I'm scared. So scared that I'll get sick again."

"It's okay. I'm scared too. But no matter how scared I am, I won't run."

Isaac had given her the strength to fight when she'd been sick. To face death with her head high. Eric gave her the strength to be alive. Fully alive. And now that she had so much to live for, she wasn't sure she could face death again.

She leaned away and wiped her tears on the hem of her T-shirt.

"I'm sorry I fell apart. I really am happy you want to marry me. Even if it is selfish of me to accept."

"I thought you'd be mad that I went out and bought your ring on my own. I woke up beside you this morning, watched you sleep for a while, and decided I couldn't wait. Do you really like it?"

"I love it. *You.* I love you."

"You'd better. I had to take out a second mortgage to afford that sucker."

She smiled, knowing that he needed a reprieve from the emotional barrage she'd just subjected him to. "Suck?" She licked her lips and reached for his fly. "Well, if you insist."

Chapter 32

REBEKAH KISSED ERIC'S CHEEK and opened the car door. She honestly wasn't looking forward to spending the evening pretending to be Isaac's doting girlfriend. Especially at a party guaranteed to be boring.

Eric caught her hand before she could get out. "I'm considering becoming a jealous prick and making a scene, just so you know."

"I might buy that if you had anything to be jealous about."

"What time will you be home?"

"Early," she promised.

He kissed her knuckles and released her hand. "Call me if you need anything."

"I'll be fine. Isaac promised he would bring me home as soon as we can get away. You and I will have plenty of fun tomorrow." On Eric's birthday.

"Why tomorrow?"

"No reason." She grinned. He'd been trying to get her to reveal something for days. She'd put together over two dozen surprises for Eric's birthday to celebrate his life and hers. Well, mostly she'd be celebrating his cock, but she didn't think he'd mind.

She kissed him good-bye and stepped from the car, smoothing her hands over her black cocktail dress to make sure everything was in place. She closed the car door and offered Eric a wave as he drove off. When Isaac opened his apartment door to answer her knock, he didn't look any too pleased to see her.

"Let's get this over with," he said.

"I'm fine, thanks, how are you?"

"I've been better."

He locked the apartment door behind him and headed for the stairwell. She followed him, seconds from telling him to forget this favor if he was going to act like an ass all night.

"What's wrong?" Rebekah asked him.

"Trey left me." He stopped dead in his tracks and Rebekah bumped into his back.

She took his arm and turned him to face her. His brow crumpled, and he took a deep shaky breath. If he starting crying, she was totally going to join him. "What? Like permanently?"

He raked a hand through his perfectly arranged loose curls, mussing them in a most charming way. "I don't know. He said until I get my head on straight. Whatever that means."

"I'm sorry. I hope you can work things out."

"It's just an excuse. I know he sees other people. When I hinted that I wanted things to be serious between us, he... lost interest."

Rebekah sighed. "Isaac, I probably should have warned you. Trey is wonderful, but he's kind of hung up on someone else."

"Brian?"

Stunned, Rebekah stared at him with her mouth hanging open. "How did you know?"

"He talks about the guy nonstop. At first I thought they were just best friends, but he even murmurs his name in his sleep." Isaac flushed. "I probably shouldn't talk about this with you."

"It's okay. I don't mind."

"You really are terrific." His soft gray eyes swept up her figure from carefully styled hair to the pink toenails peeking out of her strappy heels. "You look sensational, by the way. If I was into girls, I'd definitely be thinking inappropriate thoughts right now."

She laughed, glad the tension between them had eased. "You're quite the charmer, Dr. Crandall."

He helped her into his car, and they headed to his parents' house. He told her about some fancy diagnostic machine they'd installed at his father's clinic and how it would make the office cutting-edge. "I can't wait to be a part of it. They already have more patients than they can handle. This is an amazing opportunity for me."

"You'll be awesome," she said.

"Assuming I don't mess this up. Thanks for helping me out, angel."

"That's what friends are for."

When they arrived, a valet took Isaac's car and parked it somewhere in the next county. Isaac settled a hand on her lower back to guide her into the sprawling Mediterranean-style house. There were a lot more people at the dinner party than Rebekah expected. Isaac introduced her to so many people that her head was spinning. Everything was going well until someone noticed her engagement ring.

"My Lord, Isaac, how did you ever afford that rock on *your* salary?" a gentleman, who looked like he'd fallen off a bucket of fried chicken, asked.

Isaac grabbed Rebekah's left wrist and stared at the hefty ring. "An enormous loan," he said with a nervous laugh. "I hope Father's hiring."

The Colonel Sanders look-a-like pounded him on the back enthusiastically. "I think he might be."

Isaac steered Rebekah toward a corner. "You're *engaged?*"

Rebekah's heart fluttered, and she smiled. "Well, yeah. How did you not notice?" She lifted her left hand. "It's pretty obvious."

Isaac sighed. "I was a little distracted." He reached for her hand and tried to slip the ring from her finger. She jerked her hand away and hid it behind her back.

"What are you doing?"

"You have to take it off. It's obvious that I didn't give you that ring. I could never afford it."

"I'm not taking it off, Isaac."

"She's not taking it off, Isaac," a low voice said behind her. Before she could turn around, she was wrapped in a strong embrace, and a hard kiss hit her in the temple. "Congratulations!" She struggled against the hard body behind her. He released her, and she spun around to glare at... *Trey?*

Her mouth dropped open in shock.

"What are you doing here?" Isaac asked in a harsh whisper.

"My father conned me into coming along. Usually, I try to get out of these kinds of things, but..." He shrugged. "I thought it would be fun to see how good of an actor you are, young Dr. Crandall."

"Your father?" Rebekah questioned.

"The highly celebrated plastic surgeon of the rich and famous, Ethan Mills, MD," Trey said. He waved at a man who could have been Trey's twin had he been twenty-five years younger and traded his conventional haircut for Trey's long in the front, short in the back style.

Doctor Mills wrapped a possessive arm around a lovely woman who looked earthy, eccentric, and completely bewildered in her round glasses, peasant garb, and Birkenstocks. She had a smudge of pink paint on her tan cheek, and her waist-length, curly brown hair, which was held out of her face with a green plastic headband, looked completely untamable. She fit in with the black-tie crowd almost as well as Eric would have. Rebekah instantly loved her.

"And that sweetheart with him is the highly underrated mixed media artist, Gwen Mills, also known as my mom." Gwen must have known someone was talking about her, because her head swiveled in their direction, and her entire face lit up with delight when she noticed her son. Trey's parents headed in their direction. Isaac tried to hide behind a drapery.

"Did you find someone to talk to?" Dr. Mills asked and extended a hand in Rebekah's direction.

"Yeah, small world," Trey said. "This is Rebekah, Sinners' temporary soundboard engineer. I told you about her. Dave's little sister."

Dr. Mills' expression turned serious. "How's your brother?"

She smiled at his concern and shook his hand. "Not mobile yet, but working on it. It takes more than a broken neck to keep him down."

"And I just found out that she's Eric's fiancée," Trey added. "Check out her new rock."

Gwen took Rebekah's free hand in hers and shook it up and down vigorously. "That boy needs a nice girl to look after him. Good for you!"

"And tonight she's pretending to be Isaac's girlfriend," Trey added, "so mum's the word. Wouldn't want to make dear Isaac uncomfortable."

Trey grabbed Isaac by the arm and pulled him out from behind the gauzy drape. Scowling, Isaac shoved him.

"Don't worry," Trey said. "I already told them all about you."

Isaac turned green. "*All* about me?"

"Well, not that sexy little noise you make when—" Trey bit his lip. "Never mind."

"It's not healthy to pretend to be something you're not," Dr. Mills said to Isaac. Being Trey's father, the guy had to be incredibly open-minded. Or totally clueless.

Isaac sidled toward the drapery again.

Trey's head turned as he tracked a gorgeous cocktail waitress distributing champagne to guests. "I just wanted to say hey. I'll leave you two *pretend* lovebirds alone." He dashed off without another word and walked directly in front of the waitress. Startled, she almost dropped her tray of drinks as she skidded to a halt. With a twirl, Trey somehow managed to catch the tray in one hand and press the disoriented woman against his length with the other. "Careful," he said in that low voice that made knees go weak. Rebekah was immune by now, but the waitress sagged against him, her eyes wide, her lips slightly parted as she gawked at him.

Rebekah rolled her eyes and shook her head.

"That son of yours…" Dr. Mills muttered under his breath.

"Oh sure, he's my son when he's chasing skirts," Mrs. Mills said, "but yours when you need to impress your shallow clients. Your son, the famous electric guitarist."

"My *sons*, the famous electric guitar*ists*," Dr. Mills corrected. "Your sons, the notorious skirt chasers."

"They don't get it from me."

Dr. Mills chuckled and kissed the tip of her nose. "I stopped chasing skirts after I found the right one."

Rebekah smiled, hoping she and Eric still shared that kind of affection after thirty years of marriage, and looked over to see how Isaac was taking Trey's continual indiscretions.

Isaac had vanished. The floor-to-ceiling window behind his favorite drape was opened. Had he honestly snuck outside through the open window? Rebekah sighed and rubbed her forehead to stave off a threatening headache. She really didn't need this right now. She already wanted to go home. She had enough drama to deal with in her own life, thank you very much.

A shadow crossed Rebekah's face. "There you are, Rebekah. So good to see you again. Where'd did Isaac run off to?" Isaac's father asked. The man looked nothing like Isaac. Where Isaac was graceful and handsome, Dr. Crandall was shaped like a barrel and had a protruding forehead demarcated by a wild eyebrow. Yes, eye*brow*. Singular. The man had apparently never been introduced to tweezers. He sniffed his red, bulbous nose and swiped a hand over his receding hairline. Isaac definitely took after his mother.

"I think he's in the restroom," Rebekah lied.

"As soon as he gets back, tell him to find me so we can make his big announcement." Something caught his attention behind her. He smiled, showing yellowed teeth. "Oh good, your parents are here now. I'll go say hello."

Her *parents*? Rebekah's heart skipped a beat. She cringed and chanced a glance over her shoulder. Sure enough, there was her mother in a fuchsia evening gown two sizes too small, and her father in his tweed church suit and unfashionably wide, yellow-and-blue striped tie. What in the world were they doing here? She supposed Isaac was like a son to them. They'd want to hear his big news. She wished Isaac would have told her that he'd invited them.

"Excuse me," she said to Trey's parents and climbed out the window behind the drapery in search of her escaped date.

She found Isaac staring at a shrub trimmed into the shape of a rearing horse. She touched his lower back, and he started.

"Your father is looking for you," she said. "He says it's time to make the announcement."

He nodded slightly and bit his trembling lower lip. Her heart went out to him. She knew what heartache felt like. She'd experienced the empty, achy chasm in her chest not too long ago, due to the very man who was feeling it now.

"Trey's probably being a jerk to set you free, sweetheart. To give you a clean break before you get too attached."

"I don't want to be set free."

She rubbed his back and leaned against his arm. "Let's go get this over with and then we can leave."

"What about dinner?"

"I'll pretend to feel sick."

"I don't need to pretend."

She took his elbow and tugged him toward the house, steering away from the window to enter through the open terrace doors. "Why didn't you tell me you invited my parents?"

Isaac's brow furrowed. "I didn't. They're here?"

"Yeah."

"That's odd."

When they stepped into the main gathering room, the crowd erupted into enthusiastic applause. Rebekah smiled. Everyone was certainly excited to welcome Isaac into their fold. She was happy for him. She knew how hard he worked.

Dr. Crandall lifted his glass of champagne, and a hush fell over the crowd. "I want to thank you all for coming to my son's engagement party. It's about time the boy got hitched."

Rebekah spun and glared at Isaac, who looked as flabbergasted as she felt. "You told them we were engaged?" she said in harsh whisper.

He shook his head. "No, of course not."

Rebekah spun to the crowd. "We're not engaged. We're just friends."

"That's not true!" Rebekah's mother cried. "They are engaged. They are."

"What do you mean you're not engaged?" Dr. Crandall bellowed.

"Isaac and I are just friends," Rebekah said. "We never got back together after we broke up. In fact, I'm marrying someone else."

"But your mother said—"

Everyone turned to look at her mom, and Rebekah could tell by the wild look in her eyes that she wasn't well. Eric had tried to tell her that, but Rebekah had gotten too wrapped up in her own happiness to get her mom the help she needed.

"I'm sorry, Mom, but I'm not marrying Isaac. I'm marrying Eric."

There was a twittering of "who's Eric" throughout the crowd. Rebekah spotted Trey, and he offered a nod of encouragement. A friend in a sea of enemies.

Banshees had nothing on her mother's shriek. "No! You have to marry Isaac. You have to! If you don't, I'll… I'll… I'll…" She repeatedly clenched and unclenched both fists. Dad grabbed her arm to prevent her from flying across the room and attacking Rebekah.

"Mary," he said, glancing nervously at all the upper-class citizens staring at her. "Calm down."

"Mom, it will never work between us. Isaac's…" She caught herself before she said *gay* and glanced at Isaac, who looked paler than an anemic ghost. "…not right for me."

"You little tramp," Mom screamed. "You've been shacking up with that filthy rock star, haven't you? No wonder Isaac doesn't want you."

"Hey," Trey protested, "I happen to like that filthy rock star."

"It's not her," Isaac said quietly.

"Now you apologize to Isaac, Rebekah Esther Blake, and you beg him to take you back. You *beg* him!"

"Mother, I'm not going to marry Isaac. Get over it."

"Stop saying that. Just stop!" She turned her tearful eyes to Isaac. "Isaac, sweetheart, she doesn't mean it. She wants to marry you. Please take her back. Please! I know she's wronged you, but—"

"It's not her!" Isaac yelled. "It's me. I'm gay. Okay?" He stared directly at Trey and said, "I'm in love with a man."

Trey shook his head slightly and then turned his attention to the parquet floor.

Mom collapsed against Rebekah's father in a fit of hysterical sobs.

"What?" Dr. Crandall grabbed his son by one arm. "What did you say?"

Isaac massaged his forehead with one hand. "This isn't how I wanted to break this to you. Let's go talk about this in private."

Rebekah clutched the back of Isaac's shirt, wanting to offer him comfort and at the same time keep her head above the churning waters that threatened to drown her.

"You're gay?" Dr. Crandall bellowed. "*My* son is gay? Impossible!"

"Dad—" Isaac reached for his father's hand, but he jerked away. "Don't touch me."

"Will you listen?" Isaac said, and wiped a leaky eye on the back of his hand.

"It's not true," Mom cried, her head pressed firmly between both palms. "Not true. Not true."

"Get out of my sight," Dr. Crandall said to Isaac. "You're not my son. I never want to lay eyes on you again."

"Dad—" Isaac gripped his father's sleeve, but he shook him off.

"You are not my son."

The wounded sound Isaac made cut Rebekah's heart in two. He wavered on his feet, and she wrapped her arms around him to keep him from collapsing.

Mom was still shrieking hysterically.

Dad was still trying to calm her down in his unassuming way.

Isaac's weight was suddenly off her. "Go help your mother," Trey said quietly. "I've got him. I'll take him home."

Isaac clung to Trey, who walked him toward the front door. Rebekah turned to the unpleasant task of placating her mother.

"Don't let him leave," she was saying, one arm outstretched in Isaac's direction. "Don't let him leave without Rebekah."

"Mom," Rebekah said. She took Mom by both shoulders and gave her a harsh shake.

"Oh baby," Mom wailed. "I'm so sorry he left. I'm so sorry I couldn't save you. You're too young to die."

Sheesh, drama queen much? "I'm not going to die, Mom. Dad, go get the car."

Mom's entire body was shaking. "You are. You will. Soon. God will take you from me. I know He will."

Rebekah knew her mother was delusional, but her words still hit Rebekah like a slap in the face. "Come on, Mom. Let's go outside and get some fresh air." And wait for Dad. And get away from all the staring eyes and scandalized whispers. And get her mother some really good antipsychotic drugs.

Mom followed her outside. She clung to Rebekah like a frightened little girl, with her arms around Rebekah's waist and her head on her shoulder. Rebekah stroked Mom's hair soothingly. "It's going to be okay, Mom. Dad will get you some help." The driveway was entirely full of cars now, so she led her mom toward the street at the end of the drive. When Dad pulled up in the van a few minutes later, Rebekah helped her mom inside.

"Don't you marry that rock star guy. Don't you marry him, Rebekah," Mom was now muttering under her breath. "He's not right for you. Don't you marry him."

Dad squeezed Mom's hand and she started as if she hadn't realized he was there. He leaned over her to look at Rebekah outside the vehicle. "Sweetheart, I'll get your mother admitted, and then I'll give you a call," Dad said. "I think you should give her a couple days to pull herself together before you come visit."

Rebekah bit her lip and nodded, knowing he was right. When Mom got confused like this the last time, they'd had to isolate her for a couple days so she could sort things out and get a grip on reality. And then she'd been perfectly fine. Or so it had seemed at the time.

"Do you have a way home?"

Eric. She knew she could count on him. She nodded. "I'll be fine. Go take care of Mom."

Her eyes stinging with unshed tears, Rebekah dug her cell phone out of her evening bag and called Eric.

"What's up? Miss me already?" he answered. She could hear the smile in his voice.

"C-can y-you come g-get me?" Damn stuttering again.

He hesitated. "Yeah, of course. What happened?"

"Just h-hurry, okay? P-please."

"Are you okay?"

"Y-yes." She gulped air. He was the only thing in her life *not* falling apart, and she needed him. So much. "N-no." She gulped more air. "I don't know."

"Where are you?"

"Still at the party. Do you know how to get here?"

"Yeah." She knew he'd looked up the address when he'd been trying to convince her that she didn't have to arrive at the party in Isaac's car. "Will you tell me what's going on?"

She told him everything that happened. "Anyway… I'm stuck here without a ride and would appreciate it if you would hurry." She lowered her voice to a whisper and glanced up the driveway where a crowd of gawkers had gathered. "People are staring…"

"I'm on my way."

He arrived more quickly than she thought possible. She was so happy to see him that she didn't chastise him about his speeding. She climbed into the car, wrapped both arms around his neck, and kissed every inch of his face.

"Tomorrow I refuse to leave the house. I hope you don't mind me monopolizing your entire birthday."

He chuckled. "I have a birthday tomorrow?"

"And I have a whole slew of surprises for you."

"Surprises? What kind of surprises?"

"If I told you, they wouldn't be surprises."

"True." He took her hand and gave it an encouraging squeeze. "Do you need to talk about what happened tonight?"

"No," she said. "I'm going to pretend it never happened. On Monday I'll face reality, but for the rest of the weekend there will be nothing but me and you and all our fantasies."

He kissed her knuckles and eased the car away from the curve. "Well, if you insist."

Chapter 33

THE NEXT MORNING, ERIC opened his eyes to a bright blue box. Resting on Rebekah's vacated pillow, the box was tied shut with a thick white ribbon. He rose to look around the room and was disappointed to find himself alone. Even the cocktail dress that had been hanging from the ceiling fan when he'd passed out from exhaustion the night before was now gone. He sat cross-legged in the middle of the bed and reached for the box. It had a little card attached that said, *Happy 1st Birthday, sweetheart. Please open immediately. Rebekah*

He smiled. He'd never been greeted with a birthday present on his pillow. The guys had once woken him by smashing a birthday cake into his face. It had been one rude, but rather delicious, wake-up call.

He untied the ribbon and lifted the lid, expecting to find something sexy nestled in the tissue paper. Instead, he found a baby monitor.

"A baby monitor?"

He lifted the device from the box and found a second note tied to its short antenna. *I'm at your beck and call, birthday boy. Press the button, and let me know when you're ready for me.*

His heart thundered with anticipation. He pressed the button. "Rebekah?"

"I'll be right up," her voice came from the little speaker.

He was already up. When it came to his woman, he was always up. He covered his excitement by dropping a pillow on his lap.

A moment later the bedroom door opened and Rebekah entered carrying a tray of food. She wore a frilly little apron. *Just* a frilly little apron. Damn, she looked good enough to eat. If he hadn't already been up, this would have done the trick.

"I hope you're hungry," she said. "I made you three different types of scrambled eggs. Also, bacon. Sausage. Biscuits. Hash browns. A fruit cup and some coffee. Juice."

"It smells fantastic," he murmured. He was sure it looked fantastic too, but he couldn't take his eyes off the gentle bounce of her pert breasts as she crossed the room and set the tray on the bed beside him.

She leaned across the bed and kissed him gently on the mouth. "Happy first birthday," she said.

"*First* birthday?"

"Well, I missed twenty-seven of them, so I have a lot of birthdays to celebrate with you today."

He'd never thought he cared that no one had ever done anything special for his birthday or that he'd never had a party as a kid. The warmth spreading through his chest and his giddiness at her thoughtfulness told him that he really had cared. Rebekah had a way of making him glad for those hard times so that he treasured his time with her that much more. "I love you."

"I love you too. Now eat."

"Maybe I want you to feed me," he said.

She climbed onto the bed beside him and picked up his fork. "What do you want?"

He lifted his hand and stroked her taut nipple with his fingertips. "This." He leaned forward and flicked his tongue over the aroused skin.

"You'll get plenty of that with your other surprises," she said. "You should probably eat so you can keep up your strength."

He sucked her nipple into his mouth and then drew away. "I'll eat," he said. "You keep those hard for me."

Mesmerized, he watched her pluck her nipples, roll them between her thumb and forefinger, and lick her fingers to spread the wetness over her pink, pebbled flesh. He ate slowly, enjoying his private peep show too much to want it to end. Watching her play with herself still excited him like nothing else. When he was full, he crawled around the breakfast tray and tumbled her to the mattress beneath him. He suckled her nipples until she was clinging to his hair and moaning with need.

He lifted her apron and discovered that she'd completely shaved her mound. "I see dessert," he said.

"That's supposed to be for later."

"I can have multiple desserts today. It's my birthday." He slid down her body and suckled her smooth, swollen lips, teased her clit with his tongue, and licked at her slick hole to sample her sweet juices.

"Oh, Eric," she moaned. "I want you."

He slipped a finger inside her and rotated it in wide circles while he sucked hard on her clit.

Her back arched. "Oh wait. I'm gonna come. Eric!"

Her body shuddered with release. She strained against his hand, her pussy gripping his finger in delightful spasms. When she went limp, he pulled his finger free and placed a tender kiss on her pretty folds, loving how exposed they looked when clean-shaven. He slid up her body to smile down at her flushed face.

"It's your birthday," she said breathlessly. "I'm not supposed to get the presents."

"That was a present for both of us." He lowered his head to kiss her jaw, her neck, her ear.

She stiffened beneath him. "Wait! I've been planning this for a week, and you're messing with my agenda here."

If he hadn't been so curious about her plans, he would have said to hell with them, but he was. Curious. She slipped from beneath him and scampered off the bed. She collected his breakfast tray and nodded toward the connecting bathroom. "Your next surprise is in there."

He watched the apron ties bounce against her sweet little bottom as she trotted out of the room. As soon as she was out of sight, Eric scrambled into the bathroom. On the sink, he found a red box with a large yellow bow. *Happy 2nd Birthday, sweetheart. Please open immediately. Rebekah*

He lifted the lid and found a white poof inside. The kind she used in the shower. Beneath it was a little card. *Wait for me in the shower.*

He used the toilet and then stepped into the shower, letting the water wet his naked body. A moment later, Rebekah entered the bathroom. She was wearing a plain white T-shirt and nothing else. She stepped into the shower with him, still wearing the T-shirt. At first, he wasn't sure why, but as the T-shirt got wet, it became completely transparent and clung to her curves in a way that was somehow sexier than naked flesh.

He mumbled something incoherent and reached for her breasts, cupping them beneath the T-shirt, squeezing them so that her darkened nipples strained against the transparent wet cloth. Oh God. He wanted them. Wanted her. He lowered his head and sucked one breast, shirt and all, into his mouth. "There you go giving me presents again," she murmured in a husky voice. "Where's the present I gave you?"

He had no idea. He lifted his head to look at her, and when confronted by that wet T-shirt again, he couldn't even remember what she'd asked him. Apparently, she found what she was looking for in his left hand. She turned to retrieve a bottle of liquid soap from the caddy on the wall. His gaze drifted to the tattoo on her lower back and then the sweet curves of her naked ass. She turned again and began to draw the poof over his chest, leaving foamy suds on his skin as she washed him with slow, deliberate motions.

He couldn't keep his hands off her tits.

She soaped his shoulders. His arms. His back. His belly. It felt wonderful. He felt special and loved. And really fucking horny.

Her soapy poof moved lower. She squatted to soap his hips and thighs. The head of his cock disappeared into her hot little mouth. She sucked it gently, sending waves of pleasure rippling along his shaft while she soaped his balls and soaped them and soaped them. By the time she was done washing them, he was certain there had never been a cleaner set of balls on the planet. He was also certain that there was nothing hotter than his woman in a wet T-shirt looking at him with adoration while she sucked his cock.

Control took a backseat to need.

He bent to grab her by both arms. She let his cock pop free of her tight suction, and he hauled her to her feet. He had to fuck her. Immediately. None of the emotional, tender lovemaking that had occurred the night before. No. This would be dirty. And rough. He was much too excited to be gentle.

He grabbed her face between both palms and kissed her hard and deep. She didn't protest, even when he pressed her against the wall and moved his hands to squeeze her breasts.

She jerked her head to the side. "Rip it off me," she demanded.

He was no Hulk Hogan. He couldn't tear a T-shirt apart with his bare hands. Or could he? He noticed that she'd cut the neck-band, so he *could* rip it off her. The sexy little vixen had planned it from the start. He grabbed the fabric and pulled in both directions. It gave way with a satisfying rip. Her breasts tumbled free, and he gasped. He grabbed them and massaged them roughly. He needed to be inside her. Needed to fuck her.

Eric lifted her off the shower floor and propped her against the tile wall. Water coursed down his body in thick rivulets. He surged forward seeking her slick heat, but he didn't find it. Gritting his teeth, he cursed and tried again. Rebekah reached between their bodies, grabbed his cock, and directed it home. He thrust into her.

Hard.

Harder.

He wanted her to feel him. For it to be impossible for her to ignore him. His excitement brought him to the brink of orgasm quickly, but he wasn't ready to come. He wanted to keep going for hours. Unfortunately, gravity wasn't in agreement. His strength waning, Rebekah slipped down the wall.

He grunted in protest when he could no longer find the leverage to thrust and had to pull out. She turned around and bent forward, presenting her backside. "Put it back in, Eric. I want it so bad."

He found her easy this time, thrusting into her fast and hard from behind. She arched her back so he could hold onto her breasts while he plunged into her repeatedly.

"Oh. Oh. Oh!" Her cries echoed off the tile walls as she found release.

Eric pulled out at the last second and watched as he spurt across her lower back. She reached behind her and smeared his cum over the name tattooed on her skin. His name.

He gasped as he watched her. Could this woman possibly get any sexier? Could he love her any more than he did at that moment? He didn't think it was possible.

He drew her against his length. His belly against her back, the tattered remains of the T-shirt between them, he kissed her neck while he rubbed her breasts and belly. He eventually retrieved the poof from the shower floor, and they took turns washing each other. Touching, kissing, a bit of nibbling. When she was squeaky clean, she stepped away.

"Your next present is in the green bedroom," she whispered and climbed out of the shower. She reached for a towel and wrapped it around her amazing little body. He shut off the water and didn't even bother with a towel. Soaking wet, Eric padded down the hallway to the spare bedroom, which had been decorated in sage green. On the bed was a rectangular box—white with a red ribbon. He read the tag. *Happy 3rd Birthday, sweetheart. Open this when you'd like tea service.*

Tea service? He didn't have any idea what could be in the box. He wasn't sure if he wanted tea service or not, but he was curious. He opened the gift and found a beautiful silk robe. It was white and decorated with small pink flowers. He lifted it out of the box and held it up to his chest. If he put it on, it wouldn't even cover his ass. He didn't want to hurt Rebekah's feelings or anything, but… Um? It was a *bit* feminine. He couldn't imagine ever wearing it.

"It's beautiful, isn't it?" Rebekah said from the doorway.

"Yeah. I just don't think it's me."

She laughed. "You're not supposed to wear it. I am."

He released a relieved breath. "Oh thank God. I was starting to worry you wanted me in drag."

She took the robe from him. "I'll go slip into this and make the tea." She opened a side table drawer and pulled out another box. "You open this. Happy fourth birthday." She kissed him and handed him the box before leaving the room.

This box was relatively small, long, and flat. Inside he found a fan belt and a note that said, *As soon as we get the Camaro running, I challenge you to a race.* At the bottom of the box, he found a gift certificate from a local racetrack for one hour of private usage. "Rebekah!" he shouted. "This is so awesome!"

He turned to find her standing in the doorway, dressed in the beautiful robe. It was one of those Japanese ones. A komodo or something like that. A thick red sash tied around her middle made her waist look impossibly tiny. Her feet and sexy legs were bare. She kept her eyes downcast as she walked with small steps into the room. On a tray she carried a teapot, a small cup, and a white vase with a red flower.

"Whoa," Eric said, setting the box in his hand on the nightstand. "You look so… delicate." Nice save on not calling her adorable. "Thanks for the gift certificate. I can't wait to race you."

She nodded slightly and blushed, keeping her gaze lowered. He wasn't sure why, but her acting all shy and demure was kind of sexy.

"Please, sit," she said quietly.

He sat. The hardwood floors were cold against his bare ass, but his blood ran hot and he'd surely be overheated in no time.

She set the tray on the floor and retrieved a quilt from a wooden rack at the end of the bed. She placed it on the floor and encouraged Eric to move onto it. Kneeling beside him, she poured tea from the pot into the tiny cup. When she handed it to him, her fingertips brushed his. That seemingly accidental touch streaked up his arm and sent a shiver down his spine. She kept her eyes downcast, her body tense, as if he made her nervous. He supposed he shouldn't be surprised that he found her little act sexy. He found everything she did a total turn-on. He took a sip of the tea and it burned the hair off his tonsils.

Eyes watering, Eric sputtered and covered his mouth with the back of his hand. "It's a tad hot," he breathed.

She looked up, her bottom lip trembling. "I do not please you?"

He knew she wanted him to play a role, but he simply could not stand the devastated look, even if it was an act. He tucked a finger under her chin and moved in for a tender kiss. "You always please me. You are incapable of displeasing me."

She chuckled, dropping her act. "I think you'll need tutoring on this scenario."

"Now?"

"Unless… Do you want to open more presents?"

He hesitated, then grinned and nodded eagerly.

"Anything you want to save for another day, you can. You have a lot of presents. Probably too many to enjoy in one day."

He couldn't pretend to be anything but excited. He grabbed her in an exuberant hug. "What's next?"

"Your next present is in the kitchen. Go put on some shorts and meet me downstairs. No peeking until I join you."

He grinned. "So you don't want me naked for this one?"

"Not all your gifts are sexual in nature."

"Bummer."

"The racetrack gift certificate, for example."

He squeezed her and rooted on her neck with loud sloppy kisses until she giggled and squirmed. "That is a fucking awesome non-sexual gift, but afterward, I'm sure I'll be pretty worked up."

"You can make anything sexual, Eric."

"You're just figuring that out?"

"Nope. I'm celebrating it." She kissed him and squirmed out of his arms. "I'll see you downstairs."

She collected her tray and climbed to her feet. As soon as she was out of the room, he hurried to his bedroom to tug on a pair of shorts and took the stairs two at a time. He spotted several gift boxes in the family room on his way past and three more on the breakfast bar in the kitchen. He sat at the bar and stretched his neck so he could read the tags on each box. They were all different sizes and shapes. There was one for his fifth birthday, another for his twelfth and a third for his twenty-first. He wondered if she would make him open them in order. By the time she finally joined him, wearing an old T-shirt and jeans, he was about to explode with anticipation. She smiled when he grabbed the box labeled for his fifth birthday.

"Can I open it now?"

She nodded. He didn't know what he expected, but two boxes of hair-dye—one platinum blond, the other purple—was not it. "What's this?"

"It's time to get rid of this mousy brown color."

"I do prefer you as a blonde with blue."

"How about a blonde with purple? And I'd like to color your blue strand purple to match mine, if you'll let me."

He released a heavy breath. "Okay, I suppose my every forty-nine days tradition is pretty lame anyway."

"Am I messing up something sacred?"

"Just a stupid superstition."

"We can wait."

He shook his head. "I don't believe it brings me luck anymore."

"You still like changing the color though, right?"

"Yeah. It's kind of my trademark. There are betting pools online about what my next color will be."

"How many have their money on purple?"

He laughed. "Two little girls I met at a homeless shelter, for sure."

Eric was surprised by how fun it was to dye each other's hair. She let him choose where he wanted the purple to go in her hair. Instead of doing the under-layer, like she'd had it when they'd met, the purple strands framed her lovely face, and there were a few streaks in the back where he'd gotten a little carried away. Every stupid thing they did together made him feel closer to her.

He opened more presents, ranging from a book of Shakespearean limericks to a case of hot dogs for the tour bus. She'd put a lot of thought into all his gifts. There were several costumes for their bedroom games—a cheerleader, an angel, and a sexy pirate wench.

When he opened the Spider-Man costume that included two cans of silly string, he grabbed a can and chased Rebekah around the house until he eventually cornered her and sprayed his sticky web all over her.

He had personalized drumsticks, a new flask and some Cabo Wabo tequila to fill it, and a pair of handcuffs with the instructions: "for me or you, it's your decision." He was too overwhelmed to make any decisions at the moment. In the living room, she dropped another present in his lap and sat beside him on the sofa.

She gave his knee an encouraging squeeze as he opened the box. Inside he found a framed picture of himself and Rebekah. It was the same picture he used as his phone's screen saver, where they were simultaneously kissing, smiling, and looking at the camera. It was his favorite picture in the world. The frame was engraved with the word *family*. He got a little choked up as he ran his fingertips over the lettering. Couldn't help it.

"I love it," he said breathlessly.

Rebekah climbed from the sofa, then took a hammer and nail from an end table. "Where are we going to hang it?"

His interior decorator would have a cow if she knew he'd hung a picture in her perfectly designed living room. They hung the picture on the wall beside a Thomas Kincaid print. Both grinned at it for a good five minutes.

"We're going to add more soon," she said.

He wrapped an arm around her shoulders and tugged her against his side. "Yeah." He bent to nibble on her ear, now wishing he'd asked her to put on that cheerleading costume instead of saving it for a later date.

Hand splayed over his belly, she shuddered. "Go wait for me in the family room," she said. "Sit at the piano."

"I'm ready for some hot lovin' now," he said.

She winked at him. "You'll probably get some."

"Probably?"

She grabbed him by the hair at the nape of his neck and kissed him until his dick was so hard his stomach ached.

She pulled away and stared hungrily into his eyes. He stroked the purple strands of hair from her face.

"I'll be there in ten minutes," she promised.

He wasn't sure how she managed to get away. He sure as hell didn't want her to escape. Not even for ten minutes. He knew by now that she had something sexy planned, and half the fun was imagining what it might be. With a sigh, he went to the family room and waited at the black grand piano. The piano's lid had been lowered and several more colorful boxes were sitting there. He would never figure out how she'd managed to put this together. She had to have an accomplice. There's no way she could have done all this by herself. They were together almost constantly.

He got bored enough to play the piano while he waited. That little melody duet that he'd written for their tattoos was starting to stretch into a song.

A pair of soft, warm palms rested on his shoulders and then slid down his chest. His hands went still on the keys. One finger caught in his nipple ring. The gentle tug made his balls tighten. Her breasts pressed against his back. Unfortunately, they weren't bare.

"Happy birthday to you," Rebekah sang into his ear in a sultry, breathless voice.

Her hands slid lower, over his belly.

"Happy birthday to you," she continued.

He turned to look at her and almost fell off the piano bench. Rebekah wore a white halter dress with a long, loose skirt. It was a replica of the one Marilyn Monroe wore in *The Seven Year Itch*. The costume didn't stop at the dress; Rebekah had the wig, the makeup. She looked as hot as hell in July.

"Happy Birthday, Mister Eric Sticks," she sang in that same sexy voice.

She slid around his body to sit on his lap, her arms around his neck, her eyelids heavy as she looked at him with open invitation.

Oh dear God.

"Happy Birthday… to… you."

Heart thudding, he lowered his head to kiss her. His hand slid up one smooth leg, under her skirt, higher and higher until he knew for certain. She wasn't wearing panties. He lifted her onto the piano and ducked his head under her skirt. Her heels dug into his back as she encouraged his exploring lips and tongue. He sampled her flowing juices, tongue dancing over slick flesh, fingers digging into her hips to hold her still as he excited her to a writhing mass of feminine perfection.

Breathless with anticipation, he emerged from beneath her skirt and tugged his shorts down to free his straining cock. He jerked her body toward him, and she slid off the slick lid of the piano onto the keys, which gave a discordant clang. Finding her opening beneath her skirt, he inserted his cock carefully and then surged forward, filling her with one hard, deep thrust. Pumping into her with a steady rhythm, he opened his eyes to look at her. He tugged her wig off and ran his fingers through her soft hair. As sexy as she was when she was pretending to be someone else, he preferred the real woman.

His woman.

She was more than enough for him. Everything he would ever need.

He captured her lips with his and slowed his pace, not seeking release any longer. Seeking something more. The connection between them. The one he only felt when he was with her. His hands slid down the bare flesh of her back, and he pressed her body close. Their hearts thundered out of control, his against hers, hers against his.

She broke their kiss, and he gazed into her beautiful blue eyes. She stared at him as if in awe. Eventually, he had to ask, "What?"

She wrapped both arms around his waist and snuggled against his shoulder. "Sometimes it just hits me," she whispered. "How lucky I am to be with you."

"I'm the lucky one."

There was a crunch of gravel in the driveway. Rebekah stiffened. "What time is it?"

Outside, a car door slammed shut.

Eric checked the grandfather clock. "Um, almost six."

"Already?" she gasped. "Hurry up and come."

"I wonder who that is," he said, trying to see out in the driveway through a window on the far wall.

Looking half-panicked, Rebekah shoved him back so that his cock slipped from her body. She dropped to her knees in front of him and sucked him into her mouth. She was obviously intent on making him come as quickly as possible. He let the pleasure consume him, tenderly tucking her hair behind her ears as she bobbed her head and sucked hard. He erupted in her mouth, his body taut as he let go.

She swallowed his offering and hopped to her feet, tugging his shorts in place as the doorbell rang. "We'll do this again later," she promised. "You can take as long as you want then."

He chuckled. Six weeks ago, he never took long at all, and now she was apologizing for making him come too fast.

"I love you, woman."

She grinned. "I know. I love you too. Go answer the door. I need to find some panties."

She hurried out of the room. The doorbell rang again. "Come on, dude!" he heard Brian call from the front porch. "All this stuff is getting heavy!"

"Well, if you'd let me carry something," Myrna complained.

"You are. You're carrying my baby."

Eric opened the door, smiling at the bickering couple. "Hey, I wasn't expecting you two."

"Oh yeah," Brian said. He had a Crock-Pot under one arm, a large casserole dish in another, and several bags dangling from both hands. "Surprise!"

Myrna hugged Eric. "Happy birthday!" She slipped around his body to enter the foyer. Brian followed.

"Where's the kitchen?" Myrna asked. "I need to warm stuff up."

"I'll show you," Brian said.

"Make yourself at home," Eric called after them.

Eric honestly didn't think this day could get any better, and then another car pulled up in the driveway. It was Sed's Mercedes. Sed and Jessica took awhile to get out of the car. They were too busy making out in the front seat. Eric stood patiently on the porch so he could let them in the house when they decided they were finished sucking face, and Sed finished doing whatever he was doing with his head under the dashboard.

Rebekah appeared beside Eric and handed him another birthday present.

"Should I open it now?" he asked.

"Yeah. I don't want all the women staring at my fine piece of man meat all evening."

He laughed. As if. He opened the box and found a black T-shirt. The words Dirty Old Man were scribed across its front in white lettering. He chuckled and pulled it over his head. He kissed her temple and murmured, "Later I'll show you how dirty this old man can be."

"I'm counting on it." She reached up on tiptoes to kiss him and stroked his hair lovingly. "I'm going to help Myrna. It was so awesome of her to make us all dinner."

"Who's all?" Eric asked.

"You'll see."

He hoped *all* didn't include Isaac.

Eventually, Sed climbed out of the car and dashed around the vehicle to open the door for Jessica. They shared a few more moments of locking lips, and then Sed went to the trunk. Jessica carried gift bags and Sed carried a big container that looked suspiciously like a cake box. In a sweet little sundress and matching short-sleeved jacket, Jessica looked as smokin' hot as ever. No wonder Sed couldn't keep his hands off her.

At the same instant, Sed and Jessica noticed Eric standing on the steps waiting. "Hey," Sed said. "Happy birthday."

When the couple climbed onto the wraparound porch, Jessica lifted a hand and patted Eric's cheek. She read his shirt and laughed. "Dirty *old* man? Perfect."

Jace and Aggie arrived a few minutes later. They had presents and food too. Jace offered Eric a playful punch in the ribs. "Sorry we're late," he said. "Aggie was finishing your present."

Eric felt the blood drain from his face. "Please don't tell me it's a whip."

Jace laughed. "You'll have to wait and see."

"You look happy," Aggie commented, tucking her long, silky black hair behind both ears and kissing his cheek.

"I am happy. *Old*, but happy."

A van pulled into the drive. It took Eric a moment to recognize it as belonging to Rebekah's parents. *Great.* Eric's smile faded. No doubt they'd brought Isaac along for kicks and giggles. He'd like to kick him, that's for sure. And it would make him giggle. Trey climbed out of the drivers' seat and opened the side door to lower Dave in his wheelchair to the ground. No one else emerged from the van. Eric sighed in relief.

Dave wheeled himself through the gravel and onto the sidewalk that led to the front porch. At the bottom of the steps he stopped and looked up at Eric. "The ADA is gonna have your ass, Sticks. How am I supposed to get up the steps?"

"Getcher lazy ass out of the chair," Trey said.

Eric watched in stunned silence as Dave moved the foot pedals of his wheelchair aside, grabbed the banister, and pulled himself to his feet.

"You got it?" Trey asked him.

"Yep," Dave said breathlessly. With tremendous effort and using the handrail for support, Dave slowly climbed the four stairs to stand on the porch. Eric grabbed him in a tremendous bear hug while Trey folded Dave's wheelchair and hefted it up the steps.

"You can walk?" Eric said.

There was suddenly a smaller body participating in their hug fest. Rebekah was literally sobbing with happiness.

"Okay," Dave said. "I need to sit down again. I'm still weak as a fuckin' kitten. I can only move a few steps at a time."

They helped him back into his chair and bumped him over the threshold into the house.

"Is everyone here?" Trey asked.

Rebekah nodded. "How's Isaac?" she asked.

"He'll be okay," Trey promised. "I know just the guy for him." Everyone in the foyer stared. "No, not me. You know how I feel about serious relationships." He made a face of disgust and Rebekah laughed.

"And I wanted to date you," she said. "Good thing I didn't stay hung up on you for too long. Heartbreaker."

"Cock tease," Trey shot back.

Dave chuckled. "You've no idea how happy I am to hear him call you that."

Rebekah glanced at Eric and turned beet red.

"How's your mother doing?" Eric asked Dave, hoping to change the subject.

"Better. They're trying her on some new meds. She sounded great when I talked to her a couple hours ago. You should call her, Rebekah."

Rebekah nodded. "I will after Eric's party."

"She's not stuck in her Isaac-and-Rebekah loop anymore."

"That's a relief," Rebekah said. She stroked her brother's hair and kissed his forehead. "You had to go and one-up me, didn't you?"

"Huh?"

"I plan all this stuff for Eric's birthday, and you show up and promptly start walking." She shook her head as if annoyed. "Figures."

"Sibling rivalry at its finest." Dave grabbed her around the waist and tumbled her onto his lap so he could tickle her. She laughed and squirmed, finally landing herself in a heap on the floor. Smiling broadly, Eric helped her to her feet.

They made their way into the kitchen where Myrna was busy getting the meal heated and appropriately served. Brian was at underfoot as he tried to help. Eventually, she grabbed him by both arms and gave him a hard shake. "I know you want to help, but will you sit down and let me get this done? Back off! I'm fine. I'm not the first woman to have a baby, you know!"

"But you're the first woman to have *my* baby."

Myrna stared at her husband and then burst into tears. She hugged him against her and kissed every inch of his face. "I'm s-sorry I yelled at you. I love you so much."

"Hormones," Sed grumbled. "Hey, Jess. You aren't going to be like that when I knock you up, are you?"

Jessica poked him in the ribs. Hard. "Ask me that again, and you'll be incapable of ever having children."

Sed covered his crotch protectively with both hands.

The meal was amazing. Myrna had made her homemade lasagna. The Italian bread, with its crisp outside and melt-on-your-tongue center, was also homemade. Everything was perfect. The meal. The company. The love of his life playing footsies with him beneath the dinner table. Everything.

Perfect.

They covered Eric's cake with candles and made him blow them out. "Don't forget to make a wish," Rebekah encouraged.

He couldn't think of anything else he could possibly want or need. And then he remembered that Rebekah had her MRI the next day. He wished for perfect health for his woman and then blew out the candles. A second later, Eric found his face shoved into the cake, and then a full-fledged cake-flinging battle ensued in his kitchen. Hiding with Rebekah under the breakfast bar from the chocolate cake and buttercream frosting projectiles, Eric smiled as she began to nibble the cake and frosting off his face.

"This is delicious," she said.

He laughed and smeared his cheek against hers so he could sample his birthday cake for himself. "That is pretty good," he said, licking frosting off her face, "but these are much sweeter." He kissed her and was still kissing her when eight pairs of eyes peered under the counter to stare at them.

"Time to open presents," Sed announced.

"I could get used to this," Eric murmured and kissed Rebekah again before hauling himself from beneath the counter. He helped Rebekah to her feet and turned to find Jessica sucking frosting off Sed's huge biceps. Brian and Myrna were feeding each other bits of cake with their fingers. Aggie was nibbling on Jace's jaw, none too gently, if his raspy breathing was any indication of his level of excitement.

Trey crossed his arms over his chest. "If you all don't stop it, I'm going to have to start making out with Dave here, and no one wants to see that."

"I do," Aggie said and emitted a husky chuckle.

Damn, that woman was delightfully wicked. Eric could only imagine what she'd made him as a birthday gift. It turned out to be a custom-made black leather corset with blue butterflies embroidered down one side for Rebekah. Eric totally approved.

Sed and Jessica had bought him a personalized license plate frame for the Corvette that read *Drummers Do It with Rhythm*.

Myrna and Brian gave him a box of sex toys that came with their stamp of approval.

Trey didn't get him anything. "I practically gave you that wonderful woman of yours," he explained with a wink.

Dave gave him a new cymbal for his drum kit, which he had to try immediately.

Rebekah handed him yet another gift.

"You're spoiling me," Eric said. He laughed when he opened the box and found a pillow shaped like a pair of breasts.

"So when you're on the road, you'll have something to remind you of me. Something you can play with while you're sleeping alone. And you will be sleeping alone, Eric Sticks!"

"No, he won't," Sed said.

"What do you mean he won't?" Rebekah bellowed.

Before Eric could assure her that she had absolutely nothing to worry about, Sed said, "You'll be there with him. The band talked about it, and we decided we want you to stay on as our permanent soundboard operator."

Her smile could have lit the heavens, and then she glanced at her brother. "Dave—"

"Dave will also be our soundboard operator. That job is big enough for two people. There are things he won't be able to do for a while yet, so you can help him, but honestly, with both of you on the job, Sinners is gonna rock everyone's face off," he said in that front man roar that made the crowds go wild.

Eric was so happy he could've kissed Sed. So he did. He got slapped alongside the head for his misplaced affection, but he didn't care. He wouldn't have to be away from Rebekah for weeks on end. Or ever. She would always be by his side.

"So do you want the job?" Sed asked.

"Are you kidding?" Rebekah cried. "Of course I want the job!"

Sed didn't slap *her* alongside the head when she kissed him, but Jessica's eyes flashed a warning.

The doorbell rang. Eric glanced at Rebekah in question.

"Happy twenty-eighth birthday, baby."

"Did you get me a stripper?" Eric teased.

Trey slapped himself in the forehead. "Why didn't I think of that? Then I'd have someone to play with too."

"Go get the door," Rebekah urged.

Eric gave her a strange look. Everyone he knew was already here, but he went to answer. Jon stood on his threshold. Well, Eric's birthday had been going perfectly. Only seemed fair that something would fuck it up. Why would Rebekah invite him?

Jon smiled slightly. "Hey," he said.

"I already told you, the band is finished with you, Jon. You're not going to weasel your way back in."

Jon offered a curt nod. "Yeah, I get that. That's not why I'm here. What is that in your hair?"

Eric touched his hair and found a hunk of cake in the row of spikes down the center. "Birthday cake."

"Oh yeah. Happy birthday."

"Thanks. So what do you want?"

"Can we talk outside? It's kind of… personal."

Eric sighed. Why couldn't he just tell this guy to fuck off? To get out of his life and stay out. Maybe because he remembered him before he'd become an addict.

"Yeah. Okay." Eric closed the front door and went to sit on the porch swing.

Jon perched beside him, clasped his hands in his lap, and stared at his thumbs. "My rehab counselor said it would help to make amends."

"You're in rehab?"

"Outpatient."

"Obviously."

Jon chuckled. "When I called the house looking for you yesterday, Rebekah said I could come tonight. Own up to everything."

Eric wondered why she thought this was a good birthday present.

"I'm sorry I lied about the money in the lockbox," Jon said. "I did take it. Blew it all on a weekend's worth of quality cocaine." He looked up and met Eric's eyes. "I don't expect you to forgive me. I wouldn't forgive me. Everyone else gave up on me years ago, but you never did." His defeated smile made Eric's heart pang. Just a little. "I didn't know how else to keep you in my life, Eric, so I manipulated you into thinking you owed me. All I really wanted was to hang out with you again. Like we used to before I completely fucked up my life."

"You don't have to be in the band to hang out with me."

Jon rubbed his forehead and stared across the immaculately tended front yard. "Don't enable me again, Eric. It honestly doesn't help."

"I don't want you anywhere near me if you're using, but..."

Jon glanced at him.

"But if you get your shit together, maybe we could put a little band together. Play gigs at local bars. I've been working on some alternative rock songs. You never were heavy enough for Sinners."

Jon smiled. "That would be awesome."

"But I get to sing."

"And drum?"

"Nope, just sing. I'll need you to find a good drummer. A couple of guitarists. I won't have time. I'm fuckin' busy, you know?"

Jon's eyes sparkled with hope. "Are you serious?"

"Yeah, it'll be fun. We'll jam. Just when I'm off tour with Sinners, of course, and only if you keep your nose clean. I'm not putting up with your bullshit anymore, Jon."

Jon punched him in the arm. "I don't expect you to."

Eric nodded. "Do you want to come inside?"

Jon shook his head. "Nah. I've taken enough of your time. You'll probably get a long, boring letter from me in a couple days. Another part of my therapy. You don't have to read it, if you don't want to."

Eric laughed. "That's why you're really here, huh? To keep me from reading that letter."

"No," Jon said sheepishly. "I'm not like that anymore."

"Whatever, dude," Eric said, laughing. "I don't expect you to change overnight."

Jon climbed to his feet. "I'll give you a call once I'm sure this therapy is going to stick. I really want to succeed this time. I'm finished with that shit."

"You better. I have some songs written that are amazing, but not Sinners' style. I'd love to get them in front of an audience. I'm counting on you to make that happen."

Jon rolled his eyes. "You don't need me, Eric. You could put your own band together in ten seconds. Any musician in his right mind would give his left nut to perform with you."

"But I'm counting on you." Eric shoved Jon toward the porch steps. "Get now. I need to chase off the rest of my guests so I can have time alone with my woman."

"She's good for you."

Eric smiled. "You don't have to state the obvious."

Jon trotted down the steps and then turned to look at him. "Thanks." He didn't need to say more. Eric understood. "Happy birthday."

When Eric let himself back in the house, Rebekah was waiting in the foyer. "How did it go?"

Eric nodded. "I think he's actually going to get his life back together."

She reached up and cupped his face. "And I suppose you're going to help him with that."

"Nope. Just gave him a little incentive. My part in his recovery is entirely hands-off."

"Good," she said, "because I think it's about time you put your hands on me."

"I think it's past time for that."

Chapter 34

REBEKAH DIDN'T KNOW WHAT was worse, the actual MRI or waiting for the results. She and Eric played a word game against each other on their phones while she waited to be called to see her doctor. She was glad Eric was there to help her pass the time. Her stomach was in knots.

When they called her in, she left Eric in the waiting room. If it was bad news, she didn't want him to see her fall apart. She'd have a few minutes to pull herself together before she had to tell him.

"Are you sure you don't want me to go in with you?" he asked, clinging to her fingers with one hand.

"I'll only be a minute." She kissed his cheek and followed the nurse to Dr. Palmer's office.

The moment she entered the room, she knew it would not be good news. Dr. Palmer had two expressions. I'm on top of the world. You're going to die. He was wearing his solemn look at the moment.

"Have a seat, Miss Blake."

She sat, or more collapsed. Her legs were like wet noodles.

"Your blood work looks great. CEA levels normal," he said, but he didn't offer a smile of encouragement. "The MRI…"

Oh God, please don't say it. Please.

"There is a suspicious spot in your pelvic cavity."

Fuck. He said it.

"I want to do an immediate biopsy to take a look. It might be an artifact or excess scar tissue or—it might be a relapse of cancer."

Unable to speak, she lowered her eyes and nodded slightly.

"They're prepping a room for you upstairs. If it *is* cancer, the faster we get you on chemo, the better our chances of beating it again."

But if it was back, they hadn't beat it. Not really. "I feel fine," she said breathlessly. Well, she had. Now she felt devastated. She'd found true love, true happiness, and her body had betrayed her again.

"It might be nothing. Let's do the biopsy and see what we have to deal with before we talk about treatment options."

She nodded and somehow found the strength to climb to her feet and shuffle out of his office. The nurse told her where she should go for her biopsy, and then she went to find Eric in the waiting room. He looked almost as nauseous as she felt.

"What's wrong?"

She shook her head. "I need another test," she said breathlessly. She couldn't tell him why. She just couldn't.

"Why?"

"Because," she snapped. "Doctors like to stick long, thick needles into my body, that's why!"

"I have something long and thick I'd like to stick into your body."

She knew that he was trying to cheer her up, but it wasn't working. "Just shut up, Eric. I'm not in the mood."

He looked like she'd slapped him. "Sorry."

She squeezed her forehead between both hands, trying to stave off a threatening headache. "Let's just go get this over with."

They made Eric wait outside while they used some kind of machine to direct the needles they jabbed her with while collecting their samples. When they left her alone, she laid there on the examination table, staring at the ceiling to fight threatening tears. They told her they'd have the results of the biopsy soon. Didn't want her to leave in case they had to poke her some more. Her doctor had ordered her biopsy evaluation STAT, and there was a qualified pathologist on duty. At least she wouldn't have to wonder for long.

The door opened and Eric appeared in the doorway. "Are you decent?"

"Unfortunately," she muttered.

"I'm supposed to say that," he said, settling beside her on the padded table. He took her hand and kissed her knuckles. They sat there silently for a long while. "Are you okay?" he asked finally.

She shook her head, blinking hard, her lips pursed.

"Tell me, baby. Not knowing what's going on has to be worse than the truth."

"Worse than the cancer being back? I'd rather not know."

"It's back?" he whispered.

"I don't know. They found a suspicious spot on the MRI so they did a biopsy to see if it's cancer."

"Everything will be all right, sweetheart," he said.

She glared at him. "If the cancer has relapsed, nothing is all right, Eric. Nothing."

"I'm here," he said. "Okay? You beat this once. You can do it again."

"I don't want to go through chemotherapy again, Eric. It makes me so tired. I'll be all sick and skinny. All my hair will fall out. I won't be beautiful anymore." She squeezed her eyes and swallowed. "Or sexy."

Eric cupped her face in both hands, his thumbs stroking the tears from her cheeks. "Look at me, Rebekah."

She forced her eyes open.

"You know I think your outer package is perfect," he said, "but what's beautiful about you is in here." He pressed the fingertips of one hand to the center of her chest over her aching heart. He moved his other hand to the side of her head. "What's sexy is in here." He kissed her forehead, her temple. "I said I'd love you forever, baby. That doesn't mean I abandon you when you're sick. If you're too tired to get out of bed, I'll carry you. If your hair falls out, I'll…" He grabbed the long strand of purple resting against his collarbone. "I'll cut this off and tape it to your forehead."

She laughed, picturing herself with one long chunk of purple hair taped to her bald head.

"If you're sick, I'll take care of you. If you're skinny, I'll feed you every flavor of scrambled eggs you can imagine."

"Okay, you've gone too far with that one."

"What I won't do is let you give up. I won't bury you without a fight, Rebekah. And you're going to have to do all the fighting, sweetheart. You have to be the strong one. All I can do is hold your hand and stand beside you."

A movement behind Eric caught Rebekah's attention. Her mother stood there with tears in her eyes. Mom grabbed Eric around the neck and hugged his head against her ample bosom. Rebekah laughed at his startled expression.

"How long have you been here?" Rebekah asked her mother.

Her mom smiled. "Long enough. Doctor Palmer told me you were down here and could probably use some support while you waited for your results." She grabbed Eric by both ears and pulled him away from her chest to look at him. "I'm sorry I didn't realize how much you love my daughter. I get... *confused* sometimes. I can see you now." She ruffled his wild hair with both hands. "Not just the crazy hair and the tattoos, but what's inside."

"Blood and guts?" Eric said.

Rebekah laughed and hit him with a spare pillow.

"Well, no," Mom said, looking a tad queasy. "I don't really want to see that. I see that you love her unconditionally. I trust you to take care of her. It's a big responsibility. She's always been a difficult one. You sure you want the job?"

Eric glanced at Rebekah and smiled. "I'm sure."

"Well, hello Mrs. Blake," Doctor Palmer said as he walked into the room. "How are you feeling?"

Mom turned and smiled. "Amazing. This new prescription has made all the difference. And my daughter is getting married!"

Doctor Palmer chuckled. "I kind of figured that out on my own. Her engagement ring is huge."

"And I want to be there," Mom added. That was the real news.

Rebekah's heart warmed. With Eric and her family's support, she could get through another cycle of chemo if she had to. She stared at her doctor, feeling a strength she hadn't possessed twenty minutes ago. "Do you have the results of the biopsy?" she asked.

Eric grabbed her hand and squeezed.

Doctor Palmer beamed. "False alarm. The suspicious mass was just dense scar tissue and some entirely normal fibroblasts. No signs of cancer at all."

Eric hugged her so hard, she thought she might pass out.

When he pulled away, he wiped his tears on the hem of his T-shirt.

"Looks like I won't need your lock of purple hair after all," Rebekah said.

He laughed. "Everything that's mine is yours." He looked at the doctor. "Can she leave now? We have an appointment with a justice of the peace in twenty minutes."

"We do?" Rebekah asked.

"Yeah, just let me call and make one." He pulled his phone out of his pocket and started searching the Internet for numbers. After a moment, he looked up. "Unless you want the big fancy wedding."

She pondered for a moment. "Nope, I want a quick wedding and a big fancy reception and a lifelong honeymoon."

Eric grinned and leaned forward to kiss her. His fingertips against her jaw, his lips tugged hers with gentle suction and incomparable tenderness. When he pulled away, he offered her a tender smile. "Well, if you insist."

Read on for an excerpt from

Rock
HARD

By Olivia Cunning

JESSICA WAS THE HAPPIEST woman on the planet. Life could not have been more perfect. She snuck up behind Sed, wrapped her arms around his neck, and kissed his ear. "Hey, baby, guess what?"

"What?" he said absently.

She peeked around his shoulder to find him scowling at a stack of invoices.

"I got in!"

His scowl deepened in confusion. "You got in? Got in what?"

She pulled the acceptance letter from her back pocket and snapped it open in front of him. This would wipe the scowl from his gorgeous face.

While he read, she gazed at her recently acquired engagement ring. After all her hard work in school, her dreams were finally becoming a reality. Having a hunky rising-star rock vocalist as her fiancé was the frosting on her Pop Tart.

"Law school?" His deep voice rumbled through his back against her chest.

"Yeah. Isn't it great? I'm so excited. We have to go out and celebrate." She kissed his temple and squeezed him. "I'll go put on a skirt. We'll go sightseeing. I want you to make love to me on a crowded street. Maybe Rodeo Drive. Or Hollywood Boulevard. What do you think?"

"I can't afford to put you through law school, Jess. I can't even afford to fix the transmission in the fuckin' tour bus." He tossed her acceptance letter on his stack of invoices.

"Don't worry." She pulled out a second letter. Her financial aid award letter. "Scholarships, grants, waivers. I only have to come up with $3,000 a semester."

Sed shoved his chair away from the table and went to open the banged-up refrigerator. Finding it empty, he closed it again. "I don't have $3,000, Jessica." He didn't get it. This was her dream. He was encouraged to pursue his. Why wasn't she? Even though Sed's band, Sinners, would probably never make it as big as their front man envisioned, she believed in him. Was it so much to ask that he believed in her, too?

"I don't expect you to pay for it, Sed. I'll find a way. I just want you to be happy for me. Congratulate me. Something. This is the most important thing that's ever happened to me."

He leaned back against the counter and crossed his arms over his chest. For a second, she was struck by how attractive he was. Those broad shoulders, bulging muscles, narrow hips. Black hair, blue eyes. A face that belonged in movies. And then he opened his mouth. "I'm the most important thing that's ever happened to you. And *you* aren't going."

"What do you mean I'm not going?"

"You're not going to law school. You'll be far too busy keeping me entertained in the bedroom. When that gets boring, you'll pop out five or six kids and take care of them while I tour with the band and make us all rich and famous."

That was his big scheme for her life? Was he fucking kidding her? "I've dreamt of being a lawyer since I was a little girl, Sedric. I *am* going to law school. And you're not telling me how to live my life."

"If you want to be my wife, you're not going. I forbid it."

She stared at him in disbelief. "You did *not* just say that."

"Yeah, I did."

"Then I don't want to be your wife."

He scoffed, looking amused. "You don't mean that."

That cocksure attitude of his—the one that had attracted her to him in the first place—made her grit her teeth. She yanked the ring off her finger and flung it at him. It hit him in the chest and he caught it against his body with his hand.

"There! Go hock that cheap piece of shit, fix your precious tour bus, and make yourself famous with your stupid band, you asshole."

He stared at her in disbelief.

"We're through, Sed."

His blue eyes widened. "You're breaking up with me?" For the first time in their four months together, Jessica saw a dent in his armor of self-assurance. "No one has ever broken up with me. Ever."

Fuckin' A, he totally missed the point. "What did you expect? That I'd be happy as your little toy?"

His cocky grin returned. "Well, aren't you? You never complain in the bedroom."

She had no complaints in the bedroom. Their bodies were made for each other. Their sexual appetites perfectly in sync. It was everything else that didn't work between them. "I'm leaving, Sed."

She hesitated. This was his last chance to make things right between them. All he had to do was admit he was wrong to try to control her life. Wrong to think of her as an object instead of a person. A person he supposedly loved enough to be his wife.

She waited. Wanting him. God, she always wanted him. As overbearing and arrogant as he was, she wanted him. She did not, however, need him.

"I don't think you will." He chuckled. "You're not strong enough to leave me."

Jessica snatched her acceptance letter off the table and proved him wrong.

About the Author

New York Times and *USA Today* bestselling author, Olivia Cunning, combines her passion for naughty rock stars and erotic romance in a sweltering mix of sex, love, and rock 'n' roll. Her debut novel, *Backstage Pass*, has won numerous awards, including the Readers' Crown for Best First Book and Best Long Erotic Romance. She currently lives in Texas.

Backstage Pass

SINNERS ON TOUR

By Olivia Cunning

• •

FOR HIM, LIFE IS ALL MUSIC AND NO PLAY...

When Brian Sinclair, lead songwriter and guitarist of the hottest metal band on the scene, loses his creative spark, it will take nights of downright sinful passion to release his pent-up genius...

SHE'S THE ONE TO CALL THE TUNE...

When sexy psychologist Myrna Evans goes on tour with the Sinners, every boy in the band tries to woo her into his bed. But Brian is the only one she wants to get her hands on...

Then the two lovers' wildly shocking behavior sparks the whole band to new heights of glory... and sin...

• •

For more Olivia Cunning, visit:

www.sourcebooks.com

Sinners on Tour

Rock Hard

by Olivia Cunning

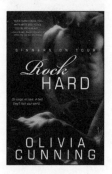

On stage, on tour, in bed, they'll rock your world…

Trapped together on the Sinners tour bus for the summer, Sed and Jessica will rediscover the millions of steamy reasons they never should have called it quits in the first place…

"A full, well rounded romance… another dazzling story of Sinners, love, sex, and rock and roll!" —Night Owl Reviews, *Reviewer Top Pick*

"Wicked, naughty, arousing, and you'll be craving the next page of this book as if you were living it for yourself!" —Dark Divas Reviews

"Hot men, rocking music, and explosive sex? What could be better?" —Seriously Reviewed

"An erotic romance that is rockin' with action and a plotline that keeps you on your toes." —Romance Fiction on Suite101.com

For more Olivia Cunning, visit:

www.sourcebooks.com

Sinners on Tour

Double Time

by Olivia Cunning

On stage, on tour, in bed, they'll rock your world...

On the rebound from the tumult of his bisexual lifestyle, notoriously sexy rock guitarist Trey Mills falls for sizzling new female guitar sensation Reagan Elliot and is swept into the hot, heady romance he never dreamed possible.

"Snappy dialogue, dizzying romance, scorching hot sex, and realistic observations about life on tour make this a winner." —Publishers Weekly

"Whether you like rockers or not, this story will get you thinking about becoming a groupie!" —Night Owl Reviews

"Hot rock stars, hotter sex, and some of the best characters I've read this year." —Guilty Pleasures Book Review

"Double Time gives us Trey's much anticipated happy ending, and all the sexual adventures along the way." —Fresh Fiction

"A sexy, steamy read about two rock stars and the man who loves them both. A great installment to this series, it left me anxiously waiting for the next one." —Romance Junkies

For more Olivia Cunning, visit:

www.sourcebooks.com

Sinners on Tour

Hot Ticket

by Olivia Cunning

On stage, on tour, in bed, they'll rock your world...

A man as talented as Sinners bass guitarist Jace Seymour needs a woman who can beat out his self-doubt. A woman as strong as Mistress V needs a man she can't always overpower. And in each other's tight embrace, an escape from harsh reality is always a welcome diversion...

"The heat and hunger between the two leads creates a palpable tension that will keep readers turning pages with reckless abandon and begging for more from this sizzling series." —RT Book Reviews

"Cunning develops her characters into real people who engage in a compelling and satisfying erotic romance. Their relationship builds amid a dramatic series of unexpected events." —Publishers Weekly

"Sizzling hot, tragically emotional, and totally rockin'. Only one more band member to go and I can hardly wait." —Fresh Fiction

"I said it for the first book and I'll say it again, these yummy guys are so hot that you'll want to rip your clothes off and join them. I hope this tour never ends." —Night Owl Reviews, *Top Pick*

"As Jace's story is told in Hot Ticket, *the reader is provided with the heart-wrenching and powerful backstory that formed the Jace we saw in the first two books of this series."* —The Romance Reviews, *Top Pick*

For more Olivia Cunning, visit:

www.sourcebooks.com